Acknowledgements

The editor and publishers wish to thank the following for permission to use copyright material:

David Campbell Publishers Ltd for Guy de Maupassant, 'The Necklace' from *Guy de Maupassant: Short Stories*, trans. Majorie Laurie, Everyman's Library (1934) pp. 38–46;

Curtis Brown, London, on behalf of the Estate of the author and Alfred A Knopf, Inc for Elizabeth Bowen, 'The Demon Lover' from *Collected Stories*. Copyright © 1946, renewed 1974 by Elizabeth Bowen;

A M Heath & Co Ltd on behalf of Robert and Olivia Temple for 'The Middle-Aged Man and His Mistresses' and 'The Old Woman and the Doctor' from *Aesop: The Complete Fables*. Translation and annotation copyright © 1988 by Olivia and Robert Temple;

Laurence Pollinger Ltd on behalf of the Estate of Frieda Ravagli and Viking Penguin, a division of Penguin Putnam Inc for D H Lawrence, 'The Rocking-Horse Winner' from *The Complete Short Stories of D H Lawrence*. Copyright © 1933 by the Estate of D H Lawrence, renewed © 1961 by Angelo Ravagli and C M Weekley, Executors of the Estate of Frieda Lawrence;

Every effort has been made to trace the copyright holders but if any have been inadvertently overlooked the publishers will be pleased to make the necessary arrangement at the first opportunity.

Contents

Evergreen Stories

Selected by Hilary Laurie

PHŒNIX

A Phoenix Paperback

This edition first published in Great Britain by
Phoenix Paperbacks in 1998
Selection © Phoenix Paperbacks 1998

All rights reserved

Orion Publishing Group
Orion House
5 Upper St Martin's Lane
London WC2H 9EA

Typeset by Deltatype Ltd, Birkenhead, Merseyside
Printed in Great Britain by
The Guernsey Press Co. Ltd, Guernsey C. I.

This book if bound as a paperback is subject to the condition
that it may not be issued on loan or otherwise except in its
original binding

British Library Cataloguing-in-Publication Data
available upon request.

ISBN 0 75380 515 4

CONTENTS

The Garden Party

KATHERINE MANSFIELD

And after all the weather was ideal. They could not have had a more perfect day for a garden party if they had ordered it. Windless, warm, the sky without a cloud. Only the blue was veiled with a haze of light gold, as it is sometimes in early summer. The gardener had been up since dawn, mowing the lawns and sweeping them, until the grass and the dark flat rosettes where the daisy plants had been seemed to shine. As for the roses, you could not help feeling they understood that roses are the only flowers that impress people at garden parties; the only flowers that everybody is certain of knowing. Hundreds, yes, literally hundreds, had come out in a single night; the green bushes bowed down as though they had been visited by archangels.

Breakfast was not yet over before the men came to put up the marquee.

'Where do you want the marquee put mother?'

'My dear child, it's no use asking me. I'm determined to leave everything to you children this year. Forget I am your mother. Treat me as an honoured guest.'

But Meg could not possibly go and supervise the men. She had washed her hair before breakfast, and she sat drinking her coffee in a green turban, with a dark wet curl stamped on each cheek. Jose, the butterfly, always came down in a silk petticoat and a kimono jacket.

'You'll have to go, Laura; you're the artistic one.'

Away Laura flew, still holding her piece of bread and butter. It's so delicious to have an excuse for eating out of doors and, besides, she loved having to arrange things; she always felt she could do it so much better than anybody else.

Four men in their shirtsleeves stood grouped together on the garden path. They carried staves covered with rolls of canvas and they had big toolbags slung on their backs. They looked impressive. Laura wished now that she was not holding that piece of bread and butter, but there was nowhere to put it and she couldn't possibly throw it away. She blushed and tried to look severe and even a little bit short-sighted as she came up to them.

'Good morning,' she said, copying her mother's voice. But that sounded so fearfully affected that she was ashamed, and stammered like a little girl, 'Oh – er – have you come – is it about the marquee?'

'That's right, miss,' said the tallest of the men, a lanky, freckled fellow, and he shifted his toolbag, knocked back his straw hat and smiled down at her. 'That's about it.'

His smile was so easy, so friendly, that Laura recovered. What nice eyes he had, small, but such a dark blue! And now she looked at the others, they were smiling too. 'Cheer up, we won't bite,' their smile seemed to say. How very nice workmen were! And what a beautiful morning! She mustn't mention the morning; she must be businesslike. The marquee.

'Well, what about the lily lawn? Would that do?'

And she pointed to the lily lawn with the hand that didn't hold the bread and butter. They turned, they stared in the direction. A little fat chap thrust out his underlip and the tall fellow frowned.

'I don't fancy it,' said he. 'Not conspicuous enough. You see, with a thing like a marquee,' and he turned to Laura in his easy way, 'you want to put it somewhere where it'll give you a bang slap in the eye, if you follow me.'

Laura's upbringing made her wonder for a moment whether it was quite respectful of a workman to talk to her of bangs slap in the eye. But she did quite follow him.

'A corner of the tennis court,' she suggested. 'But the band's going to be in one corner.'

'H'm, going to have a band, are you?' said another of the workmen. He was pale. He had a haggard look as his dark eyes scanned the tennis court. What was he thinking?

'Only a very small band,' said Laura gently. Perhaps he wouldn't mind so much if the band was quite small. But the tall fellow interrupted.

'Look here, miss, that's the place. Against those trees. Over there. That'll do fine.'

Against the karakas. Then the karaka trees would be hidden. And they were so lovely, with their broad, gleaming leaves, and their clusters of yellow fruit. They were like trees you imagined growing on a desert island, proud, solitary, lifting their leaves and fruits to the sun in a kind of silent splendour. Must they be hidden by a marquee?

They must. Already the men had shouldered their staves and were making for the place. Only the tall fellow was left. He bent down, pinched a sprig of lavender, put his thumb and forefinger to his nose and snuffed up the smell. When Laura saw that gesture she forgot all about the karakas in her wonder at him caring for things like that – caring for the smell of lavender. How many men that she knew would have done such a thing. Oh, how extraordinarily nice workmen were, she thought. Why couldn't she have workmen for friends rather than the silly boys she danced with and who came to Sunday night supper? She would get on much better with men like these.

It's all the fault, she decided, as the tall fellow drew something on the back of an envelope, something that was to be looped up or left to hang, of these absurd class distinctions. Well, for her part, she didn't feel them. Not a bit, not an atom . . . And now there came the chock-chock of wooden hammers. Someone whistled, someone sang out, 'Are you right there, matey?' 'Matey!' The friendliness of it, the – the – Just to prove how happy she was, just to show the tall fellow how at home she felt, and how she despised stupid conventions, Laura took a big bite of her bread and butter as she stared at the little drawing. She felt just like a work-girl.

'Laura, Laura, where are you? Telephone, Laura!' a voice cried from the house.

'Coming!' Away she skimmed, over the lawn, up the path, up the steps, across the veranda and into the porch. In the hall her father and Laurie were brushing their hats ready to go to the office.

'I say, Laura,' said Laurie very fast, 'you might just give a squiz at my coat before this afternoon. See if it wants pressing.'

'I will,' said she. Suddenly she couldn't stop herself. She ran at Laurie and gave him a small, quick squeeze. 'Oh, I do love parties, don't you?' gasped Laura.

'Ra-ther,' said Laurie's warm, boyish voice, and he squeezed his sister too and gave her a gentle push. 'Dash off to the telephone, old girl.'

The telephone. 'Yes, yes; oh yes. Kitty? Good morning, dear. Come to lunch? Do, dear. Delighted, of course. It will only be a very scratch meal – just the sandwich crusts and broken meringue-shells and what's left over. Yes, isn't it a perfect morning? Your white? Oh, I certainly should. One moment – hold the line. Mother's calling.' And Laura sat back. 'What, mother? Can't hear.'

Mrs Sheridan's voice floated down the stairs. 'Tell her to wear that sweet hat she had on last Sunday.'

'Mother says you're to wear that *sweet* hat you had on last Sunday. Good. One o'clock. Bye-bye.'

Laura put back the receiver, flung her arms over her head, took a deep breath, stretched and let them fall. 'Huh,' she sighed, and the moment after the sigh she sat up quickly. She was still, listening. All the doors in the house seemed to be open. The house was alive with soft, quick steps and running voices. The green baize door that led to the kitchen regions swung open and shut with a muffled thud. And now there came a long, chuckling absurd sound. It was the heavy piano being moved on its stiff castors. But the air! If you stopped to notice, was the air always like this? Little faint winds were playing chase in at the tops of the windows, out at the doors. And there were two tiny spots of sun, one on the inkpot, one on a silver photograph frame, playing too. Darling little spots. Especially the one on the inkpot lid. It was quite warm. A warm little silver star. She could have kissed it.

The front door bell pealed and there sounded the rustle of Sadie's print skirt on the stairs. A man's voice murmured; Sadie answered, careless, 'I'm sure I don't know. Wait. I'll ask Mrs Sheridan.'

'What is it, Sadie?' Laura came into the hall.

'It's the florist, Miss Laura.'

It was, indeed. There, just inside the door, stood a wide, shallow tray full of pots of pink lilies. No other kind. Nothing but lilies – canna lilies, big pink flowers, wide open, radiant, almost frighteningly alive on bright crimson stems.

'O-oh, Sadie!' said Laura, and the sound was like a little moan. She crouched down as if to warm herself at that blaze of lilies; she felt they were in her fingers, on her lips, growing in her breast.

'It's some mistake,' she said faintly. 'Nobody ever ordered so many. Sadie, go and find mother.'

But at that moment Mrs Sheridan joined them.

'It's quite right,' she said calmly. 'Yes, I ordered them. Aren't they lovely?' She pressed Laura's arm. 'I was passing the shop yesterday, and I saw them in the window. And I suddenly thought for once in my life I shall have enough canna lilies. The garden party will be a good excuse.'

'But I thought you said you didn't mean to interfere,' said Laura. Sadie had gone. The florist's man was still outside at his van. She put her arm round her mother's neck and gently, very gently, she bit her mother's ear.

'My darling child, you wouldn't like a logical mother, would you? Don't do that. Here's the man.'

He carried more lilies still, another whole tray.

'Bank them up, just inside the door, on both sides of the porch, please,' said Mrs Sheridan. 'Don't you agree, Laura?'

'Oh, I *do*, mother.'

In the drawing-room Meg, Jose and good little Hans had at last succeeded in moving the piano.

'Now, if we put this chesterfield against the wall and move everything out of the room except the chairs, don't you think?'

'Quite.'

'Hans, move these tables into the smoking-room, and bring a sweeper to take these marks of the carpet and – one moment, Hans –' Jose loved giving orders to the servants and they loved obeying her. She always made them feel they were taking part in some drama. 'Tell mother and Miss Laura to come here at once.'

'Very good, Miss Jose.'

She turned to Meg. 'I want to hear what the piano sounds like, just in case I'm asked to sing this afternoon. Let's try over "This Life is Weary." '

Pom! Ta-ta-ta *Tee*-ta! The piano burst out so passionately that Jose's face changed. She clasped her hands. She looked mournfully and enigmatically at her mother and Laura as they came in.

> This Life is *Wee*-ary,
> A Tear – a Sigh.
> A Love that *Chan*-ges,
>   This Life is *Wee*-ary,
> A Tear – a Sigh.
> A Love that *Chan*-ges,
> And then . . . Good-bye!

But at the word 'Good-bye,' and although the piano sounded

more desperate than ever, her face broke into a briliant, dreadfully unsympathetic smile.

'Aren't I in good voice, mummy?' she beamed.

> This Life is *Wee*-ary,
> Hope comes to Die.
> A Dream – a *Wa*-kening.

But now Sadie interrupted them. 'What is it, Sadie?'

'If you please, m'm, cook says have you got the flags for the sandwiches?'

'The flags for the sandwiches, Sadie?' echoed Mrs Sheridan dreamily. And the children knew by her face that she hadn't got them. 'Let me see.' And she said to Sadie firmly, 'Tell cook I'll let her have them in ten minutes.'

Sadie went.

'Now, Laura,' said her mother quickly, 'come with me into the smoking-room. I've got the names somewhere on the back of an envelope. You'll have to write them out for me. Meg, go upstairs this minute and take that wet thing off your head. Jose, run and finish dressing this instant. Do you hear me, children, or shall I have to tell your father when he comes home tonight? And – and, Jose, pacify cook if you do go into the kitchen, will you? I'm terrified of her this morning.'

The envelope was found at last behind the dining room clock, though how it had got there Mrs Sheridan could not imagine.

'One of you children must have stolen it out of my bag, because I remember vividly – cream cheese and lemon curd. Have you done that?'

'Yes.'

'Egg and –' Mrs Sheridan held the envelope away from her. 'It looks like mice. It can't be mice, can it?'

'Olive, pet,' said Laura, looking over her shoulder.

'Yes, of course, olive. What a horrible combination it sounds. Egg and olive.'

They were finished at last, and Laura took them off to the kitchen. She found Jose there pacifying the cook, who did not look at all terrifying.

'I have never seen such exquisite sandwiches,' said Jose's rapturous voice. 'How many kinds did you say there were, cook? Fifteen?'

'Fifteen, Miss Jose.'

'Well, cook, I congratulate you.'

Cook swept up crusts with the long sandwich knife, and smiled broadly.

'Godber's has come,' announced Sadie, issuing out of the pantry. She had seen the man pass the window.

That meant the cream puffs had come. Godber's were famous for their cream puffs. Nobody ever thought of making them at home.

'Bring them in and put them on the table, my girl,' ordered cook.

Sadie brought them in and went back to the door. Of course Laura and Jose were far too grown-up to really care about such things. All the same, they couldn't help agreeing that the puffs looked very attractive. Very. Cook began arranging them, shaking off the extra icing sugar.

'Don't they carry one back to all one's parties?' said Laura.

'I suppose they do,' said practical Jose, who never liked to be carried back. 'They look beautifully light and feathery, I must say.'

'Have one each, my dears,' said cook in her comfortable voice. 'Yer ma won't know.'

Oh, impossible. Fancy cream puffs so soon after breakfast. The very idea made one shudder. All the same, two minutes later Jose and Laura were licking their fingers with that absorbed inward look that only comes from whipped cream.

'Let's go into the garden, out by the back way,' suggested Laura. 'I want to see how the men are getting on with the marquee. They're such awfully nice men.'

But the back door was blocked by cook, Sadie, Godber's man and Hans.

Something had happened.

'Tuk-tuk-tuk,' clucked cook like an agitated hen. Sadie had her hand clapped to her cheek as though she had toothache. Hans's face was screwed up in the effort to understand. Only Godber's man seemed to be enjoying himself; it was his story.

'What's the matter? What's happened?'

'There's been a horrible accident,' said cook. 'A man killed.'

'A man killed! Where? How? When?'

But Godber's man wasn't going to have his story snatched from under his very nose.

'Know those little cottages just below here, miss?' Know them? Of course she knew them. 'Well, there's a young chap living there, name of Scott, a carter. His horse shied at a traction-engine, corner of Hawke Street this morning, and he was thrown out on the back of his head. Killed.'

'Dead!' Laura stared at Godber's man.

'Dead when they picked him up,' said Godber's man with relish. 'They were taking the body home as I come up here.' And he said to the cook, 'He's left a wife and five little ones.'

'Jose, come here.' Laura caught hold of her sister's sleeve and dragged her through the kitchen to the other side of the green baize door. There she paused and leaned against it. 'Jose!' she said, horrified, 'however are we going to stop everything?'

'Stop everything, Laura!' cried Jose in astonishment. 'What do you mean?'

'Stop the garden party, of course.' Why did Jose pretend?

But Jose was still more amazed. 'Stop the garden party? My dear Laura, don't be so absurd. Of course we can't do anything of the kind. Nobody expects us to. Don't be so extravagant.'

'But we can't possibly have a garden party with a man dead just outside the front gate.'

That really was extravagant, for the little cottages were in a lane to themselves at the very bottom of a steep rise that led up to the house. A broad road ran between. True, they were far too near. They were the greatest possible eyesore and they had no right to be in that neighbourhood at all. They were little mean dwellings painted a chocolate brown. In the garden patches there was nothing but cabbage stalks, sick hens and tomato cans. The very smoke coming out of their chimneys was poverty-stricken. Little rags and shreds of smoke, so unlike the great silvery plumes that uncurled from the Sheridans' chimneys. Washerwomen lived in the lane and sweeps and a cobbler and a man whose house-front was studded all over with minute birdcages. Children swarmed. When the Sheridans were little they were forbidden to set foot there because of the revolting language and of what they might catch. But since they were grown up Laura and Laurie on their prowls sometimes walked through. It was disgusting and sordid. They came out with a shudder. But still one must go everywhere; one must see everything. So through they went.

'And just think of what the band would sound like to that poor woman,' said Laura.

'Oh, Laura!' Jose began to be seriously annoyed. 'If you're going to stop a band playing every time someone has an accident, you'll lead a very strenuous life. I'm every bit as sorry about it as you. I feel just as sympathetic.' Her eyes hardened. She looked at her sister just as she used to when they were little and fighting together. 'You won't bring a drunken workman back to life by being sentimental,' she said softly.

'Drunk! Who said he was drunk?' Laura turned furiously on Jose. She said just as they had used to say on those occasions, 'I'm going straight up to tell mother.'

'Do, dear,' cooed Jose.

'Mother, can I come into your room?' Laura turned the big glass doorknob.

'Of course, child. Why, what's the matter? What's given you such a colour?' And Mrs Sheridan turned round from her dressing table. She was trying on a new hat.

'Mother, a man's been killed,' began Laura.

'*Not* in the garden?' interrupted her mother.

'No, no!'

'Oh, what a fright you gave me!' Mrs Sheridan sighed with relief and took off the big hat and held it on her knees.

'But listen, mother,' said Laura. Breathless, half choking, she told the dreadful story. 'Of course, we can't have our party, can we?' she pleaded. 'The band and everybody arriving. They'd hear us, mother; they're nearly neighbours!'

To Laura's astonishment her mother behaved just like Jose; it was harder to bear because she seemed amused. She refused to take Laura seriously.

'But, my dear child, use your common sense. It's only by accident we've heard of it. If someone had died there normally – and I can't understand how they keep alive in those poky little holes – we should still be having our party, shouldn't we?'

Laura had to say 'yes' to that, but she felt it was all wrong. She sat down on her mother's sofa and pinched the cushion frill.

'Mother, isn't it really terribly heartless of us?' she asked.

'Darling!' Mrs Sheridan got up and came over to her, carrying the hat. Before Laura could stop her she had popped it on. 'My child!' said her mother, 'the hat is yours. It's made for you. It's much too young for me. I have never seen you look such a picture. Look at yourself!' And she held up her hand-mirror.

'But, mother,' Laura began again. She couldn't look at herself; she turned aside.

This time Mrs Sheridan lost patience just as Jose had done.

'You are being very absurd, Laura,' she said coldly. 'People like that don't expect sacrifices from us. And it's not very sympathetic to spoil everybody's enjoyment as you're doing now.'

'I don't understand,' said Laura, and she walked quickly out of the room into her own bedroom. There, quite by chance, the first thing she saw was this charming girl in the mirror, in her black hat trimmed with gold daisies and a long black velvet ribbon. Never had she imagined she could look like that. Is mother right? she thought. And now she hoped her mother was right. Am I being extravagant? Perhaps it was extravagant. Just for a moment she had another glimpse of that poor woman and those little children and the body being carried into the house. But it all seemed blurred, unreal, like a picture in the newspaper. I'll remember it again after the party's over, she decided. And somehow that seemed quite the best plan . . .

Lunch was over by half past one. By half past two they were all ready for the fray. The green-coated band had arrived and was established in a corner of the tennis court.

'My dear!' trilled Kitty Maitland, 'aren't they too like frogs for words? You ought to have arranged them round the pond with the conductor in the middle on a leaf.'

Laurie arrived and hailed them on his way to dress. At the sight of him Laura remembered the accident again. She wanted to tell him. If Laurie agreed with the others, then it was bound to be all right. And she followed him into the hall.

'Laurie!'

'Hallo!' He was half-way upstairs, but when he turned round and saw Laura he suddenly puffed out his cheeks and goggled his eyes at her. 'My word, Laura! You do look stunning,' said Laurie. 'What an absolutely topping hat!'

Laura said faintly 'Is it?' and smiled up at Laurie and didn't tell him after all.

Soon after that people began coming in streams. The band

struck up; the hired waiters ran from the house to the marquee. Wherever you looked there were couples strolling, bending to the flowers, greeting, moving on over the lawn. They were like bright birds that had alighted in the Sheridans' garden for this one afternoon, on their way to – where? Ah, what happiness it is to be with people who all are happy, to press hands, press cheeks, smile into eyes.

'Darling Laura, how well you look!'

'What a becoming hat, child!'

'Laura, you look quite Spanish. I've never seen you look so striking.'

And Laura, glowing, answered softly, 'Have you had tea? Won't you have an ice? The passion fruit ices really are rather special.' She ran to her father and begged him: 'Daddy darling, can't the band have something to drink?'

And the perfect afternoon slowly ripened, slowly faded, slowly its petals closed.

'Never a more delightful garden party . . .' 'The greatest success . . .' 'Quite the most . . .'

Laura helped her mother with the goodbyes. They stood side by side in the porch till it was all over.

'All over, all over, thank heaven,' said Mrs Sheridan. 'Round up the others, Laura. Let's go and have some fresh coffee. I'm exhausted. Yes, it's been very successful. But oh, these parties, these parties! Why will you children insist on giving parties!' And they all of them sat down in the deserted marquee.

'Have a sandwich, daddy dear. I wrote the flag.'

'Thanks.' Mr Sheridan took a bite and the sandwich was gone. He took another. 'I suppose you didn't hear of a beastly accident that happened today?' he said.

'My dear,' said Mrs Sheridan, holding up her hand, 'we did. It nearly ruined the party. Laura insisted we should put it off.'

'Oh, mother!' Laura didn't want to be teased about it.

'It was a horrible affair all the same,' said Mr Sheridan. 'The chap was married too. Lived just below in the lane, and leaves a wife and half a dozen kiddies, so they say.'

An awkward little silence fell. Mrs Sheridan fidgeted with her cup. Really, it was very tactless of father . . .

Suddenly she looked up. There on the table were all those

sandwiches, cakes, puffs, all uneaten, all going to be wasted. She had one of her brilliant ideas.

'I know,' she said. 'Let's make up a basket. Let's send that poor creature some of this perfectly good food. At any rate, it will be the greatest treat for the children. Don't you agree? And she's sure to have neighbours calling in and so on. What a point to have it all ready prepared. Laura!' She jumped up. 'Get me the big basket out of the stairs cupboard.'

'But, mother, do you really think it's a good idea?' said Laura.

Again, how curious, she seemed to be different from them all. To take scraps from their party. Would the poor woman really like that?

'Of course! What's the matter with you today? An hour or two ago you were insisting on us being sympathetic.'

Oh well! Laura ran for the basket. It was filled, it was now heaped by her mother.

'Take it yourself, darling,' said she. 'Run down just as you are. No, wait, take the arum lilies too. People of that class are so impressed by arum lilies.'

'The stems will ruin her lace frock,' said practical Jose.

So they would. Just in time. 'Only the basket, then. And, Laura!' – her mother followed her out of the marquee – 'don't on any account –'

'What, mother?'

No, better not put such ideas into the child's head! 'Nothing! Run along.'

It was just growing dusky as Laura shut their garden gates. A big dog ran by like a shadow. The road gleamed white, and down below in the hollow the little cottages were in deep shade. How quiet it seemed after the afternoon. Here she was going down the hill to somewhere where a man lay dead, and she couldn't realise it. Why couldn't she? She stopped a minute. And it seemed to her that kisses, voices, tinkling spoons, laughter, the smell of crushed grass were somehow inside her. She had no room for anything else. How strange! She looked up at the pale sky, and all she thought was, 'Yes, it was the most successful party.'

Now the broad road was crossed. The lane began, smoky and dark. Women in shawls and men's tweed caps hurried by. Men hung over the palings; the children played in the doorways. A low hum came from the mean little cottages. In some of them there was a flicker of light, and a shadow, crab-like, moved across the window. Laura bent her head and hurried on. She wished now she had put on a coat. How her frock shone! And the big hat with the velvet streamer – if only it was another hat! Were the people looking at her? They must be. It was a mistake to have come; she knew all along it was a mistake. Should she go back even now?

No, too late. This was the house. It must be. A dark knot of people stood outside. Beside the gate an old, old woman with a crutch sat in a chair, watching. She had her feet on a newspaper. The voices stopped as Laura drew near. The group parted. It was as though she was expected, as though they had known she was coming here.

Laura was terribly nervous. Tossing the velvet ribbon over her shoulder, she said to a woman standing by, 'Is this Mrs Scott's house?' and the woman, smiling queerly, said, 'It is, my lass.'

Oh, to be away from this! She actually said, 'Help me, God,' as she walked up the tiny path and knocked. To be away from those staring eyes, or to be covered up in anything, one of those women's shawls even. I'll just leave the basket and go, she decided. I shan't even wait for it to be emptied.

Then the door opened. A little woman in black showed in the gloom.

Laura said, 'Are you Mrs Scott?' But to her horror the woman answered, 'Walk in, please, miss,' and she was shut in the passage.

'No,' said Laura, 'I don't want to come in. I only want to leave this basket. Mother sent –'

The little woman in the gloomy passage seemed not to have heard her. 'Step this way, please, miss,' she said in an oily voice, and Laura followed her.

She found herself in a wretched little low kitchen, lighted by a smoky lamp. There was a woman sitting before the fire.

'Em,' said the little creature who had let her in. 'Em! It's a young lady.' She turned to Laura. She said meaningly, 'I'm 'er sister, miss. You'll excuse 'er, won't you?'

'Oh, but of course!' said Laura. 'Please, please don't disturb her. I – I only want to leave –'

But at that moment the woman at the fire turned round. Her face, puffed up, red, with swollen eyes and swollen lips, looked terrible. She seemed as though she couldn't understand why Laura was there. What did it mean? Why was this stranger standing in the kitchen with a basket? What was it all about? And the poor face puckered up again.

'All right, my dear,' said the other. 'I'll thenk the young lady.'

And again she began, 'You'll excuse her, miss, I'm sure,' and her face, swollen too, tried an oily smile.

Laura only wanted to get out, to get away. She was back in the passage. The door opened. She walked straight through into the bedroom, where the dead man was lying.

'You'd like a look at 'im, wouldn't you?' said Em's sister, and she brushed past Laura over to the bed. 'Don't be afraid, my lass' – and now her voice sounded fond and sly, and fondly she drew down the sheet – ''e looks a picture. There's nothing to show. Come along, my dear.'

Laura came.

There lay a young man, fast asleep – sleeping so soundly, so deeply, that he was far, far away from them both. Oh, so remote, so peaceful. He was dreaming. Never wake him up again. His head was sunk in the pillow, his eyes were closed; they were blind under the closed eyelids. He was given up to his dream. What did garden parties and baskets and lace frocks matter to him? He was far from all those things. He was wonderful, beautiful. While they were laughing and while the band was playing, this marvel had come to the lane. Happy . . . happy . . . All is well, said that sleeping face. This is just as it should be. I am content.

But all the same you had to cry, and she couldn't go out of the room without saying something to him. Laura gave a loud childish sob.

'Forgive my hat,' she said.

And this time she didn't wait for Em's sister. She found her way out of the door, down the path past all those dark people. At the corner of the lane she met Laurie.

He stepped out of the shadow. 'Is that you, Laura?'

'Yes.'

'Mother was getting anxious. Was it all right?'

'Yes, quite, Oh, Laurie!' She took his arm, she pressed up against him.

'I say, you're not crying, are you?' asked her brother.

Laura shook her head. She was.

Laurie put his arm round her shoulder. 'Don't cry,' he said in his warm, loving voice. 'Was it awful?'

'No,' sobbed Laura. 'It was simply marvellous. But, Laurie –' She stopped, she looked at her brother. 'Isn't life,' she stammered, 'isn't life –' But what life was she couldn't explain. No matter. He quite understood.

'*Isn't* it, darling?' said Laurie.

A Jury of Her Peers

SUSAN GLASPELL

When Martha Hale opened the storm-door and got a cut of the north wind, she ran back for her big woolen scarf. As she hurriedly wound that round her head her eye made a scandalized sweep of her kitchen. It was no ordinary thing that called her away – it was probably farther from ordinary than anything that had ever happened in Dickson County. But what her eye took in was that her kitchen was in no shape for leaving: her bread all ready for mixing, half the flour sifted and half unsifted.

She hated to see things half done; but she had been at that when the team from town stopped to get Mr Hale, and then the sheriff came running in to say his wife wished Mrs Hale would come too – adding, with a grin, that he guessed she was getting scarey and wanted another woman along. So she had dropped everything right where it was.

'Martha!' now came her husband's impatient voice. 'Don't keep folks waiting out here in the cold.'

She again opened the storm-door, and this time joined the three men and the one woman waiting for her in the big, two-seated buggy.

After she had the robes tucked around her she took another look at the woman who sat beside her on the back seat. She had met Mrs Peters the year before at the county fair, and the thing she remembered about her was that she didn't seem like a sheriff's wife. She was small and thin and didn't have a strong voice. Mrs Gorman, sheriff's wife before Gorman went out and Peters came in, had a voice that somehow seemed to be backing up the law with every word. But if Mrs Peters didn't look like a sheriff's wife, Peters made it up in looking like a sheriff. He was to a dot the kind of man who could get himself elected sheriff – a heavy man with a big voice, who was particularly genial with the law-abiding, as if to make it plain that he knew the difference between criminals and non-criminals. And right there it came into Mrs Hale's mind, with a stab, that this man who was so pleasant and lively with all of them was going to the Wrights' now as a sheriff.

'The country's not very pleasant this time of year,' Mrs Peters at last ventured, as if she felt they ought to be talking as well as the men.

Mrs Hale scarcely finished her reply, for they had gone up a little hill and could see the Wright place now, and seeing it did not make her feel like talking. It looked very lonesome this cold March morning. It had always been a lonesome-looking place. It was down in a hollow, and the poplar trees around it were lonesome-looking trees. The men were looking at it and talking about what had happened. The county attorney was bending to one side of the buggy, and kept looking steadily at the place as they drew up to it.

'I'm glad you came with me,' Mrs Peters said nervously, as the two women were about to follow the men in through the kitchen door.

Even after she had her foot on the door-step, her hand on the knob, Martha Hale had a moment of feeling she could not cross that threshold. And the reason it seemed she couldn't cross it now was simply because she hadn't crossed it before. Time and time again it had been in her mind. 'I ought to go over and see Minnie Foster' – she still thought of her as Minnie Foster, though for twenty years she had been Mrs Wright. And then there was always something to do and Minnie Foster would go from her mind. But *now* she could come.

The men went over to the stove. The women stood close together by the door. Young Henderson, the county attorney, turned around and said, 'Come up to the fire, ladies.'

Mrs Peters took a step forward, then stopped. 'I'm not – cold,' she said.

And so the two women stood by the door, at first not even so much as looking around the kitchen.

The men talked for a minute about what a good thing it was the sheriff had sent his deputy out that morning to make a fire for them, and then Sheriff Peters stepped back from the stove, unbuttoned his outer coat, and leaned his hands on the kitchen table in a way that seemed to mark the beginning of official business. 'Now, Mr Hale,' he said in a sort of semi-official voice,

'before we move things about, you tell Mr Henderson just what it
was you saw when you came here yesterday morning.'

The county attorney was looking around the kitchen.

'By the way,' he said, 'has anything been moved?' He turned to
the sheriff. 'Are things just as you left them yesterday?'

Peters looked from cupboard to sink; from that to a small worn
rocker a little to one side of the kitchen table.

'It's just the same.'

'Somebody should have been left here yesterday,' said the
county attorney.

'Oh – yesterday,' returned the sheriff, with a little gesture as of
yesterday having been more than he could bear to think of.
'When I had to send Frank to Morris Center for that man who
went crazy – let me tell you, I had my hands full *yesterday*. I
knew you could get back from Omaha by today, George, and as
long as I went over everything here myself –'

'Well, Mr Hale,' said the county attorney, in a way of letting
what was past and gone go, 'tell just what happened when you
came here yesterday morning.'

Mrs Hale, still leaning against the door, had that sinking
feeling of the mother whose child is about to speak a piece. Lewis
often wandered along and got things mixed up in a story. She
hoped he would tell this straight and plain, and not say
unnecessary things that would just make things harder for
Minnie Foster. He didn't begin at once, and she noticed that he
looked queer – as if standing in that kitchen and having to tell
what he had seen there yesterday morning made him almost
sick.

'Yes, Mr Hale?' the county attorney reminded.

'Harry and I had started to town with a load of potatoes,' Mrs
Hale's husband began.

Harry was Mrs Hale's oldest boy. He wasn't with them now, for
the very good reason that those potatoes never got to town
yesterday and he was taking them this morning, so he hadn't
been home when the sheriff stopped to say he wanted Mr Hale to
come over to the Wright place and tell the county attorney his
story there, where he could point it all out. With all Mrs Hale's
other emotions came the fear now that maybe Harry wasn't
dressed warm enough – they hadn't any of them realized how
that north wind did bite.

'We come along this road,' Hale was going on, with a motion of his hand to the road over which they had just come, 'and as we got in sight of the house I says to Harry, "I'm goin' to see if I can't get John Wright to take a telephone." You see,' he explained to Henderson, 'unless I can get somebody to go in with me they won't come out this branch road except for a price I can't pay. I'd spoke to Wright about it once before; but he put me off, saying folks talked too much anyway, and all he asked was peace and quiet – guess you know about how much he talked himself. But I thought maybe if I went to the house and talked about it before his wife, and said all the women-folks liked the telephones, and that in this lonesome stretch of road it would be a good thing – well, I said to Harry that that was what I was going to say – though I said at the same time that I didn't know as what his wife wanted made much difference to John –'

Now, there he was! – saying things he didn't need to say. Mrs Hale tried to catch her husband's eye, but fortunately the county attorney interrupted with:

'Let's talk about that a little later, Mr Hale. I do want to talk about that, but I'm anxious now to get along to just what happened when you got here.'

When he began this time, it was very deliberately and carefully:

'I didn't see or hear anything. I knocked at the door. And still it was all quiet inside. I knew they must be up – it was past eight o'clock. So I knocked again, louder, and I thought I heard somebody say, "Come in." I wasn't sure – I'm not sure yet. But I opened the door – this door,' jerking a hand toward the door by which the two women stood, 'and there, in that rocker' – pointing to it – 'sat Mrs Wright.'

Everyone in the kitchen looked at the rocker. It came into Mrs Hale's mind that that rocker didn't look in the least like Minnie Foster – the Minnie Foster of twenty years before. It was a dingy red, with wooden rungs up the back, and the middle rung was gone, and the chair sagged to one side.

'How did she – look?' the county attorney was inquiring.

'Well,' said Hale, 'she looked – queer.'

'How do you mean – queer?'

As he asked it he took out a notebook and pencil. Mrs Hale did not like the sight of that pencil. She kept her eye fixed on her husband, as if to keep him from saying unnecessary things that would go into that notebook and make trouble.

Hale did speak guardedly, as if the pencil had affected him too.

'Well, as if she didn't know what she was going to do next. And kind of – done up.'

'How did she seem to feel about your coming?'

'Why, I don't think she minded – one way or other. She didn't pay much attention. I said, "Ho' do, Mrs Wright? It's cold, ain't it?" And she said, "Is it?" – and went on pleatin' at her apron.

'Well, I was surprised. She didn't ask me to come up to the stove, or to sit down, but just set there, not even lookin' at me. And so I said: "I want to see John."

'And then she – laughed. I guess you would call it a laugh.

'I thought of Harry and the team outside, so I said, a little sharp, "Can I see John?" "No," says she – kind of dull like. "Ain't he home?" says I. Then she looked at me. "Yes," says she, "he's home." "Then why can't I see him?" I asked her, out of patience with her now. "'Cause he's dead," says she, just as quiet and dull – and fell to pleatin' her apron. "Dead?" says I, like you do when you can't take in what you've heard.

'She just nodded her head, not getting a bit excited, but rockin' back and forth.

' "Why – where is he?" says I, not knowing *what* to say.

'She just pointed upstairs – like this' – pointing to the room above.

'I got up, with the idea of going up there myself. By this time I – didn't know what to do. I walked from there to here; then I says: "Why, what did he die of?"

' "He died of a rope round his neck," says she; and just went on pleatin' at her apron.'

Hale stopped speaking, and stood staring at the rocker, as if he were still seeing the woman who had sat there the morning before. Nobody spoke; it was as if every one were seeing the woman who had sat there the morning before.

'And what did you do then?' the county attorney at last broke the silence.

'I went out and called Harry. I thought I might – need help. I got Harry in, and we went upstairs.' His voice fell almost to a whisper. 'There he was – lying over the –'

'I think I'd rather have you go into that upstairs,' the county attorney interrupted, 'where you can point it all out. Just go on now with the rest of the story.'

'Well, my first thought was to get that rope off. It looked –'

He stopped, his face twitching.

'But Harry, he went up to him, and he said, "No, he's dead all right, and we'd better not touch anything." So we went downstairs.

'She was still sitting that same way. "Has anybody been notified?" I asked. "No," says she, unconcerned.

' "Who did this, Mrs Wright?" said Harry. He said it business-like, and she stopped pleatin' at her apron. "I don't know," she says. "You don't *know*?" says Harry. "Weren't you sleepin' in the bed with him?" "Yes," says she, "but I was on the inside." "Somebody slipped a rope round his neck and strangled him, and you didn't wake up?" says Harry. "I didn't wake up," she said after him.

'We may have looked as if we didn't see how that could be, for after a minute she said, "I sleep sound."

'Harry was going to ask her more questions, but I said maybe that weren't our business; maybe we ought to let her tell her story first to the coroner or the sheriff. So Harry went fast as he could over to High Road – the Rivers' place, where there's a telephone.'

'And what did she do when she knew you had gone for the coroner?' The attorney got his pencil in his hand all ready for writing.

'She moved from that chair to this one over here' – Hale pointed to a small chair in the corner – 'and just sat there with her hands held together and looking down. I got a feeling that I ought to make some conversation, so I said I had come in to see if John wanted to put in a telephone; and at that she started to laugh, and then she stopped and looked at me – scared.'

At sound of a moving pencil the man who was telling the story looked up.

'I dunno – maybe it wasn't scared,' he hastened; 'I wouldn't like to say it was. Soon Harry got back, and then Dr Lloyd came, and you, Mr Peters, and so I guess that's all I know that you don't.'

He said that last with relief, and moved a little, as if relaxing.

Everyone moved a little. The county attorney walked toward the stair door.

'I guess we'll go upstairs first – then out to the barn and around there.'

He paused and looked around the kitchen.

'You're convinced there was nothing important here?' he asked the sheriff. 'Nothing that would – point to any motive?'

The sheriff too looked all around, as if to re-convince himself.

'Nothing here but kitchen things,' he said, with a little laugh for the insignificance of kitchen things.

The county attorney was looking at the cupboard – a peculiar, ungainly structure, half closet and half cupboard, the upper part of it being built in the wall, and the lower part just the old-fashioned kitchen cupboard. As if its queerness attracted him, he got a chair and opened the upper part and looked in. After a moment he drew his hand away sticky.

'Here's a nice mess,' he said resentfully.

The two women had drawn nearer, and now the sheriff's wife spoke.

'Oh – her fruit,' she said, looking to Mrs Hale for sympathetic understanding. She turned back to the county attorney and explained: 'She worried about that when it turned so cold last night. She said the fire would go out and her jars might burst.'

Mrs Peter's husband broke into a laugh.

'Well, can you beat the woman! Held for murder, and worrying about her preserves!'

The young attorney set his lips.

'I guess before we're through with her she may have something more serious than preserves to worry about.'

'Oh, well,' said Mrs Hale's husband, with good-natured superiority, 'women are used to worrying over trifles.'

The two women moved a little closer together. Neither of them spoke. The county attorney seemed suddenly to remember his manners – and think of his future.

'And yet,' said he, with the gallantry of a young politician, 'for all their worries, what would we do without the ladies?'

The women did not speak, did not unbend. He went to the sink and began washing his hands. He turned to wipe them on the roller towel – whirled it for a cleaner place.

'Dirty towels! Not much of a housekeeper, would you say, ladies?'

He kicked his foot against some dirty pans under the sink.

'There's a great deal of work to be done on a farm,' said Mrs Hale stiffly.

'To be sure. And yet' – with a little bow at her – 'I know there are some Dickson County farm houses that do not have such roller towels.' He gave it a pull to expose its full length again.

'Those towels get dirty awful quick. Men's hands aren't always as clean as they might be.'

'Ah, loyal to your sex, I see,' he laughed. He stopped and gave her a keen look. 'But you and Mrs Wright were neighbors. I suppose you were friends, too.'

Martha Hale shook her head.

'I've seen little enough of her of late years. I've not been in this house – it's more than a year.'

'And why was that? You didn't like her?'

'I liked her well enough,' she replied with spirit. 'Farmers' wives have their hands full, Mr Henderson. And then –' She looked around the kitchen.

'Yes?' he encouraged.

'It never seemed a very cheerful place,' said she, more to herself than to him.

'No,' he agreed; 'I don't think any one would call it cheerful. I shouldn't say she had the home-making instinct.'

'Well, I don't know as Wright had, either,' she muttered.

'You mean they didn't get on very well?' he was quick to ask.

'No; I don't mean anything,' she answered, with decision. As she turned a little away from him, she added: 'But I don't think a place would be any the cheerfuler for John Wright's bein' in it.'

'I'd like to talk to you about that a little later, Mrs Hale,' he said. 'I'm anxious to get the lay of things upstairs now.'

He moved toward the stair door, followed by the two men.

'I suppose anything Mrs Peters does'll be all right?' the sheriff inquired. 'She was to take in some clothes for her, you know – and a few little things. We left in such a hurry yesterday.'

The county attorney looked at the two women whom they were leaving alone there among the kitchen things.

'Yes – Mrs Peters,' he said, his glance resting on the woman who was not Mrs Peters, the big farmer woman who stood

behind the sheriff's wife. 'Of course Mrs Peters is one of us,' he
said, in a manner of entrusting responsibility. 'And keep your eye
out, Mrs Peters, for anything that might be of use. No telling; you
women might come upon a clue to the motive – and that's the
thing we need.'

Mr Hale rubbed his face after the fashion of a show man
getting ready for a pleasantry.

'But would the women know a clue if they did come upon it?'
he said; and, having delivered himself of this, he followed the
others through the stair door.

The women stood motionless and silent, listening to the footsteps,
first upon the stairs, then in the room above them.

Then, as if releasing herself from something strange, Mrs Hale
began to arrange the dirty pans under the sink, which the county
attorney's disdainful push of the foot had deranged.

'I'd hate to have men comin' into my kitchen,' she said testily –
'snoopin' round and criticizin'.'

'Of course it's no more than their duty,' said the sheriff's wife,
in her manner of timid acquiescence.

'Duty's all right,' replied Mrs Hale bluffly; 'but I guess that
deputy sheriff that come out to make the fire might have got a
little of this on.' She gave the roller towel a pull. 'Wish I'd
thought of that sooner! Seems mean to talk about her for not
having things slicked up, when she had to come away in such a
hurry.'

She looked around the kitchen. Certainly it was not 'slicked
up.' Her eye was held by a bucket of sugar on a low shelf. The
cover was off the wooden bucket, and beside it was a paper bag –
half full.

Mrs Hale moved toward it.

'She was putting this in there,' she said to herself – slowly.

She thought of the flour in her kitchen at home – half sifted,
half not sifted. She had been interrupted, and had left things half
done. What had interrupted Minnie Foster? Why had that work
been left half done? She made a move as if to finish it, –
unfinished things always bothered her, – and then she glanced
around and saw that Mrs Peters was watching her – and she
didn't want Mrs Peters to get that feeling she had got of work
begun and then – for some reason – not finished.

'It's a shame about her fruit,' she said, and walked toward the cupboard that the county attorney had opened, and got on the chair, murmuring: 'I wonder if it's all gone.'

It was a sorry enough looking sight, but 'Here's one that's all right,' she said at last. She held it toward the light. 'This is cherries, too.' She looked again. 'I declare I believe that's the only one.'

With a sigh, she got down from the chair, went to the sink, and wiped off the bottle.

'She'll feel awful bad, after all her hard work in the hot weather. I remember the afternoon I put up my cherries last summer.'

She set the bottle on the table, and, with another sigh, started to sit down in the rocker. But she did not sit down. Something kept her from sitting down in that chair. She straightened – stepped back, and, half turned away, stood looking at it, seeing the woman who had sat there 'pleatin' at her apron.'

The thin voice of the sheriff's wife broke in upon her: 'I must be getting those things from the front room closet.' She opened the door into the other room, started in, stepped back. 'You coming with me, Mrs Hale?' she asked nervously. 'You – you could help me get them.'

They were soon back – the stark coldness of that shut-up room was not a thing to linger in.

'My!' said Mrs Peters, dropping the things on the table and hurrying to the stove.

Mrs Hale stood examining the clothes the woman who was being detained in town had said she wanted.

'Wright was close!' she exclaimed, holding up a shabby black skirt that bore the marks of much making over. 'I think maybe that's why she kept so much to herself. I s'pose she felt she couldn't do her part; and then, you don't enjoy things when you feel shabby. She used to wear pretty clothes and be lively – when she was Minnie Foster, one of the town girls, singing in the choir. But that – oh, that was twenty years ago.'

With a carefulness in which there was something tender, she folded the shabby clothes and piled them at one corner of the table. She looked up at Mrs Peters, and there was something in the other woman's look that irritated her.

'She don't care,' she said to herself. 'Much difference it makes to her whether Minnie Foster had pretty clothes when she was a girl.'

Then she looked again, and she wasn't so sure; in fact, she hadn't at any time been perfectly sure about Mrs Peters. She had that shrinking manner, and yet her eyes looked as if they could see a long way into things.

'This all you was to take in?' asked Mrs Hale.

'No,' said the sheriff's wife; 'she said she wanted an apron. Funny thing to want,' she ventured in her nervous little way, 'for there's not much to get you dirty in jail, goodness knows. But I suppose just to make her feel more natural. If you're used to wearing an apron – . She said they were in the bottom drawer of this cupboard. Yes – here they are. And then her little shawl that always hung on the stair door.'

She took the small gray shawl from behind the door leading upstairs, and stood a minute looking at it.

Suddenly Mrs Hale took a quick step toward the other woman.

'Mrs Peters!'

'Yes, Mrs Hale?'

'Do you think she – did it?'

A frightened look blurred the other thing in Mrs Peters' eyes.

'Oh, I don't know,' she said, in a voice that seemed to shrink away from the subject.

'Well, I don't think she did,' affirmed Mrs Hale stoutly. 'Asking for an apron, and her little shawl. Worryin' about her fruit.'

'Mr Peters says – .' Footsteps were heard in the room above; she stopped, looked up, then went on in a lowered voice: 'Mr Peters says – it looks bad for her. Mr Henderson is awful sarcastic in a speech, and he's going to make fun of her saying she didn't – wake up.'

For a moment Mrs Hale had no answer. Then, 'Well, I guess John Wright didn't wake up – when they was slippin' that rope under his neck,' she muttered.

'No, it's *strange*,' breathed Mrs Peters. 'They think it was such a – funny way to kill a man.'

She began to laugh; at sound of the laugh, abruptly stopped.

'That's just what Mr Hale said,' said Mrs Hale, in a resolutely natural voice. 'There was a gun in the house. He says that's what he can't understand.'

'Mr Henderson said, coming out, that what was needed for the case was a motive. Something to show anger – or sudden feeling.'

'Well, I don't see any signs of anger around here,' said Mrs Hale. 'I don't –'

She stopped. It was as if her mind tripped on something. Her eye was caught by a dish-towel in the middle of the kitchen table. Slowly she moved toward the table. One half of it was wiped clean, the other half messy. Her eyes made a slow, almost unwilling turn to the bucket of sugar and the half empty bag beside it. Things begun – and not finished.

After a moment she stepped back, and said, in that manner of releasing herself:

'Wonder how they're finding things upstairs? I hope she had it a little more red up there. You know,' – she paused, and feeling gathered, – 'it seems kind of *sneaking*: locking her up in town and coming out here to get her own house to turn against her!'

'But, Mrs Hale,' said the sheriff's wife, 'the law is the law.'

'I s'pose 'tis,' answered Mrs Hale shortly.

She turned to the stove, saying something about that fire not being much to brag of. She worked with it a minute, and when she straightened up she said aggressively:

'The law is the law – and a bad stove is a bad stove. How'd you like to cook on this?' – pointing with the poker to the broken lining. She opened the oven door and started to express her opinion of the oven; but she was swept into her own thoughts, thinking of what it would mean, year after year, to have that stove to wrestle with. The thought of Minnie Foster trying to bake in that oven – and the thought of her never going over to see Minnie Foster – .

She was startled by hearing Mrs Peters, say: 'A person gets discouraged – and loses heart.'

The sheriff's wife had looked from the stove to the sink – to the pail of water which had been carried in from outside. The two women stood there silent, above them the footsteps of the men who were looking for evidence against the woman who had worked in that kitchen. That look of seeing into things, of seeing through a thing to something else, was in the eyes of the sheriff's wife now. When Mrs Hale next spoke to her, it was gently:

'Better loosen up your things, Mrs Peters. We'll not feel them when we go out.'

Mrs Peters went to the back of the room to hang up the fur tippet she was wearing. A moment later she exclaimed, 'Why, she was piecing a quilt,' and held up a large sewing basket piled high with quilt pieces.

Mrs Hale spread some of the blocks out on the table. 'It's log-cabin pattern,' she said, putting several of them together. 'Pretty, isn't it?'

They were so engaged with the quilt that they did not hear the footsteps on the stairs. Just as the stair door opened Mrs Hale was saying:

'Do you suppose she was going to quilt it or just knot it?'

The sheriff threw up his hands.

'They wonder whether she was going to quilt it or just knot it!'

There was a laugh for the ways of women, a warming of hands over the stove, and then the county attorney said briskly:

'Well, let's go right out to the barn and get that cleared up.'

'I don't see as there's anything so strange,' Mrs Hale said resentfully, after the outside door had closed on the three men – 'our taking up our time with little things while we're waiting for them to get the evidence. I don't see as it's anything to laugh about.'

'Of course they've got awful important things on their minds,' said the sheriff's wife apologetically.

They returned to an inspection of the block for the quilt. Mrs Hale was looking at the fine, even sewing, and preoccupied with thoughts of the woman who had done that sewing, when she heard the sheriff's wife say, in a queer tone:

'Why, look at this one.'

She turned to take the block held out to her.

'The sewing,' said Mrs Peters, in a troubled way. 'All the rest of them have been so nice and even – but – this one. Why, it looks as if she didn't know what she was about!'

Their eyes met – something flashed to life, passed between them; then, as if with an effort, they seemed to pull away from each other. A moment Mrs Hale sat there, her hands folded over that sewing which was so unlike all the rest of the sewing. Then she had pulled a knot and drawn the threads.

'Oh, what are you doing, Mrs Hale?' asked the sheriff's wife, startled.

'Just pulling out a stitch or two that's not sewed very good,' said Mrs Hale mildly.

'I don't think we ought to touch things,' Mrs Peters said, a little helplessly.

'I'll just finish up this end,' answered Mrs Hale, still in that mild, matter-of-fact fashion.

She threaded a needle and started to replace bad sewing with good. For a little while she sewed in silence. Then, in that thin, timid voice, she heard:

'Mrs Hale!'

'Yes, Mrs Peters?'

'What do you suppose she was so – nervous about?'

'Oh, *I* don't know,' said Mrs Hale, as if dismissing a thing not important enough to spend much time on. 'I don't know as she was – nervous. I sew awful queer sometimes when I'm just tired.'

She cut a thread, and out of the corner of her eye looked up at Mrs Peters. The small, lean face of the sheriff's wife seemed to have tightened up. Her eyes had that look of peering into something. But next moment she moved, and said in her thin, indecisive way:

'Well, I must get those clothes wrapped. They may be through sooner than we think. I wonder where I could find a piece of paper – and string.'

'In that cupboard, maybe,' suggested Mrs Hale, after a glance around.

One piece of the crazy sewing remained unripped. Mrs Peter's back turned, Martha Hale now scrutinized that piece, compared it with the dainty, accurate sewing of the other blocks. The difference was startling. Holding this block made her feel queer, as if the distracted thoughts of the woman who had perhaps turned to it to try and quiet herself were communicating themselves to her.

Mrs Peters' voice roused her.

'Here's a bird-cage,' she said. 'Did she have a bird, Mrs Hale?'

'Why, I don't know whether she did or not.' She turned to look at the cage Mrs Peters was holding up. 'I've not been here in so long.' She sighed. 'There was a man round last year selling canaries cheap – but I don't know as she took one. Maybe she did. She used to sing real pretty herself.'

Mrs Peters looked around the kitchen.

'Seems kind of funny to think of a bird here.' She half laughed – an attempt to put up a barrier. 'But she must have had one – or why would she have a cage? I wonder what happened to it.'

'I suppose maybe the cat got it,' suggested Mrs Hale, resuming her sewing.

'No; she didn't have a cat. She's got that feeling some people have about cats – being afraid of them. When they brought her to our house yesterday, my cat got in the room, and she was real upset and asked me to take it out.'

'My sister Bessie was like that,' laughed Mrs Hale.

The sheriff's wife did not reply. The silence made Mrs Hale turn round. Mrs Peters was examining the bird-cage.

'Look at this door,' she said slowly. 'It's broke. One hinge has been pulled apart.'

Mrs Hale came nearer.

'Looks as if someone must have been – rough with it.'

Again their eyes met – startled, questioning, apprehensive. For a moment neither spoke nor stirred. Then Mrs Hale, turning away, said brusquely:

'If they're going to find any evidence, I wish they'd be about it. I don't like this place.'

'But I'm awful glad you came with me, Mrs Hale.' Mrs Peters put the bird-cage on the table and sat down. 'It would be lonesome for me – sitting here alone.'

'Yes, it would, wouldn't it?' agreed Mrs Hale, a certain determined naturalness in her voice. She had picked up the sewing, but now it dropped in her lap, and she murmured in a different voice: 'But I tell you what I *do* wish, Mrs Peters. I wish I had come over sometimes when she was here. I wish – I had.'

'But of course you were awful busy, Mrs Hale. Your house – and your children.'

'I could've come,' retorted Mrs Hale shortly. 'I stayed away because it weren't cheerful – and that's why I ought to have come. I' – she looked around – 'I've never liked this place. Maybe because it's down in a hollow and you don't see the road. I don't know what it is, but it's a lonesome place, and always was. I wish I had come over to see Minnie Foster sometimes. I can see now –' She did not put it into words.

'Well, you mustn't reproach yourself,' counseled Mrs Peters.

'Somehow, we just don't see how it is with other folks till – something comes up.'

'Not having children makes less work,' mused Mrs Hale, after a silence, 'but it makes a quiet house – and Wright out to work all day – and no company when he did come in. Did you know John Wright, Mrs Peters?'

'Not to know him. I've seen him in town. They say he was a good man.'

'Yes – good,' conceded John Wright's neighbor grimly. 'He didn't drink, and kept his word as well as most, I guess, and paid his debts. But he was a hard man, Mrs Peters. Just to pass the time of day with him – .' She stopped, shivered a little. 'Like a raw wind that gets to the bone.' Her eye fell upon the cage on the table before her, and she added, almost bitterly: 'I should think she would've wanted a bird!'

Suddenly she leaned forward, looking intently at the cage. 'But what do you s'pose went wrong with it?'

'I don't know,' returned Mrs Peters; 'unless it got sick and died.'

But after she said it she reached over and swung the broken door. Both women watched it as if somehow held by it.

'You didn't know – her?' Mrs Hale asked, a gentler note in her voice.

'Not till they brought her yesterday,' said the sheriff's wife.

'She – come to think of it, she was kind of like a bird herself. Real sweet and pretty, but kind of timid and – fluttery. How – she – did – change.'

That held her for a long time. Finally, as if struck with a happy thought and relieved to get back to everyday things, she exclaimed:

'Tell you what, Mrs Peters, why don't you take the quilt in with you? It might take up her mind.'

'Why, I think that's a real nice idea, Mrs Hale,' agreed the sheriff's wife, as if she too were glad to come into the atmosphere of a simple kindness. 'There couldn't possibly be any objection to that, could there? Now, just what will I take? I wonder if her patches are in here – and her things.'

They turned to the sewing basket.

'Here's some red,' said Mrs Hale, bringing out a roll of cloth. Underneath that was a box. 'Here, maybe her scissors are in here

– and her things.' She held it up. 'What a pretty box! I'll warrant that was something she had a long time ago – when she was a girl.'

She held it in her hand a moment; then, with a little sigh, opened it.

Instantly her hand went to her nose.

'Why – !'

Mrs Peters drew nearer – then turned away.

'There's something wrapped up in this piece of silk,' faltered Mrs Hale.

'This isn't her scissors,' said Mrs Peters, in a shrinking voice.

Her hand not steady, Mrs Hale raised the piece of silk. 'Oh, Mrs Peters!' she cried. 'It's –'

Mrs Peters bent closer.

'It's the bird,' she whispered.

'But, Mrs Peters!' cried Mrs Hale. '*Look* at it! Its *neck* – look at its neck! It's all – other side to.'

She held the box away from her.

The sheriff's wife again bent closer.

'Somebody wrung its neck,' said she, in a voice that was slow and deep.

And then again the eyes of the two women met – this time clung together in a look of dawning comprehension, of growing horror. Mrs Peters looked from the dead bird to the broken door of the cage. Again their eyes met. And just then there was a sound at the outside door.

Mrs Hale slipped the box under the quilt pieces in the basket, and sank into the chair before it. Mrs Peters stood holding to the table. The county attorney and the sheriff came in from outside.

'Well, ladies,' said the county attorney, as one turning from serious things to little pleasantries, 'have you decided whether she was going to quilt it or knot it?'

'We think,' began the sheriff's wife in a flurried voice, 'that she was going to – knot it.'

He was too preoccupied to notice the change that came in her voice on that last.

'Well, that's very interesting, I'm sure,' he said tolerantly. He caught sight of the bird-cage. 'Has the bird flown?'

'We think the cat got it,' said Mrs Hale in a voice curiously even.

He was walking up and down, as if thinking something out. 'Is there a cat?' he asked absently.

Mrs Hale shot a look up at the sheriff's wife.

'Well, not *now*,' said Mrs Peters. 'They're superstitious, you know; they leave.'

She sank into her chair.

The county attorney did not heed her. 'No sign at all of anyone having come in from the outside,' he said to Peters, in the manner of continuing an interrupted conversation. 'Their own rope. Now let's go upstairs again and go over it, piece by piece. It would have to have been someone who knew just the –'

The stair door closed behind them and their voices were lost.

The two women sat motionless, not looking at each other, but as if peering into something and at the same time holding back. When they spoke now it was as if they were afraid of what they were saying, but as if they could not help saying it.

'She liked the bird,' said Martha Hale, low and slowly. 'She was going to bury it in that pretty box.'

'When I was a girl,' said Mrs Peters, under her breath, 'my kitten – there was a boy took a hatchet, and before my eyes – before I could get there –' She covered her face an instant. 'If they hadn't held me back I would have' – she caught herself, looked upstairs where footsteps were heard, and finished weakly – 'hurt him.'

Then they sat without speaking or moving.

'I wonder how it would seem,' Mrs Hale at last began, as if feeling her way over strange ground – 'never to have had any children around?' Her eyes made a slow sweep of the kitchen, as if seeing what that kitchen had meant through all the years. 'No, Wright wouldn't like the bird,' she said after that – 'a thing that sang. She used to sing. He killed that too.' Her voice tightened.

Mrs Peters moved uneasily.

'Of course we don't know who killed the bird.'

'I knew John Wright,' was Mrs Hale's answer.

'It was an awful thing was done in this house that night, Mrs Hale,' said the sheriff's wife. 'Killing a man while he slept – slipping a thing round his neck that choked the life out of him.'

Mrs Hale's hand went out to the bird-cage.

'His neck. Choked the life out of him.'

'We don't *know* who killed him,' whispered Mrs Peters wildly. 'We don't *know*.'

Mrs Hale had not moved. 'If there had been years and years of – nothing, then a bird to sing to you, it would be awful – still – after the bird was still.'

It was as if something within her not herself had spoken, and it found in Mrs Peters something she did not know as herself.

'I know what stillness is,' she said, in a queer, monotonous voice. 'When we homesteaded in Dakota, and my first baby died – after he was two years old – and me with no other then –'

Mrs Hale stirred.

'How soon do you suppose they'll be through looking for evidence?'

'I know what stillness is,' repeated Mrs Peters, in just that same way. Then she too pulled back. 'The law has got to punish crime, Mrs Hale,' she said in her tight little way.

'I wish you'd seen Minnie Foster,' was the answer, 'when she wore a white dress with blue ribbons, and stood up there in the choir and sang.'

The picture of that girl, the fact that she had lived neighbor to that girl for twenty years, and had let her die for lack of life, was suddenly more than she could bear.

'Oh, I *wish* I'd come over here once in a while!' she cried. 'That was a crime! That was a crime! Who's going to punish that?'

'We mustn't take on,' said Mrs Peters, with a frightened look toward the stairs.

'I might 'a' *known* she needed help! I tell you, it's *queer*, Mrs Peters. We live close together, as we live far apart. We all go through the same things – it's all just a different kind of the same thing! If it weren't – why do you and I *understand*? Why do we *know* – what we know this minute?'

She dashed her hand across her eyes. Then, seeing the jar of fruit on the table, she reached for it and choked out:

'If I was you I wouldn't *tell* her her fruit was gone! Tell her it *ain't*. Tell her it's all right – all of it. Here – take this in to prove it to her! She – she may never know whether it was broke or not.'

She turned away.

Mrs Peters reached out for the bottle of fruit as if she were glad to take it – as if touching a familiar thing, having something to do, could keep her from something else. She got up, looked about for something to wrap the fruit in, took a petticoat from the pile of clothes she had brought from the front room, and nervously started winding that round the bottle.

'My!' she began, in a high, false voice, 'it's a good thing the men couldn't hear us! Getting all stirred up over a little thing like a – dead canary.' She hurried over that. 'As if that could have anything to do with – with – My, wouldn't they *laugh*?'

Footsteps were heard on the stairs.

'Maybe they would,' muttered Mrs Hale – 'maybe they wouldn't.'

'No, Peters,' said the county attorney incisively; 'it's all perfectly clear, except the reason for doing it. But you know juries when it comes to women. If there was some definite thing – something to show. Something to make a story about. A thing that would connect up with this clumsy way of doing it.'

In a covert way Mrs Hale looked at Mrs Peters. Mrs Peters was looking at her. Quickly they looked away from each other. The outer door opened and Mr Hale came in.

'I've got the team round now,' he said. 'Pretty cold out there.'

'I'm going to stay here awhile by myself,' the county attorney suddenly announced. 'You can send Frank out for me, can't you?' he asked the sheriff. 'I want to go over everything. I'm not satisfied we can't do better.'

Again, for one brief moment, the two women's eyes found one another.

The sheriff came up to the table.

'Did you want to see what Mrs Peters was going to take in?'

The county attorney picked up the apron. He laughed.

'Oh, I guess they're not very dangerous things the ladies have picked out.'

Mrs Hale's hand was on the sewing basket in which the box was concealed. She felt that she ought to take her hand off the basket. She did not seem able to. He picked up one of the quilt blocks which she had piled on to cover the box. Her eyes felt like fire. She had a feeling that if he took up the basket she would snatch it from him.

But he did not take it up. With another little laugh, he turned away, saying:

'No; Mrs Peters doesn't need supervising. For that matter, a sheriff's wife is married to the law. Ever think of it that way, Mrs Peters?'

Mrs Peters was standing beside the table. Mrs Hale shot a look up at her; but she could not see her face. Mrs Peters had turned away. When she spoke, her voice was muffled.

'Not – just that way,' she said.

'Married to the law!' chuckled Mrs Peters' husband. He moved toward the door into the front room, and said to the county attorney:

'I just want you to come in here a minute, George. We ought to take a look at these windows.'

'Oh – windows,' said the county attorney scoffingly.

'We'll be right out, Mr Hale,' said the sheriff to the farmer, who was still waiting by the door.

Hale went to look after the horses. The sheriff followed the county attorney into the other room. Again – for one final moment – the two women were alone in that kitchen.

Martha Hale sprang up, her hands tight together, looking at that other woman, with whom it rested. At first she could not see her eyes, for the sheriff's wife had not turned back since she turned away at that suggestion of being married to the law. But now Mrs Hale made her turn back. Her eyes made her turn back. Slowly, unwillingly, Mrs Peters turned her head until her eyes met the eyes of the other woman. There was a moment when they held each other in a steady, burning look in which there was no evasion nor flinching. Then Martha Hale's eyes pointed the way to the basket in which was hidden the thing that would make certain the conviction of the other woman – that woman who was not there and yet who had been there with them all through that hour.

For a moment Mrs Peters did not move. And then she did it. With a rush forward, she threw back the quilt pieces, got the box, tried to put it in her handbag. It was too big. Desperately she opened it, started to take the bird out. But there she broke – she could not touch the bird. She stood there helpless, foolish.

There was the sound of a knob turning in the inner door. Martha Hale snatched the box from the sheriff's wife, and got it in the pocket of her big coat just as the sheriff and the county attorney came back into the kitchen.

'Well, Henry,' said the county attorney facetiously, 'at least we

found out that she was not going to quilt it. She was going to –
what is it you call it, ladies?'

Mrs Hale's hand was against the pocket of her coat.

'We call it – knot it, Mr Henderson.'

Candaules and Gyges

HERODOTUS

Their rule endured for two and twenty generations of men, a space of five hundred and five years; during the whole of which period, from Agron to Candaules, the crown descended in the direct line from father to son.

Now it happened that this Candaules was in love with his own wife; and not only so, but thought her the fairest woman in the whole world. This fancy had strange consequences. There was in his body-guard a man whom he specially favoured, Gyges, the son of Dascylus. All affairs of greatest moment were entrusted by Candaules to this person, and to him he was wont to extol the surpassing beauty of his wife. So matters went on for a while. At length, one day, Candaules, who was fated to end ill, thus addressed his follower: 'I see thou dost not credit what I tell thee of my lady's loveliness; but come now, since men's ears are less credulous than their eyes, contrive some means whereby thou mayst behold her naked.' At this the other loudly exclaimed, saying, 'What most unwise speech is this, master, which thou hast uttered? Wouldst thou have me behold my mistress when she is naked? Bethink thee that a woman, with her clothes, puts off her bashfulness. Our fathers, in time past, distinguished right and wrong plainly enough, and it is our wisdom to submit to be taught by them. There is an old saying, "Let each look on his own." I hold thy wife for the fairest of all womankind. Only, I beseech thee, ask me not to do wickedly.'

Gyges thus endeavoured to decline the king's proposal, trembling lest some dreadful evil should befall him through it. But the king replied to him, 'Courage, friend; suspect me not of the design to prove thee by this discourse; nor dread thy mistress, lest mischief befall thee at her hands. Be sure I will so manage that she shall not even know that thou hast looked upon her. I will place thee behind the open door of the chamber in which we sleep. When I enter to go to rest she will follow me. There stands a chair close to the entrance, on which she will lay her clothes one by one as she takes them off. Thou wilt be able thus at thy leisure to peruse her person. Then, when she is moving from the chair toward the bed, and her back is turned on thee, be it thy care that she see thee not as thou passest through the doorway.'

Gyges, unable to escape, could but declare his readiness. Then Candaules, when bedtime came, led Gyges into his sleeping-chamber, and a moment after the queen followed. She entered, and laid her garments on the chair, and Gyges gazed on her. After a while she moved toward the bed, and her back being then turned, he glided stealthily from the apartment. As he was passing out, however, she saw him, and instantly divining what had happened, she neither screamed as her shame impelled her, nor even appeared to have noticed aught, purposing to take vengeance upon the husband who had so affronted her. For among the Lydians, and indeed among the barbarians generally, it is reckoned a deep disgrace, even to a man, to be seen naked.

No sound or sign of intelligence escaped her at the time. But in the morning, as soon as day broke, she hastened to choose from among her retinue, such as she knew to be most faithful to her, and preparing them for what was to ensue, summoned Gyges into her presence. Now it had often happened before that the queen had desired to confer with him, and he was accustomed to come to her at her call. He therefore obeyed the summons, not suspecting that she knew aught of what had occurred. Then she addressed these words to him: 'Take thy choice, Gyges, of two courses which are open to thee. Slay Candaules, and thereby become my lord, and obtain the Lydian throne, or die this moment in his room. So wilt thou not again, obeying all behests of thy master, behold what is not lawful for thee. It must needs be, that either he perish by whose counsel this thing was done, or thou, who sawest me naked, and so didst break our usages.' At these words Gyges stood awhile in mute astonishment; recovering after a time, he earnestly besought the queen that she would not compel him to so hard a choice. But finding he implored in vain, and that necessity was indeed laid on him to kill or to be killed, he made choice of life for himself, and replied by this inquiry: 'If it must be so, and thou compellest me against my will to put my lord to death, come, let me hear how thou wilt have me set on him.' 'Let him be attacked,' she answered, 'on that spot where I was by him shown naked to you, and let the assault be made when he is asleep.'

The Rocking-Horse Winner

D. H. LAWRENCE

There was a woman who was beautiful, who started with all the advantages, yet she had no luck. She married for love, and the love turned to dust. She had bonny children, yet she felt they had been thrust upon her, and she could not love them. They looked at her coldly, as if they were finding fault with her. And hurriedly she felt she must cover up some fault in herself. Yet what it was that she must cover up she never knew. Nevertheless, when her children were present, she always felt the centre of her heart go hard. This troubled her, and in her manner she was all the more gentle and anxious for her children, as if she loved them very much. Only she herself knew that at the centre of her heart was a hard little place that could not feel love, no, not for anybody. Everybody else said of her: 'She is such a good mother. She adores her children.' Only she herself, and her children themselves, knew it was not so. They read it in each other's eyes.

There were a boy and two little girls. They lived in a pleasant house, with a garden, and they had discreet servants, and felt themselves superior to anyone in the neighbourhood.

Although they lived in style, they felt always an anxiety in the house. There was never enough money. The mother had a small income, and the father had a small income, but not nearly enough for the social position which they had to keep up. The father went in to town to some office. But though he had good prospects, these prospects never materialized. There was always the grinding sense of the shortage of money, though the style was always kept up.

At last the mother said, 'I will see if *I* can't make something.' But she did not know where to begin. She racked her brains, and tried this thing and the other, but could not find anything successful. The failure made deep lines come into her face. Her children were growing up, they would have to go to school. There must be more money, there must be more money. The father, who was always very handsome and expensive in his tastes, seemed as if he never *would* be able to do anything worth doing. And the mother, who had a great belief in herself, did not succeed any better, and her tastes were just as expensive.

And so the house came to be haunted by the unspoken phrase: *There must be more money! There must be more money!* The children could hear it all the time, though nobody said it aloud. They heard it at Christmas, when the expensive and splendid toys filled the nursery. Behind the shining modern rocking-horse, behind the smart doll's-house, a voice would start whispering: 'There *must* be more money! There *must* be more money!' And the children would stop playing, to listen for a moment. They would look into each other's eyes to see if they had all heard. And each one saw in the eyes of the other two that they too had heard. 'There *must* be more money! There *must* be more money!'

It came whispering from the springs of the still-swaying rocking-horse, and even the horse, bending his wooden, champing head, heard it. The big doll, sitting so pink and smirking in her new pram, could hear it quite plainly, and seemed to be smirking all the more self-consciously because of it. The foolish puppy, too, that took the place of the teddy-bear, he was looking so extraordinarily foolish for no other reason but that he heard the secret whisper all over the house: 'There *must* be more money!'

Yet nobody ever said it aloud. The whisper was everywhere, and therefore no one spoke it. Just as no one ever says: 'We are breathing!' in spite of the fact that breath is coming and going all the time.

'Mother,' said the boy Paul one day, 'why don't we keep a car of our own? Why do we always use uncle's, or else a taxi?'

'Because we're the poor members of the family,' said the mother.

'But why *are* we, mother?'

'Well – I suppose,' she said slowly and bitterly, 'it's because your father has no luck.'

The boy was silent for some time.

'Is luck money, mother?' he asked, rather timidly.

'No, Paul. Not quite. It's what causes you to have money.'

'Oh!' said Paul vaguely. 'I thought when Uncle Oscar said *filthy lucker,* it meant money.'

'*Filthy lucre* does mean money,' said the mother. 'But it's lucre, not luck.'

'Oh!' said the boy, 'Then what *is* luck, mother?'

'It's what causes you to have money. If you're lucky you have money. That's why it's better to be born lucky than rich. If you're rich, you may lose your money. But if you're lucky, you will always get more money.'

'Oh! Will you? And is father not lucky?'

'Very unlucky, I should say,' she said bitterly.

The boy watched her with unsure eyes.

'Why?' he asked.

'I don't know. Nobody ever knows why one person is lucky and another unlucky.'

'Don't they? Nobody at all? Does *nobody* know?'

'Perhaps God. But He never tells.'

'He ought to, then. And aren't you lucky either, mother?'

'I can't be, if I married an unlucky husband.'

'But by yourself, aren't you?'

'I used to think I was, before I married. Now I think I am very unlucky indeed.'

'Why?'

'Well – never mind! Perhaps I'm not really,' she said.

The child looked at her, to see if she meant it. But he saw, by the lines of her mouth, that she was only trying to hide something from him.

'Well, anyhow,' he said stoutly, 'I'm a lucky person.'

'Why?' said his mother, with a sudden laugh.

He stared at her. He didn't even know why he had said it.

'God told me,' he asserted, brazening it out.

'I hope He did, dear!' she said, again with a laugh, but rather bitter.

'He did, mother!'

'Excellent!' said the mother, using one of her husband's exclamations.

The boy saw she did not believe him; or rather, that she paid no attention to his assertion. This angered him somewhere, and made him want to compel her attention.

He went off by himself, vaguely, in a childish way, seeking for the clue to 'luck'. Absorbed, taking no heed of other people, he went about with a sort of stealth, seeking inwardly for luck. He wanted luck, he wanted it, he wanted it. When the two girls were playing dolls in the nursery, he would sit on his big rocking-

horse, charging madly into space, with a frenzy that made the
little girls peer at him uneasily. Wildly the horse careered, the
waving dark hair of the boy tossed, his eyes had a strange glare
in them. The little girls dared not speak to him.

When he had ridden to the end of his mad little journey, he
climbed down and stood in front of his rocking-horse, staring
fixedly into its lowered face. Its red mouth was slightly open, its
big eye was wide and glassy-bright.

'Now!' he would silently command the snorting steed. 'Now,
take me to where there is luck! Now take me!'

And he would slash the horse on the neck with the little whip
he had asked Uncle Oscar for. He *knew* the horse could take him
to where there was luck, if only he forced it. So he would mount
again, and start on his furious ride, hoping at last to get there. He
knew he could get there.

'You'll break your horse, Paul!' said the nurse.

'He's always riding like that! I wish he'd leave off!' said his
elder sister Joan.

But he only glared down on them in silence. Nurse gave him
up. She could make nothing of him. Anyhow he was growing
beyond her.

One day his mother and his Uncle Oscar came in when he was
on one of his furious rides. He did not speak to them.

'Hallo, you young jockey! Riding a winner?' said his uncle.

'Aren't you growing too big for a rocking-horse? You're not a
very little boy any longer, you know,' said his mother.

But Paul only gave a blue glare from his big, rather close-set
eyes. He would speak to nobody when he was in full tilt. His
mother watched him with an anxious expression on her face.

At last he suddenly stopped forcing his horse into the
mechanical gallop, and slid down.

'Well, I got there!' he announced fiercely, his blue eyes still
flaring, and his sturdy long legs straddling apart.

'Where did you get to?' asked his mother.

'Where I wanted to go,' he flared back at her.

'That's right, son!' said Uncle Oscar. 'Don't you stop till you get
there. What's the horse's name?'

'He doesn't have a name,' said the boy.

'Gets on without all right?' asked the uncle.

'Well, he has different names. He was called Sansovino last week.'

'Sansovino, eh? Won the Ascot. How did you know his name?'

'He always talks about horse-races with Bassett,' said Joan.

The uncle was delighted to find that his small nephew was posted with all the racing news. Bassett, the young gardener, who had been wounded in the left foot in the war and had got his present job through Oscar Cresswell, whose batman he had been, was a perfect blade of the 'turf'. He lived in the racing events, and the small boy lived with him.

Oscar Cresswell got it all from Bassett.

'Master Paul comes and asks me, so I can't do more than tell him, sir,' said Bassett, his face terribly serious, as if he were speaking of religious matters.

'And does he ever put anything on a horse he fancies?'

'Well – I don't want to give him away – he's a young sport, a fine sport, sir. Would you mind asking him himself? He sort of takes a pleasure in it, and perhaps he'd feel I was giving him away, sir, if you don't mind.'

Bassett was serious as a church.

The uncle went back to his nephew, and took him off for a ride in the car.

'Say, Paul, old man, do you ever put anything on a horse?' the uncle asked.

The boy watched the handsome man closely.

'Why, do you think I oughtn't to?' he parried.

'Not a bit of it! I thought perhaps you might give me a tip for the Lincoln.'

The car sped on into the country, going down to Uncle Oscar's place in Hampshire.

'Honour bright?' said the nephew.

'Honour bright, son!' said the uncle.

'Well, then, Daffodil.'

'Daffodil! I doubt it, sonny. What about Mirza?'

'I only know the winner,' said the boy. 'That's Daffodil.'

'Daffodil, eh?'

There was a pause. Daffodil was an obscure horse comparatively.

'Uncle!'

'Yes, son?'

'You won't let it go any further, will you? I promised Bassett.'

'Bassett be damned, old man! What's he got to do with it?'

'We're partners. We've been partners from the first. Uncle, he lent me my first five shillings, which I lost. I promised him, honour bright, it was only between me and him; only you gave me that ten-shilling note I started winning with, so I thought you were lucky. You won't let it go any further, will you?'

The boy gazed at his uncle from those big, hot, blue eyes, set rather close together. The uncle stirred and laughed uneasily.

'Right you are, son! I'll keep your tip private. Daffodil, eh? How much are you putting on him?'

'All except twenty pounds,' said the boy. 'I keep that in reserve.'

The uncle thought it a good joke.

'You keep twenty pounds in reserve, do you, you young romancer? What are you betting, then?'

'I'm betting three hundred,' said the boy gravely. 'But it's between you and me, Uncle Oscar! Honour bright?'

The uncle burst into a roar of laughter.

'It's between you and me all right, you young Nat Gould,' he said, laughing. 'But where's your three hundred?'

'Bassett keeps it for me. We're partners.'

'You are, are you! And what is Bassett putting on Daffodil?'

'He won't go quite as high as I do, I expect. Perhaps he'll go a hundred and fifty.'

'What, pennies?' laughed the uncle.

'Pounds,' said the child, with a surprised look at his uncle. 'Bassett keeps a bigger reserve than I do.'

Between wonder and amusement Uncle Oscar was silent. He pursued the matter no further, but he determined to take his nephew with him to the Lincoln races.

'Now, son,' he said, 'I'm putting twenty on Mirza, and I'll put five for you on any horse you fancy. What's your pick?'

'Daffodil, uncle.'

'No, not the fiver on Daffodil!'

'I should if it was my own fiver,' said the child.

'Good! Good! Right you are! A fiver for me and a fiver for you on Daffodil.'

The child had never been to a race-meeting before, and his eyes were blue fire. He pursed his mouth tight, and watched. A

Frenchman just in front had put his money on Lancelot. Wild with excitement, he flayed his arms up and down, yelling '*Lancelot! Lancelot!*' in his French accent.

Daffodil came in first, Lancelot second, Mirza third. The child, flushed and with eyes blazing, was curiously serene. His uncle brought him four five-pounds notes, four to one.

'What am I to do with these?' he cried, waving them before the boy's eyes.

'I suppose we'll talk to Bassett,' said the boy. 'I expect I have fifteen hundred now; and twenty in reserve; and this twenty.'

His uncle studied him for some moments.

'Look here, son!' he said. 'You're not serious about Bassett and that fifteen hundred, are you?'

'Yes, I am. But it's between you and me, uncle. Honour bright!'

'Honour bright all right, son! But I must talk to Bassett.'

'If you'd like to be a partner, uncle, with Bassett and me, we could all be partners. Only, you'd have to promise, honour bright, uncle, not to let it go beyond us three. Bassett and I are lucky, and you must be lucky, because it was your ten shillings I started winning with . . .'

Uncle Oscar took both Bassett and Paul into Richmond Park for an afternoon, and there they talked.

'It's like this, you see, sir,' Bassett said. 'Master Paul would get me talking about racing events, spinning yarns, you know, sir. And he was always keen on knowing if I'd made or if I'd lost. It's about a year since, now, that I put five shillings on Blush of Dawn for him: and we lost. Then the luck turned, with that ten shillings he had from you: that we put on Singhalese. And since that time, it's been pretty steady, all things considering. What do you say, Master Paul.'

'We're all right when we're sure,' said Paul. 'It's when we're not quite sure that we go down.'

'Oh, but we're careful then,' said Bassett.

'But when are you *sure?*' smiled Uncle Oscar.

'It's Master Paul, sir,' said Bassett, in a secret, religious voice. 'It's as if he had it from heaven. Like Daffodil, now, for the Lincoln. That was as sure as eggs.'

'Did you put anything on Daffodil?' asked Oscar Cresswell.

'Yes, sir. I made my bit.'

'And my nephew?'

Bassett was obstinately silent, looking at Paul.

'I made twelve hundred, didn't I, Bassett? I told uncle I was putting three hundred on Daffodil.'

'That's right,' said Bassett, nodding.

'But where's the money?' asked the uncle.

'I keep it safe locked up, sir. Master Paul he can have it any minute he likes to ask for it.'

'What, fifteen hundred pounds?'

'And twenty! And *forty*, that is, with the twenty he made on the course.'

'It's amazing!' said the uncle.

'If Master Paul offers you to be partners, sir, I would, if I were you: if you'll excuse me,' said Bassett.

Oscar Cresswell thought about it.

'I'll see the money,' he said.

They drove home again, and, sure enough, Bassett came round to the garden-house with fifteen hundred pounds in notes. The twenty pounds reserve was left with Joe Glee, in the Turf Commission deposit.

'You see, it's all right, uncle, when I'm *sure!* Then we go strong, for all we're worth. Don't we, Bassett?'

'We do that, Master Paul.'

'And when are you sure?' said the uncle, laughing.

'Oh, well, sometimes I'm *absolutely* sure, like about Daffodil,' said the boy; 'and sometimes I have an idea; and sometimes I haven't even an idea, have I, Bassett? Then we're careful, because we mostly go down.'

'You do, do you! And when you're sure, like about Daffodil, what makes you sure, sonny?'

'Oh, well, I don't know,' said the boy uneasily. 'I'm sure, you know, uncle; that's all.'

'It's as if he had it from heaven, sir,' Bassett reiterated.

'I should say so!' said the uncle.

But he became a partner. And when the Leger was coming on Paul was 'sure' about Lively Spark, which was a quite inconsiderable horse. The boy insisted on putting a thousand on the horse, Bassett went for five hundred, and Oscar Creswell two hundred. Lively Spark came in first, and the betting had been ten to one against him. Paul had made ten thousand.

'You see,' he said, 'I was absolutely sure of him.'

Even Oscar Cresswell had cleared two thousand.

'Look here, son,' he said, 'this sort of thing makes me nervous.'

'It needn't, uncle! Perhaps I shan't be sure again for a long time.'

'But what are you going to do with your money?' asked the uncle.

'Of course,' said the boy, 'I started it for mother. She said she had no luck because father is unlucky, so I thought if *I* was lucky, it might stop whispering.'

'What might stop whispering?'

'Our house. I *hate* our house for whispering.'

'What does it whisper?'

'Why – why' – the boy fidgeted – 'why, I don't know. But it's always short of money, you know, uncle.'

'I know it, son, I know it.'

'You know people send mother writs, don't you, uncle?'

'I'm afraid I do,' said the uncle.

'And then the house whispers, like people laughing at you behind your back. It's awful, that is! I thought if I was lucky –'

'You might stop it,' added the uncle.

The boy watched him with big blue eyes, that had an uncanny cold fire in them, and he said never a word.

'Well, then!' said the uncle. 'What are we doing?'

'I shouldn't like mother to know I was lucky,' said the boy.

'Why not, son?'

'She'd stop me.'

'I don't think she would.'

'Oh!' – and the boy writhed in an odd way – 'I *don't* want her to know, uncle.'

'All right, son! We'll manage it without her knowing.'

They managed it very easily. Paul, at the other's suggestion, handed over five thousand pounds to his uncle, who deposited it with the family lawyer, who was then to inform Paul's mother that a relative had put five thousand pounds into his hands, which sum was to be paid out a thousand pounds at a time, on the mother's birthday, for the next five years.

'So she'll have a birthday present of a thousand pounds for five successive years,' said Uncle Oscar. 'I hope it won't make it all the harder for her later.'

Paul's mother had her birthday in November. The house had

been 'whispering' worse than ever lately, and, even in spite of his luck, Paul could not bear up against it. He was very anxious to see the effect of the birthday letter, telling his mother about the thousand pounds.

When there were no visitors, Paul now took his meals with his parents, as he was beyond the nursery control. His mother went into town nearly every day. She had discovered that she had an odd knack of sketching furs and dress materials, so she worked secretly in the studio of a friend who was the chief 'artist' for the leading drapers. She drew the figures of ladies in furs and ladies in silk and sequins for the newspaper advertisements. This young woman artist earned several thousand pounds a year, but Paul's mother only made several hundreds, and she was again dissatisfied. She so wanted to be first in something, and she did not succeed, even in making sketches for drapery advertisements.

She was down to breakfast on the morning of her birthday. Paul watched her face as she read her letters. He knew the lawyer's letter. As his mother read it, her face hardened and became more expressionless. Then a cold, determined look came on her mouth. She hid the letter under the pile of others, and said not a word about it.

'Didn't you have anything nice in the post for your birthday, mother?' said Paul.

'Quite moderately nice,' she said, her voice cold and absent.

She went away to town without saying more.

But in the afternoon Uncle Oscar appeared. He said Paul's mother had had a long interview with the lawyer, asking if the whole five thousand could not be advanced at once, as she was in debt.

'What do you think, uncle?' said the boy.

'I leave it to you, son.'

'Oh, let her have it, then! We can get some more with the other,' said the boy.

'A bird in the hand is worth two in the bush, laddie!' said Uncle Oscar.

'But I'm sure to *know* for the Grand National; or the Lincolnshire; or else the Derby. I'm sure to know for *one* of them,' said Paul.

So Uncle Oscar signed the agreement, and Paul's mother touched the whole five thousand. Then something very curious happened. The voices in the house suddenly went mad, like a chorus of frogs on a spring evening. There were certain new furnishings, and Paul had a tutor. He was *really* going to Eton, his father's school, in the following autumn. There were flowers in the winter, and a blossoming of the luxury Paul's mother had been used to. And yet the voices in the house, behind the sprays of mimosa and almond-blossom, and from under the piles of iridescent cushions, simply trilled and screamed in a sort of ecstasy: 'There *must* be more money! Oh-h-h; there *must* be more money. Oh, now, now-w! Now-w-w – there *must* be more money! – more than ever! More than ever!'

It frightened Paul terribly. He studied away at his Latin and Greek with his tutors. But his intense hours were spent with Bassett. The Grand National had gone by: he had not 'known', and had lost a hundred pounds. Summer was at hand. He was in agony for the Lincoln. But even for the Lincoln he didn't 'know', and he lost fifty pounds. He became wild-eyed and strange, as if something were going to explode in him.

'Let it alone, son! Don't you bother about it!' urged Uncle Oscar. But it was as if the boy couldn't really hear what his uncle was saying.

'I've got to know for the Derby! I've got to know for the Derby!' the child reiterated, his big blue eyes blazing with a sort of madness.

His mother noticed how overwrought he was.

'You'd better go to the seaside. Wouldn't you like to go now to the seaside, instead of waiting? I think you'd better,' she said, looking down at him anxiously, her heart curiously heavy because of him.

But the child lifted his uncanny blue eyes.

'I couldn't possibly go before the Derby, mother!' he said. 'I couldn't possibly!'

'Why not?' she said, her voice becoming heavy when she was opposed. 'Why not? You can still go from the seaside to see the Derby with your Uncle Oscar, if that's what you wish. No need for you to wait here. Besides, I think you care too much about these races. It's a bad sign. My family has been a gambling family, and you won't know till you grow up how much damage it has done. But it has done damage. I shall have to send Bassett away, and ask Uncle Oscar not to talk racing to you, unless you promise to be reasonable about it: go away to the seaside and forget it. You're all nerves!'

'I'll do what you like mother, so long as you don't send me away till after the Derby,' the boy said.

'Send you away from where? Just from this house?'

'Yes,' he said, gazing at her.

'Why, you curious child, what makes you care about this house so much, suddenly? I never knew you loved it.'

He gazed at her without speaking. He had a secret within a secret, something he had not divulged, even to Bassett or to his Uncle Oscar.

But his mother, after standing undecided and a little bit sullen for some moments, said:

'Very well, then! Don't go to the seaside till after the Derby, if you don't wish it. But promise me you won't let your nerves go to pieces. Promise you won't think so much about horse-racing and *events*, as you call them!'

'Oh, no,' said the boy casually. 'I won't think much about them, mother. You needn't worry. I wouldn't worry, mother, if I were you.'

'If you were me and I were you,' said his mother, 'I wonder what we *should* do!'

'But you know you needn't worry, mother, don't you?' the boy repeated.

'I should be awfully glad to know it,' she said wearily.

'Oh, well, you *can*, you know. I mean, you *ought* to know you needn't worry,' he insisted.

'Ought I? Then I'll see about it,' she said.

Paul's secret of secrets was his wooden horse, that which had no name. Since he was emancipated from a nurse and a nursery-governness, he had had his rocking-horse removed to his own bedroom at the top of the house.

'Surely, you're too big for a rocking-horse!' his mother had remonstrated.

'Well, you see, mother, till I can have a *real* horse, I like to have *some* sort of animal about,' had been his quaint answer.

'Do you feel he keeps you company?' she laughed.

'Oh, yes! He's very good, he always keeps me company, when I'm there,' said Paul.

So the horse, rather shabby, stood in an arrested prance in the boy's bedroom.

The Derby was drawing near, and the boy grew more and more tense. He hardly heard what was spoken to him, he was very frail, and his eyes were really uncanny. His mother had sudden strange seizures of uneasiness about him. Sometimes, for half an hour, she would feel a sudden anxiety about him that was almost anguish. She wanted to rush to him at once, and know he was safe.

Two nights before the Derby, she was at a big party in town, when one of her rushes of anxiety about her boy, her first-born, gripped her heart till she could hardly speak. She fought with the feeling, might and main, for she believed in common sense. But it was too strong. She had to leave the dance and go downstairs to telephone to the country. The children's nursery-governess was terribly surprised and startled at being rung up in the night.

'Are the children all right, Miss Wilmot?'

'Oh, yes, they are quite all right.'

'Master Paul? Is he all right?'

'He went to bed as right as a trivet. Shall I run up and look at him?'

'No,' said Paul's mother reluctantly. 'No! Don't trouble. It's all right. Don't sit up. We shall be home fairly soon.' She did not want her son's privacy intruded upon.

'Very good,' said the governess.

It was about one o'clock when Paul's mother and father drove up to their house. All was still. Paul's mother went to her room and slipped off her white fur cloak. She had told her maid not to wait up for her. She heard her husband downstairs, mixing a whisky and soda.

And then, because of the strange anxiety at her heart, she stole upstairs to her son's room. Noiselessly she went along the upper corridor. Was there a faint noise? What was it?

She stood, with arrested muscles, outside his door, listening. There was a strange, heavy, and yet not loud noise. Her heart stood still. It was a soundless noise, yet rushing and powerful. Something huge, in violent, hushed motion. What was it? What in God's name was it? She ought to know. She felt that she knew the noise. She knew what it was.

Yet she could not place it. She couldn't say what it was. And on and on it went, like a madness.

Softly, frozen with anxiety and fear, she turned the doorhandle. The room was dark. Yet in the space near the windows, she heard and saw something plunging to and fro. She gazed in fear and amazement.

Then suddenly she switched on the light, and saw her son, in his green pyjamas, madly surging on the rocking-horse. The blaze of light suddenly lit him up, as he urged the wooden horse, and lit her up, as she stood, blonde, in her dress of pale green and crystal, in the doorway.

'Paul!' she cried, 'Whatever are you doing?'

'It's Malabar!' he screamed, in a powerful, strange voice. 'It's Malabar!'

His eyes blazed at her for one strange and senseless second, as he ceased urging his wooden horse. Then he fell with a crash to the ground, and she, all her tormented motherhood flooding upon her, rushed to gather him up.

But he was unconscious, and unconscious he remained, with some brain-fever. He talked and tossed, and his mother sat stonily by his side.

'Malabar! It's Malabar! Bassett, Bassett, I *know*! It's Malabar!'

So the child cried, trying to get up and urge the rocking-horse that gave him his inspiration.

'What does he mean by Malabar?' asked the heart-frozen mother.

'I don't know,' said the father stonily.

'What does he mean by Malabar?' she asked her brother Oscar.

'It's one of the horses running for the Derby,' was the answer.

And, in spite of himself, Oscar Cresswell spoke to Bassett, and himself put a thousand on Malabar: at fourteen to one.

The third day of the illness was critical: they were waiting for a change. The boy, with his rather long, curly hair, was tossing ceaselessly on the pillow. He neither slept nor regained consciousness, and his eyes were like blue stones. His mother sat, feeling her heart had gone, turned actually into a stone.

In the evening, Oscar Cresswell did not come, but Bassett sent a message, saying could he come up for one moment, just one moment? Paul's mother was very angry at the intrusion, but on second thoughts she agreed. The boy was the same. Perhaps Bassett might bring him to consciousness.

The gardener, a shortish fellow with a little brown moustache, and sharp little brown eyes, tiptoed into the room, touched his imaginary cap to Paul's mother, and stole to the bedside, staring with glittering, smallish eyes at the tossing, dying child.

'Master Paul!' he whispered. 'Master Paul! Malabar came in first all right, a clean win. I did as you told me. You've made over seventy thousand pounds, you have; you've got over eighty thousand. Malabar came in all right, Master Paul.'

'Malabar! Malabar! Did I say Malabar, mother? Did I say Malabar? Do you think I'm lucky, mother? I knew Malabar, didn't I? Over eighty thousand pounds! I call that lucky, don't you, mother? Over eighty thousand pounds! I knew, didn't I know I knew? Malabar came in all right. If I ride my horse till I'm sure, then I tell you, Bassett, you can go as high as you like. Did you go for all you were worth, Bassett?'

'I went a thousand on it, Master Paul.'

'I never told you, mother, that if I can ride my horse, and *get there*, then I'm absolutely sure – oh, absolutely! Mother, did I ever tell you? I *am* lucky!'

'No, you never did,' said the mother.

But the boy died in the night.

And even as he lay dead, his mother heard her brother's voice saying to her: 'My God, Hester, you're eighty-odd thousand to the good, and a poor devil of a son to the bad. But, poor devil, poor devil, he's best gone out of a life where he rides his rocking-horse to find a winner.'

The Yellow Wallpaper

CHARLOTTE PERKINS GILMAN

It is very seldom that mere ordinary people like John and myself secure ancestral halls for the summer.

A colonial mansion, a hereditary estate, I would say a haunted house, and reach the height of romantic felicity – but that would be asking too much of fate!

Still I will proudly declare that there is something queer about it.

Else, why should it be let so cheaply? And why have stood so long untenanted?

John laughs at me, of course, but one expects that in marriage.

John is practical in the extreme. He has no patience with faith, an intense horror of superstition, and he scoffs openly at any talk of things not to be felt and seen and put down in figures.

John is a physician, and *perhaps* – (I would not say it to a living soul, of course, but this is dead paper and a great relief to my mind) – *perhaps* that is one reason I do not get well faster.

You see he does not believe I am sick!

And what can one do?

If a physician of high standing, and one's own husband, assures friends and relatives that there is really nothing the matter with one but temporary nervous depression – a slight hysterical tendency – what is one to do?

My brother is also a physician, and also of high standing, and he says the same thing.

So I take phosphates or phosphites – whichever it is, and tonics, and journeys, and air, and exercise, and am absolutely forbidden to 'work' until I am well again.

Personally, I disagree with their ideas.

Personally, I believe that congenial work, with excitement and change, would do me good.

But what is one to do?

I did write for a while in spite of them; but it *does* exhaust me a good deal – having to be so sly about it, or else meet with heavy opposition.

I sometimes fancy that in my condition if I had less opposition and more society and stimulus – but John says the very worst thing I can do is to think about my condition, and I confess it always makes me feel bad.

So I will let it alone and talk about the house.

The most beautiful place! It is quite alone, standing well back from the road, quite three miles from the village. It makes me think of English places that you read about, for there are hedges and walls and gates that lock, and lots of separate little houses for the gardeners and people.

There is a *delicious* garden! I never saw such a garden – large and shady, full of box-bordered paths, and lined with long grape-covered arbors with seats under them.

There were greenhouses, too, but they are all broken now.

There was some legal trouble, I believe, something about the heirs and coheirs; anyhow, the place has been empty for years.

That spoils my ghostliness, I am afraid, but I don't care – there is something strange about the house – I can feel it.

I even said so to John one moonlight evening, but he said what I felt was a *draught*, and shut the window.

I get unreasonably angry with John sometimes. I'm sure I never used to be so sensitive. I think it is due to this nervous condition.

But John says if I feel so, I shall neglect proper self-control; so I take pains to control myself – before him, at least, and that makes me very tired.

I don't like our room a bit. I wanted one downstairs that opened on the piazza and had roses all over the window, and such pretty old-fashioned chintz hangings! but John would not hear of it.

He said there was only one window and not room for two beds, and no near room for him if he took another.

He is very careful and loving, and hardly lets me stir without special direction.

I have a schedule prescription for each hour in the day; he takes all care from me, and so I feel basely ungrateful not to value it more.

He said we came here solely on my account, that I was to have perfect rest and all the air I could get. 'Your exercise depends on your strength, my dear,' said he, 'and your food somewhat on your appetite; but air you can absorb all the time.' So we took the nursery at the top of the house.

It is a big, airy room, the whole floor nearly, with windows that look all ways, and air and sunshine galore. It was nursery first and then playroom and gymnasium, I should judge; for the windows are barred for little children, and there are rings and things in the walls.

The paint and paper look as if a boys' school had used it. It is stripped off – the paper – in great patches all around the head of my bed, about as far as I can reach, and in a great place on the other side of the room low down. I never saw a worse paper in my life.

One of those sprawling flamboyant patterns committing every artistic sin.

It is dull enough to confuse the eye in following, pronounced enough to constantly irritate and provoke study, and when you follow the lame uncertain curves for a little distance they suddenly commit suicide – plunge off at outrageous angles, destroy themselves in unheard of contradictions.

The color is repellent, almost revolting; a smouldering unclean yellow, strangely faded by the slow-turning sunlight.

It is a dull yet lurid orange in some places, a sickly sulphur tint in others.

No wonder the children hated it! I should hate it myself if I had to live in this room long.

There comes John, and I must put this away, – he hates to have me write a word.

We have been here two weeks, and I haven't felt like writing before, since that first day.

I am sitting by the window now, up in this atrocious nursery, and there is nothing to hinder my writing as much as I please, save lack of strength.

John is away all day, and even some nights when his cases are serious.

I am glad my case is not serious!

But these nervous troubles are dreadfully depressing.

John does not know how much I really suffer. He knows there is no *reason* to suffer, and that satisfies him.

Of course it is only nervousness. It does weigh on me so not to do my duty in any way!

I meant to be such a help to John, such a real rest and comfort, and here I am a comparative burden already!

Nobody would believe what an effort it is to do what little I am able, – to dress and entertain, and order things.

It is fortunate Mary is so good with the baby. Such a dear baby!

And yet I *cannot* be with him, it makes me so nervous.

I suppose John never was nervous in his life. He laughs at me so about this wallpaper!

At first he meant to repaper the room, but afterwards he said that I was letting it get the better of me, and that nothing was worse for a nervous patient than to give way to such fancies.

He said that after the wallpaper was changed it would be the heavy bedstead, and then the barred windows, and then that gate at the head of the stairs, and so on.

'You know the place is doing you good,' he said, 'and really, dear, I don't care to renovate the house just for a three months' rental.'

'Then do let us go downstairs,' I said, 'there are such pretty rooms there.'

Then he took me in his arms and called me a blessed little goose, and said he would go down to the cellar, if I wished, and have it whitewashed into the bargain.

But he is right enough about the beds and windows and things.

It is an airy and comfortable room as any one need wish, and, of course, I would not be so silly as to make him uncomfortable just for a whim.

I'm really getting quite fond of the big room, all but that horrid paper.

Out of one window I can see the garden, those mysterious deepshaded arbors, the riotous old-fashioned flowers, and bushes and gnarly trees.

Out of another I get a lovely view of the bay and a little private wharf belonging to the estate. There is a beautiful shaded lane that runs down there from the house. I always fancy I see people walking in these numerous paths and arbors, but John has cautioned me not to give way to fancy in the least. He says that with my imaginative power and habit of story-making, a nervous weakness like mine is sure to lead to all manner of excited fancies, and that I ought to use my will and good sense to check the tendency. So I try.

I think sometimes that if I were only well enough to write a little it would relieve the press of ideas and rest me.

But I find I get pretty tired when I try.

It is so discouraging not to have any advice and companionship about my work. When I get really well, John says we will ask Cousin Henry and Julia down for a long visit; but he says he would as soon put fireworks in my pillow-case as to let me have those stimulating people about now.

I wish I could get well faster.

But I must not think about that. This paper looks to me as if it *knew* what a vicious influence it had!

There is a recurrent spot where the pattern lolls like a broken neck and two bulbous eyes stare at you upside down.

I get positively angry with the impertinence of it and the everlastingness. Up and down and sideways they crawl, and those absurd, unblinking eyes are everywhere. There is one place where two breaths didn't match, and the eyes go all up and down the line, one a little higher than the other.

I never saw so much expression in an inanimate thing before, and we all know how much expression they have! I used to lie awake as a child and get more entertainment and terror out of blank walls and plain furniture than most children could find in a toy-store.

I remember what a kindly wink the knobs of our big, old bureau used to have, and there was one chair that always seemed like a strong friend.

I used to feel that if any of the other things looked too fierce I could always hop into that chair and be safe.

The furniture in this room is no worse than inharmonious, however, for we had to bring it all from downstairs. I suppose when this was used as a playroom they had to take the nursery things out, and no wonder! I never saw such ravages as the children have made here.

The wallpaper, as I said before, is torn off in spots, and it sticketh closer than a brother – they must have had perseverance as well as hatred.

Then the floor is scratched and gouged and splintered, the

plaster itself is dug out here and there, and this great heavy bed which is all we found in the room, looks as if it had been through the wars.

But I don't mind it a bit – only the paper.

There comes John's sister. Such a dear girl as she is, and so careful of me! I must not let her find me writing.

She is a perfect and enthusiastic housekeeper, and hopes for no better profession. I verily believe she thinks it is the writing which made me sick!

But I can write when she is out, and see her a long way off from these windows.

There is one that commands the road, a lovely shaded winding road, and one that just looks off over the country. A lovely country, too, full of great elms and velvet meadows.

This wallpaper has a kind of sub-pattern in a different shade, a particularly irritating one, for you can only see it in certain lights, and not clearly then.

But in the places where it isn't faded and where the sun is just so – I can see a strange, provoking, formless sort of figure, that seems to skulk about behind that silly and conspicuous front design.

There's sister on the stairs!

Well, the Fourth of July is over! The people are all gone and I am tired out. John thought it might do me good to see a little company, so we just had Mother and Nellie and the children down for a week.

Of course I didn't do a thing, Jennie sees to everything now.

But it tired me all the same.

John says if I don't pick up faster he shall send me to Weir Mitchell in the fall.

But I don't want to go there at all. I had a friend who was in his hands once, and she says he is just like John and my brother, only more so!

Besides, it is such an undertaking to go so far.

I don't feel as if it was worth while to turn my hand over for anything, and I'm getting dreadfully fretful and querulous.

I cry at nothing, and cry most of the time.

Of course I don't when John is here, or anybody else, but when I am alone.

And I am alone a good deal just now. John is kept in town very often by serious cases, and Jennie is good and lets me alone when I want her to.

So I walk a little in the garden or down that lovely lane, sit on the porch under the roses, and lie down up here a good deal.

I'm getting really fond of the room in spite of the wallpaper. Perhaps *because* of the wallpaper.

It dwells in my mind so!

I lie here on this great immovable bed – it is nailed down, I believe – and follow that pattern about by the hour. It is as good as gymnastics, I assure you. I start, we'll say, at the bottom, down in the corner over there where it has not been touched, and I determine for the thousandth time that I *will* follow that pointless pattern to some sort of a conclusion.

I know a little of the principle of design, and I know this thing was not arranged on any laws of radiation, or alternation, or repetition, or symmetry, or anything else that I ever heard of.

It is repeated, of course, by the breadths, but not otherwise.

Looked at in one way each breadth stands alone, the bloated curves and flourishes – a kind of 'debased Romanesque' with *delirium tremens* – go waddling up and down in isolated columns of fatuity.

But, on the other hand, they connect diagonally, and the sprawling outlines run off in great slanting waves of optic horror, like a lot of wallowing seaweeds in full chase.

The whole thing goes horizontally, too, at least it seems so, and I exhaust myself in trying to distinguish the order of its going in that direction.

They have used a horizontal breadth for a frieze, and that adds wonderfully to the confusion.

There is one end of the room where it is almost intact, and there, when the crosslights fade and the low sun shines directly upon it, I can almost fancy radiation after all, – the interminable grotesques seem to form around a common centre and rush off in headlong plunges of equal distraction.

It makes me tired to follow it. I will take a nap I guess.

I don't know why I should write this.

I don't want to.

I don't feel able.

And I know John would think it absurd. But I *must* say what I feel and think in some way – it is such a relief!

But the effort is getting to be greater than the relief.

Half the time now I am awfully lazy, and lie down ever so much.

John says I mustn't lose my strength, and has me take cod liver oil and lots of tonics and things, to say nothing of ale and wine and rare meat.

Dear John! He loves me very dearly, and hates to have me sick. I tried to have a real earnest reasonable talk with him the other day, and tell him how I wish he would let me go and make a visit to Cousin Henry and Julia.

But he said I wasn't able to go, nor able to stand it after I got there; and I did not make out a very good case for myself, for I was crying before I had finished.

It is getting to be a great effort for me to think straight. Just this nervous weakness I suppose.

And dear John gathered me up in his arms, and just carried me upstairs and laid me on the bed, and sat by me and read to me till it tired my head.

He said I was his darling and his comfort and all he had, and that I must take care of myself for his sake, and keep well.

He says no one but myself can help me out of it, that I must use my will and self-control and not let any silly fancies run away with me.

There's one comfort, the baby is well and happy, and does not have to occupy this nursery with the horrid wallpaper.

If we had not used it, that blessed child would have! What a fortunate escape! Why, I wouldn't have a child of mine, an impressionable little thing, live in such a room for worlds.

I never thought of it before, but it is lucky that John kept me here after all, I can stand it so much easier than a baby, you see.

Of course I never mention it to them any more – I am too wise, – but I keep watch of it all the same.

There are things in that paper that nobody knows but me, or ever will.

Behind that outside pattern the dim shapes get clearer every day.

It is always the same shape, only very numerous.

And it is like a woman stooping down and creeping about behind that pattern. I don't like it a bit. I wonder – I begin to think – I wish John would take me away from here!

It is so hard to talk with John about my case, because he is so wise, and because he loves me so.

But I tried it last night.

It was moonlight. The moon shines in all around just as the sun does.

I hate to see it sometimes, it creeps so slowly, and always comes in by one window or another.

John was asleep and I hated to waken him, so I kept still and watched the moonlight on that undulating wallpaper till I felt creepy.

The faint figure behind seemed to shake the pattern, just as if she wanted to get out.

I got up softly and went to feel and see if the paper *did* move, and when I came back John was awake.

'What is it, little girl?' he said. 'Don't go walking about like that – you'll get cold.'

I thought it was a good time to talk, so I told him that I really was not gaining here, and that I wished he would take me away.

'Why darling!' said he, 'our lease will be up in three weeks, and I can't see how to leave before.

'The repairs are not done at home, and I cannot possibly leave town just now. Of course if you were in any danger, I could and would, but you really are better, dear, whether you can see it or not. I am a doctor, dear, and I know. You are gaining flesh and color, your appetite is better, I feel really much easier about you.'

'I don't weigh a bit more,' said I, 'nor as much; and my appetite may be better in the evening when you are here, but it is worse in the morning when you are away!'.

'Bless her little heart!' said he with a big hug, 'she shall be as sick as she pleases! But now let's improve the shining hours by going to sleep, and talk about it in the morning!'

'And you won't go away?' I asked gloomily.

'Why, how can I, dear? It is only three weeks more and then we will take a nice little trip of a few days while Jennie is getting the house ready. Really dear you are better!'

'Better in body perhaps –' I began, and stopped short, for he sat up straight and looked at me with such a stern, reproachful look that I could not say another word.

'My darling,' said he, 'I beg of you, for my sake and for our child's sake, as well as for your own, that you will never for one instant let that idea enter your mind! There is nothing so dangerous, so fascinating, to a temperament like yours. It is a false and foolish fancy. Can you not trust me as a physician when I tell you so?'

So of course I said no more on that score, and we went to sleep before long. He thought I was asleep first, but I wasn't, and lay there for hours trying to decide whether that front pattern and the back pattern really did move together or separately.

On a pattern like this, by daylight, there is a lack of sequence, a defiance of law, that is a constant irritant to a normal mind.

The color is hideous enough, and unreliable enough, and infuriating enough, but the pattern is torturing.

You think you have mastered it, but just as you get well underway in following, it turns a back-somersault and there you are. It slaps you in the face, knocks you down, and tramples upon you. It is like a bad dream.

The outside pattern is a florid arabesque, reminding one of a fungus. If you can imagine a toadstool in joints, an interminable string of toadstools, budding and sprouting in endless convolutions – why, that is something like it.

That is, sometimes!

There is one marked peculiarity about this paper, a thing nobody seems to notice but myself, and that is that it changes as the light changes.

When the sun shoots in through the east window – I always watch for that first long, straight ray – it changes so quickly that I never can quite believe it.

That is why I watch it always.

By moonlight – the moon shines in all night when there is a moon – I wouldn't know it was the same paper.

At night in any kind of light, in twilight, candle light, lamplight, and worst of all by moonlight, it becomes bars! The outside pattern I mean, and the woman behind it is as plain as can be.

I didn't realize for a long time what the thing was that showed behind, that dim sub-pattern, but now I am quite sure it is a woman.

By daylight she is subdued, quiet. I fancy it is the pattern that keeps her so still. It is so puzzling. It keeps me quiet by the hour.

I lie down ever so much now. John says it is good for me, and to sleep all I can.

Indeed he started the habit by making me lie down for an hour after each meal.

It is a very bad habit I am convinced, for you see I don't sleep.

And that cultivates deceit, for I don't tell them I'm awake – O no!

The fact is I am getting a little afraid of John.

He seems very queer sometimes, and even Jennie has an inexplicable look.

It strikes me occasionally, just as a scientific hypothesis, – that perhaps it is the paper!

I have watched John when he did not know I was looking, and come into the room suddenly on the most innocent excuses, and I've caught him several times *looking at the paper!* And Jennie too. I caught Jennie with her hand on it once.

She didn't know I was in the room, and when I asked her in a quiet, a very quiet voice, with the most restrained manner possible, what she was doing with the paper – she turned around as if she had been caught stealing, and looked quite angry – asked me why I should frighten her so!

Then she said that the paper stained everything it touched, and that she had found yellow smooches on all my clothes and John's, and she wished we would be more careful!

Did not that sound innocent? But I know she was studying that pattern, and I am determined that nobody shall find it out but myself!

Life is very much more exciting now than it used to be. You see I have something more to expect, to look forward to, to watch. I really do eat better, and am more quiet than I was.

John is so pleased to see me improve! He laughed a little the other day, and said I seemed to be flourishing in spite of my wallpaper.

I turned it off with a laugh. I had no intention of telling him it was *because* of the wallpaper – he would make fun of me. He might even want to take me away.

I don't want to leave now until I have found it out. There is a week more, and I think that will be enough.

I'm feeling ever so much better! I don't sleep much at night, for it is so interesting to watch developments; but I sleep a good deal in the daytime.

In the daytime it is tiresome and perplexing.

There are always new shoots on the fungus, and new shades of yellow all over it. I cannot keep count of them, though I have tried conscientiously.

It is the strangest yellow, that wallpaper! It makes me think of all the yellow things I ever saw – not beautiful ones like buttercups, but old foul, bad yellow things.

But there is something else about that paper – the smell! I noticed it the moment we came into the room, but with so much air and sun it was not bad. Now we have had a week of fog and rain, and whether the windows are open or not, the smell is here.

It creeps all over the house.

I find it hovering in the dining-room, skulking in the parlor, hiding in the hall, lying in wait for me on the stairs.

It gets into my hair.

Even when I go to ride, if I turn my head suddenly and surprise it – there is that smell!

Such a peculiar odor, too! I have spent hours in trying to analyze it, to find what it smelled like.

It is not bad – at first, and very gentle, but quite the subtlest, most enduring odor I ever met.

In this damp weather it is awful, I wake up in the night and find it hanging over me.

It used to disturb me at first. I thought seriously of burning the house – to reach the smell.

But now I am used to it. The only thing I can think of that it is like is the *color* of the paper! A yellow smell.

There is a very funny mark on this wall, low down, near the mopboard. A streak that runs round the room. It goes behind every piece of furniture, except the bed, a long, straight, even *smooch*, as if it had been rubbed over and over.

I wonder how it was done and who did it, and what they did it

for. Round and round and round – round and round and round –
it makes me dizzy!

I really have discovered something at last.

Through watching so much at night, when it changes so, I
have finally found out.

The front pattern *does* move – and no wonder! The woman
behind shakes it!

Sometimes I think there are a great many women behind, and
sometimes only one, and she crawls around fast, and her
crawling shakes it all over.

Then in the very bright spots she keeps still, and in the very
shady spots she just takes hold of the bars and shakes them hard.

And she is all the time trying to climb through. But nobody
could climb through that pattern – it strangles so; I think that is
why it has so many heads.

They get through, and then the pattern strangles them off and
turns them upside down, and makes their eyes white!

If those heads were covered or taken off it would not be half so
bad.

I think that woman gets out in the daytime!

And I'll tell you why – privately – I've seen her!

I can see her out of every one of my windows!

It is the same woman, I know, for she is always creeping, and
most women do not creep by daylight.

I see her on that long road under the trees, creeping along, and
when a carriage comes she hides under the blackberry vines.

I don't blame her a bit. It must be very humiliating to be
caught creeping by daylight!

I always lock the door when I creep by daylight. I can't do it at
night, for I know John would suspect something at once.

And John is so queer now, that I don't want to irritate him. I
wish he would take another room! Besides, I don't want anybody
to get that woman out at night but myself.

I often wonder if I could see her out of all the windows at once.

But, turn as fast as I can, I can only see out of one at one time.

And though I always see her, she *may* be able to creep faster
than I can turn!

I have watched her sometimes away off in the open country, creeping as fast as a cloud shadow in a high wind.

If only that top pattern could be gotten off from the under one! I mean to try it, little by little.

I have found out another funny thing, but I shan't tell it this time! It does not do to trust people too much.

There are only two more days to get this paper off, and I believe John is beginning to notice. I don't like the look in his eyes.

And I heard him ask Jennie a lot of professional questions about me. She had a very good report to give.

She said I slept a good deal in the daytime.

John knows I don't sleep very well at night, for all I'm so quiet!

He asked me all sorts of questions, too, and pretended to be very loving and kind.

As if I couldn't see through him!

Still, I don't wonder he acts so, sleeping under this paper for three months.

It only interests me, but I feel sure John and Jennie are secretly affected by it.

Hurrah! This is the last day, but it is enough. John to stay in town over night, and won't be out until this evening.

Jennie wanted to sleep with me – the sly thing! but I told her I should undoubtedly rest better for a night all alone.

That was clever, for really I wasn't alone a bit! As soon as it was moonlight and that poor thing began to crawl and shake the pattern, I got up and ran to help her.

I pulled and she shook, I shook and she pulled, and before morning we had peeled off yards of that paper.

A strip about as high as my head and half around the room.

And then when the sun came and that awful pattern began to laugh at me, I declared I would finish it today!

We go away tomorrow, and they are moving all my furniture down again to leave things as they were before.

Jennie looked at the wall in amazement, but I told her merrily that I did it out of pure spite at the vicious thing.

She laughed and said she wouldn't mind doing it herself, but I must not get tired.

How she betrayed herself that time!

But I am here, and no person touches this paper but me, – not *alive*!

She tried to get me out of the room – it was too patent! But I said it was so quiet and empty and clean now that I believed I would lie down again and sleep all I could; and not to wake me even for dinner – I would call when I woke.

So now she is gone, and the servants are gone, and the things are gone, and there is nothing left but that great bedstead nailed down, with the canvas mattress we found on it.

We shall sleep downstairs tonight, and take the boat home tomorrow.

I quite enjoy the room, now it is bare again.

How those children did tear about here!

This bedstead is fairly gnawed!

But I must get to work.

I have locked the door and thrown the key down into the front path.

I don't want to go out, and I don't want to have anybody come in, till John comes.

I want to astonish him.

I've got a rope up here that even Jennie did not find. If that woman does get out, and tries to get away, I can tie her!

But I forgot I could not reach far without anything to stand on!

This bed will *not* move!

I tried to lift and push it until I was lame, and then I got so angry I bit off a little piece at one corner – but it hurt my teeth.

Then I peeled off all the paper I could reach standing on the floor. It sticks horribly and the pattern just enjoys it! All those strangled heads and bulbous eyes and waddling fungus growths just shriek with derision!

I am getting angry enough to do something desperate. To jump out of the window would be admirable exercise, but the bars are too strong even to try.

Besides I wouldn't do it. Of course not. I know well enough that a step like that is improper and might be misconstrued.

I don't like to *look* out of the windows even – there are so many of those creeping women, and they creep so fast.

I wonder if they all came out of that wallpaper as I did?

But I am securely fastened now by my well-hidden rope – you don't get *me* out in the road there!

I suppose I shall have to get back behind the pattern when it comes night, and that is hard!

It is so pleasant to be out in this great room and creep around as I please!

I don't want to go outside. I won't, even if Jennie asks me to.

For outside you have to creep on the ground, and everything is green instead of yellow.

But here I can creep smoothly on the floor, and my shoulder just fits in that long smooch around the wall, so I cannot lose my way.

Why there's John at the door!

It is no use, young man, you can't open it!

How he does call and pound!

Now he's crying for an axe.

It would be a shame to break down that beautiful door!

'John dear!' said I in the gentlest voice, 'the key is down by the front steps, under a plantain leaf!'

That silenced him for a few moments.

Then he said – very quietly indeed, 'Open the door, my darling!'

'I can't,' said I. 'The key is down by the front door under a plantain leaf!'

And then I said it again, several times, very gently and slowly, and said it so often that he had to go and see, and he got it of course, and came in. He stopped short by the door.

'What is the matter?' he cried. 'For God's sake, what are you doing!'

I kept on creeping just the same, but I looked at him over my shoulder.

'I've got out at last,' said I, 'in spite of you and Jane. And I've pulled off most of the paper, so you can't put me back!'

Now why should that man have fainted? But he did, and right across my path by the wall, so that I had to creep over him every time!

The Wedding Gown

GEORGE MOORE

It was said, but with what truth I cannot say, that the Roche property had been owned by the O'Dwyers many years ago, several generations past, some time in the eighteenth century. Only a faint legend of this ownership remained; only once had young Mr Roche heard of it, and it was from his mother he had heard it; among the country people it was forgotten. His mother had told him that his great-great-grandfather, who had made large sums of money abroad, had increased his property by purchase from the O'Dwyers, who then owned, as well as farmed, the hillside on which the Big House stood. The O'Dwyers themselves had forgotten that they were once much greater people than they now were, but the master never spoke to them without remembering it, for though they only thought of themselves as small farmers, dependents on the squire, every one of them, boys and girls alike, retained an air of high birth, which at the first glance distinguished them from the other tenants of the estate. Though they were not aware of it, some sense of their remote origin must have survived in them, and I think that in a still more obscure way some sense of it survived in the country side, for the villagers did not think worse of the O'Dwyers because they kept themselves aloof from the pleasures of the village and its squabbles. The O'Dwyers kept themselves apart from their fellows without any show of pride, without wounding anyone's feelings.

The head of the family was a man of forty, and he was the trusted servant, almost the friend, of the young master. He was his bailiff and his steward, and he lived in a pretty cottage by the edge of the lake. O'Dwyer's aunts – they were old women of sixty-eight and seventy – lived in the Big House; the elder had been cook, and the younger housemaid, and both were now past their work, and they lived full of gratitude to the young master, to whom they thought they owed a great deal. He believed the debt to be all on his side, and when he was away he often thought of them, and when he returned home he went to greet them as he might go to the members of his own family. The family of the O'Dwyers was long-lived, and Betty and Mary had a sister far older than themselves, Margaret Kirwin, 'Granny Kirwin,' as she was called, and she lived in the cottage by the lake with her nephew, Alec O'Dwyer. She was over eighty – it was said that she was nearly ninety – but her age was not known exactly. Mary O'Dwyer said that Margaret was nearly twenty years older than she, but neither Betty nor Mary remembered the exact date of their sister's birth. They did not know much about her, for though she was their sister, she was almost a stranger to them. She had married when she was sixteen, and had gone away to another part of the country, and they had hardly heard of her for thirty years. It was said that she had been a very pretty girl, and that many men had been in love with her, and it was known for certain that she had gone away with the son of the gamekeeper of the grandfather of the present Mr Roche, so you can understand what a very long while ago it was, and how little of the story of her life had come to the knowledge of those living now.

It was certainly sixty years since she had gone away with this young man; she had lived with him in Meath for some years, nobody knew exactly how many years, maybe some nine or ten years, and then he had died suddenly, and his death, it appears, had taken away from her some part of her reason. It was known for certain that she left Meath after his death, and had remained away many years. She had returned to Meath about twenty years ago, though not to the place she had lived in before. Some said she had experienced misfortunes so great that they had unsettled her mind. She herself had forgotten her story, and one day news had come to Galway – news, but it was sad news, that she was living in some very poor cottage on the edge of Navan town where her strange behaviour and her strange life had made a scandal of her. The priest had to inquire out her relations, and it took him some time to do this, for the old woman's answers were incoherent, but he at length discovered she came from Galway, and he had written to the O'Dwyers. And immediately on receiving the priest's letter, Alec sent his wife to Navan, and she had come back with the old woman.

'And it was time indeed that I went to fetch her,' she said. 'The boys in the town used to make game of her, and follow her, and throw things at her, and they nearly lost the poor thing the little reason that was left to her. The rain was coming through the thatch, there was hardly a dry place in the cabin, and she had nothing to eat but a few scraps that the neighbours gave her. Latterly she had forgotten how to make a fire, and she ate the potatoes the neighbours gave her raw, and on her back there were only a few dirty rags. She had no care for anything except for her wedding gown. She kept that in a box covered over with paper so that no damp should get to it, and she was always folding it and seeing that the moth didn't touch it, and she was talking of it when I came in at the door. She thought that I had come to steal it from her. The neighbours told me that that was the way she always was, thinking that someone had come to steal her wedding gown.'

And this was all the news of Margaret Kirwin that Alec O'Dwyer's wife brought back with her. The old woman was given a room in the cottage, and though with food and warmth and kind treatment she became a little less bewildered, a little less like a wild, hunted creature, she never got back her memory sufficiently to tell them all that had happened to her after her husband's death. Nor did she seem as if she wanted to try to remember: she was garrulous only of her early days when the parish bells rang for her wedding, and the furze was in bloom. This was before the Big House on the hill had been built. The hill was then a fine pasture for sheep, and Margaret would often describe the tinkling of the sheep-bells in the valley, and the yellow furze, and the bells that were ringing for her wedding. She always spoke of the bells, though no one could understand where the bells came from. It was not customary to ring the parish bell for weddings, and there was no other bell, so that it was impossible to say how Margaret could have got the idea into her head that bells were ringing for her when she crossed the hill on her way to the church, dressed in the beautiful gown, which the grandmother of the present Mr Roche had dressed her in, for she had always been the favourite, she said, with the old mistress, a much greater favourite than even her two sisters had ever been. Betty and Mary were then little children and hardly remembered the wedding, and could say nothing about the bells.

Margaret Kirwin walked with a short stick, her head lifted hardly higher than the handle, and when the family were talking round the kitchen fire she would come among them for a while and say something to them, and then go away, and they felt they had seen someone from another world. She hobbled now and then as far as the garden-gate, and she frightened the peasantry, so strange did she seem among the flowers – so old and forlorn, almost cut off from this world, with only one memory to link her to it. It was the spectral look in her eyes that frightened them, for Margaret was not ugly. In spite of all her wrinkles the form of the face remained, and it was easy, especially when her little grandniece was by, to see that sixty-five years ago she must have had a long and pleasant face, such as one sees in a fox, and red hair like Molly.

Molly was sixteen, and her grey dress reached only to her ankles. Everyone was fond of the poor old woman; but it was only Molly who had no fear of her at all, and one would often see them standing together beside the pretty paling that separated the steward's garden from the high road. Chestnut trees grew about the house, and China roses over the walls, and in the course of the summer there would be lilies in the garden, and in the autumn hollyhocks and sunflowers. There were a few fruit-trees a little further on, and, lower down, a stream. A little bridge led over the stream into the meadow, and Molly and her grandaunt used to go as far as the bridge, and everyone wondered what the child and the old woman had to say to each other. Molly was never able to give any clear account of what the old woman said to her during the time they spent by the stream. She had tried once to give Molly an account of one long winter when the lake was frozen from side to side. Then there was something running in her mind about the transport of pillars in front of the Big House – how they had been drawn across the lake by oxen, and how one of the pillars was now lying at the bottom of the lake. That was how Molly took up the story from her, but she understood little of it. Molly's solicitude for the old woman was a subject of admiration, and Molly did not like to take the credit for a kindness and pity which she did not altogether feel. She had never seen anyone dead, and her secret fear was that the old woman might die before she went away to service. Her parents had promised to allow her to go away when she was eighteen, and she lived in the hope that her aunt would live two years longer, and that she would be saved the terror of seeing a dead body. And it was in this intention that she served her aunt, that she carefully minced the old woman's food and insisted on her eating often, and that she darted from her place to fetch the old woman her stick when she rose to go. When Margaret Kirwin was not in the kitchen Molly was always laughing and talking, and her father and mother often thought it was her voice that brought the old woman out of her room. So the day Molly was grieving because she could not go to the dance the old woman remained in her room, and not seeing her at tea-time they began to be afraid, and Molly was asked to go to fetch her aunt.

'Something may have happened to her, mother. I daren't go.'

And when old Margaret came into the kitchen towards evening she surprised everyone by her question:

'Why is Molly crying?'

No one else had heard Molly sob, if she had sobbed, but everyone knew the reason of her grief; indeed, she had been reproved for it many times that day.

'I will not hear any more about it,' said Mrs O'Dwyer; 'she has been very tiresome all day. Is it my fault if I cannot give her a gown to go to the dance?' And then, forgetting that old Margaret could not understand her, she told her that the servants were having a dance at the Big House, and had asked Molly to come to it. 'But what can I do? She has got no gown to go in. Even if I had the money there wouldn't be time to send for one now, nor to make one. And there are a number of English servants stopping at the house; there are people from all parts of the country, they have brought their servants with them, and I am not going to see my girl worse dressed than the others, so she cannot go. She has heard all this, she knows it. . . . I've never seen her so tiresome before.' Mrs O'Dwyer continued to chide her daughter; but her mother's reasons for not allowing her to go to the ball, though unanswerable, did not seem to console Molly, and she sat looking very miserable. 'She has been sitting like that all day,' said Mrs O'Dwyer, 'and I wish that it were tomorrow, for she will not be better until it is all over.'

'But, mother, I am saying nothing; I'll go to bed. I don't know why you're blaming me. I'm saying nothing. I can't help feeling miserable.'

'No, she don't look a bit cheerful,' the old woman said, 'and I don't like her to be disappointed.' This was the first time that old Margaret had seemed to understand since she came to live with them what was passing about her, and they all looked at her, Mrs O'Dwyer and Alec and Molly. They stood waiting for her to speak again, wondering if the old woman's speech was an accident, or if she had recovered her mind. 'It is a hard thing for a child at her age not to be able to go to the dance at the Big House, now that she has been asked. No wonder there is not a smile on her face. I remember the time that I should have been crying too for a dance, and isn't she the very same?'

'But, Granny, she can't go in the clothes she is wearing, and she has only got one other frock, the one she goes to Mass in. I can't let my daughter –'

But seeing the old woman was about to speak Alec stopped his wife.

'Let's hear what she has to say,' he whispered.

'There's my wedding gown, it's beautiful enough for anyone to wear. It hasn't been worn since the day I wore it, when the bells were ringing, and I went over the hill to be married; and I've taken such care of it that it is the same as it was that day. Molly will look very nice in it, she will look just as I looked on my wedding day.'

And they stood astonished – father, mother, and daughter – for the old woman, ever since she had come to live with them, had kept her wedding gown sacred from their eyes and hands, closing her door before taking it out to give it the air and strew it with camphor. Only once they had seen it. She had brought it out one day and shown it to them as a child might show a toy; but the moment Mrs Dwyer put out her hand to touch it, Granny had gone away with her gown, and they had heard her shutting the box it was in. Now she was going to lend it to Molly, so she said, but they fully expected her to turn away and to go to her room, forgetful of what she had said. Even if she were to let Molly put the dress on, she would not let her go out of the house with it. She would change her mind at the last minute.

'When does this dancing begin?' she asked, and when they told her she said there would be just time for her to dress Molly, and asked the girl to come into her room. Mrs O'Dwyer feared the girl would be put to a bitter disappointment, but if Molly once had the gown on she would not obliged her to take it off.

'In my gown you will be just like what I was when the bells were ringing.'

She took the gown out of its box herself, the petticoat and the stockings and the shoes.

'The old mistress gave me all these. Molly has gotten the hair I used to have, and will look like myself. Aren't they beautiful shoes? Look at the buckles, and they'll fit her, for her feet are the same size as mine were.'

Molly's feet went into the shoes just as if they had been made for her, and the gown fitted as well as the shoes, and Molly's hair was arranged according to the old woman's fancy, as she used to wear her own hair when it was thick and red like a fox's.

The girl thought that Granny would regret her gifts, and she expected the old woman to follow her into the kitchen and ask her to give back the gown as she was going out of the house. As she stood on the threshold her mother offered her the key; the ball would not be over till five, and Granny said she'd stay up for her.

'I'll doze a bit upon a chair. If I am tired I'll lie down upon my bed. I shall hear Molly; I shan't sleep much. She'll not be able to enter the house without my hearing her.'

It was extraordinary to hear her speak like this, and, a little frightened by her sudden sanity, they tried to persuade her to allow them to lock up the house; but she sat looking into the fire, seemingly so contented that they left her, and for an hour she sat dreaming, seeing Molly young and beautifully dressed in the wedding gown of more than sixty years ago.

Dream after dream went by, the fire had burned low, the sods were falling into white ashes, and the moonlight began to stream into the room. It was the chilliness that had come into the air that awoke her, and she threw several sods of turf on to the fire.

An hour passed, and old Margaret awoke. 'The bells are ringing, the bells are ringing,' she said, and went to the kitchen door; she opened it, and under the rays of the moon she stood lost in memories, for the night of her marriage was just such a night as this one, and she had stood in the garden amid the summer flowers, just as she did now.

'The day is beginning,' she said, mistaking the moonlight for the dawn, and, listening, it seemed to her that she heard once more the sound of bells coming across the hill. 'Yes, the bells are ringing,' she said; 'I can hear them quite clearly, and must hurry and get dressed – I must not keep him waiting.'

And, returning to the house, she went to her box, where her gown had lain so many years; and though no gown was there it seemed to her that there was one, and one more beautiful than the gown she had cherished. It was the same gown, only grown more beautiful. It had passed into softer silk, into a more delicate colour; it had become more beautiful, and holding the dream-gown in her hands, she sat with it in the moonlight thinking how fair he would find her in it. Once her hands went to her hair, and then she dropped them again.

'I must begin to dress myself; I mustn't keep him waiting.'

The moonlight lay still upon her knees, but little by little the moon moved up the sky, leaving her in the shadow.

It was at this moment, as the shadows grew denser about old Margaret, that the child who was dancing at the ball came to think of her who had given her her gown, and who was waiting for her. It was in the middle of a reel she was dancing, and she was dancing it with Mr Roche, that she felt that something had happened to her aunt.

'Mr Roche,' she said, 'you must let me go away; I cannot dance any more tonight. I am sure that something has happened to my aunt, the old woman, Margaret Kirwin, who lives with us in the Lodge. It was she who lent me this gown. This was her wedding gown, and for sixty-five years it has never been out of her possession. She has hardly allowed anyone to see it; but she said that I was like her, and she heard me crying because I had no gown to go to the ball, and so she lent me her wedding gown.'

'You look very nice, Molly, in the wedding gown, and this is only a fancy.' Seeing the girl was frightened and wanted to go, he said: 'But why do you think that anything has happened to your aunt?'

'She is very old.'

'But she isn't much older than she was when you left her.'

'Let me go, Mr Roche; I think I must go. I feel sure that something has happened to her. I never had such a feeling before, and I couldn't have that feeling if there was no reason for it.'

'Well, if you must go.'

She glanced to where the moon was shining and ran down the

drive, leaving Mr Roche looking after her, wondering if after all she might have had a warning of the old woman's death. The night was one of those beautiful nights in May, when the moon soars high in the sky, and all the woods and fields are clothed in the green of spring. But the stillness of the night frightened Molly, and when she stopped to pick up her dress she heard the ducks chattering in the reeds. The world seemed divided into darkness and light. The hawthorn-trees threw black shadows that reached into the hollows, and Molly did not dare to go by the path that led through a little wood, lest she should meet Death there. For now it seemed to her that she was running a race with Death, and that she must get to the cottage before him. She did not dare to take the short cut, but she ran till her breath failed her. She ran on again, but when she went through the wicket she knew that Death had been before her. She knocked twice; receiving no answer she tried the latch, and was surprised to find the door unlocked. There was a little fire among the ashes, and after blowing the sod for some time she managed to light the candle, and holding it high she looked about the kitchen.

'Auntie, are you asleep? Have the others gone to bed?'

She approached a few steps, and then a strange curiosity came over her, and though she had always feared death she now looked curiously upon death, and she thought that she saw the likeness which her aunt had often noticed.

'Yes,' she said, 'she is like me. I shall be like that some day if I live long enough.'

And then she knocked at the door of the room where her parents were sleeping.

The Lady of Shalott

ALFRED, LORD TENNYSON

Part 1

On either side the river lie
Long fields of barley and of rye,
That clothe the wold and meet the sky;
And thro' the field the road runs by
    To many-tower'd Camelot;
And up and down the people go,
Gazing where the lilies blow
Round an island there below,
    The island of Shalott.

Willows whiten, aspens quiver,
Little breezes dusk and shiver
Thro' the wave that runs for ever
By the island in the river
    Flowing down to Camelot.
Four gray walls, and four gray towers,
Overlook a space of flowers,
And the silent isle imbowers
    The Lady of Shalott.

By the margin, willow-veil'd,
Slide the heavy barges trail'd
By slow horses; and unhail'd
The shallop flitteth silken-sail'd
    Skimming down to Camelot:
But who hath seen her wave her hand?
Or at the casement seen her stand?
Or is she known in all the land,
    The Lady of Shalott?

Only reapers, reaping early
In among the bearded barley,

Hear a song that echoes cheerly
From the river winding clearly
        Down to tower'd Camelot:
And by the moon the reaper weary,
Piling sheaves in uplands airy,
Listening, whispers ''Tis the fairy
        Lady of Shalott.'

Part 2

There she weaves by night and day
A magic web with colours gay.
She has heard a whisper say,
A curse is on her if she stay
        To look down to Camelot.
She knows not what the curse may be,
And so she weaveth steadily,
And little other care hath she,
        The Lady of Shalott.

And moving thro' a mirror clear
That hangs before her all the year,
Shadows of the world appear.
There she sees the highway near
        Winding down to Camelot:
There the river eddy whirls,
And there the surly village-churls,
And the red cloaks of market girls,
        Pass onward from Shalott.

Sometimes a troop of damsels glad,
An abbot on an ambling pad,
Sometimes a curly shepherd-lad,
Or long-hair'd page in crimson clad,
        Goes by to tower'd Camelot;
And sometimes thro' the mirror blue
The knights come riding two and two:
She hath no loyal knight and true,
        The Lady of Shalott.

But in her web she still delights
To weave the mirror's magic sights,
For often thro' the silent nights
A funeral, with plumes and lights
  And music, went to Camelot:
Or when the moon was overhead,
Came two young lovers lately wed;
'I am half sick of shadows,' said
  The Lady of Shalott.

Part 3

A bow-shot from her bower-eaves,
He rode between the barley-sheaves,
The sun came dazzling thro' the leaves,
And flamed upon the brazen greaves
  Of bold Sir Lancelot.
A red-cross knight for ever kneel'd
To a lady in his shield,
That sparkled on the yellow field,
  Beside remote Shalott.

The gemmy bridle glitter'd free,
Like to some branch of stars we see
Hung in the golden Galaxy.
The bridle bells rang merrily
  As he rode down to Camelot:
And from his blazon'd baldric slung
A mighty silver bugle hung,
And as he rode his armour rung,
  Beside remote Shalott.

All in the blue unclouded weather
Thick-jewell'd shone the saddle-leather,
The helmet and the helmet-feather
Burn'd like one burning flame together,
  As he rode down to Camelot.
As often thro' the purple night,
Below the starry clusters bright,
Some bearded meteor, trailing light,

Moves over still Shalott.

His broad clear brow in sunlight glow'd;
On burnished hooves his war-horse trode;
From underneath his helmet flow'd
His coal-black curls as on he rode,
     As he rode down to Camelot.
From the bank and from the river
He flash'd into the crystal mirror,
'Tirra lirra,' by the river
     Sang Sir Lancelot.

She left the web, she left the loom,
She made three paces thro' the room,
She saw the water-lily bloom,
She saw the helmet and the plume,
     She look'd down to Camelot.
Out flew the web and floated wide;
The mirror crack'd from side to side;
'The curse is come upon me,' cried
     The Lady of Shalott.

Part 4

In the stormy east-wind straining,
The pale yellow woods were waning,
The broad stream in his banks complaining,
Heavily the low sky raining
     Over tower'd Camelot;
Down she came and found a boat
Beneath a willow left afloat,
And round about the prow she wrote
     The Lady of Shalott.

And down the river's dim expanse
Like some bold seër in a trance,
Seeing all his own mischance –
With a glassy countenance
     Did she look to Camelot.
And at the closing of the day

She loosed the chain, and down she lay;
The broad stream bore her far away,
    The Lady of Shalott.

Lying, robed in snowy white
That loosely flew to left and right –
The leaves upon her falling light –
Thro' the noises of the night
    She floated down to Camelot:
And as the boat-head wound along
The willowy hills and fields among,
They heard her singing her last song,
    The Lady of Shalott.

Heard a carol, mournful, holy,
Chanted loudly, chanted lowly,
Till her blood was frozen slowly,
And her eyes were darken'd wholly,
    Turn'd to tower'd Camelot.
For ere she reach'd upon the tide
The first house by the water-side,
Singing in her song she died,
    The Lady of Shalott.

Under tower and balcony,
By garden-wall and gallery,
A gleaming shape she floated by,
Dead-pale between the houses high,
    Silent into Camelot.
Out upon the wharfs they came,
Knight and burgher, lord and dame,
And round the prow they read her name,
    The Lady of Shalott.

Who is this? and what is here?
And in the lighted palace near
Died the sound of royal cheer;
And they cross'd themselves for fear,
    All the knights at Camelot:
But Lancelot mused a little space;

He said, 'She has a lovely face;
God in his mercy lend her grace,
　　The Lady of Shalott.'

The Withered Arm

THOMAS HARDY

I. A Lorn Milkmaid

It was an eighty-cow dairy, and the troop of milkers, regular and supernumerary, were all at work; for, though the time of year was as yet but early April, the feed lay entirely in water-meadows, and the cows were 'in full pail'. The hour was about six in the evening, and three-fourths of the large, red, rectangular animals having been finished off, there was opportunity for a little conversation.

'He do bring home his bride tomorrow, I hear. They've come as far as Anglebury today.'

The voice seemed to proceed from the belly of the cow called Cherry, but the speaker was a milking-woman, whose face was buried in the flank of that motionless beast.

'Hav' anybody seen her?' said another.

There was a negative response from the first. 'Though they say she's a rosy-cheeked, tisty-tosty little body enough,' she added; and as the milkmaid spoke she turned her face so that she could glance past her cow's tail to the other side of the barton, where a thin, fading woman of thirty milked somewhat apart from the rest.

'Years younger than he, they say,' continued the second, with also a glance of reflectiveness in the same direction.

'How old do you call him, then?'

'Thirty or so.'

'More like forty,' broke in an old milkman near, in a long white pinafore or 'wropper', and with the brim of his hat tied down, so that he looked like a woman. ''A was born before our Great Weir was builded, and I hadn't man's wages when I laved water there.'

The discussion waxed so warm that the purr of the milk-streams became jerky, till a voice from another cow's belly cried with authority, 'Now then, what the Turk do it matter to us about Farmer Lodge's age, or Farmer Lodge's new mis'ess? I shall have to pay him nine pound a year for the rent of every one of these milchers, whatever his age or hers. Get on with your work, or 'twill be dark afore we have done. The evening is pinking in a'ready.' This speaker was the dairyman himself, by whom the milkmaids and men were employed.

Nothing more was said publicly about Farmer Lodge's wedding, but the first woman murmured under her cow to her next neighbour, ''Tis hard for *she*,' signifying the thin worn milkmaid aforesaid.

'O no,' said the second. 'He ha'n't spoke to Rhoda Brook for years.'

When the milking was done they washed their pails and hung them on a many-forked stand made as usual of the peeled limb of an oak-tree, set upright in the earth, and resembling a colossal antlered horn. The majority then dispersed in various directions homeward. The thin woman who had not spoken was joined by a boy of twelve or thereabout, and the twain went away up the field also.

Their course lay apart from that of the others, to a lonely spot high above the water-meads, and not far from the border of Egdon Heath, whose dark countenance was visible in the distance as they drew nigh to their home.

'They've just been saying down in barton that your father brings his young wife home from Anglebury tomorrow,' the woman observed. 'I shall want to send you for a few things to market, and you'll be pretty sure to meet 'em.'

'Yes, mother,' said the boy. 'Is father married then?'

'Yes. . . . You can give her a look, and tell me what she's like, if you do see her.'

'Yes, mother.'

'If she's dark or fair, and if she's tall – as tall as I. And if she seems like a woman who has ever worked for a living, or one that has been always well off, and has never done anything, and shows marks of the lady on her, as I expect she do.'

'Yes.'

They crept up the hill in the twilight and entered the cottage. It was built of mud-walls, the surface of which had been washed by many rains into channels and depressions that left none of the original flat face visible; while here and there in the thatch above a rafter showed like a bone protruding through the skin.

She was kneeling down in the chimney-corner, before two pieces of turf laid together with the heather inwards, blowing at the red-hot ashes with her breath till the turves flamed. The radiance lit her pale cheek, and made her dark eyes, that had once been handsome, seem handsome anew. 'Yes,' she resumed, 'see if she is dark or fair, and if you can, notice if her hands be white; if not, see if they look as though she had ever done housework, or are milker's hands like mine.'

The boy again promised, inattentively this time, his mother not observing that he was cutting a notch with his pocket-knife in the beech-backed chair.

II. *The Young Wife*

The road from Anglebury to Holmstoke is in general level; but there is one place where a sharp ascent breaks its monotony. Farmers homeward-bound from the former market-town, who trot all the rest of the way, walk their horses up this short incline.

The next evening while the sun was yet bright a handsome new gig, with a lemon-coloured body and red wheels, was spinning westward along the level highway at the heels of a powerful mare. The driver was a yeoman in the prime of life, cleanly shaven like an actor, his face being toned to that bluish-vermilion hue which so often graces a thriving farmer's features when returning home after successive dealings in the town. Beside him sat a woman, many years his junior – almost, indeed, a girl. Her face too was fresh in colour, but it was of a totally different quality – soft and evanescent, like the light under a heap of rose-petals.

Few people travelled this way, for it was not a main road, and the long white riband of gravel that stretched before them was empty, save of one small scarce-moving speck, which presently resolved itself into the figure of a boy, who was creeping on at a snail's pace, and continually looking behind him – the heavy bundle he carried being some excuse for, if not the reason of, his dilatoriness. When the bouncing gig-party slowed at the bottom of the incline above mentioned, the pedestrian was only a few yards in front. Supporting the large bundle by putting one hand on his hip, he turned and looked straight at the farmer's wife as though he would read her through and through, pacing along abreast of the horse.

The low sun was full in her face, rendering every feature, shade, and contour distinct, from the curve of her little nostril to the colour of her eyes. The farmer, though he seemed annoyed at the boy's persistent presence, did not order him to get out of the way; and thus the lad preceded them, his hard gaze never leaving her, till they reached the top of the ascent, when the farmer trotted on with relief in his lineaments – having taken no outward notice of the boy whatever.

'How that poor lad stared at me!' said the young wife.

'Yes, dear; I saw that he did.'

'He is one of the village, I suppose?'

'One of the neighbourhood. I think he lives with his mother a mile or two off.'

'He knows who we are, no doubt?'

'O yes. You must expect to be stared at just at first, my pretty Gertrude.'

'I do, – though I think the poor boy may have looked at us in the hope we might relieve him of his heavy load, rather than from curiosity.'

'O no,' said her husband off-handedly. 'These country lads will carry a hundredweight once they get it on their backs; besides, his pack had more size than weight in it. Now, then, another mile and I shall be able to show you our house in the distance – if it is not too dark before we get there.' The wheels spun round, and particles flew from their periphery as before, till a white house of ample dimensions revealed itself, with farm-buildings and ricks at the back.

Meanwhile the boy had quickened his pace, and turning up a by-lane some mile and half short of the white farmstead, ascended towards the leaner pastures, and so on to the cottage of his mother.

She had reached home after her day's milking at the outlying dairy, and was washing cabbage at the doorway in the declining light. 'Hold up the net a moment,' she said, without preface, as the boy came up.

He flung down his bundle, held the edge of the cabbage-net, and as she filled its meshes with the dripping leaves she went on, 'Well, did you see her?'

'Yes; quite plain.'

'Is she ladylike?'

'Yes; and more. A lady complete.'

'Is she young?'

'Well, she's growed up, and her ways be quite a woman's.'

'Of course. What colour is her hair and face?'

'Her hair is lightish, and her face as comely as a live doll's.'

'Her eyes, then, are not dark like mine?'

'No – of a bluish turn, and her mouth is very nice and red; and when she smiles, her teeth show white.'

'Is she tall?' said the woman sharply.

'I couldn't see. She was sitting down.'

'Then do you go to Holmstoke church tomorrow morning: she's sure to be there. Go early and notice her walking in, and come home and tell me if she's taller than I.'

'Very well, mother. But why don't you go and see for yourself?'

'*I* go to see her! I wouldn't look up at her if she were to pass my window this instant. She was with Mr Lodge, of course. What did he say or do?'

'Just the same as usual.'

'Took no notice of you?'

'None.'

Next day the mother put a clean shirt on the boy, and started him off for Holmstoke church. He reached the ancient little pile when the door was just being opened and he was the first to enter. Taking his seat by the font, he watched all the parishioners file in. The well-to-do Farmer Lodge came nearly last, and his young wife, who accompanied him, walked up the aisle with the shyness natural to a modest woman who had appeared thus for the first time. As all other eyes were fixed upon her, the youth's stare was not noticed now.

When he reached home his mother said, 'Well?' before he had entered the room.

'She is not tall. She is rather short,' he replied.

'Ah!' said his mother, with satisfaction.

'But she's very pretty – very. In fact, she's lovely.' The youthful freshness of the yeoman's wife had evidently made an impression even on the somewhat hard nature of the boy.

'That's all I want to hear,' said his mother quickly. 'Now,

spread the tablecloth. The hare you wired is very tender; but mind that nobody catches you. – You've never told me what sort of hands she had.'

'I have never seen 'em. She never took off her gloves.'

'What did she wear this morning?'

'A white bonnet and a silver-coloured gownd. It whewed and whistled so loud when it rubbed against the pews that the lady coloured up more than ever for very shame at the noise, and pulled it in to keep it from touching; but when she pushed into her seat, it whewed more than ever. Mr Lodge, he seemed pleased, and his waistcoat stuck out, and his great golden seals hung like a lord's; but she seemed to wish her noisy gownd anywhere but on her.'

'Not she! However, that will do now.'

These descriptions of the newly-married couple were continued from time to time by the boy at his mother's request, after any chance encounter he had had with them. But Rhoda Brook, though she might easily have seen young Mrs Lodge for herself by walking a couple of miles, would never attempt an excursion towards the quarter where the farmhouse lay. Neither did she, at the daily milking in the dairyman's yard on Lodge's outlying second farm, ever speak on the subject of the recent marriage. The dairyman, who rented the cows of Lodge, and knew perfectly the tall milkmaid's history, with manly kindliness always kept the gossip in the cow-barton from annoying Rhoda. But the atmosphere thereabout was full of the subject during the first days of Mrs Lodge's arrival, and from her boy's description and the casual words of the other milkers, Rhoda Brook could raise a mental image of the unconscious Mrs Lodge that was realistic as a photograph.

III. A Vision

One night, two or three weeks after the bridal return, when the boy was gone to bed, Rhoda sat a long time over the turf ashes that she had raked out in front of her to extinguish them. She contemplated so intently the new wife, as presented to her in her mind's eye over the embers, that she forgot the lapse of time. At last, wearied with her day's work, she too retired.

But the figure which had occupied her so much during this

and the previous days was not to be banished at night. For the first time Gertrude Lodge visited the supplanted woman in her dreams. Rhoda Brook dreamed – since her assertion that she really saw, before falling asleep, was not to be believed – that the young wife, in the pale silk dress and white bonnet, but with features shockingly distorted, and wrinkled as by age, was sitting upon her chest as she lay. The pressure of Mrs Lodge's person grew heavier; the blue eyes peered cruelly into her face, and then the figure thrust forward its left hand mockingly, so as to make the wedding-ring it wore glitter in Rhoda's eyes. Maddened mentally, and nearly suffocated by pressure, the sleeper struggled; the incubus, still regarding her, withdrew to the foot of the bed, only, however, to come forward by degrees, resume her seat, and flash her left hand as before.

Gasping for breath, Rhoda, in a last desperate effort, swung out her right hand, seized the confronting spectre by its obtrusive left arm, and whirled it backward to the floor, starting up herself as she did so with a low cry.

'O, merciful heaven!' she cried, sitting on the edge of the bed in a cold sweat; 'that was not a dream – she was here!'

She could feel her antagonist's arm with her grasp even now – the very flesh and bone of it, as it seemed. She looked on the floor whither she had whirled the spectre, but there was nothing to be seen.

Rhoda Brook slept no more that night, and when she went milking at the next dawn they noticed how pale and haggard she looked. The milk that she drew quivered into the pail: her hand had not calmed even yet, and still retained the feel of the arm. She came home to breakfast as wearily as if it had been supper-time.

'What was that noise in your chimmer, mother, last night?' said her son. 'You fell off the bed, surely?'

'Did you hear anything fall? At what time?'

'Just when the clock struck two.'

She could not explain, and when the meal was done went silently about her household work, the boy assisting her, for he hated going afield on the farms, and she indulged his reluctance. Between eleven and twelve the garden-gate clicked, and she lifted her eyes to the window. At the bottom of the garden, within the gate, stood the woman of her vision. Rhoda seemed transfixed.

'Ah, she said she would come!' exclaimed the boy, also observing her.

'Said so – when? How does she know us?'

'I have seen and spoken to her. I talked to her yesterday.'

'I told you,' said the mother, flushing indignantly, 'never to speak to anybody in that house, or go near the place.'

'I did not speak to her till she spoke to me. And I did not go near the place. I met her in the road.'

'What did you tell her?'

'Nothing. She said, "Are you the poor boy who had to bring the heavy load from market?" And she looked at my boots, and said they would not keep my feet dry if it came on wet, because they were so cracked. I told her I lived with my mother, and we had enough to do to keep ourselves, and that's how it was; and she said then, "I'll come and bring you some better boots, and see your mother." She gives away things to other folks in the meads besides us.'

Mrs Lodge was by this time close to the door – not in her silk, as Rhoda had dreamt of in the bed-chamber, but in a morning hat, and gown of common light material, which became her better than silk. On her arm she carried a basket.

The impression remaining from the night's experience was still strong. Brook had almost expected to see the wrinkles, the scorn, and the cruelty on her visitor's face. She would have escaped an interview had escape been possible. There was, however, no backdoor to the cottage, and in an instant the boy had lifted the latch to Mrs Lodge's gentle knock.

'I see I have come to the right house,' she said, glancing at the lad, and smiling. 'But I was not sure till you opened the door.'

The figure and action were those of the phantom; but her voice was so indescribably sweet, her glance so winning, her smile so tender, so unlike that of Rhoda's midnight visitant, that the latter could hardly believe the evidence of her senses. She was truly glad that she had not hidden away in sheer aversion, as she had been inclined to do. In her basket Mrs Lodge brought the pair of boots that she had promised to the boy, and other useful articles.

At these proofs of a kindly feeling towards her and hers Rhoda's heart reproached her bitterly. This innocent young thing should have her blessing and not her curse. When she left them a light seemed gone from the dwelling. Two days later she came again to know if the boots fitted, and less than a fortnight after that paid Rhoda another call. On this occasion the boy was absent.

'I walk a good deal,' said Mrs Lodge, 'and your house is the nearest outside our own parish. I hope you are well. You don't look quite well.'

Rhoda said she was well enough, and, indeed, though the paler of the two, there was more of the strength that endures in her well-defined features and large frame than in the soft-cheeked young woman before her. The conversation became quite confidential as regarded their powers and weaknesses; and when Mrs Lodge was leaving, Rhoda said, 'I hope you will find this air agree with you, ma'am, and not suffer from the damp of the water-meads.'

The younger one replied that there was not much doubt of it, her general health being usually good. 'Though, now you remind me,' she added, 'I have one little ailment which puzzles me. It is nothing serious, but I cannot make it out.'

She uncovered her left hand and arm, and their outline confronted Rhoda's gaze as the exact original of the limb she had beheld and seized in her dream. Upon the pink round surface of the arm were faint marks of an unhealthy colour, as if produced by a rough grasp. Rhoda's eyes became riveted on the discolorations; she fancied that she discerned in them the shape of her own four fingers.

'How did it happen?' she said mechanically.

'I cannot tell,' replied Mrs Lodge, shaking her head. 'One night when I was sound asleep, dreaming I was away in some strange place, a pain suddenly shot into my arm there, and was so keen as to awaken me. I must have struck it in the daytime, I suppose, though I don't remember doing so.' She added, laughing, 'I tell my dear husband that it looks just as if he had flown into a rage and struck me there. O, I daresay it will soon disappear.'

'Ha, ha! Yes. . . . On what night did it come?'

Mrs Lodge considered, and said it would be a fortnight ago on the morrow. 'When I awoke I could not remember where I was,' she added, 'till the clock striking two reminded me.'

She had named the night and the hour of Rhoda's spectral encounter, and Brook felt like a guilty thing. The artless disclosure startled her; she did not reason on the freaks of coincidence, and all the scenery of that ghastly night returned with double vividness to her mind.

'O, can it be,' she said to herself, when her visitor had departed, 'that I exercise a malignant power over people against my own will?' She knew that she had been slily called a witch since her fall; but never having understood why that particular stigma had been attached to her, it had passed disregarded. Could this be the explanation, and had such things as this ever happened before?

IV. A Suggestion

The summer drew on, and Rhoda Brook almost dreaded to meet Mrs Lodge again, notwithstanding that her feeling for the young wife amounted wellnigh to affection. Something in her own individuality seemed to convict Rhoda of crime. Yet a fatality sometimes would direct the steps of the latter to the outskirts of Holmstoke whenever she left her house for any other purpose than her daily work, and hence it happened that their next encounter was out of doors. Rhoda could not avoid the subject which had so mystified her, and after the first few words, she stammered, 'I hope your – arm is well again, ma'am?' She had perceived with consternation that Gertrude Lodge carried her left arm stiffly.

'No; it is not quite well. Indeed, it is no better at all; it is rather worse. It pains me dreadfully sometimes.'

'Perhaps you had better go to a doctor, ma'am.'

She replied that she had already seen a doctor. Her husband had insisted upon her going to one. But the surgeon had not seemed to understand the afflicted limb at all; he had told her to bathe it in hot water, and she had bathed it, but the treatment had done no good.

'Will you let me see it?' said the milkwoman.

Mrs Lodge pushed up her sleeve and disclosed the place, which was a few inches above the wrist. As soon as Rhoda Brook saw it, she could hardly preserve her composure. There was nothing of the nature of a wound, but the arm at that point had a shrivelled look, and the outline of the four fingers appeared more distinct than at the former time. Moreover, she fancied that they were imprinted in precisely the relative position of her clutch upon the arm in the trance: the first finger towards Gertrude's wrist, and the fourth towards her elbow.

What the impress resembled seemed to have struck Gertrude herself since their last meeting. 'It looks almost like fingermarks,' she said; adding with a faint laugh, 'My husband says it is as if some witch, or the devil himself, had taken hold of me there, and blasted the flesh.'

Rhoda shivered. 'That's fancy,' she said hurriedly. 'I wouldn't mind it, if I were you.'

'I shouldn't so much mind it,' said the younger, with hesitation, 'if – if I hadn't a notion that it makes my husband – dislike me – no, love me less. Men think so much of personal appearance.'

'Some do – he for one.'

'Yes; and he was very proud of mine, at first.'

'Keep your arm covered from his sight.'

'Ah – he knows the disfigurement is there!' She tried to hide the tears that filled her eyes.

'Well, ma'am, I earnestly hope it will go away soon.'

And so the milkwoman's mind was chained anew to the subject by a horrid sort of spell as she returned home. The sense of having been guilty of an act of malignity increased, affect as she might to ridicule her superstition. In her secret heart Rhoda did not altogether object to a slight diminution of her successor's beauty, by whatever means it had come about; but she did not wish to inflict upon her physical pain. For though this pretty young woman had rendered impossible any reparation which Lodge might have made Rhoda for his past conduct, everything like resentment at the unconscious usurpation had quite passed away from the elder's mind.

If the sweet and kindly Gertrude Lodge only knew of the dream-scene in the bed-chamber, what would she think? Not to inform her of it seemed treachery in the presence of her friendliness; but tell she could not of her own accord – neither could she devise a remedy.

She mused upon the matter the greater part of the night, and the next day, after the morning milking, set out to obtain another glimpse of Gertrude Lodge if she could, being held to her by a gruesome fascination. By watching the house from a distance the milkmaid was presently able to discern the farmer's wife in a ride she was taking alone – probably to join her husband in some distant field. Mrs Lodge perceived her, and cantered in her direction.

'Good morning, Rhoda!' Gertrude said, when she had come up. 'I was going to call.'

Rhoda noticed that Mrs Lodge held the reins with some difficulty.

'I hope – the bad arm,' said Rhoda.

'They tell me there is possibly one way by which I might be able to find out the cause, and so perhaps the cure, of it,' replied the other anxiously. 'It is by going to some clever man over in Egdon Heath. They did not know if he was still alive – and I cannot remember his name at this moment; but they said that you knew more of his movements than anybody else hereabout, and could tell me if he were still to be consulted. Dear me – what was his name? But you know.'

'Not Conjuror Trendle?' said her thin companion, turning pale.

'Trendle – yes. Is he alive?'

'I believe so,' said Rhoda, with reluctance.

'Why do you call him conjuror?'

'Well – they say – they used to say he was a – he had powers other folks have not.'

'Oh, how could my people be so superstitious as to recommend a man of that sort! I thought they meant some medical man. I shall think no more of him.'

Rhoda looked relieved, and Mrs Lodge rode on. The milk-woman had inwardly seen, from the moment she heard of her having been mentioned as a reference for this man, that there must exist a sarcastic feeling among the workfolk that a sorceress would know the whereabouts of the exorcist. They suspected her, then. A short time ago this would have given no concern to a woman of her common sense. But she had a haunting reason to be superstitious now; and she had been seized with sudden dread that this Conjuror Trendle might name her as the malignant influence which was blasting the fair person of Gertrude and so lead her friend to hate her for ever, and to treat her as some fiend in human shape.

But all was not over. Two days after, a shadow intruded into the window-pattern thrown on Rhoda Brook's floor by the afternoon sun. The woman opened the door at once, almost breathlessly.

'Are you alone?' said Gertrude. She seemed to be no less harassed and anxious than Brook herself.

'Yes,' said Rhoda.

'The place on my arm seems worse, and troubles me!' the young farmer's wife went on. 'It is so mysterious! I do hope it will not be an incurable wound. I have again been thinking of what they said about Conjuror Trendle. I don't really believe in such men, but I should not mind just visiting him, for curiosity – though on no account must my husband know. Is it far to where he lives?'

'Yes – five miles,' said Rhoda backwardly. 'In the heart of Egdon.'

'Well, I should have to walk. Could not you go with me to show the way – say tomorrow afternoon?'

'O, not I – that is,' the milkwoman murmured, with a start of dismay. Again the dread seized her that something to do with her fierce act in the dream might be revealed, and her character in the eyes of the most useful friend she had ever had be ruined irretrievably.

Mrs Lodge urged, and Rhoda finally assented, though with much misgiving. Sad as the journey would be to her, she could not conscientiously stand in the way of a possible remedy for her patron's strange affliction. It was agreed that, to escape suspicion of their mystic intent, they should meet at the edge of the heath at the corner of a plantation which was visible from the spot where they now stood.

V. Conjuror Trendle

By the next afternoon Rhoda would have done anything to escape this inquiry. But she had promised to go. Moreover, there was a horrid fascination at times in becoming instrumental in throwing such possible light on her own character as would reveal her to be something greater in the occult world than she had ever herself suspected.

She started just before the time of day mentioned between them, and half-an-hour's brisk walking brought her to the south-eastern extension of the Egdon tract of country, where the fir plantation was. A slight figure, cloaked and veiled, was already there. Rhoda recognized, almost with a shudder, that Mrs Lodge bore her left arm in a sling.

They hardly spoke to each other, and immediately set out on their climb into the interior of this solemn country, which stood high above the rich alluvial soil they had left half-an-hour before. It was a long walk; thick clouds made the atmosphere dark, though it was as yet only early afternoon; and the wind howled dismally over the slopes of the heath – not improbably the same heath which had witnessed the agony of the Wessex King Ina, presented to after-ages as Lear. Gertrude Lodge talked most, Rhoda replying with monosyllabic preoccupation. She had a strange dislike to walking on the side of her companion where hung the afflicted arm, moving round to the other when inadvertently near it. Much heather had been brushed by their feet when they descended upon a cart-track, beside which stood the house of the man they sought.

He did not profess his remedial practices openly, or care anything about their continuance, his direct interests being those of a dealer in furze, turf, 'sharp sand', and other local products. Indeed, he affected not to believe largely in his own powers, and when warts that had been shown him for cure miraculously disappeared – which it must be owned they infallibly did – he would say lightly, 'O, I only drink a glass of grog upon 'em at your expense – perhaps it's all chance,' and immediately turn the subject.

He was at home when they arrived, having in fact seen them descending into his valley. He was a grey-bearded man, with a reddish face, and he looked singularly at Rhoda the first moment he beheld her. Mrs Lodge told him her errand; and then with words of self-disparagement he examined her arm.

'Medicine can't cure it,' he said promptly. ''Tis the work of an enemy.'

Rhoda shrank into herself, and drew back.

'An enemy? What enemy?' asked Mrs Lodge.

He shook his head. 'That's best known to yourself,' he said. 'If you like, I can show the person to you, though I shall not myself know who it is. I can do no more; and don't wish to do that.'

She pressed him; on which he told Rhoda to wait outside where she stood, and took Mrs Lodge into the room. It opened immediately from the door; and, as the latter remained ajar, Rhoda Brook could see the proceedings without taking part in them. He brought a tumbler from the dresser, nearly filled it with water, and fetching an egg, prepared it in some private way; after which he broke it on the edge of the glass, so that the white went in and the yolk remained. As it was getting gloomy, he took the glass and its contents to the window, and told Gertrude to watch the mixture closely. They leant over the table together, and the milkwoman could see the opaline hue of the egg-fluid changing form as it sank in the water, but she was not near enough to define the shape that it assumed.

'Do you catch the likeness of any face or figure as you look?' demanded the conjuror of the young woman.

She murmured a reply, in tones so low as to be inaudible to Rhoda, and continued to gaze intently into the glass. Rhoda turned, and walked a few steps away.

When Mrs Lodge came out, and her face was met by the light, it appeared exceedingly pale – as pale as Rhoda's – against the sad dun shades of the upland's garniture. Trendle shut the door behind her, and they at once started homeward together. But Rhoda perceived that her companion had quite changed.

'Did he charge much?' she asked tentatively.

'O no – nothing. He would not take a farthing,' said Gertrude.

'And what did you see?' inquired Rhoda.

'Nothing I – care to speak of.' The constraint in her manner was remarkable; her face was so rigid as to wear an oldened aspect, faintly suggestive of the face in Rhoda's bed-chamber.

'Was it you who first proposed coming here?' Mrs Lodge suddenly inquired, after a long pause. 'How very odd, if you did!'

'No. But I am not sorry we have come, all things considered,' she replied. For the first time a sense of triumph possessed her, and she did not altogether deplore that the young thing at her side should learn that their lives had been antagonized by other influences than their own.

The subject was no more alluded to during the long and dreary walk home. But in some way or other a story was whispered about the many-dairied lowland that winter that Mrs Lodge's gradual loss of the use of her left arm was owing to her being 'overlooked' by Rhoda Brook. The latter kept her own counsel about the incubus, but her face grew sadder and thinner; and in the spring she and her boy disappeared from the neighbourhood of Holmstoke.

VI. A Second Attempt

Half a dozen years passed away, and Mr and Mrs Lodge's married experience sank into prosiness, and worse. The farmer was usually gloomy and silent; the woman whom he had wooed for her grace and beauty was contorted and disfigured in the left limb; moreover, she had brought him no child, which rendered it likely that he would be the last of a family who had occupied that valley for some two hundred years. He thought of Rhoda Brook and her son; and feared this might be a judgment from heaven upon him.

The once blithe-hearted and enlightened Gertrude was changing into an irritable, superstitious woman, whose whole time was given to experimenting upon her ailment with every quack remedy she came across. She was honestly attached to her husband, and was ever secretly hoping against hope to win back his heart again by regaining some at least of her personal beauty. Hence it arose that her closet was lined with bottles, packets and ointment-pots of every description – nay, bunches of mystic herbs, charms, and books of necromancy, which in her schoolgirl time she would have ridiculed as folly.

'Damned if you won't poison yourself with these apothecary messes and witch mixtures some time or other,' said her husband, when his eyes chanced to fall upon the multitudinous array.

She did not reply, but turned her sad, soft glance upon him in such heart-swollen reproach that he looked sorry for his words, and added, 'I only meant it for your good, you know Gertrude.'

'I'll clear out the whole lot, and destroy them,' she said huskily, 'and try such remedies no more!'

'You want somebody to cheer you,' he observed. 'I once thought of adopting a boy; but he is too old now. And he is gone away I don't know where.'

She guessed to whom he alluded; for Rhoda Brook's story had in the course of years become known to her; though not a word had ever passed between her husband and herself on the subject.

Neither had she ever spoken to him of her visit to Conjuror Trendle, and of what was revealed to her, or she thought was revealed to her, by that solitary heathman.

She was now five-and-twenty; but she seemed older. 'Six years of marriage, and only a few months of love,' she sometimes whispered to herself. And then she thought of the apparent cause, and said, with a tragic glance at her withering limb, 'If I could only again be as I was when he first saw me!'

She obediently destroyed her nostrums and charms; but there remained a hankering wish to try something else – some other sort of cure altogether. She had never revisited Trendle since she had been conducted to the house of the solitary by Rhoda against her will; but it now suddenly occurred to Gertrude that she would, in a last desperate effort at deliverance from this seeming curse, again seek out the man, if he yet lived. He was entitled to a certain credence, for the indistinct form he had raised in the glass had undoubtedly resembled the only woman in the world who – as she now knew, though not then – could have a reason for bearing her ill-will. The visit should be paid.

This time she went alone, though she nearly got lost on the heath, and roamed a considerable distance out of her way. Trendle's house was reached at last, however; he was not indoors, and instead of waiting at the cottage, she went to where his bent figure was pointed out to her at work a long way off. Trendle remembered her, and laying down the handful of furze-roots which he was gathering and throwing into a heap, he offered to accompany her in her homeward direction, as the distance was considerable and the days were short. So they walked together, his head bowed nearly to the earth, and his form of a colour with it.

'You can send away warts and other excrescences, I know,' she said; 'why can't you send away this?' And the arm was uncovered.

'You think too much of my powers!' said Trendle; 'and I am old and weak now, too. No, no; it is too much for me to attempt in my own person. What have ye tried?'

She named to him some of the hundred medicaments and counter-spells which she had adopted from time to time. He shook his head.

'Some were good enough,' he said approvingly; 'but not many of them for such as this. This is of the nature of a blight, not of the nature of a wound, and if you ever do throw it off, it will be all at once.'

'If I only could!'

'There is only one chance of doing it known to me. It has never failed in kindred afflictions – that I can declare. But it is hard to carry out, and especially for a woman.'

'Tell me!' said she.

'You must touch with the limb the neck of a man who's been hanged.'

She started a little at the image he had raised.

'Before he's cold – just after he's cut down,' continued the conjuror impassively.

'How can that do good?'

'It will turn the blood and change the constitution. But, as I say, to do it is hard. You must go to the jail when there's a hanging, and wait for him when he's brought off the gallows. Lots have done it, though perhaps not such pretty women as you. I used to send dozens for skin complaints. But that was in former times. The last I sent was in '13 – near twelve years ago.'

He had no more to tell her, and, when he had put her into a straight track homeward, turned and left her, refusing all money as at first.

VII. A Ride

The communication sank deep into Gertrude's mind. Her nature was rather a timid one; and probably of all remedies that the white wizard could have suggested there was not one which would have filled her with so much aversion as this, not to speak of the immense obstacles in the way of its adoption.

Casterbridge, the county-town, was a dozen or fifteen miles off; and though in those days, when men were executed for horse-stealing, arson, and burglary, an assize seldom passed without a hanging, it was not likely that she could get access to the body of the criminal unaided. And the fear of her husband's anger made her reluctant to breathe a word of Trendle's suggestion to him or to anybody about him.

She did nothing for months, and patiently bore her disfigurement as before. But her woman's nature, craving for renewed love, through the medium of renewed beauty (she was but twenty-five), was ever stimulating her to try what, at any rate, could hardly do her any harm. 'What came by a spell will go by a spell surely,' she would say. Whenever her imagination pictured the act she shrank in terror from the possibility of it; then the words of the conjuror, 'It will turn your blood,' were seen to be capable of a scientific no less than a ghastly interpretation; the mastering desire returned, and urged her on again.

There was at this time but one county paper, and that her husband only occasionally borrowed. But old-fashioned days had old-fashioned means, and news was extensively conveyed by word of mouth from market to market, or from fair to fair, so that, whenever such an event as execution was about to take place, few within a radius of twenty miles were ignorant of the coming sight; and so far as Holmstoke was concerned, some enthusiasts had been known to walk all the way to Casterbridge and back in one day, solely to witness the spectacle. The next assizes were in March; and when Gertrude Lodge heard that they had been held, she inquired stealthily at the inn as to the result, as soon as she could find opportunity.

She was, however, too late. The time at which the sentences were to be carried out had arrived, and to make the journey and obtain admission at such short notice required at least her husband's assistance. She dared not tell him, for she had found by delicate experiment that these smouldering village beliefs made him furious if mentioned, partly because he half entertained them himself. It was therefore necessary to wait for another opportunity.

Her determination received a fillip from learning that two epileptic children had attended from this very village of Holmstoke many years before with beneficial results, though the experiment had been strongly condemned by the neighbouring clergy. April, May, June passed; and it is no overstatement to say that by the end of the last-named month Gertrude wellnigh longed for the death of a fellow-creature. Instead of her formal prayers each night, her unconscious prayer was, 'O Lord, hang some guilty or innocent person soon!'

This time she made earlier inquiries, and was altogether more systematic in her proceedings. Moreover, the season was summer, between the haymaking and the harvest, and in the leisure thus afforded him her husband had been holiday-taking away from home.

The assizes were in July, and she went to the inn as before. There was to be one execution – only one – for arson.

Her greatest problem was not how to get to Casterbridge, but what means she should adopt for obtaining admission to the jail. Though access for such purposes had formerly never been denied, the custom had fallen into desuetide; and in contemplating her possible difficulties, she was again almost driven to fall back upon her husband. But, on sounding him about the assizes, he was so uncommunicative, so more than usually cold, that she did not proceed, and decided that whatever she did she would do alone.

Fortune, obdurate hitherto, showed her unexpected favour. On the Thursday before the Saturday fixed for the execution, Lodge remarked to her that he was going away from home for another day or two on business at a fair, and that he was sorry he could not take her with him.

She exhibited on this occasion so much readiness to stay at home that he looked at her in surprise. Time had been when she would have shown deep disappointment at the loss of such a jaunt. However, he lapsed into his usual taciturnity, and on the day named left Holmstoke.

It was now her turn. She at first had thought of driving, but on reflection held that driving would not do, since it would necessitate her keeping to the turnpike-road, and so increase by tenfold the risk of her ghastly errand being found out. She decided to ride, and avoid the beaten track, notwithstanding that in her husband's stables there was no animal just at present which by any stretch of imagination could be considered a lady's mount, in spite of his promise before marriage to always keep a mare for her. He had, however, many carthorses, fine ones of their kind; and among the rest was a serviceable creature, an equine Amazon, with a back as broad as a sofa, on which Gertrude had occasionally taken an airing when unwell. This horse she chose.

On Friday afternoon one of the men brought it round. She was dressed, and before going down looked at her shrivelled arm. 'Ah!' she said to it, 'if it had not been for you this terrible ordeal would have been saved me!'

When strapping up the bundle in which she carried a few articles of clothing, she took occasion to say to the servant, 'I take these in case I should not get back tonight from the person I am going to visit. Don't be alarmed if I am not in by ten, and close up the house as usual. I shall be at home tomorrow for certain.' She meant then to tell her husband privately; the deed accomplished was not like the deed projected. He would almost certainly forgive her.

And then the pretty palpitating Gertrude Lodge went from her husband's homestead; but though her goal was Casterbridge she did not take the direct route thither through Stickleford. Her cunning course at first was in precisely the opposite direction. As soon as she was out of sight, however, she turned to the left, by a road which led into Egdon, and on entering the heath wheeled round, and set out in the true course, due westerly. A more private way down the county could not be imagined; and as to direction, she had merely to keep her horse's head to a point a little to the right of the sun. She knew that she would light upon a furze-cutter or cottager of some sort from time to time, from whom she might correct her bearing.

Though the date was comparatively recent, Egdon was much less fragmentary in character than now. The attempts – successful and otherwise – at cultivation on the lower slopes, which intrude and break up the original heath into small detached heaths, had not been carried far; Enclosure Acts had not taken effect, and the banks and fences which now exclude the cattle of those villagers who formerly enjoyed rights of commonage thereon, and the carts of those who had turbary privileges which kept them in firing all the year round, were not erected. Gertrude, therefore, rode along with no other obstacles than the prickly furze-bushes, the mats of heather, the white water-courses, and the natural steeps and declivities of the ground.

Her horse was sure, if heavy-footed and slow, and though a draught animal, was easy-paced; had it been otherwise, she was not a woman who could have ventured to ride over such a bit of country with a half-dead arm. It was therefore nearly eight o'clock when she drew rein to breathe her bearer on the last outlying high point of heath-land towards Casterbridge, previous to leaving Egdon for the cultivated valleys.

She halted before a pool called Rushy-pond, flanked by the ends of two hedges; a railing ran through the centre of the pond, dividing it in half. Over the railing she saw the low green country; over the green trees the roofs of the town; over the roofs a white flat façade, denoting the entrance to the county jail. On the roof of this front specks were moving about; they seemed to be workmen erecting something. Her flesh crept. She descended slowly, and was soon amid corn-fields and pastures. In another half-hour, when it was almost dark, Gertrude reached the White Hart, the first inn of the town on that side.

Little surprise was excited by her arrival; farmers' wives rode on horseback then more than they do now; though, for that matter, Mrs Lodge was not imagined to be a wife at all; the innkeeper supposed her some harum-skarum young woman who had come to attend 'hang-fair' next day. Neither her husband nor herself ever dealt in Casterbridge market, so that she was unknown. While dismounting she beheld a crowd of boys standing at the door of a harness-maker's shop just above the inn, looking inside it with deep interest.

'What is going on there?' she asked of the ostler.

'Making the rope for tomorrow.'

She throbbed responsively, and contracted her arm.

''Tis sold by the inch afterwards,' the man continued. 'I could get you a bit, miss, for nothing, if you'd like?'

She hastily repudiated any such wish, all the more from a curious creeping feeling that the condemned wretch's destiny was becoming interwoven with her own; and having engaged a room for the night, sat down to think.

Up to this time she had formed but the vaguest notions about her means of obtaining access to the prison. The words of the cunning-man returned to her mind. He had implied that she should use her beauty, impaired though it was, as a pass-key. In her inexperience she knew little about jail functionaries; she had heard of a high-sheriff and an under-sheriff, but dimly only. She knew, however, that there must be a hangman, and to the hangman she determined to apply.

VIII. A Water-Side Hermit

At this date, and for several years after, there was a hangman to almost every jail. Gertrude found, on inquiry, that the Caster-bridge official dwelt in a lonely cottage by a deep slow river flowing under the cliff on which the prison buildings were situate – the stream being the self-same one, though she did not know it, which watered the Stickleford and Holmstoke meads lower down in its course.

Having changed her dress, and before she had eaten or drunk – for she could not take her ease till she had ascertained some particulars – Gertrude pursued her way by a path along the water-side to the cottage indicated. Passing thus the outskirts of the jail, she discerned on the level roof over the gateway three rectangular lines against the sky, where the specks had been moving in her distant view; she recognized what the erection was, and passed quickly on. Another hundred yards brought her to the executioner's house, which a boy pointed out. It stood close to the same stream, and was hard by a weir, the waters of which emitted a steady roar.

While she stood hesitating the door opened, and an old man came forth, shading a candle with one hand. Locking the door on the outside, he turned to a flight of wooden steps fixed against the end of the cottage, and began to ascend them, this being evidently the staircase to his bedroom. Gertrude hastened forward, but by the time she reached the foot of the ladder he was at the top. She called to him loudly enough to be heard above the roar of the weir; he looked down and said, 'What d'ye want here?'

'To speak to you a minute.'

The candlelight, such as it was, fell upon her imploring, pale, upturned face, and Davies (as the hangman was called) backed down the ladder. 'I was just going to bed,' he said. ' "Early to bed and early to rise," but I don't mind stopping a minute for such a one as you. Come into house.' He reopened the door, and preceded her to the room within.

The implements of his daily work, which was that of a jobbing gardener, stood in a corner, and seeing probably that she looked rural, he said, 'If you want me to undertake country work I can't come, for I never leave Casterbridge for gentle nor simple – not I. My real calling is officer of justice,' he added formally.

'Yes, yes! That's it. Tomorrow!'

'Ah! I thought so. Well, what's the matter about that? 'Tis no use to come here about the knot – folks do come continually, but I tell 'em one knot is as merciful as another if ye keep it under the ear. Is the unfortunate man a relation; or, I should say, perhaps' (looking at her dress) 'a person who's been in your employ?'

'No. What time is the execution?'

'The same as usual – twelve o'clock, or as soon after as the London mail-coach gets in. We always wait for that, in case of a reprieve.'

'O – a reprieve – I hope not!' she said involuntarily.

'Well, – hee, hee! – as a matter of business, so do I! But still, if ever a young fellow deserved to be let off, this one does; only just turned eighteen, and only present by chance when the rick was fired. Howsomever, there's not much risk of it, as they are obliged to make an example of him, there having been so much destruction of property that way lately.'

'I mean,' she explained, 'that I want to touch him for a charm, a cure of an affliction, by the advice of a man who has proved the virtue of the remedy.'

'O yes, miss! Now I understand. I've had such people come in past years. But it didn't strike me that you looked of a sort to require blood-turning. What's the complaint? The wrong kind for this, I'll be bound.'

'My arm.' She reluctantly showed the withered skin.

'Ah! – 'tis all a-scram!' said the hangman, examining it.

'Yes,' said she.

'Well,' he continued, with interest, 'that *is* the class o' subject, I'm bound to admit! I like the look of the wownd; it is truly as suitable for the cure as any I ever saw. 'Twas a knowing-man that sent 'ee, whoever he was.'

'You can contrive for me all that's necessary?' she said breathlessly.

'You should really have gone to the governor of the jail, and your doctor with 'ee, and given your name and address – that's how it used to be done, if I recollect. Still, perhaps, I can manage it for a trifling fee.'

'O, thank you! I would rather do it this way, as I should like it kept private.'

'Lover not to know, eh?'

'No – husband.'

'Aha! Very well. I'll get 'ee a touch of the corpse.'

'Where is it now?' she said, shuddering.

'It? – *he*, you mean; he's living yet. Just inside that little small winder up there in the glum.' He signified the jail on the cliff above.

She thought of her husband and her friends. 'Yes, of course,' she said; 'and how am I to proceed?'

He took her to the door. 'Now, do you be waiting at the little wicket in the wall, that you'll find up there in the lane, not later than one o'clock. I will open it from the inside, as I shan't come home to dinner till he's cut down. Good-night. Be punctual; and if you don't want anybody to know 'ee, wear a veil. Ah – once I had such a daughter as you!'

She went away, and climbed the path above, to assure herself that she would be able to find the wicket next day. Its outline was soon visible to her – a narrow opening in the outer wall of the prison precincts. The steep was so great that, having reached the wicket, she stopped a moment to breathe; and, looking back upon the water-side cot, saw the hangman again ascending his outdoor staircase. He entered the loft or chamber to which it led, and in a few minutes extinguished his light.

The town clock struck ten, and she returned to the White Hart as she had come.

IX. A Rencounter

It was one o'clock on Saturday. Gertrude Lodge, having been admitted to the jail as above described, was sitting in a waiting-room within the second gate, which stood under a classic archway of ashlar, then comparatively modern, and bearing the inscription, 'COVNTY JAIL; 1793'. This had been the façade she saw from the heath the day before. Near at hand was a passage to the roof on which the gallows stood.

The town was thronged, and the market suspended; but Gertrude had seen scarcely a soul. Having kept her room till the hour of the appointment, she had proceeded to the spot by a way which avoided the open space below the cliff where the spectators had gathered; but she could, even now, hear the multitudinous babble of their voices, out of which rose at intervals the hoarse croak of a single voice uttering the words, 'Last dying speech and confession!' There had been no reprieve, and the execution was over; but the crowd still waited to see the body taken down.

Soon the persistent woman heard a trampling overhead, then a hand beckoned to her, and, following directions, she went out and crossed the inner paved court beyond the gatehouse, her knees trembling so that she could scarcely walk. One of her arms was out of its sleeve, and only covered by her shawl.

On the spot at which she had now arrived were two trestles, and before she could think of their purpose she heard heavy feet descending stairs somewhere at her back. Turn her head she would not, or could not, and, rigid in this position, she was conscious of a rough coffin passing her shoulder, borne by four men. It was open, and in it lay the body of a young man, wearing the smockfrock of a rustic, and fustian breeches. The corpse had been thrown into the coffin so hastily that the skirt of the smockfrock was hanging over. The burden was temporarily deposited on the trestles.

By this time the young woman's state was such that a grey mist seemed to float before her eyes, on account of which, and the veil she wore, she could scarcely discern anything: it was as though she had nearly died, but was held up by a sort of galvanism.

'Now!' said a voice close at hand, and she was just conscious that the word had been addressed to her.

By a last strenuous effort she advanced, at the same time hearing persons approaching behind her. She bared her poor curst arm; and Davies, uncovering the face of the corpse, took Gertrude's hand, and held it so that her arm lay across the dead man's neck, upon a line the colour of an unripe blackberry, which surrounded it.

Gertrude shrieked: 'the turn o' the blood', predicted by the conjuror, had taken place. But at that moment a second shriek rent the air of the enclosure: it was not Gertrude's, and its effect upon her was to make her start round.

Immediately behind her stood Rhoda Brook, her face drawn, and her eyes red with weeping. Behind Rhoda stood Gertrude's own husband; his countenance lined, his eyes dim, but without a tear.

'D–n you! what are you doing here?' he said hoarsely.

'Hussy – to come between us and our child now!' cried Rhoda. 'This is the meaning of what Satan showed me in the vision! You are like her at last!' And clutching the bare arm of the younger woman, she pulled her unresistingly back against the wall. Immediately Brook had loosened her hold the fragile young Gertrude slid down against the feet of her husband. When he lifted her up she was unconscious.

The mere sight of the twain had been enough to suggest to her that the dead young man was Rhoda's son. At that time the relatives of an executed convict had the privilege of claiming the body for burial, if they chose to do so; and it was for this purpose that Lodge was awaiting the inquest with Rhoda. He had been summoned by her as soon as the young man was taken in the crime, and at different times since; and he had attended in court during the trial. This was the 'holiday' he had been indulging in of late. The two wretched parents had wished to avoid exposure; and hence had come themselves for the body, a waggon and sheet for its conveyance and covering being in waiting outside.

Gertrude's case was so serious that it was deemed advisable to call to her the surgeon who was at hand. She was taken out of the jail into the town; but she never reached home alive. Her delicate vitality, sapped perhaps by the paralyzed arm, collapsed under the double shock that followed the severe strain, physical and mental, to which she had subjected herself during the previous twenty-four hours. Her blood had been 'turned' indeed – too far. Her death took place in the town three days after.

Her husband was never seen in Casterbridge again; once only in the old market-place at Anglebury, which he had so much frequented, and very seldom in public anywhere. Burdened at first with moodiness and remorse, he eventually changed for the better, and appeared as a chastened and thoughtful man. Soon after attending the funeral of his poor young wife he took steps towards giving up the farms in Holmstoke and the adjoining parish, and, having sold every head of his stock, he went away to Port-Bredy, at the other end of the county, living there in solitary lodgings till his death two years later of a painless decline. It was then found that he had bequeathed the whole of his not inconsiderable property to a reformatory for boys, subject to the payment of a small annuity to Rhoda Brook, if she could be found to claim it.

For some time she could not be found; but eventually she reappeared in her old parish, – absolutely refusing, however, to have anything to do with the provision made for her. Her monotonous milking at the dairy was resumed, and followed for many long years, till her form became bent, and her once abundant dark hair white and worn away at the forehead – perhaps by long pressure against the cows. Here, sometimes, those who knew her experiences would stand and observe her, and wonder what sombre thoughts were beating inside that impassive, wrinkled brow, to the rhythm of the alternating milk-streams.

Sredni Vashtar

'SAKI'

Conradin was ten years old, and the doctor had pronounced his professional opinion that the boy would not live another five years. The doctor was silky and effete, and counted for little, but his opinion was endorsed by Mrs De Ropp, who counted for nearly everything. Mrs De Ropp was Conradin's cousin and guardian, and in his eyes she represented those three-fifths of the world that are necessary and disagreeable and real; the other two-fifths, in perpetual antagonism to the foregoing, were summed up in himself and his imagination. One of these days Conradin supposed he would succumb to the mastering pressure of wearisome necessary things – such as illness and coddling restrictions and drawn-out dullness. Without his imagination, which was rampant under the spur of loneliness, he would have succumbed long ago.

Mrs De Ropp would never, in her honestest moments, have confessed to herself that she disliked Conradin, though she might have been dimly aware that thwarting him 'for his good' was a duty which she did not find particularly irksome. Conradin hated her with a desperate sincerity which he was perfectly able to mask. Such few pleasures as he could contrive for himself gained an added relish from the likelihood that they would be displeasing to his guardian, and from the realm of his imagination she was locked out – an unclean thing, which should find no entrance.

In the dull, cheerless garden, overlooked by so many windows that were ready to open with a message not to do this or that, or a reminder that medicines were due, he found little attraction. The few fruit-trees that it contained were set jealously apart from his plucking, as though they were rare specimens of their kind blooming in an arid waste; it would probably have been difficult to find a market-gardener who would have offered ten shillings for their entire yearly produce. In a forgotten corner, however, almost hidden behind a dismal shrubbery, was a disused tool-shed of respectable proportions, and within is walls Conradin found a haven, something that took on the varying aspects of a playroom and a cathedral. He had peopled it with a legion of familiar phantoms, evoked partly from fragments of history and partly from his own brain, but it also boasted two inmates of flesh and blood. In one corner lived a ragged-plumaged Houdan hen, on which the boy lavished an affection that had scarcely another outlet. Further back in the gloom stood a large hutch, divided into two compartments, one of which was fronted with close iron bars. This was the abode of a large polecat-ferret, which a friendly butcher-boy had once smuggled, cage and all, into its present quarters, in exchange for a long-secreted hoard of small silver. Conradin was dreadfully afraid of the lithe, sharp-fanged beast, but it was his most treasured possession. Its very presence in the tool-shed was a secret and fearful joy, to be kept scrupulously from the knowledge of the Woman, as he privately dubbed his cousin. And one day, out of Heaven knows what material, he spun the beast a wonderful name, and from that moment it grew into a god and a religion. The Woman indulged in religion once a week at a church near by, and took Conradin with her, but to him the church service was an alien rite in the House of Rimmon. Every Thursday, in the dim and musty silence of the tool-shed, he worshipped with mystic and elaborate ceremonial before the wooden hutch where dwelt Sredni Vashtar, the great ferret. Red flowers in their season and scarlet berries in the wintertime were offered at his shrine, for he was a god who laid some special stress on the fierce impatient side of things, as opposed to the Woman's religion, which, as far as Conradin could observe, went to great lengths in the contrary direction. And on great festivals powdered nutmeg was strewn in front of his hutch, an important feature of the offering being that the nutmeg had to be stolen. These festivals were of irregular occurrence, and were chiefly appointed to celebrate some passing event. On one occasion, when Mrs De Ropp suffered from acute toothache for three days, Conradin kept up the festival during the entire three days, and almost succeeded in persuading himself that Sredni Vashtar was personally responsible for the toothache. If the malady had lasted for another day the supply of nutmeg would have given out.

The Houdan hen was never drawn into the cult of Sredni Vashtar. Conradin had long ago settled that she was an

Anabaptist. He did not pretend to have the remotest knowledge as to what an Anabaptist was, but he privately hoped that it was dashing and not very respectable. Mrs De Ropp was the ground plan on which he based and detested all respectability.

After a while Conradin's absorption in the tool-shed began to attract the notice of his guardian. 'It is not good for him to be pottering down there in all weathers,' she promptly decided, and at breakfast one morning she announced that the Houdan hen had been sold and taken away overnight. With her short-sighted eyes she peered at Conradin, waiting for an outbreak of rage and sorrow, which she was ready to rebuke with a flow of excellent precepts and reasoning. But Conradin said nothing: there was nothing to be said. Something perhaps in his white set face gave her a momentary qualm, for at tea that afternoon there was toast on the table, a delicacy which she usually banned on the ground that it was bad for him; also because the making of it 'gave trouble', a deadly offence in the middle-class feminine eye.

'I thought you liked toast,' she exclaimed, with an injured air, observing that he did not touch it.

'Sometimes,' said Conradin.

In the shed that evening there was an innovation in the worship of the hutch-god. Conradin had been wont to chant his praises, tonight he asked a boon.

'Do one thing for me, Sredni Vashtar.'

The thing was not specified. As Sredni Vashtar was a god he must be supposed to know. And choking back a sob as he looked at that other empty corner, Conradin went back to the world he so hated.

And every night, in the welcome darkness of his bedroom, and every evening in the dusk of the tool-shed, Conradin's bitter litany went up: 'Do one thing for me, Sredni Vashtar.'

Mrs De Ropp noticed that the visits to the shed did not cease, and one day she made a further journey of inspection.

'What are you keeping in that locked hutch?' she asked. 'I believe it's guinea-pigs. I'll have them all cleared away.'

Conradin shut his lips tight, but the Woman ransacked his bedroom till she found the carefully hidden key, and forthwith marched down to the shed to complete her discovery. It was a cold afternoon, and Conradin had been bidden to keep to the house. From the furthest window of the dining-room the door of the shed could just be seen beyond the corner of the shrubbery, and there Conradin stationed himself. He saw the Woman enter, and then he imagined her opening the door of the sacred hutch and peering down with her short-sighted eyes into the thick straw bed where his god lay hidden. Perhaps she would prod at the straw in her clumsy impatience. And Conradin fervently breathed his prayer for the last time. But he knew as he prayed that he did not believe. He knew that the Woman would come out presently with that pursed smile he loathed so well on her face, and that in an hour or two the gardener would carry away his wonderful god, a god no longer, but a simple brown ferret in a hutch. And he knew that the Woman would triumph always as she triumphed now, and that he would grow ever more sickly under her pestering and domineering and superior wisdom, till one day nothing would matter much more with him, and the doctor would be proved right. And in the sting and misery of his defeat, he began to chant loudly and defiantly the hymn of his threatened idol:

> Sredni Vashtar went forth,
> His thoughts were red thoughts and his teeth were white.
> His enemies called for peace, but he brought them death.
> Sredni Vashtar the Beautiful.

And then of a sudden he stopped his chanting and drew closer to the window-pane. The door of the shed still stood ajar as it had been left, and the minutes were slipping by. They were long minutes, but they slipped by nevertheless. He watched the starlings running and flying in little parties across the lawn; he counted them over and over again, with one eye always on that swinging door. A sour-faced maid came in to lay the table for tea, and still Conradin stood and waited and watched. Hope had crept by inches into his heart, and now a look of triumph began to blaze in his eyes that had only known the wistful patience of defeat. Under his breath, with a furtive exultation, he began once again the paean of victory and devastation. And presently his eyes were rewarded; out through that doorway came a long, low, yellow-and-brown beast, with eyes a-blink at the waning day-light, and dark wet stains around the fur of jaws and throat. Conradin dropped on his knees. The great polecat-ferret made its way down to a small brook at the foot of the garden, drank for a moment, then crossed a little plank bridge and was lost to sight in the bushes. Such was the passing of Sredni Vashtar.

'Tea is ready,' said the sour-faced maid; 'where is the mistress?'

'She went down to the shed some time ago,' said Conradin.

And while the maid went to summon her mistress to tea, Conradin fished a toasting-fork out of the sideboard drawer and proceeded to toast himself a piece of bread. And during the toasting of it and the buttering of it with much butter and the slow enjoyment of eating it, Conradin listened to the noises and silences which fell in quick spasms beyond the dining-room door. The loud foolish screaming of the maid, the answering chorus of wondering ejaculations from the kitchen region, the scuttering footsteps and hurried embassies for outside help, and then, after a lull, the scared sobbings and the shuffling tread of those who bore a heavy burden into the house.

'Whoever will break it to the poor child? I couldn't for the life of me!' exclaimed a shrill voice. And while they debated the matter among themselves, Conradin made himself another piece of toast.

The Necklace

GUY DE MAUPASSANT

She was one of those pretty and charming girls who, by some freak of destiny, are born into families that have always held subordinate appointments. Possessing neither dowry nor expectations, she had no hope of meeting some man of wealth and distinction, who would understand her, fall in love with her, and wed her. So she consented to marry a small clerk in the Ministry of Public Instruction.

She dressed plainly, because she could not afford to be elegant, but she felt as unhappy as if she had married beneath her. Women are dependent on neither caste nor ancestry. With them, beauty, grace, and charm take the place of birth and breeding. In their case, natural delicacy, instinctive refinement, and adaptability constitute their claims to aristocracy and raise girls of the lower classes to an equality with the greatest of great ladies. She was eternally restive under the conviction that she had been born to enjoy every refinement and luxury. Depressed by her humble surroundings, the sordid walls of her dwelling, its worn furniture and shabby fabrics were a torment to her. Details which another woman of her class would scarcely have noticed, tortured her and filled her with resentment. The sight of her little Breton maid-of-all-work roused in her forlorn repinings and frantic yearnings. She pictured to herself silent antechambers, upholstered with oriental tapestry, lighted by great bronze standard lamps, where two tall footmen in knee-breeches slumbered in huge arm-chairs, overcome by the oppressive heat from the stove. She dreamed of spacious drawing-rooms with hangings of antique silk, and beautiful tables laden with priceless ornaments: of fragrant and coquettish boudoirs, exquisitely adapted for afternoon chats with intimate friends, men of note and distinction, whose attentions are coveted by every woman.

She would sit down to dinner at the round table, its cloth already three days old, while her husband, seated opposite to her, removed the lid from the soup tureen and exclaimed, '*Pot-au-feu!* How splendid! My favourite soup!' But her own thoughts were dallying with the idea of exquisite dinners and shining silver, in rooms whose tapestried walls were gay with antique figures and grotesque birds in fairy forests. She would dream of delicious dishes served on wonderful plate, of soft, whispered nothings, which evoke a sphinx-like smile, while one trifles with the pink flesh of a trout or the wing of a plump pullet.

She had no pretty gowns, no jewels, nothing – and yet she cared for nothing else. She felt that it was for such things as these that she had been born. What joy it would have given her to attract, to charm, to be envied by women, courted by men! She had a wealthy friend, who had been at school at the same convent, but after a time she refused to go and see her, because she suffered so acutely after each visit. She spent whole days in tears of grief, regret, despair, and misery.

One evening her husband returned home in triumph with a large envelope in his hand.

'Here is something for you,' he cried.

Hastily she tore open the envelope and drew out a printed card with the following inscription:

'The Minister of Public Instruction and Madame Georges Ramponneau have the honour to request the company of Monsieur and Madame Loisel at an At Home at the Education Office on Monday, 18th January.'

Instead of being delighted as her husband had hoped, she flung the invitation irritably on the table, exclaiming:

'What good is that to me?'

'Why, my dear, I thought you would be pleased. You never go anywhere, and this is a really splendid chance for you. I had no end of trouble in getting it. Everybody is trying to get an invitation. It's very select, and only a few invitations are issued to the clerks. You will see all the officials there.'

She looked at him in exasperation, and exclaimed petulantly:

'What do you expect me to wear at a reception like that?'

He had not considered the matter, but he replied hesitatingly:

'Why, that dress you always wear to the theatre seems to me very nice indeed . . .'

He broke off. To his horror and consternation he saw that his wife was in tears. Two large drops were rolling slowly down her cheeks.

'What on earth is the matter?' he gasped.

With a violent effort she controlled her emotion, and drying her wet cheeks said in a calm voice:

'Nothing. Only I haven't a frock, and so I can't go to the reception. Give your invitation to some friend in your office, whose wife is better dressed than I am.'

He was greatly distressed.

'Let us talk it over, Mathilde. How much do you think a proper frock would cost, something quite simple that would come in useful for other occasions afterwards?'

She considered the matter for a few moments, busy with her calculations, and wondering how large a sum she might venture to name without shocking the little clerk's instincts of economy and provoking a prompt refusal.

'I hardly know,' she said at last, doubtfully, 'But I think I could manage with four hundred francs.'

He turned a little pale. She had named the exact sum that he had saved for buying a gun and treating himself to some Sunday shooting parties the following summer with some friends, who were going to shoot larks in the plain of Nanterre.

But he replied:

'Very well, I'll give you four hundred francs. But mind you buy a really handsome gown.'

The day of the party drew near. But although her gown was finished Madame Loisel seemed depressed and dissatisfied.

'What is the matter?' asked her husband one evening. 'You haven't been at all yourself the last three days.'

She answered: 'It vexes me to think that I haven't any jewellery to wear, not even a brooch. I shall feel like a perfect pauper. I would almost rather not go to the party.'

'You can wear some fresh flowers. They are very fashionable this year. For ten francs you can get two or three splendid roses.'

She was not convinced.

'No, there is nothing more humiliating than to have an air of poverty among a crowd of rich women.'

'How silly you are!' exclaimed her husband. 'Why don't you ask your friend, Madame Forestier, to lend you some jewellery. You know her quite well enough for that.'

She uttered a cry of joy.

'Yes, of course, it never occurred to me.'

The next day she paid her friend a visit and explained her predicament.

Madame Forestier went to her wardrobe, took out a large jewel case and placed it open before her friend.

'Help yourself, my dear,' she said.

Madame Loisel saw some bracelets, a pearl necklace, a Venetian cross exquisitely worked in gold and jewels. She tried on these ornaments in front of the mirror and hesitated, reluctant to take them off and give them back.

'Have you nothing else?' she kept asking.

'Oh, yes, look for yourself. I don't know what you would prefer.'

At length, she discovered a black satin case containing a superb diamond necklace, and her heart began to beat with frantic desire. With trembling hands she took it out, fastened it over her high-necked gown, and stood gazing at herself in rapture.

Then, in an agony of doubt, she said:'

'Will you lend me this? I shouldn't want anything else.'

'Yes, certainly.'

She threw her arms round her friend's neck, kissed her effusively, and then fled with her treasure.

It was the night of the reception. Madame Loisel's triumph was complete. All smiles and graciousness, in her exquisite gown, she was the prettiest woman in the room. Her head was in a whirl of joy. All the men stared at her and inquired her name and begged for an introduction; all the junior staff asked her for waltzes. She even attracted the attention of the minister himself.

Carried away by her enjoyment, glorying in her beauty and her success, she threw herself ecstatically into the dance. She moved as in a beatific dream, wherein were mingled all the homage and admiration she had evoked, all the desires she had kindled, all that complete and perfect triumph, so dear to a woman's heart.

It was close on four before she could tear herself away. Ever since midnight her husband had been dozing in a little, deserted drawing-room together with three other men whose wives were enjoying themselves immensely.

He threw her outdoor wraps round her shoulders, unpretentious, every-day garments, whose shabbiness contrasted strangely with the elegance of her ball dress. Conscious of the incongruity, she was eager to be gone, in order to escape the notice of the other women in their luxurious furs. Loisel tried to restrain her.

'Wait here while I fetch a cab. You will catch cold outside.'

But she would not listen to him and hurried down the staircase. They went out into the street, but there was no cab to be seen. They continued their search, vainly hailing drivers whom they caught sight of in the distance. Shivering with cold and in desperation they made their way towards the Seine. At last, on the quay, they found one of those old vehicles which are only seen in Paris after nightfall, as if ashamed to display their shabbiness by daylight.

The cab took them to their door in the Rue des Martyrs and they gloomily climbed the stairs to their dwelling. All was over for her. As for him, he was thinking that he would have to be in the office by ten o'clock.

She took off her wraps in front of the mirror, for the sake of one last glance at herself in all her glory. But suddenly she uttered a cry. The diamonds were no longer round her neck.

'What is the matter?' asked her husband, who was already half undressed.

She turned to him in horror. 'I ... I've ... lost Madame Forestier's necklace.'

He started in dismay. 'What? Lost the necklace? Impossible!'

They searched the pleats of the gown, the folds of the cloak, and all the pockets, but in vain.

'You are sure you had it on when you came away from the ball?'

'Yes, I remember feeling it in the lobby at the Education Office.'

'But if you had lost it in the street we should have heard it drop. It must be in the cab.'

'Yes. I expect it is. Did you take the number?'

'No. Did you?'

'No.'

They gazed at each other, utterly appalled. In the end Loisel put on his clothes again.

'I will go over the ground that we covered on foot and see if I cannot find it.'

He left the house. Lacking the strength to go to bed, unable to think, she collapsed into a chair and remained there in her evening gown, without a fire.

About seven o'clock her husband returned. He had not found the diamonds.

He applied to the police, advertised a reward in the newspapers, made inquiries of all the hackney cab offices; he visited every place that seemed to hold out a vestige of hope.

His wife waited all day long in the same distracted condition, overwhelmed by this appalling calamity.

Loisel returned home in the evening, pale and hollow-cheeked. His efforts had been in vain.

'You must write to your friend,' he said, 'and tell her that you have broken the catch of the necklace and that you are having it mended. That will give us time to think things over.'

She wrote a letter to his dictation.

After a week had elapsed, they gave up all hope. Loisel, who looked five years older, said:

'We must take steps to replace the diamonds.'

On the following day they took the empty case to the jeweller whose name was inside the lid. He consulted his books.

'The necklace was not bought here, madam; I can only have supplied the case.'

They went from jeweller to jeweller, in an endeavour to find a necklace exactly like the one they had lost, comparing their recollections. Both of them were ill with grief and despair.

At last in a shop in the Palais-Royal they found a diamond necklace, which seemed to them exactly like the other. Its price was forty thousand francs. The jeweller agreed to sell it to them for thirty-six. They begged him not to dispose of it for three days, and they stipulated for the right to sell it back for thirty-four thousand francs, if the original necklace was found before the end of February.

Loisel had eighteen thousand francs left to him by his father. The balance of the sum he proposed to borrow. He raised loans in all quarters, a thousand francs from one man, five hundred from another, five louis here, three louis there. He gave promissory notes, agreed to exorbitant terms, had dealings with usurers, and with all the money-lending hordes. He compromised his whole future, and had to risk his signature, hardly knowing if he would be able to honour it. Overwhelmed by the prospect of future suffering, the black misery which was about to come upon him, the physical privations and moral torments, he went to fetch the new necklace, and laid his thirty-six thousand francs down on the jeweller's counter.

When Madame Loisel brought back the necklace, Madame Forestier said reproachfully:

'You ought to have returned it sooner; I might have wanted to wear it.'

To Madame Loisel's relief she did not open the case. Supposing she had noticed the exchange, what would she have thought? What would she have said? Perhaps she would have taken her for a thief.

Madame Loisel now became acquainted with the horrors of extreme poverty. She made up her mind to it, and played her part heroically. This appalling debt had to be paid, and pay it she would. The maid was dismissed; the flat was given up, and they moved to a garret. She undertook all the rough household work and the odious duties of the kitchen. She washed up after meals and ruined her pink finger-nails scrubbing greasy dishes and saucepans. She washed the linen, the shirts, and the dusters, and hung them out on the line to dry. Every morning she carried down the sweepings to the street, and brought up the water, pausing for breath at each landing. Dressed like a working woman, she went with her basket on her arm to the greengrocer, the grocer, and the butcher, bargaining, wrangling, and fighting for every farthing.

Each month some of the promissory notes had to be redeemed, and others renewed, in order to gain time.

Her husband spent his evenings working at some tradesman's accounts, and at night he would often copy papers at five sous a page.

This existence went on for ten years.

At the end of that time they had paid off everything to the last penny, including the usurious rates and the accumulations of interest.

Madame Loisel now looked an old woman. She had become the typical poor man's wife, rough, coarse, hardbitten. Her hair was neglected, her skirts hung awry, and her hands were red. Her voice was no longer gentle, and she washed down the floors vigorously. But now and then, when her husband was at the office, she would sit by the window and her thoughts would wander back to that far-away evening, the evening of her beauty and her triumph.

What would have been the end of it if she had not lost the necklace? Who could say? Who could say? How strange, how variable are the chances of life! How small a thing can serve to save or ruin you!

One Sunday she went for a stroll in the Champs-Élysées, for the sake of relaxation after the week's work, and she caught sight of a lady with a child. She recognized Madame Forestier, who looked as young, as pretty, and as attractive as ever. Madame Loisel felt a thrill of emotion. Should she speak to her? Why not? Now that the debt was paid, why should she not tell her the whole story? She went up to her.

'Good morning, Jeanne.'

Her friend did not recognize her and was surprised at being addressed so familiarly by this homely person.

'I am afraid I do not know you – you must have made a mistake,' she said hesitatingly.

'No. I am Mathilde Loisel.'

Her friend uttered a cry.

'Oh, my poor, dear Mathilde, how you have changed!'

'Yes, I have been through a very hard time since I saw you last, no end of trouble, and all through you.'

'Through me? What do you mean?'

'You remember the diamond necklace you lent me to wear at the reception at the Education Office?'

'Yes. Well?'

'Well, I lost it.'

'I don't understand; you brought it back to me.'

'What I brought you back was another one, exactly like it. And for the last ten years we have been paying for it. You will understand that it was not an easy matter for people like us, who hadn't a penny. However, it's all over now. I can't tell you what a relief it is.'

Madame Forestier stopped dead.

'You mean to say that you bought a diamond necklace to replace mine?'

'Yes. And you never noticed it? They were certainly very much alike.'

She smiled with ingenuous pride and satisfaction.

Madame Forestier seized both her hands in great distress.

'Oh, my poor, dear Mathilde! Why, mine was only imitation. At the most it was worth five hundred francs!'

The Middle-Aged Man and His Mistresses

AESOP

A middle-aged man who was going grey had two mistresses, one young and the other old. Now she who was advanced in years had a sense of shame at having sexual intercourse with a lover younger than herself. And so she did not fail, each time that he came to her house, to pull out all of his black hairs.

The young mistress, on her part, recoiled from the idea of having an old lover, and so she pulled out his white hairs.

Thus it happened that, plucked in turn by the one and then the other, he became bald.

That which is ill-matched always gets into difficulties.

The Manchester Marriage

ELIZABETH GASKELL

Mr and Mrs Openshaw came from Manchester to settle in London. He had been, what is called in Lancashire, a salesman for a large manufacturing firm, who were extending their business, and opening a warehouse in the city; where Mr Openshaw was now to superintend their affairs. He rather enjoyed the change; having a kind of curiosity about London, which he had never yet been able to gratify in his brief visits to the metropolis. At the same time, he had an odd, shrewd contempt for the inhabitants, whom he always pictured to himself as fine, lazy people, caring nothing but for fashion and aristocracy, and lounging away their days in Bond Street, and such places; ruining good English, and ready in their turn to despise him as a provincial. The hours that the men of business kept in the city scandalized him too, accustomed as he was to the early dinners of Manchester folk and the consequently far longer evenings. Still, he was pleased to go to London, though he would not for the world have confessed it, even to himself, and always spoke of the step to his friends as one demanded of him by the interests of his employers, and sweetened to him by a considerable increase of salary. This, indeed, was so liberal that he might have been justified in taking a much larger house than the one he did, had he not thought himself bound to set an example to Londoners of how little a Manchester man of business cared for show. Inside, however, he furnished it with an unusual degree of comfort, and, in the winter-time, he insisted on keeping up as large fires as the grates would allow, in every room where the temperature was in the least chilly. Moreover, his northern sense of hospitality was such that, if he were at home, he could hardly suffer a visitor to leave the house without forcing meat and drink upon him. Every servant in the house was well warmed, well fed, and kindly treated; for their master scorned all petty saving in aught that conduced to comfort; while he amused himself by following out all his accustomed habits and individual ways, in defiance of what any of his new neighbours might think.

His wife was a pretty, gentle woman, of suitable age and character. He was forty-two, she thirty-five. He was loud and decided; she soft and yielding. They had two children; or rather, I should say, she had two; for the elder, a girl of eleven, was Mrs Openshaw's child by Frank Wilson, her first husband. The younger was a little boy, Edwin, who could just prattle, and to whom his father delighted to speak in the broadest and most unintelligible Lancashire dialect, in order to keep up what he called the true Saxon accent.

Mrs Openshaw's Christian name was Alice, and her first husband had been her own cousin. She was the orphan niece of a sea-captain in Liverpool; a quiet, grave little creature, of great personal attraction when she was fifteen or sixteen, with regular features and a blooming complexion. But she was very shy, and believed herself to be very stupid and awkward; and was frequently scolded by her aunt, her own uncle's second wife. So when her cousin, Frank Wilson, came home from a long absence at sea, and first was kind and protective to her; secondly, attentive; and thirdly, desperately in love with her, she hardly knew how to be grateful enough to him. It is true, she would have preferred his remaining in the first or second stages of behaviour; for his violent love puzzled and frightened her. Her uncle neither helped nor hindered the love affair, though it was going on under his own eyes. Frank's stepmother had such a variable temper, that there was no knowing whether what she liked one day she would like the next, or not. At length she went to such extremes of crossness that Alice was only too glad to shut her eyes and rush blindly at the chance of escape from domestic tyranny offered her by a marriage with her cousin; and, liking him better than any one in the world, except her uncle (who was at this time at sea), she went off one morning and was married to him, her only bridesmaid being the housemaid at her aunt's. The consequence was that Frank and his wife went into lodgings, and Mrs Wilson refused to see them, and turned away Norah, the warm-hearted housemaid, whom they accordingly took into their service. When Captain Wilson returned from his voyage he was very cordial with the young couple, and spent many an evening at their lodgings, smoking his pipe and sipping his grog; but he told them, for quietness' sake, he could not ask them to his own house; for his wife was bitter against them. They were not, however, very unhappy about this.

The seed of future unhappiness lay rather in Frank's vehement, passionate disposition, which led him to resent his wife's shyness and want of demonstrativeness as failures in conjugal duty. He was already tormenting himself, and her too in a slighter degree, by apprehensions and imaginations of what might befall her during his approaching absence at sea. At last, he went to his father and urged him to insist upon Alice's being once more received under his roof; the more especially as there was now a prospect of her confinement while her husband was away on his voyage. Captain Wilson was, as he himself expressed it, 'breaking up', and unwilling to undergo the excitement of a scene; yet he felt that what his son said was true. So he went to his wife. And before Frank set sail, he had the comfort of seeing his wife installed in her old little garret in his father's house. To have placed her in the one best spare room was a step beyond Mrs Wilson's powers of submission or generosity. The worst part about it, however, was that the faithful Norah had to be dismissed. Her place as housemaid had been filled up; and, even if it had not, she had forfeited Mrs Wilson's good opinion for ever. She comforted her young master and mistress by pleasant prophecies of the time when they would have a household of their own; of which, whatever service she might be in meanwhile, she should be sure to form a part. Almost the last action Frank did, before setting sail, was going with Alice to see Norah once more at her mother's house; and then he went away.

Alice's father-in-law grew more and more feeble as winter advanced. She was of great use to her stepmother in nursing and amusing him; and although there was anxiety enough in the household, there was, perhaps, more of peace than there had been for years, for Mrs Wilson had not a bad heart, and was softened by the visible approach of death to one whom she loved, and touched by the lonely condition of the young creature expecting her first confinement in her husband's absence. To this relenting mood Norah owed the permission to come and nurse Alice when her baby was born, and to remain and attend on Captain Wilson.

Before one letter had been received from Frank (who had sailed for the East Indies and China), his father died. Alice was always glad to remember that he had held her baby in his arms, and kissed and blessed it before his death. After that, and the consequent examination into the state of his affairs, it was found that he had left far less property than people had been led by his style of living to expect; and what money there was, was settled all upon his wife, and at her disposal after her death. This did not signify much to Alice, as Frank was now first mate of his ship, and, in another voyage or two, would be captain. Meanwhile he had left her rather more than two hundred pounds (all his savings) in the bank.

It became time for Alice to hear from her husband. One letter from the Cape she had already received. The next was to announce his arrival in India. As week after week passed over, and no intelligence of the ship having got there reached the office of the owners, and the captain's wife was in the same state of ignorant suspense as Alice herself, her fears grew most oppressive. At length the day came when, in reply to her inquiry at the shipping office, they told her that the owners had given up hope of ever hearing more of the *Betsy-Jane*, and had sent in their claim upon the underwriters. Now that he was gone for ever, she first felt a yearning, longing love for the kind cousin, the dear friend, the sympathizing protector, whom she should never see again; – first felt a passionate desire to show him his child, whom she had hitherto rather craved to have all to herself – her own sole possession. Her grief was, however, noiseless and quiet – rather to the scandal of Mrs Wilson who bewailed her stepson as if he and she had always lived together in perfect harmony, and who evidently thought it her duty to burst into fresh tears at every strange face she saw; dwelling on his poor young widow's desolate state, and the helplessness of the fatherless child, with an unction as if she liked the excitement of the sorrowful story.

So passed away the first days of Alice's widowhood. By and by things subsided into their natural and tranquil course. But, as if the young creature was always to be in some heavy trouble, her ewe-lamb began to be ailing, pining, and sickly. The child's mysterious illness turned out to be some affection of the spine, likely to affect health but not to shorten life – at least, so the doctors said. But the long, dreary suffering of one whom a mother loves as Alice loved her only child, is hard to look forward to. Only Norah guessed what Alice suffered; no one but God knew.

And so it fell out, that when Mrs Wilson, the elder, came to her one day, in violent distress, occasioned by a very material diminution in the value of the property that her husband had left her – a diminution which made her income barely enough to support herself, much less Alice – the latter could hardly understand how anything which did not touch health or life could cause such grief; and she received the intelligence with irritating composure. But when, that afternoon, the little sick child was brought in, and the grandmother – who, after all, loved it well – began a fresh moan over her losses to its unconscious ears – saying how she had planned to consult this or that doctor, and to give it this or that comfort or luxury in after years, but that now all chance of this had passed away – Alice's heart was touched, and she drew near to Mrs Wilson with unwonted caresses, and, in a spirit not unlike to that of Ruth, entreated that, come what would, they might remain together. After much discussion in succeeding days, it was arranged that Mrs Wilson should take a house in Manchester, furnishing it partly with what furniture she had, and providing the rest with Alice's remaining two hundred pounds. Mrs Wilson was herself a Manchester woman, and naturally longed to return to her native town; some connexions of her own, too, at that time required lodgings, for which they were willing to pay pretty handsomely. Alice undertook the active superintendence and superior work of the household; Norah – willing, faithful Norah – offered to cook, scour, do anything in short, so that she might but remain with them.

The plan succeeded. For some years their first lodgers remained with them, and all went smoothly – with that one sad exception of the little girl's increasing deformity. How that mother loved that child, it is not for words to tell!

Then came a break of misfortune. Their lodgers left, and no one succeeded to them. After some months, it became necessary to remove to a smaller house; and Alice's tender conscience was torn by the idea that she ought not to be a burden to her mother-in-law, but to go out and seek her own maintenance. And leave her child! The thought came like the sweeping boom of a funeral-bell over her heart.

By and by, Mr Openshaw came to lodge with them. He had started in life as the errand-boy and sweeper-out of a warehouse; had struggled up through all the grades of employment in it, fighting his way through the hard, striving Manchester life with strong, pushing energy of character. Every spare moment of time had been sternly given up to self-teaching. He was a capital accountant, a good French and German scholar, a keen, far-seeing tradesman – understanding markets and the bearing of events, both near and distant, on trade; and yet, with such vivid attention to present details, that I do not think he ever saw a group of flowers in the fields without thinking whether their colour would, or would not, form harmonious contrasts in the coming spring muslins and prints. He went to debating societies, and threw himself with all his heart and soul into politics; esteeming, it must be owned, every man a fool or a knave who differed from him, and overthrowing his opponents rather by the loud strength of his language than the calm strength of his logic. There was something of the Yankee in all this. Indeed, his theory ran parallel to the famous Yankee motto – 'England flogs creation, and Manchester flogs England.' Such a man, as may be fancied, had had no time for falling in love, or any such nonsense. At the age when most young men go through their courting and matrimony, he had not the means of keeping a wife, and was far too practical to think of having one. And now that he was in easy circumstances, a rising man, he considered women almost as encumbrances to the world, with whom a man had better have as little to do as possible. His first impression of Alice was indistinct, and he did not care enough about her to make it distinct. 'A pretty, yea-nay kind of woman', would have been his description of her, if he had been pushed into a corner. He was rather afraid, in the beginning, that her quiet ways arose from a listlessness and laziness of character, which would have been exceedingly discordant to his active, energetic nature. But, when he found out the punctuality with which his wishes were attended to, and her work was done; when he was called in the morning at the very stroke of the clock, his shaving-water scalding hot, his fire bright, his coffee made exactly as his peculiar fancy dictated (for he was a man who had his theory about everything based upon what he knew of science, and often perfectly original) – then he began to think: not that Alice had any particular merit, but that he had got into remarkably good lodgings; his restlessness wore away, and he began to consider himself as almost settled for life in them.

Mr Openshaw had been too busy, all his days, to be introspective. He did not know that he had any tenderness in his nature; and if he had become conscious of its abstract existence he would have considered it as a manifestation of disease in some part of him. But he was decoyed into pity unawares; and pity led on to tenderness. That little helpless child – always carried about by one of the three busy women of the house, or else patiently threading coloured beads in the chair from which, by no effort of its own, could it ever move – the great grave blue eyes, full of serious, not uncheerful, expression, giving to the small delicate face a look beyond its years – the soft plaintive voice dropping out but few words, so unlike the continual prattle of a child – caught Mr Openshaw's attention in spite of himself. One day – he half scorned himself for doing so – he cut short his dinner-hour to go in search of some toy, which should take the place of those eternal beads. I forget what he bought; but, when he gave the present (which he took care to do in a short abrupt manner, and when no one was by to see him), he was almost thrilled by the flash of delight that came over that child's face, and he could not help, all through that afternoon, going over and over again the picture left on his memory, by the bright effect of unexpected joy on the little girl's face. When he returned home, he found his slippers placed by his sitting-room fire; and even more careful attention paid to his fancies than was habitual in those model lodgings. When Alice had taken the last of his tea-things away – she had been silent as usual till then – she stood for an instant with the door in her hand. Mr Openshaw looked as if he were deep in his book, though in fact he did not see a line; but was heartily wishing the woman would go, and not make any palaver of gratitude. But she only said:

'I am very much obliged to you, sir. Thank you very much,' and was gone, even before he could send her away with a 'There, my good woman, that's enough!'

For some time longer he took no apparent notice of the child. He even hardened his heart into disregarding her sudden flash of colour and little timid smile of recognition, when he saw her by chance. But, after all, this could not last for ever; and, having a second time given way to tenderness, there was no relapse. The insidious enemy having thus entered his heart, in the guise of compassion to the child, soon assumed the more dangerous form of interest in the mother. He was aware of this change of feeling – despised himself for it – struggled with it; nay, internally yielded to it and cherished it, long before he suffered the slightest expression of it, by word, action, or look to escape him. He watched Alice's docile, obedient ways to her stepmother; the love which she had inspired in the rough Norah (roughened by the wear and tear of sorrow and years); but, above all, he saw the wild, deep, passionate affection existing between her and her child. They spoke little to anyone else, or when anyone else was by; but, when alone together, they talked, and murmured, and cooed, and chattered so continually, that Mr Openshaw first wondered what they could find to say to each other, and next became irritated because they were always so grave and silent with him. All this time he was perpetually devising small new pleasures for the child. His thoughts ran, in a pertinacious way, upon the desolate life before her; and often he came back from his day's work loaded with the very thing Alice had been longing for, but had not been able to procure. One time, it was a little chair for drawing the little sufferer along the streets; and, many an evening that following summer, Mr Openshaw drew her along himself, regardless of the remarks of his acquaintances. One day in autumn, he put down his newspaper, as Alice came in with the breakfast, and said, in as indifferent a voice as he could assume:

'Mrs Frank, is there any reason why we two should not put up our horses together?'

Alice stood still in perplexed wonder. What did he mean? He had resumed the reading of his newspaper, as if he did not expect any answer; so she found silence her safest course, and went on quietly arranging his breakfast, without another word passing between them. Just as he was leaving the house, to go to the warehouse as usual, he turned back and put his head into the bright, neat, tidy kitchen, where all the women breakfasted in the morning:

'You'll think of what I said, Mrs Frank' (this was her name with the lodgers), 'and let me have your opinion upon it tonight.'

Alice was thankful that her mother and Norah were too busy

talking together to attend much to this speech. She determined not to think about it at all through the day; and, of course, the effort not to think made her think all the more. At night she sent up Norah with his tea. But Mr Openshaw almost knocked Norah down as she was going out at the door, by pushing past her and calling out, 'Mrs Frank!' in an impatient voice, at the top of the stairs.

Alice went up, rather than seem to have affixed too much meaning to his words.

'Well, Mrs Frank,' he said, 'what answer? Don't make it too long; for I have lots of office work to get through tonight.'

'I hardly know what you meant, sir,' said truthful Alice.

'Well! I should have thought you might have guessed. You're not new at this sort of work, and I am. However, I'll make it plain this time. Will you have me to be thy wedded husband, and serve me, and love me, and honour me, and all that sort of thing? Because, if you will, I will do as much by you, and be a father to your child – and that's more than is put in the prayer-book. Now, I'm a man of my word; and what I say, I feel; and what I promise, I'll do. Now, for your answer!'

Alice was silent. He began to make the tea, as if her reply was a matter of perfect indifference to him; but, as soon as that was done, he became impatient.

'Well?' said he.

'How long, sir, may I have to think over it?'

'Three minutes!' (looking at his watch). 'You've had two already – that makes five. Be a sensible woman, say Yes, and sit down to tea with me, and we'll talk it over together; for, after tea, I shall be busy; say No' (he hesitated a moment to try and keep his voice in the same tone), 'and I shan't say another word about it, but pay up a year's rent for my rooms tomorrow, and be off. Time's up! Yes or no?'

'If you please, sir – you have been so good to little Ailsie –'

'There, sit down comfortably by me on the sofa, and let's have our tea together. I am glad to find you are as good and sensible as I took you for.'

And this was Alice Wilson's second wooing.

Mr Openshaw's will was too strong, and his circumstances too good, for him not to carry all before him. He settled Mrs Wilson in a comfortable house of her own, and made her quite independent of lodgers. The little that Alice said with regard to future plans was in Norah's behalf.

'No,' said Mr Openshaw. 'Norah shall take care of the old lady as long as she lives; and, after that, she shall either come and live with us, or, if she likes it better, she shall have a provision for life – for your sake, missus. No one who has been good to you or the child shall go unrewarded. But even the little one will be better for some fresh stuff about her. Get her a bright, sensible girl as a nurse; one who won't go rubbing her with calf's-foot jelly as Norah does; wasting good stuff outside that ought to go in, but will follow doctors' directions; which, as you must see pretty clearly by this time, Norah won't; because they give the poor little wench pain. Now, I'm not above being nesh for other folks myself. I can stand a good blow, and never change colour; but, set me in the operating room in the infirmary, and I turn as sick as a girl. Yet, if need were, I would hold the little wench on my knees while she screeched with pain, if it were to do her poor back good. Nay, nay, wench! keep your white looks for the time when it comes – I don't say it ever will. But this I know, Norah will spare the child and cheat the doctor, if she can. Now, I say, give the bairn a year or two's chance, and then, when the pack of doctors have done their best – and, maybe, the old lady has gone – we'll have Norah back or do better for her.'

The pack of doctors could do no good to little Ailsie. She was beyond their power. But her father (for so he insisted on being called, and also on Alice's no longer retaining the appellation of Mamma, but becoming henceforward Mother), by his healthy cheerfulness of manner, his clear decision of purpose, his odd turns and quirks of humour, added to his real strong love for the helpless little girl, infused a new element of brightness and confidence into her life; and, though her back remained the same, her general health was strengthened, and Alice – never going beyond a smile herself – had the pleasure of seeing her child taught to laugh.

As for Alice's own life, it was happier than it had ever been before. Mr Openshaw required no demonstration, no expressions of affection from her. Indeed, these would rather have disgusted him. Alice could love deeply, but could not talk about it. The perpetual requirement of loving words, looks, and caresses, and misconstruing their absence into absence of love, had been the great trial of her former married life. Now, all went on clear and straight, under the guidance of her husband's strong sense, warm heart, and powerful will. Year by year their worldly prosperity increased. At Mrs Wilson's death, Norah came back to them as nurse to the newly-born little Edwin; into which post she was not installed without a pretty strong oration on the part of the proud and happy father, who declared that if he found out that Norah ever tried to screen the boy by a falsehood, or to make him nesh either in body or mind, she should go that very day. Norah and Mr Openshaw were not on the most thoroughly cordial terms; neither of them fully recognizing or appreciating the other's best qualities.

This was the previous history of the Lancashire family who had now removed to London.

They had been there about a year, when Mr Openshaw suddenly informed his wife that he had determined to heal long-standing feuds, and had asked his uncle and aunt Chadwick to come and pay them a visit and see London. Mrs Openshaw had never seen his uncle and aunt of her husband's. Years before she had married him, there had been a quarrel. All she knew was, that Mr Chadwick was a small manufacturer in a country town in South Lancashire. She was extremely pleased that the breach was to be healed, and began making preparations to render their visit pleasant.

They arrived at last. Going to see London was such an event to them, that Mrs Chadwick had made all new linen fresh for the occasion – from night-caps downwards; and as for gowns, ribbons, and collars, she might have been going into the wilds of Canada where never a shop is, so large was her stock. A fortnight before the day of her departure for London, she had formally called to take leave of all her acquaintance; saying she should need every bit of the intermediate time for packing up. It was like a second wedding in her imagination; and, to complete the resemblance which an entirely new wardrobe made between the two events, her husband brought her back from Manchester, on the last market-day before they set off, a gorgeous pearl and amethyst brooch, saying, 'Lunnon should see that Lancashire folks knew a handsome thing when they saw it.'

For some time after Mr and Mrs Chadwick arrived at the Openshaws' there was no opportunity for wearing this brooch;

but at length they obtained an order to see Buckingham Palace, and the spirit of loyalty demanded that Mrs Chadwick should wear her best clothes in visiting the abode of her sovereign. On her return she hastily changed her dress; for Mr Openshaw had planned that they should go to Richmond, drink tea, and return by moonlight. Accordingly, about five o'clock, Mr and Mrs Openshaw and Mr and Mrs Chadwick set off.

The housemaid and cook sat below, Norah hardly knew where. She was always engrossed in the nursery in tending her two children, and in sitting by the restless, excitable Ailsie till she fell asleep. By and by the housemaid Bessy tapped gently at the door. Norah went to her, and they spoke in whispers.

'Nurse! there's someone downstairs wants you.'

'Wants me! who is it?'

'A gentleman –'

'A gentleman? Nonsense!'

'Well! a man, then, and he asks for you, and he rang at the front-door bell, and has walked into the dining-room.'

'You should never have let him,' exclaimed Norah. 'Master and missus out –'

'I did not want him to come in; but, when he heard you lived here, he walked past me, and sat down on the first chair, and said, "Tell her to come and speak to me." There is no gas lighted in the room, and supper is all set out.'

'He'll be off with the spoons!' exclaimed Norah, putting the housemaid's fear into words, and preparing to leave the room; first, however, giving a look to Ailsie, sleeping soundly and calmly.

Downstairs she went, uneasy fears stirring in her bosom. Before she entered the dining-room she provided herself with a candle, and, with it in her hand, she went in, looking around her in the darkness for her visitor.

He was standing up, holding by the table. Norah and he looked at each other; gradual recognition coming into their eyes.

'Norah?' at length he asked.

'Who are you?' asked Norah, with the sharp tones of alarm and incredulity. 'I don't know you'; trying, by futile words of disbelief, to do away with the terrible fact before her.

'Am I so changed?' he said pathetically. 'I dare say I am. But,

Norah, tell me!' he breathed hard, 'where is my wife? Is she – is she alive?'

He came nearer to Norah, and would have taken her hand; but she backed away from him; looking at him all the time with staring eyes, as if he were some horrible object. Yet he was a handsome, bronzed, good-looking fellow, with beard and moustache, giving him a foreign-looking aspect; but his eyes! there was no mistaking those eager, beautiful eyes – the very same that Norah had watched not half an hour ago, till sleep stole softly over them.

'Tell me, Norah – I can bear it – I have feared it so often. Is she dead?' Norah still kept silence. 'She is dead!' He hung on Norah's words and looks, as if for confirmation or contradiction.

'What shall I do?' groaned Norah. 'Oh, sir! why did you come? how did you find me out? where have you been? We thought you dead, we did indeed!' She poured out words and questions to gain time, as if time would help her.

'Norah! answer me this question straight, by yes or no – Is my wife dead?'

'No, she is not,' said Norah, slowly and heavily.

'Oh, what a relief! Did she receive my letters? But perhaps you don't know. Why did you leave her? Where is she? Oh, Norah, tell me all quickly!'

'Mr Frank!' said Norah at last, almost driven to bay by her terror lest her mistress should return at any moment and find him there – unable to consider what was best to be done or said – rushing at something decisive, because she could not endure her present state: 'Mr Frank! we never heard a line from you, and the shipowners said you had gone down, you and everyone else. We thought you were dead, if ever man was, and poor Miss Alice and her little sick, helpless child! Oh, sir, you must guess it,' cried the poor creature at last, bursting out into a passionate fit of crying, 'for indeed I cannot tell it. But it was no one's fault. God help us all this night!'

Norah had sat down. She trembled too much to stand. He took her hands in his. He squeezed them hard, as if, by physical pressure, the truth could be wrung out.

'Norah.' This time his tone was calm, stagnant as despair. 'She has married again!'

Norah shook her head sadly. The grasp slowly relaxed. The man had fainted.

There was brandy in the room. Norah forced some drops into Mr Frank's mouth, chafed his hands, and – when mere animal life returned, before the mind poured in its flood of memories and thoughts – she lifted him up, and rested his head against her knees. Then she put a few crumbs of bread taken from the supper-table, soaked in brandy, into his mouth. Suddenly he sprang to his feet.

'Where is she? Tell me this instant.' He looked so wild, so mad, so desperate, that Norah felt herself to be in bodily danger; but her time of dread had gone by. She had been afraid to tell him the truth, and then she had been a coward. Now, her wits were sharpened by the sense of his desperate state. He must leave the house. She would pity him afterwards; but now she must rather command and upbraid; for he must leave the house before her mistress came home. That one necessity stood clear before her.

'She is not here: that is enough for you to know. Nor can I say exactly where she is' (which was true to the letter if not to the spirit). 'Go away, and tell me where to find you tomorrow, and I will tell you all. My master and mistress may come back at any minute, and then what would become of me, with a strange man in the house?'

Such an argument was too petty to touch his excited mind.

'I don't care for your master and mistress. If your master is a man, he must feel for me – poor shipwrecked sailor that I am – kept for years a prisoner amongst savages, always, always, always thinking of my wife and my home – dreaming of her by night, talking to her though she could not hear, by day. I loved her more than all heaven and earth put together. Tell me where she is, this instant, you wretched woman, who salved over her wickedness to her, as you do to me!'

The clock struck ten. Desperate positions require desperate measures.

'If you will leave the house now, I will come to you tomorrow and tell you all. What is more, you shall see your child now. She lies sleeping upstairs. Oh, sir, you have a child, you do not know that as yet – a little weakly girl – with just a heart and soul beyond her years. We have reared her up with such care! We watched her, for we thought for many a year she might die any day, and we tended her, and no hard thing has come near her, and no rough word has ever been said to her. And now you come and will take her life into your hand, and will crush it. Strangers to her have been kind to her; but her own father – Mr Frank, I am her nurse, and I love her, and I tend her, and I would do anything for her that I could. Her mother's heart beats as hers beats; and, if she suffers a pain, her mother trembles all over. If she is happy, it is her mother that smiles and is glad. If she is growing stronger, her mother is healthy: if she dwindles, her mother languishes. If she dies – well, I don't know; it is not everyone can lie down and die when they wish it. Come upstairs, Mr Frank, and see your child. Seeing her will do good to your poor heart. Then go away, in God's name, just this one night; tomorrow, if need be, you can do anything – kill us all if you will, or show yourself a great, grand man, whom God will bless for ever and ever. Come, Mr Frank, the look of a sleeping child is sure to give peace.'

She led him upstairs; at first almost helping his steps, till they came near the nursery door. She had wellnigh forgotten the existence of little Edwin. It struck upon her with affright as the shaded light fell over the other cot; but she skulfully threw that corner of the room into darkness, and let the light fall on the sleeping Ailsie. The child had thrown down the coverings, and her deformity, as she lay with her back to them, was plainly visible through her slight nightgown. Her little face, deprived of the lustre of her eyes, looked wan and pinched, and had a pathetic expression in it, even as she slept. The poor father looked and looked with hungry, wistful eyes, into which the big tears came swelling up slowly and dropped heavily down, as he stood trembling and shaking all over. Norah was angry with herself for growing impatient of the length of time that long lingering gaze lasted. She thought that she waited for full half an hour before Frank stirred. And then – instead of going away – he sank down on his knees by the bedside, and buried his face in the clothes. Little Ailsie stirred uneasily. Norah pulled him up in terror. She could afford no more time, even for prayer, in her extremity of fear; for surely the next moment would bring her mistress home. She took him forcibly by the arm; but, as he was going, his eye lighted on the other bed; he stopped. Intelligence came back into his face. His hands clenched.

'His child?' he asked.

'Her child,' replied Norah. 'God watches over him,' she said instinctively; for Frank's looks excited her fears, and she needed to remind herself of the Protector of the helpless.

'God has not watched over me,' he said, in despair; his thoughts apparently recoiling on his own desolate, deserted state. But Norah had no time for pity. Tomorrow she would be as compassionate as her heart prompted. At length she guided him downstairs, and shut the outer door, and bolted it – as if by bolts to keep out facts.

Then she went back into the dining-room, and effaced all traces of his presence, as far as she could. She went upstairs to the nursery and sat there, her head on her hand, thinking what was to come of all this misery. It seemed to her very long before her master and mistress returned; yet it was hardly eleven o'clock. She heard the loud, hearty Lancashire voices on the stairs; and, for the first time, she understood the contrast of the desolation of the poor man who had so lately gone forth in lonely despair.

It almost put her out of patience to see Mrs Openshaw come in, calmly smiling, handsomely dressed, happy, easy, to inquire after her children.

'Did Ailsie go to sleep comfortably?' she whispered to Norah. 'Yes.'

Her mother bent over her, looking at her slumbers with the soft eyes of love. How little she dreamed who had looked on her last! Then she went to Edwin, with perhaps less wistful anxiety in her countenance, but more of pride. She took off her things, to go down to supper. Norah saw her no more that night.

Beside having a door into the passage, the sleeping-nursery opened out of Mr and Mrs Openshaw's room, in order that they might have the children more immediately under their own eyes. Early the next summer's morning, Mrs Openshaw was awakened by Ailsie's startled call of 'Mother! mother!' She sprang up, put on her dressing-gown, and went to her child. Ailsie was only half awake, and in a not unusual state of terror.

'Who was he, mother? Tell me!'

'Who, my darling? No one is here. You have been dreaming, love. Waken up quite. See, it is broad daylight.'

'Yes,' said Ailsie, looking round her; then clinging to her mother, 'but a man was here in the night, mother.'

'Nonsense, little goose. No man has ever come near you!'

'Yes, he did. He stood there. Just by Norah. A man with hair and a beard. And he knelt down and said his prayers. Norah knows he was here, mother' (half angrily, as Mrs Openshaw shook her head in smiling incredulity).

'Well! we will ask Norah when she comes,' said Mrs Openshaw, soothingly. 'But we won't talk any more about him now. It is not five o'clock; it is too early for you to get up. Shall I fetch you a book and read to you?'

'Don't leave me, mother,' said the child, clinging to her. So Mrs Openshaw sat on the bedside talking to Ailsie, and telling her of what they had done at Richmond the evening before, until the little girl's eyes slowly closed and she once more fell asleep.

'What was the matter?' asked Mr Openshaw, as his wife returned to bed.

'Ailsie wakened up in a fright, with some story of a man having been in the room to say his prayers – a dream, I suppose.' And no more was said at the time.

Mrs Openshaw had almost forgotten the whole affair when she got up about seven o'clock. But, by and by, she heard a sharp altercation going on in the nursery – Norah speaking angrily to Ailsie, a most unusual thing. Both Mr and Mrs Openshaw listened in astonishment.

'Hold your tongue, Ailsie! let me hear none of your dreams; never let me hear you tell that story again!'

Ailsie began to cry.

Mr Openshaw opened the door of communication, before his wife could say a word.

'Norah, come here!'

The nurse stood at the door, defiant. She perceived she had been heard, but she was desperate.

'Don't let me hear you speak in that manner to Ailsie again,' he said sternly, and shut the door.

Norah was infinitely relieved; for she had dreaded some questioning; and a little blame for sharp speaking was what she could well bear, if cross-examination was let alone.

Downstairs they went, Mr Openshaw carrying Ailsie; the sturdy Edwin coming step by step, right foot foremost, always holding his mother's hand. Each child was placed in a chair by the breakfast-table, and then Mr and Mrs Openshaw stood together at the window, awaiting their visitors' appearance and making plans for the day. There was a pause. Suddenly Mr Openshaw turned to Ailsie, and said:

'What a little goosy somebody is with her dreams, wakening up poor, tired mother in the middle of the night, with a story of a man being in the room.'

'Father! I'm sure I saw him,' said Ailsie, half-crying. 'I don't want to make Norah angry; but I was not asleep, for all she says I was. I had been asleep – and I wakened up quite wide awake, though I was so frightened. I kept my eyes nearly shut, and I saw the man quite plain. A great brown man with a beard. He said his prayers. And then looked at Edwin. And then Norah took him by the arm and led him away, after they had whispered a bit together.'

'Now, my little woman must be reasonable,' said Mr Openshaw, who was always patient with Ailsie. 'There was no man in the house last night at all. No man comes into the house, as you know, if you think; much less goes up into the nursery. But sometimes we dream something has happened, and the dream is so like reality, that you are not the first person, little woman, who has stood out that the thing has really happened.'

'But, indeed, it was not a dream!' said Ailsie, beginning to cry.

Just then Mr and Mrs Chadwick came down, looking grave and discomposed. All during breakfast-time they were silent and uncomfortable. As soon as the breakfast things were taken away, and the children had been carried upstairs, Mr Chadwick began, in an evidently preconcerted manner, to inquire if his nephew was certain that all his servants were honest; for, that Mrs Chadwick had that morning missed a very valuable brooch, which she had worn the day before. She remembered taking it off when she came home from Buckingham Palace. Mr Openshaw's face contracted into hard lines; grew like what it was before he had known his wife and her child. He rang the bell, even before his uncle had done speaking. It was answered by the housemaid.

'Mary, was anyone here last night, while we were away?'

'A man, sir, came to speak to Norah.'

'To speak to Norah! Who was he? How long did he stay?'

'I'm sure I can't tell, sir. He came – perhaps about nine. I went

up to tell Norah in the nursery, and she came down to speak to
him. She let him out, sir. She will know who he was, and how
long he stayed.'

She waited a moment to be asked any more questions, but she
was not, so she went away.

A minute afterwards Mr Openshaw made as though he were
going out of the room; but his wife laid her hand on his arm.

'Do not speak to her before the children,' she said, in her low,
quiet voice. 'I will go up and question her.'

'No! I must speak to her. You must know,' said he, turning to
his uncle and aunt, 'my missus has an old servant, as faithful as
ever woman was, I do believe, as far as love goes, – but at the
same time, who does not speak truth, as even the missus must
allow. Now, my notion is, that this Norah of ours has been come
over by some good-for-nothing chap (for she's at the time o' life
when they say women pray for husbands – "any, good Lord,
any") and has let him into our house, and the chap has made off
with your brooch, and m'appen many another thing beside. It's
only saying that Norah is soft-hearted and doesn't stick at a
white lie – that's all, missus.'

It was curious to notice how his tone, his eye, his whole face
was changed, as he spoke to his wife; but he was the resolute
man through all. She knew better than to oppose him; so she
went upstairs, and told Norah that her master wanted to speak to
her, and that she would take care of the children in the
meanwhile.

Norah rose to go, without a word. Her thoughts were these:
'If they tear me to pieces, they shall never know through me.
He may come – and then, just Lord have mercy upon us all! for
some of us are dead folk to a certainty. But *he* shall do it; not me.'

You may fancy, now, her look of determination, as she faced
her master alone in the dining-room; Mr and Mrs Chadwick
having left the affair in their nephew's hands, seeing that he took
it up with such vehemence.

'Norah! Who was that man that came to my house last night?'

'Man, sir!' As if infinitely surprised; but it was only to gain
time.

'Yes; the man that Mary let in; that she went upstairs to the
nursery to tell you about; that you came down to speak to; the
same chap, I make no doubt, that you took into the nursery to

have your talk out with; the one Ailsie saw, and afterwards dreamed about; thinking, poor wench! she saw him say his prayers, when nothing, I'll be bound, was further from his thoughts; the one that took Mrs Chadwick's brooch, value ten pounds. Now, Norah! Don't go off. I'm as sure as my name's Thomas Openshaw that you knew nothing of this robbery. But I do think you've been imposed on, and that's the truth. Some good-for-nothing chap has been making up to you, and you've been just like all other women, and have turned a soft place in your heart to him; and he came last night a-lovyering, and you had him up in the nursery, and he made use of his opportunities, and made off with a few things on his way down! Come, now, Norah; it's no blame to you, only you must not be such a fool again! Tell us,' he continued, 'what name he gave you, Norah. I'll be bound, it was not the right one; but it will be a clue for the police.'

Norah drew herself up. 'You may ask that question, and taunt me with my being single, and with my credulity, as you will, Master Openshaw. You'll get no answer from me. As for the brooch, and the story of theft and burglary; if any friend ever came to see me (which I defy you to prove, and deny), he'd be just as much above doing such a thing as you yourself, Mr Openshaw – and more so, too; for I'm not at all sure as everything you have is rightly come by, or would be yours long, if every man had his own.' She meant, of course, his wife; but he understood her to refer to his property in goods and chattels.

'Now, my good woman,' said he, 'I'll just tell you truly, I never trusted you out and out; but my wife liked you, and I thought you had many a good point about you. If you once begin to sauce me, I'll have the police to you, and get out the truth in a court of justice, if you'll not tell it me quietly and civilly here. Now, the best thing you can do is quietly to tell me who the fellow is. Look here! a man comes to my house; asks for you; you take him upstairs; a valuable brooch is missing next day; we know that you, and Mary, and cook, are honest; but you refuse to tell us who the man is. Indeed, you've told me one lie already about him, saying no one was here last night. Now, I just put it to you, what do you think a policeman would say to this, or a magistrate? A magistrate would soon make you tell the truth, my good woman.'

'There's never the creature born that should get it out of me,' said Norah. 'Not unless I choose to tell.'

'I've a great mind to see,' said Mr Openshaw, growing angry, at the defiance. Then, checking himself, he thought before the spoke again:

'Norah, for your missus' sake I don't want to go to extremities. Be a sensible woman, if you can. It's no great disgrace, after all, to have been taken in. I ask you once more – as a friend – who was this man that you let into my house last night?'

No answer. He repeated the question in an impatient tone. Still no answer. Norah's lips were set in determination not to speak.

'Then there is but one thing to be done. I shall send for a policeman.'

'You will not,' said Norah, starting forward. 'You shall not, sir! No policeman shall touch me. I know nothing of the brooch, but I know this: ever since I was four-and-twenty, I have thought more of your wife than of myself: ever since I saw her, a poor motherless girl, put upon in her uncle's house, I have thought more of serving her than of serving myself! I have cared for her and her child, as nobody ever cared for me. I don't cast blame on you, sir, but I say it's ill giving up one's life to anyone; for, at the end, they will turn round upon you, and forsake you. Why does not my missus come herself to suspect me? Maybe, she is gone for the police? But I don't stay here, either for police, or magistrate, or master. You're an unlucky lot. I believe there's a curse on you. I'll leave you this very day. Yes! I'll leave that poor Ailsie, too. I will! No good ever will come to you!'

Mr Openshaw was utterly astonished at this speech; most of which was completely unintelligible to him, as may easily be supposed. Before he could make up his mind what to say, or what to do, Norah had left the room. I do not think he had ever really intended to send for the police to this old servant of his wife's; for he had never for a moment doubted her perfect honesty. But he had intended to compel her to tell him who the man was, and in this he was baffled. He was, consequently, much irritated. He returned to his uncle and aunt in a state of great annoyance and perplexity, and told them he could get nothing out of the woman; that some man had been in the house the night before; but that she refused to tell who he was. At this moment his wife came in, greatly agitated, and asked what had happened to Norah; for that she had put on her things in passionate haste, and left the house.

'This looks suspicious,' said Mr Chadwick. 'It is not the way in which an honest person would have acted.'

Mr Openshaw kept silence. He was sorely perplexed. But Mrs Openshaw turned round on Mr Chadwick, with a sudden fierceness no one ever saw in her before.

'You don't know Norah, uncle! She is gone because she is deeply hurt at being suspected. Oh, I wish I had seen her – that I had spoken to her myself. She would have told me anything.' Alice wrung her hands.

'I must confess,' continued Mr Chadwick to his nephew, in a lower voice, 'I can't make you out. You used to be a word and a blow, and oftenest the blow first; and now, when there is every cause for suspicion, you just do nought. Your missus is a very good woman, I grant; but she may have been put upon as well as other folk, I suppose. If you don't send for the police, I shall.'

'Very well,' replied Mr Openshaw, surlily. 'I can't clear Norah. She won't clear herself, as I believe she might if she would. Only I wash my hands of it; for I am sure the woman herself is honest, and she's lived a long time with my wife, and I don't like her to come to shame.'

'But she will then be forced to clear herself. That, at any rate, will be a good thing.'

'Very well, very well! I am heart-sick of the whole business. Come, Alice, come up to the babies; they'll be in a sore way. I tell you, uncle,' he said, turning round once more to Mr Chadwick, suddenly and sharply, after his eye had fallen on Alice's wan, tearful, anxious face, 'I'll have no sending for the police, after all. I'll buy my aunt twice as handsome a brooch this very day; but I'll not have Norah suspected, and my missus plagued. There's for you!'

He and his wife left the room. Mr Chadwick quietly waited till he was out of hearing, and then said to his wife, 'For all Tom's heroics, I'm just quietly going for a detective, wench. Thou need'st know nought about it.'

He went to the police-station and made a statement of the case. He was gratified by the impression which the evidence against Norah seemed to make. The men all agreed in his opinion, and steps were to be immediately taken to find out where she was.

Most probably, as they suggested, she had gone at once to the man, who, to all appearance, was her lover. When Mr Chadwick asked how they would find her out, they smiled, shook their heads, and spoke of mysterious but infallible ways and means. He returned to his nephew's house with a very comfortable opinion of his own sagacity. He was met by his wife with a penitent face.

'Oh, master, I've found my brooch! It was just sticking by its pin in the flounce of my brown silk, that I wore yesterday. I took it off in a hurry, and it must have caught in it; and I hung up my gown in the closet. Just now, when I was going to fold it up, there was the brooch! I am very vexed, but I never dreamt but what it was lost!'

Her husband, muttering something very like 'Confound thee and thy brooch too! I wish I'd never given it thee,' snatched up his hat, and rushed back to the station, hoping to be in time to stop the police from searching for Norah. But a detective was already gone off on the errand.

Where was Norah? Half mad with the strain of the fearful secret, she had hardly slept through the night for thinking what must be done. Upon this terrible state of mind had come Ailsie's questions, showing that she had seen the Man, as the unconscious child called her father. Lastly came the suspicion of her honesty. She was little less than crazy as she ran upstairs and dashed on her bonnet and shawl; leaving all else, even her purse, behind her. In that house she would not stay. That was all she knew or was clear about. She would not even see the children again, for fear it should weaken her. She dreaded above everything Mr Frank's return to claim his wife. She could not tell what remedy there was for a sorrow so tremendous, for her to stay to witness. The desire of escaping from the coming event was a stronger motive for her departure, than her soreness about the suspicions directed against her; although this last had been the final goad to the course she took. She walked away almost at headlong speed; sobbing as she went, as she had not dared to do during the past night for fear of exciting wonder in those who might hear her. Then she stopped. An idea came into her mind that she would leave London altogether, and betake herself to her native town of Liverpool. She felt in her pocket for her purse as she drew near the Euston Square station with this intention. She had left it at home. Her poor head aching, her eyes swollen with crying, she had to stand still, and think, as well as she could, where next she should bend her steps. Suddenly the thought flashed into her mind that she would go and find out poor Mr Frank. She had been hardly kind to him the night before, though her heart had bled for him ever since. She remembered his telling her, when she inquired for his address, almost as she had pushed him out of the door, of some hotel in a street not far distant from Euston Square. Thither she went: with what intention she scarcely knew, but to assuage her conscience by telling him how much she pitied him. In her present state she felt herself unfit to counsel, or restrain, or assist, or to do aught else but sympathize and weep. The people of the inn said such a person had been there; had arrived only the day before; had gone out soon after arrival, leaving his luggage in their care; but had never come back. Norah asked for leave to sit down, and await the gentleman's return. The landlady – pretty secure in the deposit of luggage against any probable injury – showed her into a room, and quietly locked the door on the outside. Norah was utterly worn out, and fell asleep – a shivering, starting, uneasy slumber, which lasted for hours.

The detective, meanwhile, had come up with her some time before she entered the hotel, into which he followed her. Asking the landlady to detain her for an hour or so, without giving any reason beyond showing his authority (which made the landlady applaud herself a good deal for having locked her in), he went back to the police-station to report his proceedings. He could have taken her directly; but his object was, if possible, to trace out the man who was supposed to have committed the robbery. Then he heard of the discovery of the brooch; and consequently did not care to return.

Norah slept till even the summer evening began to close in. Then started up. Someone was at the door. It would be Mr Frank; and she dizzily pushed back her ruffled grey hair which had fallen over her eyes, and stood looking to see him. Instead, there came in Mr Openshaw and a policeman.

'This is Norah Kennedy,' said Mr Openshaw.

'Oh, sir,' said Norah, 'I did not touch the brooch; indeed I did not. Oh, sir, I cannot live to be thought so badly of'; and very sick and faint, she suddenly sank down to the ground. To her surprise, Mr Openshaw raised her up very tenderly. Even the policeman helped to lay her on the sofa; and, at Mr Openshaw's desire, he went for some wine and sandwiches; for the poor gaunt woman lay there almost as if dead with weariness and exhaustion.

'Norah,' said Mr Openshaw, in his kindest voice, 'the brooch is found. It was hanging to Mrs Chadwick's gown. I beg your pardon. Most truly I beg your pardon, for having troubled you about it. My wife is almost broken-hearted. Eat, Norah – or, stay, first drink this glass of wine,' said he, lifting her head, and pouring a little down her throat.

As she drank, she remembered where she was, and who she was waiting for. She suddenly pushed Mr Openshaw away, saying, 'Oh, sir, you must go. You must not stop a minute. If he comes back, he will kill you.'

'Alas, Norah! I do not know who "he" is. But someone is gone away who will never come back: someone who knew you, and whom I am afraid you cared for.'

'I don't understand you, sir,' said Norah, her master's kind and sorrowful manner bewildering her yet more than his words. The policeman had left the room at Mr Openshaw's desire, and they two were alone.

'You know what I mean, when I say someone is gone who will never come back. I mean that he is dead!'

'Who?' said Norah, trembling all over.

'A poor man has been found in the Thames this morning – drowned.'

'Did he drown himself?' asked Norah, solemnly.

'God only knows,' replied Mr Openshaw, in the same tone. 'Your name and address at our house were found in his pocket; that, and his purse, were the only things that were found upon him. I am sorry to say it, my poor Norah; but you are required to go and identify him.'

'To what?' asked Norah.

'To say who it is. It is always done, in order that some reason may be discovered for the suicide – if suicide it was. I make no doubt, he was the man who came to see you at our house last night. It is very sad, I know.' He made pauses between each little clause, in order to try and bring back her senses, which he feared were wandering – so wild and sad was her look.

'Master Openshaw,' said she, at last, 'I've a dreadful secret to tell you – only you must never breathe it to anyone, and you and I must hide it away for ever. I thought to have done it all by myself, but I see I cannot. Yon poor man – yes! the dead, drowned creature is, I fear, Mr Frank, my mistress's first husband!'

Mr Openshaw sat down, as if shot. He did not speak; but, after a while, he signed to Norah to go on.

'He came to me the other night, when – God be thanked! – you were all away at Richmond. He asked me if his wife was dead or alive. I was a brute, and thought more of your all coming home than of his sore trial; I spoke out sharp, and said she was married again, and very content and happy. I all but turned him away: and now he lies dead and cold.'

'God forgive me!' said Mr Openshaw.

'God forgive us all!' said Norah. 'Yon poor man needs forgiveness, perhaps, less than any one among us. He had been among the savages – shipwrecked – I know not what – and he had written letters which had never reached my poor missus.'

'He saw his child!'

'He saw her – yes! I took him up, to give his thoughts another start; for I believed he was going mad on my hands. I came to seek him here, as I more than half promised. My mind misgave me when I heard he never came in. Oh, sir, it must be him!'

Mr Openshaw rang the bell. Norah was almost too much stunned to wonder at what he did. He asked for writing materials, wrote a letter, and then said to Norah:

'I am writing to Alice, to say I shall be unavoidably absent for a few days; that I have found you; that you are well, and send her your love, and will come home tomorrow. You must go with me to the police court; you must identify the body; I will pay high to keep names and details out of the papers.'

'But where are you going, sir?'

He did not answer her directly. Then he said:

'Norah! I must go with you, and look on the face of the man whom I have so injured – unwittingly, it is true; but it seems to me as if I had killed him. I will lay his head in the grave as if he were my only brother: and how he must have hated me! I cannot go home to my wife till all that I can do for him is done. Then I go with a dreadful secret on my mind. I shall never speak of it again, after these days are over. I know you will not, either.' He shook hands with her; and they never named the subject again, the one to the other.

Norah went home to Alice the next day. Not a word was said on the cause of her abrupt departure a day or two before. Alice had been charged by her husband, in his letter, not to allude to the supposed theft of the brooch; so she, implicitly obedient to those whom she loved both by nature and habit, was entirely silent on the subject, only treated Norah with the most tender respect, as if to make up for unjust suspicion.

Nor did Alice inquire into the reason why Mr Openshaw had been absent during his uncle and aunt's visit, after he had once said that it was unavoidable. He came back grave and quiet; and from that time forth was curiously changed. More thoughtful, and perhaps less active; quite as decided in conduct, but with new and different rules for the guidance of that conduct. Towards Alice he could hardly be more kind than he had always been; but he now seemed to look upon her as someone sacred, and to be treated with reverence, as well as tenderness. He throve in business, and made a large fortune, one half of which was settled upon her.

Long years after these events – a few months after her mother died – Ailsie and her 'father' (as she always called Mr Openshaw) drove to a cemetery a little way out of town, and she was carried to a certain mound by her maid, who was then sent back to the carriage. There was a headstone, with F. W. and a date upon it. That was all. Sitting by the grave, Mr Openshaw told her the story; and for the sad fate of that poor father whom she had never seen, he shed the only tears she ever saw fall from his eyes.

Souls Belated

EDITH WHARTON

Their railway carriage had been full when the train left Bologna; but at the first station beyond Milan their only remaining companion – a courtly person who ate garlic out of a carpet-bag – had left his crumb-strewn seat with a bow.

Lydia's eye regretfully followed the shiny broadcloth of his retreating back till it lost itself in the cloud of touts and cab drivers hanging about the station; then she glanced across at Gannett and caught the same regret in his look. They were both sorry to be alone.

'*Par-ten-za!*' shouted the guard. The train vibrated to a sudden slamming of doors; a waiter ran along the platform with a tray of fossilized sandwiches; a belated porter flung a bundle of shawls and band-boxes into a third-class carriage; the guard snapped out a brief *Partenza!* which indicated the purely ornamental nature of his first shout; and the train swung out of the station.

The direction of the road had changed, and a shaft of sunlight struck across the dusty red-velvet seats into Lydia's corner. Gannett did not notice it. He had returned to his *Revue de Paris*, and she had to rise and lower the shade of the farther window. Against the vast horizon of their leisure such incidents stood out sharply.

Having lowered the shade, Lydia sat down, leaving the length of the carriage between herself and Gannett. At length he missed her and looked up.

'I moved out of the sun,' she hastily explained.

He looked at her curiously: the sun was beating on her through the shade.

'Very well,' he said pleasantly; adding, 'You don't mind?' as he drew a cigarette case from his pocket.

It was a refreshing touch, relieving the tension of her spirit with the suggestion that, after all, if he could *smoke* – ! The relief was only momentary. Her experience of smokers was limited (her husband had disapproved of the use of tobacco) but she knew from hearsay that men sometimes smoked to get away from things; that a cigar might be the masculine equivalent of darkened windows and a headache. Gannett, after a puff or two, returned to his review.

It was just as she had foreseen; he feared to speak as much as she did. It was one of the misfortunes of their situation that they were never busy enough to necessitate, or even to justify, the postponement of unpleasant discussions. If they avoided a question it was obviously, unconcealably because the question was disagreeable. They had unlimited leisure and an accumulation of mental energy to devote to any subject that presented itself; new topics were in fact at a premium. Lydia sometimes had premonitions of a famine-stricken period when there would be nothing left to talk about, and she had already caught herself doling out piecemeal what, in the first prodigality of their confidences, she would have flung to him in a breath. Their silence therefore might simply mean that they had nothing to say; but it was another disadvantage of their position that it allowed infinite opportunity for the classification of minute differences. Lydia had learned to distinguish between real and factitious silences; and under Gannett's she now detected a hum of speech to which her own thoughts made breathless answer.

How could it be otherwise, with that thing between them? She glanced up at the rack overhead. The *thing* was there, in her dressing bag, symbolically suspended over her head and his. He was thinking of it now, just as she was; they had been thinking of it in unison ever since they had entered the train. While the carriage had held other travelers they had screened her from his thoughts; but now that he and she were alone she knew exactly what was passing through his mind; she could almost hear him asking himself what he should say to her.

The thing had come that morning, brought up to her in an innocent-looking envelope with the rest of their letters, as they were leaving the hotel at Bologna. As she tore it open, she and Gannett were laughing over some ineptitude of the local guide-book – they had been driven, of late, to make the most of such incidental humors of travel. Even when she had unfolded the document she took it for some unimportant business paper sent abroad for her signature, and her eye traveled inattentively over the curly *Whereases* of the preamble until a word arrested her:

Divorce. There it stood, an impassible barrier, between her husband's name and hers.

She had been prepared for it, of course, as healthy people are said to be prepared for death, in the sense of knowing it must come without in the least expecting that it will. She had known from the first that Tillotson meant to divorce her – but what did it matter? Nothing mattered, in those first days of supreme deliverance, but the fact that she was free; and not so much (she had begun to be aware) that freedom had released her from Tillotson as that it had given her to Gannett. This discovery had not been agreeable to her self-esteem. She had preferred to think that Tillotson had himself embodied all her reasons for leaving him; and those he represented had seemed cogent enough to stand in no need of reinforcement. Yet she had not left him till she met Gannett. It was her love for Gannett that had made life with Tillotson so poor and incomplete a business. If she had never, from the first, regarded her marriage as a full canceling of her claims upon life, she had at least, for a number of years, accepted it as a provisional compensation, – she had made it 'do'. Existence in the commodious Tillotson mansion in Fifth Avenue – with Mrs Tillotson senior commanding the approaches from the second-story front windows – had been reduced to a series of purely automatic acts. The moral atmosphere of the Tillotson interior was as carefully screened and curtained as the house itself: Mrs Tillotson senior dreaded ideas as much as a draft in her back. Prudent people liked an even temperature; and to do anything unexpected was as foolish as going out in the rain. One of the chief advantages of being rich was that one need not be exposed to unforeseen contingencies: by the use of ordinary firmness and common sense one could make sure of doing exactly the same thing every day at the same hour. These doctrines, reverentially imbibed with his mother's milk, Tillotson (a model son who had never given his parents an hour's anxiety) complacently expounded to his wife, testifying to his sense of their importance by the regularity with which he wore galoshes on damp days, his punctuality at meals, and his elaborate precautions against burglars and contagious diseases. Lydia, coming from a smaller town, and entering New York through the portals of the Tillotson mansion, had mechanically accepted this point of view as inseparable from having a front pew in church and a parterre box at the opera. All the people who came to the house revolved in the same small circle of prejudices. It was the kind of society in which, after dinner, the ladies compared the exorbitant charges of their children's teachers, and agreed that, even with the new duties on French clothes, it was cheaper in the end to get everything from Worth; while the husbands, over their cigars, lamented municipal corruption, and decided that the men to start a reform were those who had no private interests at stake.

To Lydia this view of life had become a matter of course, just as lumbering about in her mother-in-law's landau had come to seem the only possible means of locomotion, and listening every Sunday to a fashionable Presbyterian divine the inevitable atonement for having thought oneself bored on the other six days of the week. Before she met Gannett her life had seemed merely dull; his coming made it appear like one of those dismal Cruikshank prints in which the people are all ugly and all engaged in occupations that are either vulgar or stupid.

It was natural that Tillotson should be the chief sufferer from this readjustment of focus. Gannett's nearness had made her husband ridiculous, and a part of the ridicule had been reflected on herself. Her tolerance laid her open to a suspicion of obtuseness from which she must, at all costs, clear herself in Gannett's eyes.

She did not understand this until afterwards. At the time she fancied that she had merely reached the limits of endurance. In so large a charter of liberties as the mere act of leaving Tillotson seemed to confer, the small question of divorce or no divorce did not count. It was when she saw that she had left her husband only to be with Gannett that she perceived the significance of anything affecting their relations. Her husband, in casting her off, had virtually flung her at Gannett: it was thus that the world viewed it. The measure of alacrity with which Gannett would receive her would be the subject of curious speculation over afternoon tea tables and in club corners. She knew what would be said – she had heard it so often of others! The recollection bathed her in misery. The men would probably back Gannett to 'do the decent thing'; but the ladies' eyebrows would emphasize the worthlessness of such enforced fidelity; and after all, they would be right. She had put herself in a position where Gannett 'owed' her something; where, as a gentleman, he was bound to 'stand the damage'. The idea of accepting such compensation had never crossed her mind; the so-called rehabilitation of such a marriage had always seemed to her the only real disgrace. What she dreaded was the necessity of having to explain herself; of having to combat his arguments; of calculating, in spite of herself, the exact measure of insistence with which he pressed them. She knew not whether she most shrank from his insisting too much or too little. In such a case the nicest sense of proportion might be at fault; and how easily to fall into the error of taking her resistance for a test of his sincerity! Whichever way she turned, an ironical implication confronted her: she had the exasperated sense of having walked into the trap of some stupid practical joke.

Beneath all these preoccupations lurked the dread of what he was thinking. Sooner or later, of course, he would have to speak; but that, in the meantime, he should think, even for a moment, that there was any use in speaking, seemed to her simply unendurable. Her sensitiveness on this point was aggravated by another fear, as yet barely on the level of consciousness; the fear of unwillingly involving Gannett in the trammels of her dependence. To look upon him as the instrument of her liberation; to resist in herself the least tendency to a wifely taking possession of his future; had seemed to Lydia the one way of maintaining the dignity of their relation. Her view had not changed, but she was aware of a growing inability to keep her thoughts fixed on the essential point – the point of parting with Gannett. It was easy to face as long as she kept it sufficiently far off: but what was this act of mental postponement but a gradual encroachment on his future? What was needful was the courage to recognize the moment when, by some word or look, their voluntary fellowship should be transformed into a bondage the more wearing that it was based on none of those common obligations which make the most imperfect marriage in some sort a center of gravity.

When the porter, at the next station, threw the door open, Lydia drew back, making way for the hoped-for intruder; but none came, and the train took up its leisurely progress through the spring wheat fields and budding copses. She now began to hope that Gannett would speak before the next station. She watched him furtively, half-disposed to return to the seat opposite his, but there was an artificiality about his absorption that

restrained her. She had never before seen him read with so
conspicuous an air of warding off interruption. What could he be
thinking of? Why should he be afraid to speak? Or was it her
answer that he dreaded?

The train paused for the passing of an express, and he put
down his book and leaned out of the window. Presently he
turned to her with a smile.

'There's a jolly old villa out here,' he said.

His easy tone relieved her, and she smiled back at him as she
crossed over to his corner.

Beyond the embankment, through the opening in a mossy
wall, she caught sight of the villa, with its broken balustrades, its
stagnant fountains, and the stone satyr closing the perspective of
a dusky grass walk.

'How should you like to live there?' he asked as the train
moved on.

'There?'

'In some such place, I mean. One might do worse, don't you
think so? There must be at least two centuries of solitude under
those yew trees. Shouldn't you like it?'

'I – I don't know,' she faltered. She knew now that he meant to
speak.

He lit another cigarette. 'We shall have to live somewhere, you
know,' he said as he bent above the match.

Lydia tried to speak carelessly. '*Je n'en vois pas la nécessité!* Why
not live everywhere, as we have been doing?'

'But we can't travel forever, can we?'

'Oh, forever's a long word,' she objected, picking up the review
he had thrown aside.

'For the rest of our lives then,' he said, moving nearer.

She made a slight gesture which caused his hand to slip from
hers.

'Why should we make plans? I thought you agreed with me
that it's pleasanter to drift.'

He looked at her hesitatingly. 'It's been pleasant, certainly; but
I suppose I shall have to get at my work again some day. You
know I haven't written a line since – all this time,' he hastily
amended.

She flamed with sympathy and self-reproach. 'Oh, if you mean *that* – if you want to write – of course we must settle down. How stupid of me not to have thought of it sooner! Where shall we go? Where do you think you could work best? We oughtn't to lose any more time.'

He hesitated again. 'I had thought of a villa in these parts. It's quiet; we shouldn't be bothered. Should you like it?'

'Of course I should like it.' She paused and looked away. 'But I thought – I remember your telling me once that your best work had been done in a crowd – in big cities. Why should you shut yourself up in a desert?'

Gannett, for a moment, made no reply. At length he said, avoiding her eye as carefully as she avoided his: 'It might be different now; I can't tell, of course, till I try. A writer ought not to be dependent on his *milieu*; it's a mistake to humor oneself in that way; and I thought that just at first you might prefer to be –'

She faced him. 'To be what?'

'Well – quiet. I mean –'

'What do you mean by "at first"?' she interrupted.

He paused again. 'I mean after we are married.'

She thrust up her chin and turned toward the window. 'Thank you!' she tossed back at him.

'Lydia!' he exclaimed blankly; and she felt in every fiber of her averted person that he had made the inconceivable, the unpardonable mistake of anticipating her acquiescence.

The train rattled on and he groped for a third cigarette. Lydia remained silent.

'I haven't offended you?' he ventured at length, in the tone of a man who feels his way.

She shook her head with a sigh. 'I thought you understood,' she moaned. Their eyes met and she moved back to his side.

'Do you want to know how not to offend me? By taking it for granted, once for all, that you've said your say on the odious question and that I've said mine, and that we stand just where we did this morning before that – that hateful paper came to spoil everything between us!'

'To spoil everything between us? What on earth do you mean? Aren't you glad to be free?'

'I was free before.'

'Not to marry me,' he suggested.

'But I don't *want* to marry you!' she cried.

She saw that he turned pale. 'I'm obtuse, I suppose,' he said slowly. 'I confess I don't see what you're driving at. Are you tired of the whole business? Or was I simply a – an excuse for getting away? Perhaps you didn't care to travel alone? Was that it? And now you want to chuck me?' His voice had grown harsh. 'You owe me a straight answer, you know; don't be tenderhearted!'

Her eyes swam as she leaned to him. 'Don't you see it's because I care – because I care so much? Oh, Ralph! Can't you see how it would humiliate me? Try to feel it as a woman would! Don't you see the misery of being made your wife in this way? If I'd known you as a girl – that would have been a real marriage! But now – this vulgar fraud upon society – and upon a society we despised and laughed at – this sneaking back into a position that we've voluntarily forfeited: don't you see what a cheap compromise it is? We neither of us believe in the abstract 'sacredness' of marriage; we both know that no ceremony is needed to consecrate our love for each other; what object can we have in marrying, except the secret fear of each that the other may escape, or the secret longing to work our way back gradually – oh, very gradually – into the esteem of the people whose conventional morality we have always ridiculed and hated? And the very fact that, after a decent interval, these same people would come and dine with us – the women who talk about the indissolubility of marriage, and who would let me die in a gutter today because I am "leading a life of sin" – doesn't that disgust you more than their turning their backs on us now? I can stand being cut by them, but I couldn't stand their coming to call and asking what I meant to do about visiting that unfortunate Mrs So-and-so!'

She paused, and Gannett maintained a perplexed silence.

'You judge things too theoretically,' he said at length, slowly. 'Life is made up of compromises.'

'The life we ran away from – yes! If we had been willing to accept them' – she flushed – 'we might have gone on meeting each other at Mrs Tillotson's dinners.'

He smiled slightly. 'I didn't know that we ran away to found a new system of ethics. I supposed it was because we loved each other.'

'Life is complex, of course; isn't it the very recognition of that fact that separates us from the people who see it *tout d'une pièce?* If *they* are right – if marriage is sacred in itself and the individual must always be sacrificed to the family – then there can be no real marriage between us, since our – our being together is a protest against the sacrifice of the individual to the family.' She interrupted herself with a laugh. 'You'll say now that I'm giving you a lecture on sociology! Of course one acts as one can – as one must, perhaps – pulled by all sorts of invisible threads; but at least one needn't pretend, for social advantages, to subscribe to a creed that ignores the complexity of human motives – that classifies people by arbitrary signs, and puts it in everybody's reach to be on Mrs Tillotson's visiting list. It may be necessary that the world should be ruled by conventions – but if we believed in them, why did we break through them? And if we don't believe in them, is it honest to take advantage of the protection they afford?'

Gannett hesitated. 'One may believe in them or not; but as long as they do rule the world it is only by taking advantage of their protection that one can find a *modus vivendi.*'

'Do outlaws need a *modus vivendi?*'

He looked at her hopelessly. Nothing is more perplexing to man than the mental process of a woman who reasons her emotions.

She thought she had scored a point and followed it up passionately. 'You do understand, don't you? You see how the very thought of the thing humiliates me! We are together today because we choose to be – don't let us look any farther than that!' She caught his hands. '*Promise* me you'll never speak of it again; promise me you'll never *think* of it even,' she implored, with a tearful prodigality of italics.

Through what followed – his protests, his arguments, his final unconvinced submission to her wishes – she had a sense of his but half-discerning all that, for her, had made the moment so tumultuous. They had reached that memorable point in every heart history when, for the first time, the man seems obtuse and the woman irrational. It was the abundance of his intentions that consoled her, on reflection, for what they lacked in quality. After all, it would have been worse, incalculably worse, to have detected any overreadiness to understand her.

II

When the train at nightfall brought them to their journey's end at the edge of one of the lakes, Lydia was glad that they were not, as usual, to pass from one solitude to another. Their wanderings during the year had indeed been like the flights of outlaws: through Sicily, Dalmatia, Transylvania and Southern Italy they had persisted in their tacit avoidance of their kind. Isolation, at first, had deepened the flavor of their happiness, as night intensifies the scent of certain flowers; but in the new phase on which they were entering, Lydia's chief wish was that they should be less abnormally exposed to the action of each other's thoughts.

She shrank, nevertheless, as the brightly-looming bulk of the fashionable Anglo-American hotel on the water's brink began to radiate toward their advancing boat its vivid suggestion of social order, visitors' lists, Church services, and the bland inquisition of the *table d'hôte*. The mere fact that in a moment or two she must take her place on the hotel register as Mrs Gannett seemed to weaken the springs of her resistance.

They had meant to stay for a night only, on their way to a lofty village among the glaciers of Monte Rosa; but after the first plunge into publicity, when they entered the dining room, Lydia felt the relief of being lost in a crowd, of ceasing for a moment to be the center of Gannett's scrutiny; and in his face she caught the reflection of her feeling. After dinner, when she went upstairs, he strolled into the smoking room, and an hour or two later, sitting in the darkness of her window, she heard his voice below and saw him walking up and down the terrace with a companion cigar at his side. When he came up he told her he had been talking to the hotel chaplain – a very good sort of fellow.

'Queer little microcosms, these hotels! Most of these people live here all summer and then migrate to Italy or the Riviera. The English are the only people who can lead that kind of life with dignity – those soft-voiced old ladies in Shetland shawls somehow carry the British Empire under their caps. *Civis Romanus sum.* It's a curious study – there might be some good things to work up here.'

He stood before her with the vivid preoccupied stare of the novelist on the trail of a 'subject'. With a relief that was half painful she noticed that, for the first time since they had been together, he was hardly aware of her presence.

'Do you think you could write here?'

'Here? I don't know.' His stare dropped. 'After being out of things so long one's first impressions are bound to be tremendously vivid, you know. I see a dozen threads already that one might follow –'

He broke off with a touch of embarrassment.

'Then follow them. We'll stay,' she said with sudden decision.

'Stay here?' He glanced at her in surprise, and then, walking to the window, looked out upon the dusky slumber of the garden.

'Why not?' she said at length, in a tone of veiled irritation.

'The place is full of old cats in caps who gossip with the chaplain. Shall you like – I mean, it would be different if –'

She flamed up.

'Do you suppose I care? It's none of their business.'

'Of course not; but you won't get them to think so.'

'They may think what they please.'

He looked at her doubtfully.

'It's for you to decide.'

'We'll stay,' she repeated.

Gannett, before they met, had made himself known as a successful writer of short stories and of a novel which had achieved the distinction of being widely discussed. The reviewers called him 'promising', and Lydia now accused herself of having too long interfered with the fulfilment of his promise. There was a special irony in the fact, since his passionate assurances that only the stimulus of her companionship could bring out his latent faculty had almost given the dignity of a 'vocation' to her course: there had been moments when she had felt unable to assume, before posterity, the responsibility of thwarting his career. And, after all, he had not written a line since they had been together: his first desire to write had come from renewed contact with the world! Was it all a mistake then? Must the most intelligent choice work more disastrously than the blundering combinations of chance? Or was there a still more humiliating answer to her perplexities? His sudden impulse of activity so exactly coincided with her own wish to withdraw, for a time, from the range of his observation, that she wondered if he too were not seeking sanctuary from intolerable problems.

'You must begin tomorrow!' she cried, hiding a tremor under the laugh with which she added, 'I wonder if there's any ink in the ink-stand?'

Whatever else they had at the Hotel Bellosguardo, they had, as Miss Pinsent said, 'a certain tone'. It was to Lady Susan Condit that they owed this inestimable benefit; an advantage ranking in Miss Pinsent's opinion above even the lawn tennis courts and the resident chaplain. It was the fact of Lady Susan's annual visit that made the hotel what it was. Miss Pinsent was certainly the last to underrate such a privilege: 'It's so important, my dear, forming as we do a little family, that there should be someone to give *the tone*; and no one could do it better than Lady Susan – an earl's daughter and a person of such determination. Dear Mrs Ainger now – who really *ought*, you know, when Lady Susan's away – absolutely refuses to assert herself.' Miss Pinsent sniffed derisively. 'A bishop's niece! – my dear, I saw her once actually give in to some South Americans – and before us all. She gave up her seat at table to oblige them – such a lack of dignity! Lady Susan spoke to her very plainly about it afterwards.'

Miss Pinsent glanced across the lake and adjusted her auburn front.

'But of course I don't deny that the stand Lady Susan takes is not always easy to live up to – for the rest of us, I mean. Monsieur Grossart, our good proprietor, finds it trying at times, I know – he has said as much, privately, to Mrs Ainger and me. After all, the poor man is not to blame for wanting to fill his hotel, is he? And Lady Susan is so difficult – so very difficult – about new people. One might almost say that she disapproves of them beforehand, on principle. And yet she's had warnings – she very nearly made a dreadful mistake once with the Duchess of Levens, who dyed her hair and – well, swore and smoked. One would have thought that might have been a lesson to Lady Susan.' Miss Pinsent resumed her knitting with a sigh. 'There are exceptions, of course. She took at once to you and Mr Gannett – it was quite remarkable, really. Oh, I don't mean that either – of course not! It was perfectly natural – we *all* thought you so charming and interesting from the first day – we knew at once that Mr Gannett was intellectual, by the magazines you took in; but you know what I mean. Lady Susan is so very – well, I won't say prejudiced, as Mrs Ainger does – but so prepared *not* to like new people, that her taking to you in that way was a surprise to us all, I confess.'

Miss Pinsent sent a significant glance down the long laurustinus alley from the other end of which two people – a lady and gentleman – were strolling toward them through the smiling neglect of the garden.

'In this case, of course, it's very different; that I'm willing to admit. Their looks are against them; but, as Mrs Ainger says, one can't exactly tell them so.'

'She's very handsome,' Lydia ventured, with her eyes on the lady, who showed, under the dome of a vivid sunshade, the hourglass figure and superlative coloring of a Christmas chromo.

'That's the worst of it. She's too handsome.'

'Well, after all, she can't help that.'

'Other people manage to,' said Miss Pinsent skeptically.

'But isn't it rather unfair of Lady Susan – considering that nothing is known about them?'

'But, my dear, that's the very thing that's against them. It's infinitely worse than any actual knowledge.'

Lydia mentally agreed that, in the case of Mrs Linton, it possibly might be.

'I wonder why they came here?' she mused.

'That's against them too. It's always a bad sign when loud people come to a quiet place. And they've brought van loads of boxes – her maid told Mrs Ainger's that they meant to stop indefinitely.'

'And Lady Susan actually turned her back on her in the salon?'

'My dear, she said it was for our sakes: that makes it so unanswerable! But poor Grossart *is* in a way! The Lintons have taken his most expensive suite, you know – the yellow damask drawing room above the portico – and they have champagne with every meal!'

They were silent as Mr and Mrs Linton sauntered by; the lady with tempestuous brows and challenging chin; the gentleman, a blond stripling, trailing after her, head downward, like a reluctant child dragged by his nurse.

'What does your husband think of them, my dear?' Miss Pinsent whispered as they passed out of earshot.

Lydia stooped to pick a violet in the border.

'He hasn't told me.'

'Of your speaking to them, I mean. Would he approve of that? I know how very particular nice Americans are. I think your action might make a difference; it would certainly carry weight with Lady Susan.'

'Dear Miss Pinsent, you flatter me!'

Lydia rose and gathered up her book and sunshade.

'Well, if you're asked for an opinion – if Lady Susan asks you for one – I think you ought to be prepared,' Miss Pinsent admonished her as she moved away.

III

Lady Susan held her own. She ignored the Lintons, and her little family, as Miss Pinsent phrased it, followed suit. Even Mrs Ainger agreed that it was obligatory. If Lady Susan owed it to the others not to speak to the Lintons, the others clearly owed it to Lady Susan to back her up. It was generally found expedient, at the Hotel Bellosguardo, to adopt this form of reasoning.

Whatever effect this combined action may have had upon the Lintons, it did not at least have that of driving them away. Monsieur Grossart, after a few days of suspense, had the satisfaction of seeing them settle down in his yellow damask *premier* with what looked like a permanent installation of palm trees and silk cushions, and a gratifying continuance in the consumption of champagne. Mrs Linton trailed her Doucet draperies up and down the garden with the same challenging air, while her husband, smoking innumerable cigarettes, dragged himself dejectedly in her wake; but neither of them, after the first encounter with Lady Susan, made any attempt to extend their acquaintance. They simply ignored their ignorers. As Miss Pinsent resentfully observed, they behaved exactly as though the hotel were empty.

It was therefore a matter of surprise, as well as of displeasure, to Lydia, to find, on glancing up one day from her seat in the garden, that the shadow which had fallen across her book was that of the enigmatic Mrs Linton.

'I want to speak to you,' that lady said, in a rich hard voice that seemed the audible expression of her gown and her complexion.

Lydia started. She certainly did not want to speak to Mrs
Linton.

'Shall I sit down here?' the latter continued, fixing her
intensely-shaded eyes on Lydia's face, 'or are you afraid of being
seen with me?'

'Afraid?' Lydia colored. 'Sit down, please. What is it that you
wish to say?'

Mrs Linton, with a smile, drew up a garden chair and crossed
one openwork ankle above the other.

'I want you to tell me what my husband said to your husband
last night.'

Lydia turned pale.

'My husband – to yours?' she faltered, staring at the other.

'Didn't you know they were closeted together for hours in the
smoking room after you went upstairs? My man didn't get to bed
until nearly two o'clock and when he did I couldn't get a word
out of him. When he wants to be aggravating I'll back him
against anybody living!' Her teeth and eyes flashed persuasively
upon Lydia. 'But you'll tell me what they were talking about,
won't you? I know I can trust you – you look so awfully kind.
And it's for his own good. He's such a precious donkey and I'm
so afraid he's got into some beastly scrape or other. If he'd only
trust his own old woman! But they're always writing to him and
setting him against me. And I've got nobody to turn to.' She laid
her hand on Lydia's with a rattle of bracelets. 'You'll help me,
won't you?'

Lydia drew back from the smiling fierceness of her brows.

'I'm sorry – but I don't think I understand. My husband has
said nothing to me of – of yours.'

The great black crescents above Mrs Linton's eyes met angrily.

'I say – is that true?' she demanded.

Lydia rose from her seat.

'Oh, look here, I didn't mean that, you know – you mustn't
take one up so! Can't you see how rattled I am?'

Lydia saw that, in fact, her beautiful mouth was quivering
beneath softened eyes.

'I'm beside myself!' the splendid creature wailed, dropping into
her seat.

'I'm so sorry,' Lydia repeated, forcing herself to speak kindly;
'but how can I help you?'

Mrs Linton raised her head sharply.

'By finding out – there's a darling!'

'Finding what out?'

'What Trevenna told him.'

'Trevanna – ?' Lydia echoed in bewilderment.

Mrs Linton clapped her hand to her mouth.

'Oh, Lord – there, it's out! What a fool I am! But I supposed of course you knew; I supposed everybody knew.' She dried her eyes and bridled. 'Don't you know that he's Lord Trevenna! I'm Mrs Cope.'

Lydia recognized the names. They had figured in a flamboyant elopement which had thrilled fashionable London some six months earlier.

'Now you see how it is – you understand, don't you?' Mrs Cope continued on a note of appeal. 'I knew you would – that's the reason I came to you. I suppose *he* felt the same thing about your husband; he's not spoken to another soul in the place.' Her face grew anxious again. 'He's awfully sensitive, generally – he feels our position, he says – as if it wasn't *my* place to feel that! But when he does get talking there's no knowing what he'll say. I know he's been brooding over someting lately, and I *must* find out what it is – it's to his interest that I should. I always tell him that I think only of his interest; if he'd only trust me! But he's been so odd lately – I can't think what he's plotting. You will help me, dear?'

Lydia, who had remained standing, looked away uncomfortably.

'If you mean by finding out what Lord Trevanna has told my husband, I'm afraid it's impossible.'

'Why impossible?'

'Because I infer that it was told in confidence.'

Mrs Cope stared incredulously.

'Well, what of that? Your husband looks such a dear – anyone can see he's awfully gone on you. What's to prevent your getting it out of him?'

Lydia flushed.

'I'm not a spy!' she exclaimed.

'A spy – a spy? how dare you?' Mrs Cope flamed out. 'Oh, I don't mean that either! Don't be angry with me – I'm so miserable.' She essayed a softer note. 'Do you call that spying –

for one woman to help out another? I do need help so dreadfully! I'm at my wits' end with Trevanna, I am indeed. He's such a boy – a mere baby, you know; he's only two-and-twenty.' She dropped her orbed lids. 'He's younger than me – only fancy, a few months younger. I tell him he ought to listen to me as if I was his mother; oughtn't he now? But he won't, he won't! All his people are at him, you see – oh, I know *their* little game! Trying to get him away from me before I can get my divorce – that's what they're up to. At first he wouldn't listen to them; he used to toss their letters over to me to read; but now he reads them himself, and answers 'em too, I fancy; he's always shut up in his room, writing. If I only knew what his plan is I could stop him fast enough – he's such a simpleton. But he's dreadfully deep too – at times I can't make him out. But I know he's told your husband everything – I knew that last night the minute I laid eyes on him. And I *must* find out – you must help me – I've got no one else to turn to!'

She caught Lydia's fingers in a stormy pressure.

'Say you'll help me – you and your husband.'

Lydia tried to free herself.

'What you ask is impossible; you must see that it is. No one could interfere in – in the way you ask.'

Mrs Cope's clutch tightened.

'You won't, then? You won't?'

'Certainly not. Let me go, please.'

Mrs Cope released her with a laugh.

'Oh, go by all means – pray don't let me detain you! Shall you go and tell Lady Susan Condit that there's a pair of us – or shall I save you the trouble of enlightening her?'

Lydia stood still in the middle of the path, seeing her antagonist through a mist of terror. Mrs Cope was still laughing.

'Oh, I'm not spiteful by nature, my dear; but you're a little more than flesh and blood can stand! It's impossible, is it? Let you go, indeed! You're too good to be mixed up in my affairs, are you? Why, you little fool, the first day I laid eyes on you I saw that you and I were both in the same box – that's the reason I spoke to you.'

She stepped nearer, her smile dilating on Lydia like a lamp through a fog.

'You can take your choice, you know; I always play fair. If you'll tell I'll promise not to. Now then, which is it to be?'

Lydia, involuntarily, had begun to move away from the pelting storm of words; but at this she turned and sat down again.

'You may go,' she said simply. 'I shall stay here.'

IV

She stayed there for a long time, in the hypnotized contemplation, not of Mrs Cope's present, but of her own past, Gannett, early that morning, had gone off on a long walk – he had fallen into the habit of taking these mountain tramps with various fellow lodgers; but even had he been within reach she could not have gone to him just then. She had to deal with herself first. She was surprised to find how, in the last months, she had lost the habit of introspection. Since their coming to the Hotel Bellosguardo she and Gannett had tacitly avoided themselves and each other.

She was aroused by the whistle of the three o'clock steamboat as it neared the landing just beyond the hotel gates. Three o'clock! Then Gannett would soon be back – he had told her to expect him before four. She rose hurriedly, her face averted from the inquisitorial façade of the hotel. She could not see him just yet; she could not go indoors. She slipped through one of the overgrown garden alleys and climbed a steep path to the hills.

It was dark when she opened their sitting-room door. Gannett was sitting on the window ledge smoking a cigarette. Cigarettes were now his chief resource: he had not written a line during the two months they had spent at the Hotel Bellosguardo. In that respect, it had turned out not to be the right *milieu* after all.

He started up at Lydia's entrance.

'Where have you been? I was getting anxious.'

She sat down in a chair near the door.

'Up the mountain,' she said wearily.

'Alone?'

'Yes.'

Gannett threw away his cigarette: the sound of her voice made him want to see her face.

'Shall we have a little light?' he suggested.

She made no answer and he lifted the globe from the lamp and put a match to the wick. Then he looked at her.

'Anything wrong? You look done up.'

She sat glancing vaguely about the little sitting room, dimly lit by the pallid-globed lamp, which left in twilight the outlines of the furniture, of its writing table heaped with books and papers, of the tea roses and jasmine drooping on the mantelpiece. How like home it had all grown – how like home!

'Lydia, what is wrong?' he repeated.

She moved away from him, feeling for her hatpins and turning to lay her hat and sunshade on the table.

Suddenly she said: 'That woman has been talking to me.'

Gannett stared.

'That woman? What woman?'

'Mrs Linton – Mrs Cope.'

He gave a start of annoyance, still, as she perceived, not grasping the full import of her words.

'The deuce! She told you – ?'

'She told me everything.'

Gannett looked at her anxiously.

'What impudence! I'm so sorry that you should have been exposed to this, dear.'

'Exposed!' Lydia laughed.

Gannett's brow clouded and they looked away from each other.

'Do you know *why* she told me? She had the best of reasons. The first time she laid eyes on me she saw that we were both in the same box.'

'Lydia!'

'So it was natural, of course, that she should turn to me in a difficulty.'

'What difficulty?'

'It seems she has reason to think that Lord Trevenna's people are trying to get him away from her before she gets her divorce –'

'Well?'

'And she fancied he had been consulting with you last night as to – as to the best way of escaping from her.'

Gannett stood up with an angry forehead.

'Well – what concern of yours was all this dirty business? Why should she go to you?'

'Don't you see? It's so simple. I was to wheedle his secret out of you.'

'To oblige that woman?'

'Yes; or, if I was unwilling to oblige her, then to protect myself.'

'To protect yourself? Against whom?'

'Against her telling everyone in the hotel that she and I are in the same box.'

'She threatened that?'

'She left me the choice of telling it myself or of doing it for me.'

'The beast!'

There was a long silence. Lydia had seated herself on the sofa, beyond the radius of the lamp, and he leaned against the window. His next question surprised her.

'When did this happen? At what time, I mean?'

She looked at him vaguely.

'I don't know – after luncheon, I think. Yes, I remember; it must have been at about three o'clock.'

He stepped into the middle of the room and as he approached the light she saw that his brow had cleared.

'Why do you ask?' she said.

'Because when I came in, at about half-past three, the mail was just being distributed, and Mrs Cope was waiting as usual to pounce on her letters; you know she was always watching for the postman. She was standing so close to me that I couldn't help seeing a big official-looking envelope that was handed to her. She tore it open, gave one look at the inside, and rushed off upstairs like a whirlwind, with the director shouting after her that she had left all her other letters behind. I don't believe she ever thought of you again after that paper was put into her hand.'

'Why?'

'Because she was too busy. I was sitting in the window, watching for you, when the five o'clock boat left, and who should go on board, bag and baggage, valet and maid, dressing bags and poodle, but Mrs Cope and Trevanna. Just an hour and a half to pack up in! And you should have seen her when they started. She was radiant – shaking hands with everybody – waving her handkerchief from the deck – distributing bows and smiles like an empress. If ever a woman got what she wanted just in the nick of time that woman did. She'll be Lady Trevanna within a week, I'll wager.'

'You think she has her divorce?'

'I'm sure of it. And she must have got it just after her talk with you.'

Lydia was silent.

At length she said, with a kind of reluctance. 'She was horribly angry when she left me. It wouldn't have taken long to tell Lady Susan Condit.'

'Lady Susan Condit has not been told.'

'How do you know?'

'Because when I went downstairs half an hour ago I met Lady Susan on her way –'

He stopped, half smiling.

'Well?'

'And she stopped to ask if I thought you would act as patroness to a charity concert she is getting up.'

In spite of themselves they both broke into a laugh. Lydia's ended in sobs and she sank down with her face hidden. Gannett bent over her, seeking her hands.

'That vile woman – I ought to have warned you to keep away from her; I can't forgive myself! But he spoke to me in confidence; and I never dreamed – well, it's all over now.'

Lydia lifted her head.

'Not for me. It's only just beginning.'

'What do you mean?'

She put him gently aside and moved in her turn to the window. Then she went on, with her face turned toward the shimmering blackness of the lake, 'You see of course that it might happen again at any moment.'

'What?'

'This – this risk of being found out. And we could hardly count again on such a lucky combination of chances, could we?'

He sat down with a groan.

Still keeping her face toward the darkness, she said, 'I want you to go and tell Lady Susan – and the others.'

Gannett, who had moved towards her, paused a few feet off.

'Why do you wish me to do this?' he said at length, with less surprise in his voice than she had been prepared for.

'Because I've behaved basely, abominably, since we came here: letting these people believe we were married – lying with every breath I drew –'

'Yes, I've felt that too,' Gannett exclaimed with sudden energy.

The words shook her like a tempest: all her thoughts seemed to fall about her in ruins.

'You – you've felt so?'

'Of course I have.' He spoke with low-voiced vehemence. 'Do you suppose I like playing the sneak any better than you do? It's damnable.'

He had dropped on the arm of a chair, and they stared at each other like blind people who suddenly see.

'But you have liked it here,' she faltered.

'Oh, I've liked it – I've liked it.' He moved impatiently. 'Haven't you?'

'Yes,' she burst out; 'that's the worst of it – that's what I can't bear. I fancied it was for your sake that I insisted on staying – because you thought you could write here; and perhaps just at first that really was the reason. But afterwards I wanted to stay myself – I loved it.' She broke into a laugh. 'Oh, do you see the full derision of it? These people – the very prototypes of the bores you took me away from, with the same fenced-in view of life, the same keep-off-the-grass morality, the same little cautious virtues and the same little frightened vices – well, I've clung to them, I've delighted in them, I've done my best to please them. I've toadied Lady Susan, I've gossiped with Miss Pinsent, I've pretended to be shocked with Mrs Ainger. Respectability! It was the one thing in life that I was sure I didn't care about, and it's grown so precious to me that I've stolen it because I couldn't get it in any other way.'

She moved across the room and returned to his side with another laugh.

'I who used to fancy myself unconventional! I must have been born with a cardcase in my hand. You should have seen me with that poor woman in the garden. She came to me for help, poor creature, because she fancied that, having "sinned", as they call it, I might feel some pity for others who had been tempted in the same way. Not I! She didn't know me. Lady Susan would have been kinder, because Lady Susan wouldn't have been afraid. I hated the woman – my one thought was not to be seen with her – I could have killed her for guessing my secret. The one thing that mattered to me at that moment was my standing with Lady Susan!'

Gannett did not speak.

'And you – you've felt it too!' she broke out accusingly. 'You've enjoyed being with these people as much as I have; you've let the chaplain talk to you by the hour about The Reign of Law and Professor Drummond. When they asked you to hand the plate in church I was watching you – *you wanted to accept.*'

She stepped close, laying her hand on his arm.

'Do you know, I begin to see what marriage is for. It's to keep people away from each other. Sometimes I think that two people who love each other can be saved from madness only by the things that come between them – children, duties, visits, bores, relations – the things that protect married people from each other. We've been too close together – that has been our sin. We've seen the nakedness of each other's souls.'

She sank again on the sofa, hiding her face in her hands.

Gannett stood above her perplexedly: he felt as though she were being swept away by some implacable current while he stood helpless on its bank.

At length he said, 'Lydia, don't think me a brute – but don't you see yourself that it won't do?'

'Yes, I see it won't do,' she said without raising her head.

His face cleared.

'Then we'll go tomorrow.'

'Go – where?'

'To Paris; to be married.'

For a long time she made no answer; then she asked slowly, 'Would they have us here if we were married?'

'Have us here?'

'I mean Lady Susan – and the others.'

'Have us here? Of course they would.'

'Not if they knew – at least, not unless they could pretend not to know.'

He made an impatient gesture.

'We shouldn't come back here, of course; and other people needn't know – no one need know.'

She sighed. 'Then it's only another form of deception and a meaner one. Don't you see that?'

'I see that we're not accountable to any Lady Susans on earth!'

'Then why are you ashamed of what we are doing here?'

'Because I'm sick of pretending that you're my wife when you're not – when you won't be.'

She looked at him sadly.

'If I were your wife you'd have to go on pretending. You'd have to pretend that I'd never been – anything else. And our friends would have to pretend that they believed what you pretended.'

Gannett pulled off the sofa tassel and flung it away.

'You're impossible,' he groaned.

'It's not I – it's our being together that's impossible. I only want you to see that marriage won't help it.'

'What will help it then?'

She raised her head.

'My leaving you.'

'Your leaving me?' He sat motionless, staring at the tassel which lay at the other end of the room. At length some impulse of retaliation for the pain she was inflicting made him say deliberately:

'And where would you go if you left me?'

'Oh!' she cried.

He was at her side in an instant.

'Lydia – Lydia – you know I didn't mean it; I couldn't mean it! But you've driven me out of my senses; I don't know what I'm saying. Can't you get out of this labyrinth of self-torture? It's destroying us both.'

'That's why I must leave you.'

'How easily you say it!' He drew her hands down and made her face him. 'You're very scrupulous about yourself – and others. But have you thought of me? You have no right to leave me unless you've ceased to care –'

'It's because I care –'

'Then I have a right to be heard. If you love me you can't leave me.'

Her eyed defied him.

'Why not?'

He dropped her hands and rose from her side.

'Can you?' he said sadly.

The hour was late and the lamp flickered and sank. She stood up with a shiver and turned toward the door of her room.

V

At daylight a sound in Lydia's room woke Gannett from a troubled sleep. He sat up and listened. She was moving about softly, as though fearful of disturbing him. He heard her push back one of the creaking shutters; then there was a moment's silence, which seemed to indicate that she was waiting to see if the noise had roused him.

Presently she began to move again. She had spent a sleepless night, probably, and was dressing to go down to the garden for a breath of air. Gannett rose also; but some undefinable instinct made his movements as cautious as hers. He stole to his window and looked out through the slats of the shutter.

It had rained in the night and the dawn was gray and lifeless. The cloud-muffled hills across the lake were reflected in its surface as in a tarnished mirror. In the garden, the birds were beginning to shake the drops from the motionless laurustinus boughs.

An immense pity for Lydia filled Gannett's soul. Her seeming intellectual independence had blinded him for a time to the feminine cast of her mind. He had never thought of her as a woman who wept and clung: there was a lucidity in her intuitions that made them appear to be the result of reasoning. Now he saw the cruelty he had committed in detaching her from the normal conditions of life; he felt, too, the insight with which she had hit upon the real cause of their suffering. Their life was 'impossible', as she had said – and its worst penalty was that it had made any other life impossible for them. Even had his love lessened, he was bound to her now by a hundred ties of pity and self-reproach; and she, poor child, must turn back to him as Latude returned to his cell.

A new sound startled him: it was the stealthy closing of Lydia's door. He crept to his own and heard her footsteps passing down the corridor. Then he went back to the window and looked out.

A minute or two later he saw her go down the steps of the porch and enter the garden. From his post of observation her face was invisible, but something about her appearance struck him. She wore a long traveling cloak and under its folds he detected the outline of a bag or bundle. He drew a deep breath and stood watching her.

She walked quickly down the laurustinus alley toward the gate; there she paused a moment, glancing about the little shady square. The stone benches under the trees were empty, and she seemed to gather resolution from the solitude about her, for she crossed the square to the steamboat landing, and he saw her pause before the ticket office at the head of the wharf. Now she was buying her ticket. Gannett turned his head a moment to look at the clock: the boat was due in five minutes. He had time to jump into his clothes and overtake her –

He made no attempt to move; an obscure reluctance restrained him. If any thought emerged from the tumult of his sensations, it was that he must let her go if she wished it. He had spoken last night of his rights: what were they? At the last issue, he and she were two separate beings, not made one by the miracle of common forbearances, duties, abnegations, but bound together in a *noyade* of passion that left them resisting yet clinging as they went down.

After buying her ticket, Lydia had stood for a moment looking out across the lake; then he saw her seat herself on one of the benches near the landing. He and she, at that moment, were both listening for the same sound: the whistle of the boat as it rounded the nearest promontory. Gannett turned again to glance at the clock: the boat was due now.

Where would she go? What would her life be when she had left him? She had no near relations and few friends. There was money enough ... but she asked so much of life, in ways so complex and immaterial. He thought of her as walking bare-footed through a stony waste. No one would understand her – no one would pity her – and he, who did both, was powerless to come to her aid.

He saw that she had risen from the bench and walked toward the edge of the lake. She stood looking in the direction from which the steamboat was to come; then she turned to the ticket office, doubtless to ask the cause of the delay. After that she went back to the bench and sat down with bent head. What was she thinking of?

The whistle sounded; she started up, and Gannett involuntarily made a movement toward the door. But he turned back and continued to watch her. She stood motionless, her eyes on the trail of smoke that preceded the appearance of the boat. Then the little craft rounded the point, a dead white object on the leaden water: a minute later it was puffing and backing at the wharf.

The few passengers who were waiting – two or three peasants and a snuffy priest – were clustered near the ticket office. Lydia stood apart under the trees.

The boat lay alongside now; the gangplank was run out and the peasants went on board with their baskets of vegetables, followed by the priest. Still Lydia did not move. A bell began to ring querulously; there was a shriek of steam, and someone must have called to her that she would be late, for she started forward, as though in answer to a summons. She moved waveringly, and at the edge of the wharf she paused. Gannett saw a sailor beckon to her; the bell rang again and she stepped upon the gangplank.

Halfway down the short incline to the deck she stopped again; then she turned and ran back to the land. The gangplank was drawn in, the bell ceased to ring, and the boat backed out into the lake. Lydia, with slow steps, was walking toward the garden.

As she approached the hotel she looked up furtively and Gannett drew back into the room. He sat down beside a table; a Bradshaw lay at his elbow, and mechanically, without knowing what he did, he began looking out the trains to Paris.

Goblin Market

CHRISTINA ROSSETTI

Morning and evening
Maids heard the goblins cry:
'Come buy our orchard fruits,
Come buy, come buy:
Apples and quinces,
Lemons and oranges,
Plump unpecked cherries,
Melons and raspberries,
Bloom-down-cheeked peaches,
Swart-headed mulberries,
Wild free-born cranberries,
Crab-apples, dewberries,
Pine-apples, blackberries,
Apricots, strawberries; –
All ripe together
In summer weather, –
Morns that pass by,
Fair eves that fly;
Come buy, come buy:
Our grapes fresh from the vine,
Pomegranates full and fine,
Dates and sharp bullaces,
Rare pears and greengages,
Damsons and bilberries,
Taste them and try:
Currants and gooseberries,
Bright-fire-like barberries,
Figs to fill your mouth,
Citrons from the South,
Sweet to tongue and sound to eye;
Come buy, come buy.'

Evening by evening
Among the brookside rushes,

Laura bowed her head to hear,
Lizzie veiled her blushes:
Crouching close together
In the cooling weather,
With clasping arms and cautioning lips,
With tingling cheeks and finger tips.
'Lie close,' Laura said,
Pricking up her golden head:
'We must not look at goblin men,
We must not buy their fruits:
Who knows upon what soil they fed
Their hungry thirsty roots?'
'Come buy,' call the goblins
Hobbling down the glen.
'Oh,' cried Lizzie, 'Laura, Laura,
You should not peep at goblin men.'
Lizzie covered up her eyes,
Covered close lest they should look;
Laura reared her glossy head,
And whispered like the restless brook:
'Look, Lizzie, look, Lizzie,
Down the glen tramp little men.
One hauls a basket,
One bears a plate,
One lugs a golden dish
Of many pounds' weight.
How fair the vine must grow
Whose grapes are so luscious;
How warm the wind must blow
Through those fruit bushes.'
'No,' said Lizzie: 'No, no, no;
Their offers should not charm us,
Their evil gifts would harm us.'
She thrust a dimpled finger
In each ear, shut eyes and ran:
Curious Laura chose to linger
Wondering at each merchant man.
One had a cat's face,
One whisked a tail,
One tramped at a rat's pace,

One crawled like a snail,
One like a wombat prowled obtuse and furry,
One like a ratel tumbled hurry skurry.
She heard a voice like voice of doves
Cooing all together:
They sounded kind and full of loves
In the pleasant weather.

Laura stretched her gleaming neck
Like a rush-imbedded swan,
Like a lily from the beck,
Like a moonlit poplar branch,
Like a vessel at the launch
When its last restraint is gone.

Backwards up the mossy glen
Turned and trooped the goblin men,
With their shrill repeated cry,
'Come buy, come buy.'
When they reached where Laura was
They stood stock still upon the moss,
Leering at each other,
Brother with queer brother;
Signalling each other,
Brother with sly brother.
One set his basket down,
One reared his plate;
One began to weave a crown
Of tendrils, leaves, and rough nuts brown
(Men sell not such in any town);
One heaved the golden weight
Of dish and fruit to offer her:
'Come buy, come buy,' was still their cry.
Laura stared but did not stir,
Longed but had no money.
The whisk-tailed merchant bade her taste
In tones as smooth as honey,
The cat-faced purr'd,
The rat-paced spoke a word
Of welcome, and the snail-paced even was heard;

One parrot-voiced and jolly
Cried 'Pretty Goblin' still for 'Pretty Polly';
One whistled like a bird.
But sweet-tooth Laura spoke in haste:
'Good Folk, I have no coin;
To take were to purloin:
I have no copper in my purse,
I have no silver either,
And all my gold is on the furze
That shakes in windy weather
Above the rusty heather.'
'You have much gold upon your head,'
They answered all together:
'Buy from us with a golden curl.'
She clipped a precious golden lock,
She dropped a tear more rare than pearl,
Then sucked their fruit globes fair or red.
Sweeter than honey from the rock,
Stronger than man-rejoicing wine,
Clearer than water flowed that juice;
She never tasted such before,
How should it cloy with length of use?
She sucked and sucked and sucked the more
Fruits which that unknown orchard bore;
She sucked until her lips were sore;
Then flung the emptied rinds away
But gathered up one kernel stone,
And knew not was it night or day
As she turned home alone.

Lizzie met her at the gate
Full of wise upbraidings:
'Dear, you should not stay so late,
Twilight is not good for maidens;
Should not loiter in the glen
In the haunts of goblin men.
Do you not remember Jeanie,
How she met them in the moonlight,
Took their gifts both choice and many,
Ate their fruits and wore their flowers

Plucked from bowers
Where summer ripens at all hours?
But ever in the noonlight
She pined and pined away;
Sought them by night and day,
Found them no more, but dwindled and grew grey;
Then fell with the first snow,
While to this day no grass will grow
Where she lies low:
I planted daisies there a year ago
That never blow.
You should not loiter so.'
'Nay, hush,' said Laura:
'Nay, hush, my sister:
I ate and ate my fill,
Yet my mouth waters still:
Tomorrow night I will
Buy more'; and kissed her.
'Have done with sorrow;
I'll bring you plums tomorrow
Fresh on their mother twigs,
Cherries worth getting;
You cannot think what figs
My teeth have met in,
What melons icy-cold
Piled on a dish of gold
Too huge for me to hold,
What peaches with a velvet nap,
Pellucid grapes without one seed:
Odorous indeed must be the mead
Whereon they grow, and pure the wave they drink
With lilies at the brink,
And sugar-sweet their sap.'

Golden head by golden head,
Like two pigeons in one nest
Folded in each other's wings,
They lay down in their curtained bed:
Like two blossoms on one stem,
Like two flakes of new-fall'n snow,

Like two wands of ivory
Tipped with gold for awful kings.
Moon and stars gazed in at them,
Wind sang to them lullaby,
Lumbering owls forebore to fly,
Not a bat flapped to and fro
Round their rest:
Cheek to cheek and breast to breast
Locked together in one rest.

Early in the morning
When the first cock crowed his warning,
Neat like bees, as sweet and busy,
Laura rose with Lizzie:
Fetched in honey, milked the cows,
Aired and set to rights the house,
Kneaded cakes of whitest wheat,
Cakes for dainty mouths to eat,
Next churned butter, whipped up cream,
Fed their poultry, sat and sewed;
Talked as modest maidens should:
Lizzie with an open heart,
Laura in an absent dream,
One content, one sick in part;
One warbling for the mere bright day's delight,
One longing for the night.

At length slow evening came:
They went with pitchers to the reedy brook;
Lizzie most placid in her look,
Laura most like a leaping flame.
They drew the gurgling water from its deep.
Lizzie plucked purple and rich golden flags,
Then turning homeward said: 'The sunset flushes
Those furthest loftiest crags;
Come, Laura, not another maiden lags.
No wilful squirrel wags,
The beasts and birds are fast asleep.'
But Laura loitered still among the rushes,
And said the bank was steep.

And said the hour was early still,
The dew not fall'n, the wind not chill;
Listening ever, but not catching
The customary cry,
'Come buy, come buy,'
With its iterated jingle
Of sugar-baited words:
Not for all her watching
Once discerning even one goblin
Racing, whisking, tumbling, hobbling –
Let alone the herds
That used to tramp along the glen,
In groups or single,
Of brisk fruit-merchant men.

Till Lizzie urged, 'O Laura, come;
I hear the fruit-call, but I dare not look:
You should not loiter longer at this brook:
Come with me home.
The stars rise, the moon bends her arc,
Each glow-worm winks her spark,
Let us get home before the night grows dark:
For clouds may gather
Though this is summer weather,
Put out the lights and drench us through;
Then if we lost our way what should we do?'

Laura turned cold as stone
To find her sister heard that cry alone,
That goblin cry,
'Come buy our fruits, come buy.'
Must she then buy no more such dainty fruit?
Must she no more such succous pasture find,
Gone deaf and blind?
Her tree of life drooped from the root:
She said not one word in her heart's sore ache:
But peering thro' the dimness, nought discerning,
Trudged home, her pitcher dripping all the way;
So crept to bed, and lay
Silent till Lizzie slept;

Then sat up in a passionate yearning,
And gnashed her teeth for baulked desire, and wept
As if her heart would break.
Day after day, night after night,
Laura kept watch in vain
In sullen silence of exceeding pain.
She never caught again the goblin cry,
'Come buy, come buy'; –
She never spied the goblin men
Hawking their fruits along the glen:
But when the noon waxed bright
Her hair grew thin and grey;
She dwindled, as the fair full moon doth turn
To swift decay and burn
Her fire away.

One day remembering her kernel-stone
She set it by a wall that faced the south;
Dewed it with tears, hoped for a root,
Watched for a waxing shoot,
But there came none.
It never saw the sun,
It never felt the trickling moisture run:
While with sunk eyes and faded mouth
She dreamed of melons, as a traveller sees
False waves in desert drouth
With shade of leaf-crowned trees,
And burns the thirstier in the sandful breeze.

She no more swept the house,
Tended the fowls or cows,
Fetched honey, kneaded cakes of wheat,
Brought water from the brook:
But sat down listless in the chimney-nook
And would not eat.

Tender Lizzie could not bear
To watch her sister's cankerous care,
Yet not to share.
She night and morning

Caught the goblins' cry:
'Come buy our orchard fruits,
Come buy, come buy:' –
Beside the brook, along the glen,
She heard the tramp of goblin men,
The voice and stir
Poor Laura could not hear;
Longed to buy fruit to comfort her,
But feared to pay too dear.
She thought of Jeanie in her grave,
Who should have been a bride;
But who for joys brides hope to have
Fell sick and died
In her gay prime,
In earliest winter time,
With the first glazing rime,
With the first snow-fall of crisp winter time.

Till Laura dwindling
Seemed knocking at Death's door.
Then Lizzie weighed no more
Better and worse;
But put a silver penny in her purse,
Kissed Laura, crossed the heath with clumps of furze
At twilight, halted by the brook:
And for the first time in her life
Began to listen and look.

Laughed every goblin
When they spied her peeping:
Came towards her hobbling,
Flying, running, leaping,
Puffing and blowing,
Chuckling, clapping, crowing,
Clucking and gobbling,
Mopping and mowing,
Full of airs and graces,
Pulling wry faces,
Demure grimaces,
Cat-like and rat-like,

Ratel- and wombat-like,
Snail-paced in a hurry,
Parrot-voiced and whistler,
Helter skelter, hurry skurry,
Chattering like magpies,
Fluttering like pigeons,
Gliding like fishes, –
Hugged her and kissed her:
Squeezed and caressed her:
Stretched up their dishes,
Panniers, and plates:
'Look at our apples
Russet and dun,
Bob at our cherries,
Bite at our peaches,
Citrons and dates,
Grapes for the asking,
Pears red with basking
Out in the sun,
Plums on their twigs;
Pluck them and suck them, –
Pomegranates, figs.'

'Good folk,' said Lizzie,
Mindful of Jeanie:
'Give me much and many:'
Held out her apron,
Tossed them her penny.
'Nay, take a seat with us,
Honour and eat with us,'
They answered grinning:
'Our feast is but beginning.
Night yet is early,
Warm and dew-pearly,
Wakeful and starry:
Such fruits as these
No man can carry;
Half their bloom would fly,
Half their dew would dry,
Half their flavour would pass by.

Sit down and feast with us,
Be welcome guest with us,
Cheer you and rest with us.' –
'Thank you,' said Lizzie: 'But one waits
At home alone for me:
So without further parleying,
If you will not sell me any
Of your fruits though much and many,
Give me back my silver penny
I tossed you for a fee.' –
They began to scratch their pates,
No longer wagging, purring,
But visibly demurring,
Grunting and snarling.
One called her proud,
Cross-grained, uncivil;
Their tones waxed loud,
Their looks were evil.
Lashing their tails
They trod and hustled her,
Elbowed and jostled her,
Clawed with their nails,
Barking, mewing, hissing, mocking,
Tore her gown and soiled her stocking,
Twitched her hair out by the roots,
Stamped upon her tender feet,
Held her hands and squeezed their fruits
Against her mouth to make her eat.

White and golden Lizzie stood,
Like a lily in a flood, –
Like a rock of blue-veined stone
Lashed by tides obstreperously, –
Like a beacon left alone
In a hoary roaring sea,
Sending up a golden fire, –
Like a fruit-crowned orange-tree
White with blossoms honey-sweet
Sore beset by wasp and bee, –
Like a royal virgin town

Topped with gilded dome and spire
Close beleaguered by a fleet
Mad to tug her standard down.
One may lead a horse to water,
Twenty cannot make him drink.
Though the goblins cuffed and caught her,
Coaxed and fought her,
Bullied and besought her,
Scratched her, pinched her black as ink,
Kicked and knocked her,
Mauled and mocked her,
Lizzie uttered not a word;
Would not open lip from lip
Lest they should cram a mouthful in:
But laughed in heart to feel the drip
Of juice that syruped all her face,
And lodged in dimples of her chin,
And streaked her neck which quaked like curd.
At last the evil people,
Worn out by her resistance,
Flung back her penny, kicked their fruit
Along whichever road they took,
Not leaving root or stone or shoot;
Some writhed into the ground,
Some dived into the brook
With ring and ripple,
Some scudded on the gale without a sound,
Some vanished in the distance.

In a smart, ache, tingle,
Lizzie went her way;
Knew not was it night or day;
Sprang up the bank, tore thro' the furze,
Threaded copse and dingle,
And heard her penny jingle
Bouncing in her purse, –
Its bounce was music to her ear.
She ran and ran
As if she feared some goblin man
Dogged her with gibe or curse

Or something worse:
But not one goblin skurried after,
Nor was she pricked by fear;
The kind heart made her windy-paced
That urged her home quite out of breath with haste
And inward laughter.

She cried, 'Laura,' up the garden.
'Did you miss me?
Come and kiss me.
Never mind my bruises,
Hug me, kiss me, suck my juices
Squeezed from goblin fruits for you,
Goblin pulp and goblin dew.
Eat me, drink me, love me;
Laura, make much of me;
For your sake I have braved the glen
And had to do with goblin merchant men.'

Laura started from her chair,
Flung her arms up in the air,
Clutched her hair:
'Lizzie, Lizzie, have you tasted
For my sake the fruit forbidden?
Must your light like mine be hidden,
Your young life like mine be wasted,
Undone in mine undoing,
And ruined in my ruin,
Thirsty, cankered, goblin-ridden?' –
She clung about her sister,
Kissed and kissed and kissed her:
Tears once again
Refreshed her shrunken eyes,
Dropping like rain
After long sultry drouth;
Shaking with aguish fear, and pain,
She kissed and kissed her with a hungry mouth.

Her lips began to scorch,
That juice was wormwood to her tongue,

She loathed the feast:
Writhing as one possessed she leaped and sung,
Rent all her robe, and wrung
Her hands in lamentable haste,
And beat her breast.
Her locks streamed like the torch
Borne by a racer at full speed,
Or like the mane of horses in their flight,
Or like an eagle when she stems the light
Straight toward the sun,
Or like a caged thing freed,
Or like a flying flag when armies run.

Swift fire spread through her veins, knocked at her heart
Met the fire smouldering there
And overbore its lesser flame;
She gorged on bitterness without a name:
Ah fool, to choose such part
Of soul-consuming care!
Sense failed in the mortal strife:
Like the watch-tower of a town
Which an earthquake shatters down,
Like a lightning-stricken mast,
Like a wind-uprooted tree
Spun about,
Like a foam-topped waterspout
Cast down headlong in the sea,
She fell at last;
Pleasure past and anguish past,
Is it death or is it life?

Life out of death.
That night long Lizzie watched by her,
Counted her pulse's flagging stir,
Felt for her breath,
Held water to her lips, and cooled her face
With tears and fanning leaves.
But when the first birds chirped about their eaves,
And early reapers plodded to the place
Of golden sheaves,

And dew-wet grass
Bowed in the morning winds so brisk to pass,
And new buds with new day
Opened of cup-like lilies on the stream,
Laura awoke as from a dream,
Laughed in the innocent old way,
Hugged Lizzie but not twice or thrice;
Her gleaming locks showed not one thread of grey,
Her breath was sweet as May,
And light danced in her eyes.

Days, weeks, months, years
Afterwards, when both were wives
With children of their own;
Their mother-hearts beset with fears,
Their lives bound up in tender lives;
Laura would call the little ones
And tell them of her early prime,
Those pleasant days long gone
Of not-returning time:
Would talk about the haunted glen,
The wicked quaint fruit-merchant men,
Their fruits like honey to the throat
But poison in the blood
(Men sell not such in any town):
Would tell them how her sister stood
In deadly peril to do her good,
And win the fiery antidote:
Then joining hands to little hands
Would bid them cling together, –
'For there is no friend like a sister
In calm or stormy weather;
To cheer one on the tedious way,
To fetch one if one goes astray,
To lift one if one totters down,
To strengthen whilst one stands.'

The Parson's Daughter of Oxney Colne

ANTHONY TROLLOPE

The prettiest scenery in all England – and if I am contradicted in
that assertion, I will say in all Europe – is in Devonshire, on the
southern and southeastern skirts of Dartmoor, where the rivers
Dart and Avon and Teign form themselves, and where the broken
moor is half cultivated, and the wild-looking uplands fields are
half moor. In making this assertion I am often met with much
doubt, but it is by persons who do not really know the locality.
Men and women talk to me on the matter who have travelled
down the line of railway from Exeter to Plymouth, who have
spent a fortnight at Torquay, and perhaps made an excursion
from Tavistock to the convict prison on Dartmoor. But who
knows the glories of Chagford? Who has walked through the
parish of Manaton? Who is conversant with Lustleigh Cleeves
and Withycombe in the moor? Who has explored Holne Chase?
Gentle reader, believe me that you will be rash in contradicting
me unless you have done these things.

There or thereabouts – I will not say by the waters of which
little river it is washed – is the parish of Oxney Colne. And for
those who would wish to see all the beauties of this lovely
country a sojourn in Oxney Colne would be most desirable,
seeing that the sojourner would then be brought nearer to all
that he would delight to visit, than at any other spot in the
country. But there is an objection to any such arrangement.
There are only two decent houses in the whole parish, and these
are – or were when I knew the locality – small and fully occupied
by their possessors. The larger and better is the parsonage in
which lived the parson and his daughter; and the smaller is the
freehold residence of a certain Miss Le Smyrger, who owned a
farm of a hundred acres which was rented by one Farmer
Cloysey, and who also possessed some thirty acres round her own
house which she managed herself, regarding herself to be quite
as great in cream as Mr Cloysey, and altogether superior to him
in the article of cider. 'But yeu have to pay no rent, Miss,' Farmer
Cloysey would say, when Miss Le Smyrger expressed this opinion

of her art in a manner too defiant. 'Yeu pays no rent, or yeu couldn't do it.' Miss Le Smyrger was an old maid, with a pedigree and blood of her own, a hundred and thirty acres of fee-simple land on the borders of Dartmoor, fifty years of age, a constitution of iron, and an opinion of her own on every subject under the sun.

And now for the parson and his daughter. The parson's name was Woolsworthy – or Wolathy as it was pronounced by all those who lived around him – the Rev. Saul Woolsworthy; and his daughter was Patience Woolsworthy, or Miss Patty, as she was known to the Devonshire world of those parts. That name of Patience had not been well chosen for her for she was a hot-tempered damsel, warm in her convictions, and inclined to express them freely. She had but two closely intimate friends in the world, and by both of them this freedom of expression had been fully permitted to her since she was a child. Miss Le Smyrger and her father were well accustomed to her ways, and on the whole well satisfied with them. The former was equally free and equally warm-tempered as herself, and as Mr Woolsworthy was allowed by his daughter to be quite paramount on his own subject – for he had a subject – he did not object to his daughter being paramount on all others. A pretty girl was Patience Woolsworthy at the time of which I am writing, and one who possessed much that was worthy of remark and admiration had she lived where beauty meets with admiration, or where force of character is remarked. But at Oxney Colne, on the borders of Dartmoor, there were few to appreciate her, and it seemed as though she herself had but little idea of carrying her talent further afield, so that it might not remain for ever wrapped in a blanket.

She was a pretty girl, tall and slender, with dark eyes and black hair. Her eyes were perhaps too round for regular beauty, and her hair was perhaps too crisp; her mouth was large and expressive; her nose was finely formed, though a critic in female form might have declared it to be somewhat broad. But her countenance altogether was very attractive – if only it might be seen without that resolution for dominion which occasionally marred it, though sometimes it even added to her attractions.

It must be confessed on behalf of Patience Woolsworthy that the circumstances of her life had peremptorily called upon her to exercise dominion. She had lost her mother when she was sixteen, and had had neither brother nor sister. She had no neighbours near her fit either from education or rank to interfere in the conduct of her life, excepting always Miss Le Smyrger. Miss Le Smyrger would have done anything for her, including the whole management of her morals and of the parsonage household, had Patience been content with such an arrangement. But much as Patience had ever loved Miss Le Smyrger, she was not content with this, and therefore she had been called on to put forth a strong hand of her own. She had put forth this strong hand early, and hence had come the character which I am attempting to describe. But I must say on behalf of this girl that it was not only over others that she thus exercised dominion. In acquiring that power she had also acquired the much greater power of exercising rule over herself.

But why should her father have been ignored in these family arrangements? Perhaps it may almost suffice to say, that of all living men her father was the man best conversant with the antiquities of the county in which he lived. He was the Jonathan Oldbuck of Devonshire, and especially of Dartmoor, – but without that decision of character which enabled Oldbuck to keep his womenkind in some kind of subjection, and probably enabled him also to see that his weekly bill did not pass their proper limits. Our Mr Oldbuck, of Oxney Colne, was sadly deficient in these respects. As a parish pastor with but a small cure he did his duty with sufficient energy to keep him, at any rate, from reproach. He was kind and charitable to the poor, punctual in his services, forbearing with the farmers around him, mild with his brother clergymen, and indifferent to aught that bishop or archdeacon might think or say of him. I do not name this latter attribute as a virtue, but as a fact. But all these points were as nothing in the known character of Mr Woolsworthy, of Oxney Colne. He was the antiquarian of Dartmoor. That was his line of life. It was in that capacity that he was known to the Devonshire world; it was as such that he journeyed about with his humble carpetbag, staying away from his parsonage a night or two at a time; it was in that character that he received now and again stray visitors in the single spare bedroom – not friends asked to see him and his girl because of their friendship – but men who knew something as to this buried stone, or that old land-mark. In all these things his daughter let him have his own way, assisting and encouraging him. That was his line of life, and therefore she respected it. But in all other matters she chose to be paramount at the parsonage.

Mr Woolsworthy was a little man, who always wore, except on Sundays, grey clothes – clothes of so light a grey that they would hardly have been regarded as clerical in a district less remote. He had now reached a goodly age, being full seventy years old; but still he was wiry and active, and shewed but few symptoms of decay. His head was bald, and the few remaining locks that surrounded it were nearly white. But there was a look of energy about his mouth, and a humour in his light grey eye, which forbade those who knew him to regard him altogether as an old man. As it was, he could walk from Oxney Colne to Priestown, fifteen long Devonshire miles across the moor; and he who could do that could hardly be regarded as too old for work.

But our present story will have more to do with his daughter than with him. A pretty girl, I have said, was Patience Woolsworthy; and one, too, in many ways remarkable. She had taken her outlook into life, weighing the things which she had and those which she had not, in a manner very unusual, and, as a rule, not always desirable for a young lady. The things which she had not were very many. She had not society; she had not a fortune; she had not any assurance of future means of livelihood; she had not high hope of procuring for herself a position in life by marriage; she had not that excitement and pleasure in life which she read of in such books as found their way down to Oxney Colne Parsonage. It would be easy to add to the list of the things which she had not; and this list against herself she made out with the utmost vigour. The things which she had, or those rather which she assured herself of having, were much more easily counted. She had the birth and education of a lady, the strength of a healthy woman, and a will of her own. Such was the list as she made it out for herself, and I protest that I assert no more than the truth in saying that she never added to it either beauty, wit, or talent.

I began these descriptions by saying that Oxney Colne would, of all places, be the best spot from which a tourist could visit those parts of Devonshire, but for the fact that he could obtain there none of the accommodation which tourists require. A brother antiquarian might, perhaps, in those days have done so, seeing that there was, as I have said, a spare bedroom at the parsonage. Any intimate friend of Miss Le Smyrger's might be as fortunate, for she was also so provided at Oxney Combe, by which name her house was known. But Miss Le Smyrger was not given to extensive hospitality, and it was only to those who were bound to her, either by ties of blood or of very old friendship, that she delighted to open her doors. As her old friends were very few in number, as those few lived at a distance, and as her nearest relations were higher in the world than she was, and were said by herself to look down upon her, the visits made to Oxney Combe were few and far between.

But now, at the period of which I am writing, such a visit was about to be made. Miss Le Smyrger had a younger sister who had inherited a property in the parish of Oxney Colne equal to that of the lady who lived there; but this younger sister had inherited beauty also, and she therefore, in early life, had found sundry lovers, one of whom became her husband. She had married a man even then well to do in the world, but now rich and almost mighty; a Member of Parliament, a Lord of this and that board, a man who had a house in Eaton Square, and a park in the north of England; and in this way her course of life had been very much divided from that of our Miss Le Smyrger. But the Lord of the Government board had been blessed with various children, and perhaps it was now thought expedient to look after Aunt Penelope's Devonshire acres. Aunt Penelope was empowered to leave them to whom she pleased; and though it was thought in Eaton Square that she must, as a matter of course, leave them to one of the family, nevertheless a little cousinly intercourse might make the thing more certain. I will not say that this was the sole cause for such a visit, but in these days a visit was to be made by Captain Broughton to his aunt. Now Captain John Broughton was the second son of Alfonso Broughton, of Clapham Park and Eaton Square, Member of Parliament, and Lord of the aforesaid Government Board.

And what do you mean to do with him? Patience Woolsworthy asked of Miss Le Smyrger when that lady walked over from the Combe to say that her nephew John was to arrive on the following morning.

'Do with him? Why, I shall bring him over here to talk to your father.'

'He'll be too fashionable for that, and papa won't trouble his head about him if he finds that he doesn't care for Dartmoor.'

'Then he may fall in love with you, my dear.'

'Well, yes; there's that resource at any rate, and for your sake I dare say I should be more civil to him than papa. But he'll soon get tired of making love to me, and what you'll do then I cannot imagine.'

That Miss Woolsworthy felt no interest in the coming of the Captain I will not pretend to say. The advent of any stranger with whom she would be called on to associate must be matter of interest to her in that secluded place; and she was not so absolutely unlike other young ladies that the arrival of an unmarried young man would be the same to her as the advent of some patriarchal pater-familias. In taking that outlook into life of which I have spoken she had never said to herself that she despised those things from which other girls received the excitement, the joys, and the disappointment of their lives. She had simply given herself to understand that very little of such things would come in her way, and that it behoved her to live – to live happily if such might be possible – without experiencing the need of them. She had heard, when there was no thought of any such visit to Oxney Colne, that John Broughton was a handsome clever man – one who thought much of himself and was thought much of by others – that there had been some talk of his marrying a great heiress, which marriage, however had not taken place through unwillingness on his part, and that he was on the whole a man of more mark in the world than the ordinary captains of ordinary regiments.

Captain Broughton came to Oxney Combe, stayed there a fortnight – the intended period for his projected visit having been fixed at three or four days – and then went his way. He went his way back to his London haunts, the time of the year then being the close of the Easter holy-days; but as he did so he told his aunt that he should assuredly return to her in the autumn.

'And assuredly I shall be happy to see you, John – if you come with a certain purpose. If you have no such purpose, you had better remain away.'

'I shall assuredly come,' the Captain had replied, and then he had gone on his journey.

The summer passed rapidly by, and very little was said

between Miss Le Smyrger and Miss Woolsworthy about Captain Broughton. In many respects – nay, I may say, as to all ordinary matters, – no two women could well be more intimate with each other than they were; and more than that, they had the courage each to talk to the other with absolute truth as to things concerning themselves – a courage in which dear friends often fail. But, nevertheless, very little was said between them about Captain John Broughton. All that was said may be here repeated.

'John says that he shall return here in August,' Miss Le Smyrger said as Patience was sitting with her in the parlour at Oxney Combe, on the morning after that gentleman's departure.

'He told me so himself,' said Patience; and as she spoke her round dark eyes assumed a look of more than ordinary self-will. If Miss Le Smyrger had intended to carry the conversation any further she changed her mind as she looked at her companion. Then, as I said, the summer ran by, and towards the close of the warm days of July, Miss Le Smyrger, sitting in the same chair in the same room, again took up the conversation.

'I got a letter from John this morning. He says that he shall be here on the third.'

'Does he?'

'He is very punctual to the time he named.'

'Yes; I fancy that he is a punctual man,' said Patience.

'I hope that you will be glad to see him,' said Miss Le Smyrger.

'Very glad to see him,' said Patience, with a bold clear voice; and then the conversation was again dropped, and nothing further was said till after Captain Broughton's second arrival in the parish.

Four months had then passed since his departure, and during that time Miss Woolsworthy had performed all her usual daily duties in their accustomed course. No one could discover that she had been less careful in her household matters than had been her wont, less willing to go among her poor neighbours, or less assiduous in her attentions to her father. But not the less was there a feeling in the minds of those around her that some great change had come upon her. She would sit during the long summer evenings on a certain spot outside the parsonage orchard, at the top of a small sloping field in which their solitary cow was always pastured, with a book on her knees before her, but rarely reading. There she would sit, with the beautiful view

down to the winding river below her, watching the setting sun,
and thinking, thinking, thinking – thinking of something of
which she had never spoken. Often would Miss Le Smyrger come
upon her there, and sometimes would pass her even without a
word; but never – never once did she dare to ask of the matter of
her thoughts. But she knew the matter well enough. No
confession was necessary to inform her that Patience Woolsworthy was in love with John Broughton – ay, in love, to the full and
entire loss of her whole heart.

On one evening she was so sitting till the July sun had fallen
and hidden himself for the night, when her father came upon her
as he returned from one of his rambles on the moor. 'Patty,' he
said, 'you are always sitting there now. Is it not late? Will you not
be cold?'

'No papa,' she said, 'I shall not be cold.'

'But won't you come to the house? I miss you when you come
in so late that there's no time to say a word before we go to bed.'

She got up and followed him into the parsonage, and when
they were in the sitting-room together, and the door was closed,
she came up to him and kissed him. 'Papa,' she said, 'would it
make you very unhappy if I were to leave you?'

'Leave me!' he said, startled by the serious and almost solemn
tone of her voice. 'Do you mean for always?'

'If I were to marry, papa?'

'Oh, marry! No; that would not make me unhappy. It would
make me very happy, Patty, to see your married to a man you
would love; – very, very happy; though my days would be
desolate without you.'

'That is it, papa. What would you do if I went from you?'

'What would it matter, Patty? I should be free, at any rate,
from a load which often presses heavy on me now. What will you
do when I shall leave you? A few more years and all will be over
with me. But who is it, love? Has anybody said anything to you?'

'It was only an idea, papa. I don't often think of such a thing;
but I did think of it then.' And so the subject was allowed to pass
by. This had happened before the day of the second arrival had
been absolutely fixed and made known to Miss Woolsworthy.

And then that second arrival took place. The reader may have
understood from the words with which Miss Le Smyrger
authorized her nephew to make his second visit to Oxney Combe

that Miss Woolsworthy's passion was not altogether unauthorized. Captain Broughton had been told that he was not to come unless he came with a certain purpose; and having been so told, he still persisted in coming. There can be no doubt but that he well understood the purport to which his aunt alluded. 'I shall assuredly come,' he had said. And true to his word, he was now there.

Patience knew exactly the hour at which he must arrive at the station at Newton Abbot, and the time also which it would take to travel over those twelve up-hill miles from the station to Oxney. It need hardly be said that she paid no visit to Miss Le Smyrger's house on that afternoon; but she might have known something of Captain Broughton's approach without going thither. His road to the Combe passed by the parsonage-gate, and had Patience sat even at her bedroom window she must have seen him. But on such an evening she would not sit at her bedroom window; – she would do nothing which would force her to accuse herself of a restless longing for her lover's coming. It was for him to seek her. If he chose to do so, he knew the way to the parsonage.

Miss Le Smyrger – good, dear, honest, hearty Miss Le Smyrger, was in a fever of anxiety on behalf of her friend. It was not that she wished her nephew to marry Patience, – or rather that she had entertained any such wish when he first came among them. She was not given to match-making, and moreover thought, or had thought within herself, that they of Oxney Colne could do very well without any admixture from Eaton Square. Her plan of life had been that when old Mr Woolsworthy was taken away from Dartmoor, Patience should live with her, and that when she also shuffled off her coil, then Patience Woolsworthy should be the maiden-mistress of Oxney Combe – of Oxney Combe and of Mr Cloysey's farm – to the utter detriment of all the Broughtons. Such had been her plan before nephew John had come among them – a plan not to be spoken of till the coming of that dark day which should make Patience an orphan. But now her nephew had been there, and all was to be altered. Miss Le Smyrger's plan would have provided a companion for her old age; but that had not been her chief object. She had thought more of Patience than of herself, and now it seemed that a prospect of a higher happiness was opening for her friend.

'John,' she said, as soon as the first greetings were over, 'do you remember the last words that I said to you before you went away?' Now, for myself, I much admire Miss Le Smyrger's heartiness, but I do not think much of her discretion. It would have been better, perhaps, had she allowed things to take their course.

'I can't say that I do,' said the Captain. At the same time, the Captain did remember very well what those last words had been.

'I am so glad to see you, so delighted to see you, if – if – if – ,' and then she paused, for with all her courage she hardly dared to ask her nephew whether he had come there with the express purport of asking Miss Woolsworthy to marry him.

To tell the truth – for there is no room for mystery within the limits of this short story, – to tell, I say, at a word the plain and simple truth, Captain Broughton has already asked that question. On the day before he left Oxney Colne he had in set terms proposed to the parson's daughter, and indeed the words, the hot and frequent words, which previously to that had fallen like sweetest honey into the ears of Patience Woolsworthy, had made it imperative on him to do so. When a man in such a place as that has talked to a girl of love day after day, must not he talk of it to some definite purpose on the day on which he leaves her? Or if he do not, must he not submit to be regarded as false, selfish, and almost fraudulent? Captain Broughton, however, had asked the question honestly and truly. He had done so honestly and truly, but in words, or, perhaps, simply with a tone, that had hardly sufficed to satisfy the proud spirit of the girl he loved. She by that time had confessed to herself that she loved him with all her heart; but she had made no such confession to him. To him she had spoken no word, granted no favour, that any lover might rightfully regard as a token of love returned. She had listened to him as he spoke, and bade him keep such sayings for the drawing-rooms of his fashionable friends. Then he had spoken out and had asked for that hand, – not, perhaps, as a suitor tremulous with hope, – but as a rich man who knows that he can command that which he desires to purchase.

'You should think more of this,' she had said to him at last. 'If you would really have me for your wife, it will not be much to you to return here again when time for thinking of it shall have passed by.' With these words she had dismissed him, and now he had again come back to Oxney Colne. But still she would not place herself at the window to look for him, nor dress herself in other than her simple morning country dress, nor omit one item of her daily work. If he wished to take her at all, he should wish to take her as she really was, in her plain country life, but he should take her also with full observance of all those privileges which maidens are allowed to claim from their lovers. He should curtail no ceremonious observance because she was the daughter of a poor country parson who would come to him without a shilling, whereas he stood high in the world's books. He had asked her to give him all that she had, and that all she was ready to give, without stint. But the gift must be valued before it could be given or received. He also was to give her as much, and she would accept it as being beyond all price. But she would not allow that that which was offered to her was in any degree the more precious because of his outward worldly standing.

She would not pretend to herself that she thought he would come to her that afternoon, and therefore she busied herself in the kitchen and about the house, giving directions to her two maids as though the day would pass as all other days did pass in that household. They usually dined at four, and she rarely, in these summer months, went far from the house before that hour. At four precisely she sat down with her father, and then said that she was going up as far as Helpholme after dinner. Helpholme was a solitary farmhouse in another parish, on the border of the moor, and Mr Woolsworthy asked her whether he should accompany her.

'Do, papa,' she said, 'if you are not too tired.' And yet she had thought how probable it might be that she should meet John Broughton on her walk. And so it was arranged; but, just as dinner was over, Mr Woolsworthy remembered himself.

'Gracious me,' he said, 'how my memory is going! Gribbles, from Ivybridge, and old John Poulter, from Bovey, are coming to meet here by appointment. You can't put Helpholme off till tomorrow?'

Patience, however, never put off anything, and therefore at six o'clock, when her father had finished his slender modicum of toddy, she tied on her hat and went on her walk. She started forth with a quick step, and left no word to say by which route she would go. As she passed up along the little lane which led towards Oxney Combe she would not even look to see if he was coming towards her; and when she left the road, passing over a stone stile into a little path which ran first through the upland fields, and then across the moor ground towards Helpholme, she did not look back once, or listen for his coming step.

She paid her visit, remaining upwards of an hour with the old bedridden mother of the farmer of Helpholme. 'God bless you, my darling!' said the old lady as she left her; 'and send you someone to make your own path bright and happy through the world.' These words were still ringing in her ears with all their significance as she saw John Broughton waiting for her at the first stile which she had to pass after leaving the farmer's haggard.

'Patty,' he said, as he took her hand, and held it close within both his own, 'what a chase I have had after you!'

'And who asked you, Captain Broughton?' she answered, smiling. 'If the journey was too much for your poor London strength, could you not have waited till tomorrow morning, when you would have found me at the parsonage?' But she did not draw her hand away from him, or in any way pretend that he had not a right to accost her as a lover.

'No, I could not wait. I am more eager to see those I love than you seem to be.'

'How do you know whom I love, or how eager I might be to see them? There is an old woman there whom I love, and I have thought nothing of this walk with the object of seeing her.' And now, slowly drawing her hand away from him, she pointed to the farmhouse which she had left.

'Patty,' he said, after a minute's pause, during which she had looked full into his face with all the force of her bright eyes; 'I have come from London today, straight down here to Oxney, and from my aunt's house close upon your footsteps after you to ask you that one question. Do you love me?'

'What a Hercules?' she said, again laughing. 'Do you really mean that you left London only this morning? Why, you must have been five hours in a railway carriage and two in a post-chaise, not to talk of the walk afterwards. You ought to take more care of yourself, Captain Broughton!'

He would have been angry with her, – for he did not like to be quizzed, – had she not put her hand on his arm as she spoke, and the softness of her touch had redeemed the offence of her words.

'All that have I done,' said he, 'that I may hear one word from you.'

'That any word of mine should have such potency! But, let us walk on, or my father will take us for some of the standing stones of the moor. How have you found your aunt? If you only knew the cares that have sat on her dear shoulders for the last week past, in order that your high mightyness might have a sufficiency to eat and drink in these desolate half-starved regions.'

'She might have saved herself such anxiety. No one can care less for such things than I do.'

'And yet I think I have heard you boast of the cook of your club.' And then again there was silence for a minute or two.

'Patty,' said he, stopping again in the path; 'answer my question. I have a right to demand an answer. Do you love me?'

'And what if I do? What if I have been so silly as to allow your perfections to be too many for my weak heart? What then, Captain Broughton?'

'It cannot be that you love me, or you would not joke now.'

'Perhaps not, indeed,' she said. It seemed as though she were resolved not to yield an inch in her own humour. And then again they walked on.

'Patty,' he said once more, 'I shall get an answer from you tonight, – this evening; now, during this walk, or I shall return tomorrow, and never revisit this spot again.'

'Oh, Captain Broughton, how should we ever manage to live without you?'

'Very well,' he said; 'up to the end of this walk I can bear it all; – and one word spoken then will mend it all.'

During the whole of this time she felt that she was ill-using him. She knew that she loved him with all her heart; that it would nearly kill her to part with him; that she had heard his renewed offer with an ecstasy of joy. She acknowledged to herself that he was giving proof of his devotion as strong as any which a girl could receive from her lover. And yet she could hardly bring herself to say the word he longed to hear. That word once said, and then she knew that she must succumb to her love for ever! That word once said, and there would be nothing for her but to spoil him with her idolatry! That word once said, and she must continue to repeat it into his ears, till perhaps he might be tired of hearing it! And now he had threatened her, and how could she speak it after that? She certainly would not speak it unless he asked her again without such threat. And so they walked on again in silence.

'Patty,' he said at last. 'By the heavens above us you shall answer me. Do you love me?'

She now stood still, and almost trembled as she looked up into his face. She stood opposite to him for a moment, and then placing her two hands on his shoulders, she answered him. 'I do, I do, I do,' she said, 'with all my heart; with all my heart – with all my heart and strength.' And then her head fell upon his breast.

Captain Broughton was almost as much surprised as delighted by the warmth of the acknowledgement made by the eager-hearted passionate girl whom he now held within his arms. She had said it now; the words had been spoken; and there was nothing for her but to swear to him over and over again with her sweetest oaths, that those words were true – true as her soul. And very sweet was the walk down from thence to the parsonage gate. He spoke no more of the distance of the ground, or the length of his day's journey. But he stopped her at every turn that he might press her arm the closer to his own, that he might look into the brightness of her eyes, and prolong his hour of delight. There were no more gibes now on her tongue, no raillery at his London finery, no laughing comments on his coming and going. With downright honesty she told him everything: how she had loved him before her heart was warranted in such a passion; how, with much thinking, she had resolved that it would be unwise to take him at his first word, and had thought it better that he should return to London, and then think over it; how she had almost repented of her courage when she had feared, during those long summer days, that he would forget her; and how her heart had leapt for joy when her old friend had told her that he was coming.

'And yet,' said he, 'you were not glad to see me!'

'Oh, was I not glad? You cannot understand the feelings of a girl who has lived secluded as I have done. Glad is no word for the joy I felt. But it was not seeing you that I cared for so much. It was the knowledge that you were near me once again. I almost wish now that I had not seen you till tomorrow.' But as she spoke she pressed his arm, and his caress gave the lie to her last words.

'No, do not come in tonight,' she said, when she reached the little wicket that led up the parsonage. 'Indeed you shall not. I could not behave myself properly if you did.'

'But I don't want you to behave properly.'

'Oh! I am to keep that for London, am I? But, nevertheless, Captain Broughton, I will not invite you either to tea or to supper tonight.'

'Surely I may shake hands with your father.'

'Not tonight – not till –. John, I may tell him, may I not? I must tell him at once.'

'Certainly,' said he.

'And then you shall see him tomorrow. Let me see – at what hour shall I bid you come?'

'To breakfast.'

'No, indeed. What on earth would your aunt do with her broiled turkey and the cold pie? I have got no cold pie for you.'

'I hate cold pie.'

'What a pity! But, John, I should be forced to leave you directly after breakfast. Come down – come down at two, or three; and then I will go back with you to Aunt Penelope. I must see her tomorrow.' And so at last the matter was settled, and the happy Captain, as he left her, was hardly resisted in his attempt to press her lips to his own.

When she entered the parlour in which her father was sitting, there still were Gribbles and Poulter discussing some knotty point of Devon lore. So Patience took off her hat, and sat herself down, waiting till they should go. For full an hour she had to wait, and then Gribbles and Poulter did go. But it was not in such matters as this that Patience Woolsworthy was impatient. She could wait, and wait, and wait, curbing herself for weeks and months, while the thing waited for was in her eyes good; but she could not curb her hot thoughts or her hot words when things came to be discussed which she did not think to be good.

'Papa,' she said, when Gribbles' long-drawn last word had been spoken at the door. 'Do you remember how I asked you the other day what you would say if I were to leave you?'

'Yes, surely,' he replied, looking up at her in astonishment.

'I am going to leave you now,' she said. 'Dear, dearest father, how am I to go from you?'

'Going to leave me,' said he, thinking of her visit to Helpholme, and thinking of nothing else.

Now there had been a story about Helpholme. That bed-ridden old lady there had a stalwart son, who was now the owner of the Helpholme pastures. But though owner in fee of all those wild acres and of the cattle which they supported, he was not much above the farmers around him, either in manners or education. He had his merits, however; for he was honest, well to do in the world, and modest withal. How strong love had grown up, springing from neighbourly kindness, between our Patience and his mother, it needs not here to tell; but rising from it had come another love – or an ambition which might have grown to love. The young man, after much thought, had not dared to speak to Miss Woolsworthy, but he had sent a message by Miss Le Smyrger. If there could be any hope for him, he would present himself as a suitor – on trial. He did not owe a shilling in the world, and had money by him – saved. He wouldn't ask the parson for a shilling of fortune. Such had been the tenor of his message, and Miss Le Smyrger had delivered it faithfully. 'He does not mean it,' Patience had said with her stern voice. 'Indeed he does, my dear. You may be sure he is in earnest,' Miss Le Smyrger had replied; 'and there is not an honester man in these parts.'

'Tell him,' said Patience, not attending to the latter portion of her friend's last speech, 'that it cannot be, – make him understand, you know – and tell him also that the matter shall be thought of no more.' The matter had, at any rate, been spoken of no more, but the young farmer still remained a bachelor, and Helpholme still wanted a mistress. But all this came back upon the parson's mind when his daughter told him that she was about to leave him.

'Yes, dearest,' she said; and as she spoke, she now knelt at his knees. 'I have been asked in marriage, and I have given myself away.'

'Well, my love, if you will be happy –'

'I hope I shall; I think I shall. But you, papa?'

'You will not be far from us.'

'Oh, yes; in London.'

'In London.'

'Captain Broughton lives in London generally.'

'And has Captain Broughton asked you to marry him?'

'Yes, papa – who else? Is he not good? Will you not love him? Oh, papa, do not say that I am wrong to love him?'

He never told her his mistake, or explained to her that he had not thought it possible that the high-placed son of the London great man shall have fallen in love with his undowered daughter; but he embraced her, and told her, with all his enthusiasm, that he rejoiced in her joy, and would be happy in her happiness. 'My own Patty,' he said, 'I have ever known that you were too good for this life of ours here.' And then the evening wore away into the night, with many tears but still with much happiness.

Captain Broughton, as he walked back to Oxney Combe, made up his mind that he would say nothing on the matter to his aunt till the next morning. He wanted to think over it all, and to think it over, if possible, by himself. He had taken a step in life, the most important that a man is ever called on to take, and he had to reflect whether or no he had taken it with wisdom.

'Have you seen her?' said Miss Le Smyrger, very anxiously, when he came into the drawing-room.

'Miss Woolsworthy you mean,' said he. 'Yes, I've seen her. As I found her out I took a long walk and happened to meet her. Do you know, aunt, I think I'll go to bed; I was up at five this morning, and have been on the move ever since.'

Miss Le Smyrger perceived that she was to hear nothing that evening, so she handed him his candlestick and allowed him to go to his room.

But Captain Broughton did not immediately retire to bed, nor when he did so was he able to sleep at once. Had this step that he had taken been a wise one? He was not a man who, in worldly matters, had allowed things to arrange themselves for him, as in the case with so many men. He had formed views for himself, and had a theory of life. Money for money's sake he had declared to himself to be bad. Money, as a concomitant to things which were in themselves good, he had declared to himself to be good also. That concomitant in this affair of his marriage, he had now missed. Well; he had made up his mind to that, and would put up with the loss. He had means of living of his own, though means not so extensive as might have been desirable. That it would be

well for him to become a married man, looking merely to that
state of life as opposed to his present state, he had fully resolved.
On that point, therefore, there was nothing to repent. That Patty
Woolsworthy was good, affectionate, clever, and beautiful, he
was sufficiently satisfied. It would be odd indeed if he were not so
satisfied now, seeing that for the last four months he had declared
to himself daily that she was so with many inward assevera-
tions. And yet though he repeated now again that he was
satisfied, I do not think that he was so fully satisfied of it as he
had been throughout the whole of those four months. It is sad to
say so, but I fear – I fear that such was the case. When you have
your plaything how much of the anticipated pleasure vanishes,
especially if it have been won easily!

He had told none of his family what were his intentions in this
second visit to Devonshire, and now he had to bethink himself
whether they would be satisfied. What would his sister say, she
who had married the Honourable Augustus Gumbleton, gold-
stick-in-waiting to Her Majesty's Privy Council? Would she
receive Patience with open arms, and make much of her about
London? And then how far would London suit Patience, or would
Patience suit London? There would be much for him to do in
teaching her, and it would be well for him to set about the lesson
without loss of time. So far he got that night, but when the
morning came he went a step further, and began mentally to
criticize her manner to himself. It had been very sweet, that
warm, that full, that ready declaration of love. Yes; it had been
very sweet; but – but – ; when, after her little jokes, she did
confess her love, had she not been a little too free for feminine
excellence? A man likes to be told that he is loved, but he hardly
wishes that the girl he is to marry should fling herself at his head!

Ah me! yes; it was thus he argued to himself as on that
morning he went through the arrangements of his toilet. 'Then
he was a brute,' you say, my pretty reader. I have never said that
he was not a brute. But this I remark, that many such brutes are
to be met with in the beaten paths of the world's high highway.
When Patience Woolsworthy had answered him coldly, bidding
him go back to London and think over his love; while it seemed
from her manner that at any rate as yet she did not care for him;
while he was absent from her, and, therefore, longing for her, the
possession of her charms, her talent, and bright honesty of

purpose had seemed to him a thing most desirable. Now they were his own. They had, in fact, been his own from the first. The heart of this country-bred girl had fallen at the first word from his mouth. Had she not so confessed to him? She was very nice, – very nice indeed. He loved her dearly. But had he not sold himself too cheaply?

I by no means say that he was not a brute. But whether brute or no he was an honest man, and had no remotest dream, either then, on that morning, or during the following days on which such thoughts pressed more thickly on his mind – of breaking away from his pledged word. At breakfast on that morning he told all to Miss Le Smyrger, and that lady, with warm and gracious intentions, confided to him her purpose regarding her property. 'I have always regarded Patience as my heir,' she said, 'and shall do so still.'

'Oh, indeed,' said Captain Broughton.

'But it is a great, great pleasure to me to think that she will give back the little property to my sister's child. You will have your mother's, and thus it will all come together again.'

'Ah!' said Captain Broughton. He had his own ideas about property, and did not, even under existing circumstances, like to hear that his aunt considered herself at liberty to leave the acres away to one who was by blood quite a stranger to the family.

'Does Patience know of this?' he asked.

'Not a word,' said Miss Le Smyrger. And then nothing more was said upon the subject.

On that afternoon he went down and received the parson's benediction and congratulations with a good grace. Patience said very little on the occasion, and indeed was absent during the greater part of the interview. The two lovers then walked up to Oxney Combe, and there were more benedictions and more congratulations. 'All went merry as a marriage bell', at any rate as far as Patience was concerned. Not a word had yet fallen from that dear mouth, not a look had yet come over that handsome face, which tended in any way to mar her bliss. Her first day of acknowledged love was a day altogether happy, and when she prayed for him as she knelt beside her bed there was no feeling in her mind that any fear need disturb her joy.

I will pass over the next three or four days very quickly, merely saying that Patience did not find them so pleasant as that first day after her engagement. There was something in her lover's manner – something which at first she could not define – which by degrees seemed to grate against her feelings. He was sufficiently affectionate, that being a matter on which she did not require much demonstration; but joined to his affection there seemed to be – ; she hardly liked to suggest to herself a harsh word, but could it be possible that he was beginning to think that she was not good enough for him? And then she asked herself the question – was she good enough for him? If there were doubt about that, the match should be broken off, though she tore her own heart out in the struggle. The truth, however, was this, – that he had begun that teaching which he had already found to be so necessary. Now, had any one essayed to teach Patience German or mathematics, with that young lady's free consent, I believe that she would have been found a meek scholar. But it was not probable that she would be meek when she found a self-appointed tutor teaching her manners and conduct without her consent.

So matters went on for four or five days, and on the evening of the fifth day, Captain Broughton and his aunt drank tea at the parsonage. Nothing very especial occurred; but as the parson and Miss Le Smyrger insisted on playing backgammon with devoted perseverance during the whole evening, Broughton had a good opportunity of saying a word or two about those changes in his lady-love which a life in London would require – and some word he said also – some single slight word, as to the higher station in life to which he would exalt his bride. Patience bore it – for her father and Miss Le Smyrger were in the room – she bore it well, speaking no syllable of anger, and enduring, for the moment, the implied scorn of the old parsonage. Then the evening broke up, and Captain Broughton walked back to Oxney Combe with his aunt. 'Patty,' her father said to her before they went to bed, 'he seems to me to be a most excellent young man.' 'Dear papa,' she answered, kissing him. 'And terribly deep in love,' said Mr Woolsworthy. 'Oh, I don't know about that,' she answered, as she left him with her sweetest smile. But though she could thus smile at her father's joke, she had already made up her mind that there was still something to be learned as to her promised husband before she could place herself altogether in his hands. She would ask him whether he thought himself liable to injury from this proposed marriage; and though he should deny any such thought, she would know from the manner of his denial what his true feelings were.

And he, too, on that night, during his silent walk with Miss Le Smyrger, had entertained some similar thoughts. 'I fear she is obstinate', he had said to himself, and then he had half accused her of being sullen also. 'If that be her temper, what a life of misery I have before me!'

'Have you fixed a day yet?' his aunt asked him as they came near to her house.

'No, not yet; I don't know whether it will suit me to fix it before I leave.'

'Why, it was but the other day you were in such a hurry.'

'Ah – yes – I have thought more about it since then.'

'I should have imagined that this would depend on what Patty thinks,' said Miss Le Smyrger, standing up for the privileges of her sex. 'It is presumed that the gentleman is always ready as soon as the lady will consent.'

'Yes, in ordinary cases it is so; but when a girl is taken out of her own sphere –'

'Her own sphere! Let me caution you, Master John, not to talk to Patty about her own sphere.'

'Aunt Penelope, as Patience is to be my wife and not yours, I must claim permission to speak to her on such subjects as may seem suitable to me.' And then they parted – not in the best humour with each other.

On the following day Captain Broughton and Miss Woolsworthy did not meet till the evening. She had said, before those few ill-omened words had passed her lover's lips, that she would probably be at Miss Le Smyrger's house on the following morning. Those ill-omened words did pass her lover's lips, and then she remained at home. This did not come from sullenness, nor even from anger, but from a conviction that it would be well that she should think much before she met him again. Nor was he anxious to hurry a meeting. His thought – his base thought – was this; that she would be sure to come up to the Combe after him; but she did not come, and therefore in the evening he went down to her, and asked her to walk with him.

They went away by the path that led by Helpholme, and little was said between them till they had walked some mile together.

Patience, as she went along the path, remembered almost to the letter the sweet words which had greeted her ears as she came down that way with him on the night of his arrival; but he remembered nothing of that sweetness then. Had he not made an ass of himself during these last six months? That was the thought which very much had possession of his mind.

'Patience,' he said at last, having hitherto spoken only an indifferent word now and again since they had left the parsonage, 'Patience, I hope you realize the importance of the step which you and I are about to take?'

'Of course I do,' she answered: 'What an odd question that is for you to ask!'

'Because,' said he, 'sometimes I almost doubt it. It seems to me as though you thought you could remove yourself from here to your new home with no more trouble than when you go from home up to the Combe.'

'Is that meant for a reproach, John?'

'No, not for a reproach, but for advice. Certainly not for a reproach.'

'I am glad of that.'

'But I should wish to make you think how great is the leap in the world which you are about to take.' Then again they walked on for many steps before she answered him.

'Tell me, then, John,' she said, when she had sufficiently considered what words she would speak; – and as she spoke a dark bright colour suffused her face, and her eyes flashed almost with anger. 'What leap do you mean? Do you mean a leap upwards?'

'Well, yes; I hope it will be so.'

'In one sense, certainly, it would be a leap upwards. To be the wife of the man I loved; to have the privilege of holding his happiness in my hand; to know that I was his own – the companion whom he had chosen out of all the world – that would, indeed, be a leap upward; a leap almost to heaven, if all that were so. But if you mean upwards in any other sense –'

'I was thinking of the social scale.'

'Then, Captain Broughton, your thoughts were doing me dishonour.'

'Doing you dishonour!'

'Yes, doing me dishonour. That your father is, in the world's esteem, a greater man than mine is doubtless true enough. That you, as a man, are richer than I am as a woman is doubtless also true. But you dishonour me, and yourself also, if these things can weigh with you now.'

'Patience, – I think you can hardly know what words you are saying to me.'

'Pardon me, but I think I do. Nothing that you can give me – no gifts of that description – can weigh aught against that which I am giving you. If you had all the wealth and rank of the greatest lord in the land, it would count as nothing in such a scale. If – as I have not doubted – if in return for my heart you have given me yours, then – then – then, you have paid me fully. But when gifts such as those are going, nothing else can count even as a make-weight.'

'I do not quite understand you,' he answered, after a pause. 'I fear you are a little high-flown.' And then, while the evening was still early, they walked back to the parsonage almost without another word.

Captain Broughton at this time had only one more full day to remain at Oxney Combe. On the afternoon following that he was to go as far as Exeter, and thence return to London. Of course it was to be expected, that the wedding day would be fixed before he went, and much had been said about it during the first day or two of his engagement. Then he had pressed for an early time, and Patience, with a girl's usual diffidence, had asked for some little delay. But now nothing was said on the subject; and how was it probable that such a matter could be settled after such a conversation as that which I have related? That evening, Miss Le Smyrger asked whether the day had been fixed. 'No,' said Captain Broughton harshly; 'nothing has been fixed.' 'But it will be arranged before you go.' 'Probably not,' he said; and then the subject was dropped for the time.

'John,' she said, just before she went to bed, 'if there be anything wrong between you and Patience, I conjure you to tell me.'

'You had better ask her,' he replied. 'I can tell you nothing.'

On the following morning he was much surprised by seeing Patience on the gravel path before Miss Le Smyrger's gate immediately after breakfast. He went to the door to open it for her, and she, as she gave him her hand, told him that she came up to speak to him. There was no hesitation in her manner, nor any look of anger in her face. But there was in her gait and form, in her voice and countenance, a fixedness of purpose which he had never seen before, or at any rate had never acknowledged.

'Certainly,' said he. 'Shall I come out with you, or will you come upstairs?'

'We can sit down in the summer-house,' she said; and thither they both went.

'Captain Broughton,' she said – and she began her task the moment that they were both seated – 'You and I have engaged ourselves as man and wife, but perhaps we have been over rash.'

'How so?' said he.

'It may be – and indeed I will say more – it is the case that we have made this engagement without knowing enough of each other's character.'

'I have not thought so.'

'The time will perhaps come when you will so think, but for the sake of all that we most value, let it come before it is too late. What would be our fate – how terrible would be our misery, if such a thought should come to either of us after we have linked our lots together.'

There was a solemnity about her as she thus spoke which almost repressed him, – which for a time did prevent him from taking that tone of authority which on such a subject he would choose to adopt. But he recovered himself. 'I hardly think that this comes well from you,' he said.

'From whom else should it come? Who else can fight my battle for me; and, John, who else can fight that same battle on your behalf? I tell you this, that with your mind standing towards me as it does stand at present you could not give me your hand at the altar with true words and a happy conscience. Is it not true? You have half repented of your bargain already. Is it not so?'

He did not answer her; but getting up from his seat walked to the front of the summer-house, and stood there with his back turned upon her. It was not that he meant to be ungracious, but in truth he did not know how to answer her. He had half repented of his bargain.

'John,' she said, getting up and following him so that she could put her hand upon his arm, 'I have been very angry with you.'

'Angry with me!' he said, turning sharp upon her.

'Yes, angry with you. You would have treated me like a child. But that feeling has gone now. I am not angry now. There is my hand; – the hand of a friend. Let the words that have been spoken between us be as though they had not been spoken. Let us both be free.'

'Do you mean it?' he asked.

'Certainly I mean it.' As she spoke these words her eyes were filled with tears in spite of all the efforts she could make to restrain them; but he was not looking at her, and her efforts had sufficed to prevent any sob from being audible.

'With all my heart,' he said; and it was manifest from his tone that he had no thought of her happiness as he spoke. It was true that she had been angry with him – angry, as she had herself declared; but nevertheless, in what she had said and what she had done, she had thought more of his happiness than of her own. Now she was angry once again.

'With all your heart, Captain Broughton! Well, so be it. If with all your heart, then is the necessity so much the greater. You go tomorrow. Shall we say farewell now?'

'Patience, I am not going to be lectured.'

'Certainly not by me. Shall we say farewell now?'

'Yes, if you are determined.'

'I am determined. Farewell, Captain Broughton. You have all my wishes for your happiness.' And she held out her hand to him.

'Patience!' he said. And he looked at her with a dark frown, as though he would strive to frighten her into submission. If so, he might have saved himself any such attempt.

'Farewell, Captain Broughton. Give me your hand, for I cannot stay.' He gave her his hand, hardly knowing why he did so. She lifted it to her lips and kissed it, and then, leaving him, passed from the summer-house down through the wicket-gate, and straight home to the parsonage.

During the whole of that day she said no word to anyone of what had occurred. When she was once more at home she went about her household affairs as she had done on that day of his arrival. When she sat down to dinner with her father he observed nothing to make him think that she was unhappy, nor during the evening was there any expression in her face, or any tone in her voice, which excited his attention. On the following morning

Captain Broughton called at the parsonage, and the servant-girl brought word to her mistress that he was in the parlour. But she would not see him. 'Laws miss, you ain't a quarrelled with your beau?' the poor girl said. 'No, not quarrelled,' she said; 'but give him that.' It was a scrap of paper containing a word or two in pencil. 'It is better that we should not meet again. God bless you.' And from that day to this, now more than ten years, they have never met.

'Papa,' she said to her father that afternoon, 'dear papa, do not be angry with me. It is all over between me and John Broughton. Dearest, you and I will not be separated.'

It would be useless here to tell how great was the old man's surprise and how true his sorrow. As the tale was told to him no cause was given for anger with anyone. Not a word was spoken against the suitor who had on that day returned to London with a full conviction that now at least he was relieved from his engagement. 'Patty, my darling child,' he said, 'may God grant that it be for the best!'

'It is for the best,' she answered stoutly. 'For this place I am fit; and I much doubt whether I am fit for any other.'

On that day she did not see Miss Le Smyrger, but on the following morning, knowing that Captain Broughton had gone off, – having heard the wheels of the carriage as they passed by the parsonage gate on his way to the station, – she walked up to the Combe.

'He has told you, I suppose?' said she.

'Yes,' said Miss Le Smyrger. 'And I will never see him again unless he asks your pardon on his knees. I have told him so. I would not even give him my hand as he went.'

'But why so, thou kindest one? The fault was mine more than his.'

'I understand. I have eyes in my head,' said the old maid. 'I have watched him for the last four or five days. If you could have kept the truth to yourself and bade him keep off from you, he would have been at your feet now, licking the dust from your shoes.'

'But, dear friend, I do not want a man to lick dust from my shoes.'

'Ah, you are a fool. You do not know the value of your own wealth.'

'True; I have been a fool. I was a fool to think that one coming from such a life as he has led could be happy with such as I am. I know the truth now. I have bought the lesson dearly – but perhaps not too dearly, seeing that it will never be forgotten.'

There was but little more said about the matter between our three friends at Oxney Combe. What, indeed, could be said? Miss Le Smyrger for a year or two still expected that her nephew would return and claim his bride; but he has never done so, nor has there been any correspondence between them. Patience Woolsworthy had learned her lesson dearly. She had given her whole heart to the man; and, though she so bore herself that no one was aware of the violence of the struggle, nevertheless the struggle within her bosom was very violent. She never told herself that she had done wrong; she never regretted her loss; but yet – yet! – the loss was very hard to bear. He also had loved her, but he was not capable of a love which could much injure his daily peace. Her daily peace was gone for many a day to come.

Her father is still living; but there is a curate now in the parish. In conjunction with him and with Miss Le Smyrger she spends her time in the concern of the parish. In her own eyes she is a confirmed old maid; and such is my opinion also. The romance of her life was played out in that summer. She never sits now lonely on the hillside thinking how much she might do for one whom she really loved. But with a large heart she loves many, and, with no romance, she works hard to lighten the burdens of those she loves.

As for Captain Broughton, all the world knows that he did marry that great heiress with whom his name was once before connected, and that he is now a useful member of Parliament, working on committees three or four days a week with zeal that is indefatigable. Sometimes, not often, as he thinks of Patience Woolsworthy a smile comes across his face.

The Birthmark

NATHANIEL HAWTHORNE

In the latter part of the last century there lived a man of science, an eminent proficient in every branch of natural philosophy, who not long before our story opens had made experience of a spiritual affinity more attractive than any chemical one. He had left his laboratory to the care of an assistant, cleared his fine countenance from the furnace smoke, washed the stain of acids from his fingers, and persuaded a beautiful woman to become his wife. In those days when the comparatively recent discovery of electricity and other kindred mysteries of Nature seemed to open paths into the region of miracle, it was not unusual for the love of science to rival the love of woman in its depth and absorbing energy. The higher intellect, the imagination, the spirit, and even the heart might all find their congenial aliment in pursuits which, as some of their ardent votaries believed, would ascend from one step of powerful intelligence to another, until the philosopher should lay his hand on the secret of creative force and perhaps make new worlds for himself. We know not whether Aylmer possessed this degree of faith in man's ultimate control over Nature. He had devoted himself, however, too unreservedly to scientific studies ever to be weaned from them by any second passion. His love for his young wife might prove the stronger of the two; but it could only be by intertwining itself with his love of science, and uniting the strength of the latter to his own.

Such a union accordingly took place, and was attended with truly remarkable consequences and a deeply impressive moral. One day, very soon after their marriage, Aylmer sat gazing at his wife with a trouble in his countenance that grew stronger until he spoke.

'Georgiana,' said he, 'has it never occurred to you that the mark upon your cheek might be removed?'

'No, indeed,' said she, smiling; but perceiving the seriousness of his manner, she blushed deeply. 'To tell you the truth it has been so often called a charm that I was simple enough to imagine it might be so.'

'Ah, upon another face perhaps it might,' replied her husband; 'but never on yours. No, dearest Georgiana, you came so nearly perfect from the hand of Nature that this slightest possible defect, which we hesitate whether to term a defect or a beauty, shocks me, as being the visible mark of earthly imperfection.'

'Shocks you, my husband!' cried Georgiana, deeply hurt; at first reddening with momentary anger, but then bursting into tears. 'Then why did you take me from my mother's side? You cannot love what shocks you!'

To explain this conversation it must be mentioned that in the centre of Georgiana's left cheek there was a singular mark, deeply interwoven, as it were, with the texture and substance of her face. In the usual state of her complexion – a healthy though delicate bloom – the mark wore a tint of deeper crimson, which imperfectly defined its shape amid the surrounding rosiness. When she blushed it gradually became more indistinct, and finally vanished amid the triumphant rush of blood that bathed the whole cheek with its brilliant glow. But if any shifting motion caused her to turn pale there was the mark again, a crimson stain upon the snow, in what Aylmer sometimes deemed an almost fearful distinctness. Its shape bore not a little similarity to the human hand, though of the smallest pygmy size. Georgiana's lovers were wont to say that some fairy at her birth hour had laid her tiny hand upon the infant's cheek, and left this impress there in token of the magic endowments that were to give her such sway over all hearts. Many a desperate swain would have risked life for the privilege of pressing his lips to the mysterious hand. It must not be concealed, however, that the impression wrought by this fairy sign manual varied exceedingly, according to the difference of temperament in the beholders. Some fastidious persons – but they were exclusively of her own sex – affirmed that the bloody hand, as they chose to call it, quite destroyed the effect of Georgiana's beauty, and rendered her countenance even hideous. But it would be as reasonable to say that one of those small blue stains which sometimes occur in the purest statuary marble would convert the Eve of Powers to a monster. Masculine observers, if the birthmark did not heighten their admiration, contented themselves with wishing it away, that the world might possess one living specimen of ideal loveliness without the semblance of a flaw. After his marriage, – for he thought little or nothing of the matter before, – Aylmer discovered that this was the case with himself.

Had she been less beautiful, – if Envy's self could have found aught else to sneer at, – he might have felt his affection heightened by the prettiness of this mimic hand, now vaguely portrayed, now lost, now stealing forth again and glimmering to and fro with every pulse of emotion that throbbed within her heart; but seeing her otherwise so perfect, he found this one defect grow more and more intolerable with every moment of their united lives. It was the fatal flaw of humanity which Nature, in one shape or another, stamps ineffaceably on all her productions, either to imply that they are temporary and finite, or that their perfection must be wrought by toil and pain. The crimson hand expressed the ineludible gripe in which mortality clutches the highest and purest of earthly mould, degrading them into kindred with the lowest, and even with the very brutes, like whom their visible frames return to dust. In this manner, selecting it as the symbol of his wife's liability to sin, sorrow, decay, and death, Aylmer's sombre imagination was not long in rendering the birthmark a frightful object, causing him more trouble and horror than ever Georgiana's beauty, whether of soul or sense, had given him delight.

At all the seasons which should have been their happiest, he invariably and without intending it, nay, in spite of a purpose to the contrary, reverted to this one disastrous topic. Trifling as it at first appeared, it so connected itself with innumerable trains of thought and modes of feeling that it became the central point of all. With the morning twilight Aylmer opened his eyes upon his wife's face and recognized the symbol of imperfection; and when they sat together at the evening hearth his eyes wandered stealthily to her cheek, and beheld, flickering with the blaze of the wood fire, the spectral hand that wrote mortality where he would fain have worshipped. Georgiana soon learned to shudder at his gaze. It needed but a glance with the peculiar expression that his face often wore to change the roses of her cheek into a deathlike paleness, amid which the crimson hand was brought strongly out, like a bas-relief of ruby on the whitest marble.

Late one night when the lights were growing dim, so as hardly to betray the stain on the poor wife's cheek, she herself, for the first time, voluntarily took up the subject.

'Do you remember, my dear Aylmer,' said she, with a feeble attempt at a smile, 'have you any recollection of a dream last night about this odious hand?'

'None! none whatever!' replied Aylmer, starting; but then he added, in a dry, cold tone, affected for the sake of concealing the real depth of his emotion, 'I might well dream of it; for before I fell asleep it had taken a pretty firm hold of my fancy.'

'And you did dream of it?' continued Georgiana, hastily; for she dreaded lest a gush of tears should interrupt what she had to say. 'A terrible dream! I wonder that you can forget it. Is it possible to forget this one expression? – "It is in her heart now; we must have it out!" Reflect, my husband; for by all means I would have you recall that dream.'

The mind is in a sad state when Sleep, the all-involving, cannot confine her spectres within the dim region of her sway, but suffers them to break forth, affrighting this actual life with secrets that perchance belong to a deeper one. Aylmer now remembered his dream. He had fancied himself with his servant Aminadab, attempting an operation for the removal of the birthmark; but the deeper went the knife, the deeper sank the hand, until at length its tiny grasp appeared to have caught hold of Georgiana's heart; whence, however, her husband was inexorably resolved to cut or wrench it away.

When the dream had shaped itself perfectly in his memory, Aylmer sat in his wife's presence with a guilty feeling. Truth often finds its way to the mind close muffled in robes of sleep, and then speaks with uncompromising directness of matters in regard to which we practise an unconscious self-deception during our waking moments. Until now he had not been aware of the tyrannizing influence acquired by one idea over his mind, and of the lengths which he might find in his heart to go for the sake of giving himself peace.

'Aylmer,' resumed Georgiana, solemnly, 'I know not what may be the cost to both of us to rid me of this fatal birthmark. Perhaps its removal may cause cureless deformity; or it may be the stain goes as deep as life itself. Again: do we know that there is a possibility, on any terms, of unclasping the firm gripe of this little hand which was laid upon me before I came into the world?'

'Dearest Georgiana, I have spent much thought upon the

subject,' hastily interrupted Aylmer. 'I am convinced of the perfect practicability of its removal.'

'If there be the remotest possibility of it,' continued Georgiana, 'let the attempt be made at whatever risk. Danger is nothing to me; for life, while this hateful mark makes me the object of your horror and disgust, – life is a burden which I would fling down with joy. Either remove this dreadful hand, or take my wretched life! You have deep science. All the world bears witness of it. You have achieved great wonders. Cannot you remove this little, little mark, which I cover with the tips of two small fingers? Is this beyond your power, for the sake of your own peace, and to save your poor wife from madness?'

'Noblest, dearest, tenderest wife,' cried Aylmer, rapturously, 'doubt not my power. I have already given this matter the deepest thought – thought which might almost have enlightened me to create a being less perfect than yourself. Georgiana, you have led me deeper than ever into the heart of science. I feel myself fully competent to render this dear cheek as faultless as its fellow; and then, most beloved, what will be my triumph when I shall have corrected what Nature left imperfect in her fairest work! Even Pygmalion, when his sculptured woman assumed life, felt not greater ecstasy than mine will be.'

'It is resolved, then,' said Georgiana, faintly smiling. 'And, Aylmer, spare me not, though you should find the birthmark take refuge in my heart at last.'

Her husband tenderly kissed her cheek – her right cheek – not that which bore the impress of the crimson hand.

The next day Aylmer apprised his wife of a plan that he had formed whereby he might have opportunity for the intense thought and constant watchfulness which the proposed opera- tion would require; while Georgiana, likewise, would enjoy the perfect repose essential to its success. They were to seclude themselves in the extensive apartments occupied by Aylmer as a laboratory, and where, during his toilsome youth, he had made discoveries in the elemental powers of Nature that had roused the admiration of all the learned societies in Europe. Seated calmly in this laboratory, the pale philosopher had investigated the secrets of the highest cloud region and of the profoundest mines; he had satisfied himself of the causes that kindled and kept alive the fires of the volcano; and had explained the mystery of fountains, and how it is that they gush forth, some so bright and pure, and others with such rich medicinal virtues, from the dark bosom of the earth. Here, too, at an earlier period, he had studied the wonders of the human frame, and attempted to fathom the very process by which Nature assimilates all her precious influences from earth and air, and from the spiritual world, to create and foster man, her masterpiece. The latter pursuit, however, Aylmer had long laid aside in unwilling recognition of the truth – against which all seekers sooner or later stumble – that our great creative Mother, while she amuses us with apparently working in the broadest sunshine, is yet severely careful to keep her own secrets, and, in spite of her pretended openness, shows us nothing but results. She permits us, indeed, to mar, but seldom to mend, and, like a jealous patentee, on no account to make. Now, however, Aylmer resumed these half-forgotten investigations; not, of course, with such hopes or wishes as first suggested them; but because they involved much physiological truth and lay in the path of his proposed scheme for the treatment of Georgiana.

As he led her over the threshold of the laboratory, Georgiana was cold and tremulous. Aylmer looked cheerfully into her face, with intent to reassure her, but was so startled with the intense glow of the birthmark upon the whiteness of her cheek that he could not restrain a strong convulsive shudder. His wife fainted.

'Aminadab! Aminadab!' shouted Aylmer, stamping violently on the floor.

Forthwith there issued from an inner apartment a man of low stature, but bulky frame, with shaggy hair hanging about his visage, which was grimed with the vapors of the furnace. This personage had been Aylmer's underworker during his whole scientific career, and was admirably fitted for that office by his great mechanical readiness, and the skill with which, while incapable of comprehending a single principle, he executed all the details of his master's experiments. With his vast strength, his shaggy hair, his smoky aspect, and the indescribable earthiness that incrusted him, he seemed to represent man's physical nature; while Aylmer's slender figure, and pale, intellectual face, were no less apt a type of the spiritual element.

'Throw open the door of the boudoir, Aminadab,' said Aylmer, 'and burn a pastil.'

'Yes, master,' answered Aminadab, looking intently at the

lifeless form of Georgiana; and then he muttered to himself, 'If she were my wife, I'd never part with that birthmark.'

When Georgiana recovered consciousness she found herself breathing an atmosphere of penetrating fragrance, the gentle potency of which had recalled her from her deathlike faintness. The scene around her looked like enchantment. Aylmer had converted those smoky, dingy, sombre rooms, where he had spent his brightest years in recondite pursuits, into a series of beautiful apartments not unfit to be the secluded abode of a lovely woman. The walls were hung with gorgeous curtains, which imparted the combination of grandeur and grace that no other species of adornment can achieve; and as they fell from the ceiling to the floor, their rich and ponderous folds, concealing all angles and straight lines, appeared to shut in the scene from infinite space. For aught Georgiana knew, it might be a pavilion among the clouds. And Aylmer, excluding the sunshine, which would have interfered with his chemical processes, had supplied its place with perfumed lamps, emitting flames of various hue, but all uniting in a soft, impurpled radiance. He now knelt by his wife's side, watching her earnestly, but without alarm; for he was confident in his science, and felt that he could draw a magic circle round her within which no evil might intrude.

'Where am I? Ah, I remember,' said Georgiana, faintly; and she placed her hand over her cheek to hide the terrible mark from her husband's eyes.

'Fear not, dearest!' exclaimed he. 'Do not shrink from me! Believe me, Georgiana, I even rejoice in this single imperfection, since it will be such a rapture to remove it.'

'Oh, spare me!' sadly replied his wife. 'Pray do not look at it again. I never can forget that convulsive shudder.'

In order to soothe Georgiana, and, as it were, to release her mind from the burden of actual things, Aylmer now put in practice some of the light and playful secrets which science had taught him among its profounder lore. Airy figures, absolutely bodiless ideas, and forms of unsubstantial beauty came and danced before her, imprinting their momentary footsteps on beams of light. Though she had some indistinct idea of the method of these optical phenomena, still the illusion was almost perfect enough to warrant the belief that her husband possessed sway over the spiritual world. Then again, when she felt a wish to look forth from her seclusion, immmediately, as if her thoughts were answered, the procession of external existence flitted across a screen. The scenery and the figures of actual life were perfectly represented, but with that bewitching, yet indescribable difference which always makes a picture, an image, or a shadow so much more attractive than the original. When wearied of this, Aylmer bade her cast her eyes upon a vessel containing a quantity of earth. She did so, with little interest at first; but was soon startled to perceive the germ of a plant shooting upward from the soil. Then came the slender stalk; the leaves gradually unfolded themselves; and amid them was a perfect and lovely flower.

'It is magical!' cried Georgiana. 'I dare not touch it.'

'Nay, pluck it,' answered Aylmer, – 'pluck it, and inhale its brief perfume while you may. The flower will wither in a few moments and leave nothing save its brown seed vessels; but thence may be perpetuated a race as ephemeral as itself.'

But Georgiana had no sooner touched the flower than the whole plant suffered a blight, its leaves turning coal-black as if by the agency of fire.

'There was too powerful a stimulus,' said Aylmer, thoughtfully.

To make up for this abortive experiment, he proposed to take her portrait by a scientific process of his own invention. It was to be effected by rays of light striking upon a polished plate of metal. Georgiana assented; but, on looking at the result, was affrighted to find the features of the portrait blurred and indefinable; while the minute figure of a hand appeared where the cheek should have been. Aylmer snatched the metallic plate and threw it into a jar of corrosive acid.

Soon, however, he forgot these mortifying failures. In the intervals of study and chemical experiment he came to her flushed and exhausted, but seemed invigorated by her presence, and spoke in glowing language of the resources of his art. He gave a history of the long dynasty of the alchemists, who spent so many ages in quest of the universal solvent by which the golden principle might be elicited from all things vile and base. Aylmer appeared to believe that, by the plainest scientific logic, it was altogether within the limits of possibility to discover this long-sought medium; 'but,' he added, 'a philosopher who should go

deep enough to acquire the power would attain too lofty a
wisdom to stoop to the exercise of it'. Not less singular were his
opinions in regard to the elixir vitae. He more than intimated
that it was at his option to concoct a liquid that should prolong
life for years, perhaps interminably; but that it would produce a
discord in Nature which all the world, and chiefly the quaffer of
the immortal nostrum, would find cause to curse.

'Aylmer, are you in earnest?' asked Georgiana, looking at him
with amazement and fear. 'It is terrible to possess such power, or
even to dream of possessing it.'

'Oh, do not tremble, my love,' said her husband. 'I would not
wrong either you or myself by working such inharmonious
effects upon our lives; but I would have you consider how trifling,
in comparison, is the skill requisite to remove this little hand.'

At the mention of the birthmark, Georgiana, as usual, shrank
as if a red-hot iron had touched her cheek.

Again Aylmer applied himself to his labors. She could hear his
voice in the distant furnace room giving directions to Aminadab,
whose harsh, uncouth, misshapen tones were audible in
response, more like the grunt or growl of a brute than human
speech. After hours of absence, Aylmer reappeared and proposed
that she should now examine his cabinet of chemical products
and natural treasures of the earth. Among the former he showed
her a small vial, in which, he remarked, was contained a gentle
yet most powerful fragrance, capable of impregnating all the
breezes that blow across a kingdom. They were of inestimable
value, the contents of that little vial; and, as he said so, he threw
some of the perfume into the air and filled the room with piercing
and invigorating delight.

'And what is this?' asked Georgiana, pointing to a small crystal
globe containing a gold-colored liquid. 'It is so beautiful to the
eye that I could imagine it the elixir of life.'

'In one sense it is,' replied Aylmer; 'or, rather, the elixir of
immortality. It is the most precious poison that ever was
concocted in this world. By its aid I could apportion the lifetime of
any mortal at whom you might point your finger. The strength of
the dose would determine whether he were to linger out years, or
drop dead in the midst of a breath. No king on his guarded throne
could keep his life if I, in my private station, should deem that the
welfare of millions justified me in depriving him of it.'

'Why do you keep such a terrific drug?' inquired Georgiana in horror.

'Do not mistrust me, dearest,' said her husband, smiling; 'its virtuous potency is yet greater than its harmful one. But see! here is a powerful cosmetic. With a few drops of this in a vase of water, freckles may be washed away as easily as the hands are cleansed. A stronger infusion would take the blood out of the cheek, and leave the rosiest beauty a pale ghost.'

'Is it with this lotion that you intend to bathe my cheek?' asked Georgiana, anxiously.

'Oh, no,' hastily replied her husband; 'this is merely superficial. Your case demands a remedy that shall go deeper.'

In his interviews with Georgiana, Aylmer generally made minute inquiries as to her sensations and whether the confinement of the rooms and the temperature of the atmosphere agreed with her. These questions had such a particular drift that Georgiana began to conjecture that she was already subjected to certain physical influences, either breathed in with the fragrant air or taken with her food. She fancied likewise, but it might be altogether fancy, that there was a stirring up of her system – a strange, indefinite sensation creeping through her veins, and tingling, half painfully, half pleasurably, at her heart. Still, whenever she dared to look into the mirror, there she beheld herself pale as a white rose and with the crimson birthmark stamped upon her cheek. Not even Aylmer now hated it so much as she.

To dispel the tedium of the hours which her husband found it necessary to devote to the processes of combination and analysis, Georgiana turned over the volumes of his scientific library. In many dark old tomes she met with chapters full of romance and poetry. There were the works of the philosophers of the middle ages, such as Albertus Magnus, Cornelius Agrippa, Paracelsus, and the famous friar who created the prophetic Brazen Head. All these antique naturalists stood in advance of their centuries, yet were imbued with some of their credulity, and therefore were believed, and perhaps imagined themselves to have acquired from the investigation of Nature a power above Nature, and from physics a sway over the spiritual world. Hardly less curious and imaginative were the early volumes of the Transactions of the Royal Society, in which the members, knowing little of the limits of natural possibility, were continually recording wonders or proposing methods whereby wonders might be wrought.

But to Georgiana the most engrossing volume was a large folio from her husband's own hand, in which he had recorded every experiment of his scientific career, its original aim, the methods adopted for its development, and its final success or failure, with the circumstances to which either event was attributable. The book, in truth, was both the history and emblem of his ardent, ambitious, imaginative, yet practical and laborious life. He handled physical details as if there were nothing beyond them; yet spiritualized them all, and redeemed himself from materialism by his strong and eager aspiration towards the infinite. In his grasp the veriest clod of earth assumed a soul. Georgiana, as she read, reverenced Aylmer and loved him more profoundly than ever, but with a less entire dependence on his judgment than heretofore. Much as he had accomplished, she could not but observe that his most splendid successes were almost invariably failures, if compared with the ideal at which he aimed. His brightest diamonds were the merest pebbles, and felt to be so by himself, in comparison with the inestimable gems which lay hidden beyond his reach. The volume, rich with achievements that had won renown for its author, was yet as melancholy a record as ever mortal hand had penned. It was the sad confession and continual exemplification of the shortcomings of the composite man, the spirit burdened with clay and working in matter, and of the despair that assails the higher nature at finding itself so miserably thwarted by the earthly part. Perhaps every man of genius in whatever sphere might recognize the image of his own experience in Aylmer's journal.

So deeply did these reflections affect Georgiana that she laid her face upon the open volume and burst into tears. In this situation she was found by her husband.

'It is dangerous to read in a sorcerer's book,' said he, with a smile, though his countenance was uneasy and displeased. 'Georgiana, there are pages in that volume which I can scarcely glance over and keep my senses. Take heed lest it prove as detrimental to you.'

'It has made me worship you more than ever,' said she.

'Ah, wait for this one success,' rejoined he, 'then worship me if you will. I shall deem myself hardly unworthy of it. But come, I have sought you for the luxury of your voice. Sing to me, dearest.'

So she poured out the liquid music of her voice to quench the thirst of his spirit. He then took his leave with a boyish exuberance of gayety, assuring her that her seclusion would endure but a little longer, and that the result was already certain. Scarcely had he departed when Georgiana felt irresistibly impelled to follow him. She had forgotten to inform Aylmer of a symptom which for two or three hours past had begun to excite her attention. It was a sensation in the fatal birthmark, not painful, but which induced a restlessness throughout her system. Hastening after her husband, she intruded for the first time into the laboratory.

The first thing that struck her eye was the furnace, that hot and feverish worker, with the intense glow of its fire, which by the quantities of soot clustered above it seemed to have been burning for ages. There was a distilling apparatus in full operation. Around the room were retorts, tubes, cylinders, crucibles, and other apparatus of chemical research. An electrical machine stood ready for immediate use. The atmosphere felt oppressively close, and was tainted with gaseous odors which had been tormented forth by the processes of science. The severe and homely simplicity of the apartment, with its naked walls and brick pavement, looked strange, accustomed as Georgiana had become to the fantastic elegance of her boudoir. But what chiefly, indeed almost solely, drew her attention, was the aspect of Aylmer himself.

He was pale as death, anxious and absorbed, and hung over the furnace as if it depended upon his utmost watchfulness whether the liquid which it was distilling should be the draught of immortal happiness or misery. How different from the sanguine and joyous mien that he had assumed for Georgiana's encouragement!

'Carefully now, Aminadab; carefully, thou human machine; carefully, thou man of clay!' muttered Aylmer, more to himself than his assistant. 'Now, if there be a thought too much or too little, it is all over.'

'Ho! ho!' mumbled Aminadab. 'Look, master! look!'

Aylmer raised his eyes hastily, and at first reddened, then grew paler than ever, on beholding Georgiana. He rushed towards her and seized her arm with a gripe that left the print of his fingers upon it.

'Why do you come hither? Have you no trust in your husband?' cried he, impetuously. 'Would you throw the blight of that fatal birthmark over my labors? It is not well done. Go, prying woman, go!'

'Nay, Aylmer,' said Georgiana with the firmness of which she possessed no stinted endowment, 'it is not you that have a right to complain. You mistrust your wife; you have concealed the anxiety with which you watch the development of this experiment. Think not so unworthy of me, my husband. Tell me all the risk we run, and fear not that I shall shrink; for my share in it is far less than your own.'

'No, no, Georgiana!' said Aylmer, impatiently, 'it must not be.'

'I submit,' replied she calmly. 'And, Aylmer, I shall quaff whatever draught you bring me; but it will be on the same principle that would induce me to take a dose of poison if offered by your hand.'

'My noble wife,' said Aylmer, deeply moved, 'I knew not the height and depth of your nature until now. Nothing shall be concealed. Know, then, that this crimson hand, superficial as it seems, has clutched its grasp into your being with a strength of which I had no previous conception. I have already administered agents powerful enough to do aught except to change your entire physical system. Only one thing remains to be tried. If that fail us we are ruined.'

'Why did you hesitate to tell me this?' asked she.

'Because, Georgiana,' said Aylmer, in a low voice, 'there is danger.'

'Danger? There is but one danger – that this horrible stigma shall be left upon my cheek!' cried Georgiana. 'Remove it, remove it, whatever be the cost, or we shall both go mad!'

'Heaven knows your words are too true,' said Aylmer, sadly. 'And now, dearest, return to your boudoir. In a little while all will be tested.'

He conducted her back and took leave of her with a solemn tenderness which spoke far more than his words how much was now at stake. After his departure Georgiana became rapt in musings. She considered the character of Aylmer, and did it completer justice than at any previous moment. Her heart exulted, while it trembled, at his honorable love – so pure and lofty that it would accept nothing less than perfection nor miserably make itself contented with an earthlier nature than he had dreamed of. She felt how much more precious was such a sentiment than that meaner kind which would have borne with the imperfection for her sake, and have been guilty of treason to holy love by degrading its perfect idea to the level of the actual; and with her whole spirit she prayed that, for a single moment, she might satisfy his highest and deepest conception. Longer than one moment she well knew it could not be; for his spirit was ever on the march, ever ascending, and each instant required something that was beyond the scope of the instant before.

The sound of her husband's footsteps aroused her. He bore a crystal goblet containing a liquor colorless as water, but bright enough to be the draught of immortality. Aylmer was pale; but it seemed rather the consequence of a highly-wrought state of mind and tension of spirit than of fear or doubt.

'The concoction of the draught has been perfect,' said he, in answer to Georgiana's look. 'Unless all my science have deceived me, it cannot fail.'

'Save on your account, my dearest Aylmer,' observed his wife, 'I might wish to put off this birthmark of mortality by relinquishing mortality itself in preference to any other mode. Life is but a sad possession to those who have attained precisely the degree of moral advancement at which I stand. Were I weaker and blinder it might be happiness. Were I stronger, it might be endured hopefully. But, being what I find myself, methinks I am of all mortals the most fit to die.'

'You are fit for heaven without tasting death!' replied her husband. 'But why do we speak of dying? The draught cannot fail. Behold its effect upon this plant.'

On the window seat there stood a geranium diseased with yellow blotches, which had overspread all its leaves. Aylmer poured a small quantity of the liquid upon the soil in which it grew. In a little time, when the roots of the plant had taken up the moisture, the unsightly blotches began to be extinguished in a living verdure.

'There needed no proof,' said Georgiana, quietly. 'Give me the goblet. I joyfully stake all upon your word.'

'Drink, then, thou lofty creature!' exclaimed Aylmer, with

fervid admiration. 'There is no taint of imperfection on thy spirit. Thy sensible frame, too, shall soon be all perfect.'

She quaffed the liquid and returned the goblet to his hand.

'It is grateful,' said she with a placid smile. 'Methinks it is like water from a heavenly fountain, for it contains I know not what of unobtrusive fragrance and deliciousness. It allays a feverish thirst that had parched me for many days. Now, dearest, let me sleep. My earthly senses are closing over my spirit like the leaves around the heart of a rose at sunset.'

She spoke the last words with a gentle reluctance, as if it required almost more energy than she could command to pronounce the faint and lingering syllables. Scarcely had they loitered through her lips ere she was lost in slumber. Aylmer sat by her side, watching her aspect with the emotions proper to a man the whole value of whose existence was involved in the process now to be tested. Mingled with this mood, however, was the philosophic investigation characteristic of the man of science. Not the minutest symptom escaped him. A heightened flush of the cheek, a slight irregularity of breath, a quiver of the eyelid, a hardly perceptible tremor through the frame, – such were the details which, as the moments passed, he wrote down in his folio volume. Intense thought had set its stamp upon every previous page of that volume, but the thoughts of years were all concentrated upon the last.

While thus employed, he failed not to gaze often at the fatal hand, and not without a shudder. Yet once, by a strange and unaccountable impulse, he pressed it with his lips. His spirit recoiled, however, in the very act; and Georgiana, out of the midst of her deep sleep, moved uneasily and murmured as if in remonstrance. Again Aylmer resumed his watch. Nor was it without avail. The crimson hand, which at first had been strongly visible upon the marble paleness of Georgiana's cheek, now grew more faintly outlined. She remained not less pale than ever; but the birthmark, with every breath that came and went, lost somewhat of its former distinctness. Its presence had been awful; its departure was more awful still. Watch the stain of the rainbow fading out of the sky, and you will know how that mysterious symbol passed away.

'By Heaven! it is well-nigh gone!' said Aylmer to himself, in almost irrepressible ecstasy. 'I can scarcely trace it now. Success!

success! And now it is like the faintest rose color. The lightest flush of blood across her cheek would overcome it. But she is so pale!'

He drew aside the window curtain and suffered the light of natural day to fall into the room and rest upon her cheek. At the same time he heard a gross, hoarse chuckle, which he had long known as his servant Aminadab's expression of delight.

'Ah, clod! ah, earthly mass!' cried Aylmer, laughing in a sort of frenzy, 'you have served me well! Matter and spirit – earth and heaven – have both done their part in this! Laugh, thing of the senses! You have earned the right to laugh.'

These exclamations broke Georgiana's sleep. She slowly unclosed her eyes and gazed into the mirror which her husband had arranged for that purpose. A faint smile flitted over her lips when she recognized how barely perceptible was now that crimson hand which had once blazed forth with such disastrous brilliancy as to scare away all their happiness. But then her eyes sought Aylmer's face with a trouble and anxiety that he could by no means account for.

'My poor Aylmer!' murmured she.

'Poor? Nay, richest, happiest, most favored!' exclaimed he. 'My peerless bride, it is successful! You are perfect!'

'My poor Aylmer,' she repeated, with a more than human tenderness, 'you have aimed loftily; you have done nobly. Do not repent that with so high and pure a feeling, you have rejected the best the earth could offer. Aylmer, dearest Aylmer, I am dying!'

Alas! it was too true! The fatal hand had grappled with the mystery of life, and was the bond by which an angelic spirit kept itself in union with a mortal frame. As the last crimson tint of the birthmark – that sole token of human imperfection – faded from her cheek, the parting breath of the now perfect woman passed into the atmosphere, and her soul, lingering a moment near her husband, took its heavenward flight. Then a hoarse, chuckling laugh was heard again! Thus ever does the gross fatality of earth exult in its invariable triumph over the immortal essence which, in this dim sphere of half development, demands the completeness of a higher state. Yet, had Aylmer reached a profounder wisdom, he need not thus have flung away the happiness which would have woven his mortal life of the selfsame texture with the celestial. The momentary circumstance was too strong for him;

The Old Woman and the Doctor

AESOP

An old woman whose eyes were failing summoned a doctor for a certain fee. He went to her house and, each time, he treated her eyes with unguent. On each occasion while her eyes were thus shut, he stole her furniture piece by piece. When he had removed everything, the eye treatment came to an end and he demanded his agreed fee. The old woman refused to pay him so he took her before the judge. She then declared that she had indeed promised him a fee if he restored her sight, but since the doctor's course of treatment her condition was worse than before. For, she said, 'Previously I could see all the furniture at home, but now I can't see any of it.'

Thus it is that dishonest people, thinking only of their greed, furnish evidence of their own guilt.

The Demon Lover

ELIZABETH BOWEN

Towards the end of her day in London Mrs Drover went round to her shut-up house to look for several things she wanted to take away. Some belonged to herself, some to her family, who were by now used to their country life. It was late August; it had been a steamy, showery day: at the moment the trees down the pavement glittered in an escape of humid yellow afternoon sun. Against the next batch of clouds, already piling up ink-dark, broken chimneys and parapets stood out. In her once familiar street, as in any unused channel, an unfamiliar queerness had silted up; a cat wove itself in and out of railings, but no human eye watched Mrs Drover's return. Shifting some parcels under her arm, she slowly forced round her latchkey in an unwilling lock, then gave the door, which had warped, a push with her knee. Dead air came out to meet her as she went in.

The staircase window having been boarded up, no light came down into the hall. But one door, she could just see, stood ajar, so she went quickly through into the room and unshuttered the big window in there. Now the prosaic woman, looking about her, was more perplexed than she knew by everything that she saw, by traces of her long former habit of life – the yellow smoke-stain up the white marble mantelpiece, the ring left by a vase on the top of the escritoire; the bruise in the wallpaper where, on the door being thrown open widely, the china handle had always hit the wall. The piano, having gone away to be stored, had left what looked like claw-marks on its part of the parquet. Though not much dust had seeped in, each object wore a film of another kind; and, the only ventilation being the chimney, the whole drawing-room smelled of the cold hearth. Mrs Drover put down her parcels on the escritoire and left the room to proceed upstairs; the things she wanted were in a bedroom chest.

She had been anxious to see how the house was – the part-time caretaker she shared with some neighbours was away this week on his holiday, known to be not yet back. At the best of times he did not look in often, and she was never sure that she trusted him. There were some cracks in the structure, left by the last bombing, on which she was anxious to keep an eye. Not that one could do anything –

A shaft of refracted daylight now lay across the hall. She stopped dead and stared at the hall table – on this lay a letter addressed to her.

She thought first – then the caretaker *must* be back. All the same, who, seeing the house shuttered, would have dropped a letter in at the box? It was not a circular, it was not a bill. And the post office redirected, to the address in the country, everything for her that came through the post. The caretaker (even if he *were* back) did not know she was due in London today – her call here had been planned to be a surprise – so his negligence in the manner of this letter, leaving it to wait in the dusk and the dust, annoyed her. Annoyed, she picked up the letter, which bore no stamp. But it cannot be important, or they would know . . . She took the letter rapidly upstairs with her, without a stop to look at the writing till she reached what had been her bedroom, where she let in light. The room looked over the garden and other gardens: the sun had gone in; as the clouds sharpened and lowered, the trees and rank lawns seemed already to smoke with dark. Her reluctance to look again at the letter came from the fact that she felt intruded upon – and by someone contemptuous of her ways. However, in the tenseness preceding the fall of rain she read it: it was a few lines.

Dear Kathleen,

You will not have forgotten that today is our anniversary, and the day we said. The years have gone by at once slowly and fast. In view of the fact that nothing has changed, I shall rely upon you to keep your promise. I was sorry to see you leave London, but was satisfied that you would be back in time. You may expect me, therefore, at the hour arranged.

Until then . . .

K.

Mrs Drover looked for the date: it was today's. She dropped the letter on to the bed-springs, then picked it up to see the writing again – her lips, beneath the remains of lipstick, beginning to go white. She felt so much the change in her own face that she went to the mirror, polished a clear patch in it and looked at once urgently and stealthily in. She was confronted by a woman of forty-four, with eyes starting out under a hat-brim that had been rather carelessly pulled down. She had not put on any more powder since she left the shop where she ate her solitary tea. The pearls her husband had given her on their marriage hung loose round her now rather thinner throat, slipping into the V of the pink wool jumper her sister knitted last autumn as they sat round the fire. Mrs Drover's most normal expression was one of controlled worry, but of assent. Since the birth of the third of her little boys, attended by a quite serious illness, she had had an intermittent muscular flicker to the left of her mouth, but in spite of this she could always sustain a manner that was at once energetic and calm.

Turning from her own face as precipitately as she had gone to meet it, she went to the chest where the things were, unlocked it, threw up the lid and knelt to search. But as rain began to come crashing down she could not keep from looking over her shoulder at the stripped bed on which the letter lay. Behind the blanket of rain the clock of the church that still stood struck six – with rapidly heightening apprehension she counted each of the slow strokes. 'The hour arranged ... My God,' she said, '*what* hour? How should I . . ? After twenty-five years ...'

The young girl talking to the soldier in the garden had not ever completely seen his face. It was dark; they were saying good-bye under a tree. Now and then – for it felt, from not seeing him at this intense moment, as though she had never seen him at all – she verified his presence for these few moments longer by putting out a hand, which he each time pressed, without very much kindness, and painfully, on to one of the breast buttons of his uniform. That cut of the button on the palm of her hand was, principally, what she was to carry away. This was so near the end of a leave from France that she could only wish him already gone. It was August 1916. Being not kissed, being drawn away from and looked at intimidated Kathleen till she imagined spectral glitters in the place of his eyes. Turning away and looking back up the lawn she saw, through branches of trees, the drawing-room window alight: she caught a breath for the moment when she could go running back there into the safe arms of her mother and sister, and cry: 'What shall I do, what shall I do? He has gone.'

Hearing her catch her breath, her fiancé said, without feeling: 'Cold?'

'You're going away such a long way.'

'Not so far as you think.'

'I don't understand?'

'You don't have to,' he said. 'You will. You know what we said.'

'But that was – suppose you – I mean, suppose.'

'I shall be with you,' he said, 'sooner or later. You won't forget that. You need do nothing but wait.'

Only a little more than a minute later she was free to run up the silent lawn. Looking in through the window at her mother and sister, who did not for the moment perceive her, she already felt that unnatural promise drive down between her and the rest of all humankind. No other way of having given herself could have made her feel so apart, lost and foresworn. She could not have plighted a more sinister troth.

Kathleen behaved well when, some months later, her fiancé was reported missing, presumed killed. Her family not only supported her but were able to praise her courage without stint because they could not regret, as a husband for her, the man they knew almost nothing about. They hoped she would, in a year or two, console herself – and had it been only a question of consolation things might have gone much straighter ahead. But her trouble, behind just a little grief, was a complete dislocation from everything. She did not reject other lovers, for these failed to appear: for years she failed to attract men – and with the approach of her thirties she became natural enough to share her family's anxiousness on this score. She began to put herself out, to wonder; and at thirty-two she was very greatly relieved to find herself being courted by William Drover. She married him, and the two of them settled down in this quiet, arboreal part of Kensington: in this house the years piled up, her children were born and they all lived till they were driven out by the bombs of the next war. Her movements as Mrs Drover were circumscribed, and she dismissed any idea that they were still watched.

As things were – dead or living the letter-writer sent her only a threat. Unable, for some minutes, to go on kneeling with her back exposed to the empty room, Mrs Drover rose from the chest to sit on an upright chair whose back was firmly against the wall. The desuetude of her former bedroom, her married London home's whole air of being a cracked cup from which memory, with its reassuring power, had either evaporated or leaked away, made a crisis – and at just this crisis the letter-writer had, knowledgeably, struck. The hollowness of the house this evening cancelled years on years of voices, habits and steps. Through the shut windows she only heard rain fall on the roofs around. To rally herself, she said she was in a mood – and, for two or three seconds shutting her eyes, told herself that she had imagined the letter. But she opened them – there it lay on the bed.

On the supernatural side of the letter's entrance she was not permitting her mind to dwell. Who, in London, knew she meant to call at the house today? Evidently, however, this has been known. The caretaker, *had* he come back, had had no cause to expect her: he would have taken the letter in his pocket, to forward it, at his own time, through the post. There was no other sign that the caretaker had been in – but, if not? Letters dropped in at doors of deserted houses do not fly or walk to tables in halls. They do not sit on the dust of empty tables with the air of certainty that they will be found. There is needed some human hand – but nobody but the caretaker had a key. Under circumstances she did not care to consider, a house can be entered without a key. It was possible that she was not alone now. She might be being waited for, downstairs. Waited for – until when? Until 'the hour arranged'. At least that was not six o'clock: six has struck.

She rose from the chair and went over and locked the door.

The thing was, to get out. To fly? No, not that: she had to catch her train. As a woman whose utter dependability was the keystone of her family life she was not willing to return to the country, to her husband, her little boys and her sister, without the objects she had come up to fetch. Resuming work at the chest she set about making up a number of parcels in a rapid, fumbling-decisive way. These, with her shopping parcels, would be too much to carry; these meant a taxi – at the thought of the taxi her heart went up and her normal breathing resumed. I will ring up the taxi now; the taxi cannot come too soon: I shall hear the taxi out there running its engine, till I walk calmly down to it

through the hall. I'll ring up – But no: the telephone is cut off. . . .
She tugged at a knot she had tied wrong.

The idea of flight. . . . He was never kind to me, not really. I
don't remember him kind at all. Mother said he never considered
me. He was set on me, that was what it was – not love. Not love,
not meaning a person well. What did he do, to make me promise
like that? I can't remember – But she found that she could.

She remembered with such dreadful acuteness that the twenty-
five years since then dissolved like smoke and she instinctively
looked for the weal left by the button on the palm of her hand.
She remembered not only all that he said and did but the
complete suspension of *her* existence during that August week. *I
was not myself* – they all told me so at the time. She remembered
– but with one white burning blank as where acid has dropped
on a photograph: *under no conditions* could she remember his face.

So, wherever he may be waiting, I shall not know him. You
have no time to run from a face you do not expect.

The thing was to get to the taxi before any clock struck what
could be the hour. She would slip down the street and round the
side of the square to where the square gave on the main road.
She would return in the taxi, safe, to her own door, and bring the
solid driver into the house with her to pick up the parcels from
room to room. The idea of the taxi driver made her decisive, bold:
she unlocked her door, went to the top of the staircase and
listened down.

She heard nothing – but while she was hearing nothing the
passé air of the staircase was disturbed by a draught that travelled
up to her face. It emanated from the basement: down there a
door or window was being opened by someone who chose this
moment to leave the house.

The rain had stopped; the pavements steamily shone as Mrs
Drover let herself out by inches from her own front door into the
empty street. The unoccupied houses opposite continued to meet
her look with their damaged stare. Making towards the thor-
oughfare and the taxi, she tried not to keep looking behind.
Indeed, the silence was so intense – one of those creeks of London
silence exaggerated this summer by the damage of war – that no
tread could have gained on hers unheard. Where her street
debouched on the square where people went on living, she grew
conscious of, and checked, her unnatural pace. Across the open

end of the square two buses impassively passed each other: women, a perambulator, cyclists, a man wheeling a barrow signalized, once again, the ordinary flow of life. At the square's most populous corner should be – and was – the short taxi rank. This evening, only one taxi – but this, although it presented its black rump, appeared already to be alertly waiting for her. Indeed, without looking round the driver started his engine as she panted up from behind and put her hand on the door. As she did so, the clock struck seven. The taxi faced the main road: to make the trip back to her house it would have to turn – she had settled back on the seat and the taxi *had* turned before she, surprised by its knowing movement, recollected that she had not 'said where'. She leaned forward to scratch at the glass panel that divided the driver's head from her own.

The driver braked to what was almost a stop, turned round and slid the glass panel back: the jolt of this flung Mrs Drover forward till her face was almost into the glass. Through the aperture driver and passenger, not six inches between them, remained for an eternity eye to eye. Mrs Drover's mouth hung open for some seconds before she could issue her first scream. After that she continued to scream freely and to beat with her gloved hands on the glass all round at the taxi, accelerating without mercy, made off with her into the hinterland of deserted streets.